From international bestselling author Posie Graeme-Evans comes the passionate tale of a woman ahead of her time.

RAISED IN RURAL NORFOLK, ELLEN GOWAN'S childhood was poor but blessed with affection. Resilience, spirit, and one great talent will eventually carry her far from her humble beginnings. In time, she will become the witty, celebrated, and very beautiful Madame Ellen, dressmaker to the nobility of England, the Great Six Hundred.

Yet Ellen has secrets. At fifteen, she falls for Raoul de Valentin, the dangerous descendant of French aristocrats. Raoul marries Ellen for her brilliance as a designer but abandons his wife when she becomes pregnant. Determined that she and her daughter will survive, Ellen begins her long climb to success. Toiling first in a clothing sweatshop, she later opens her own salon in fashionable Berkeley Square though she tells the world—and her daughter—she's a widow. One single dress, a ball gown created for the enigmatic Countess of Hawksmoor, the leader of London society, transforms Ellen's fortunes and, as the years pass, business thrives. But then Raoul de Valentin returns and threatens to destroy all that Ellen has achieved.

A meeting of the romance of Jane Austen, the social commentary of Charles Dickens, and the very contemporary voice of Posie Graeme-Evans, *The Dressmaker* plunges the reader deep into Victorian England in all its rich and spectacular detail.

ALSO BY POSIE GRAEME-EVANS

The Innocent

The Exiled

The Uncrowned Queen

The Dressmaker

A NOVEL

POSIE GRAEME-EVANS

ATRIA PAPERBACK

NEW YORK   LONDON   TORONTO   SYDNEY

ATRIA PAPERBACK

A Division of Simon & Schuster, Inc.
1230 Avenue of the Americas
New York, NY 10020

First Atria Paperback edition October 2010

ATRIA PAPERBACK and colophon are trademarks of Simon & Schuster, Inc.

For information about special discounts for bulk purchases, please contact Simon & Schuster Special Sales at 1-866-506-1949 or business@simonandschuster.com.

The Simon & Schuster Speakers Bureau can bring authors to your live event. For more information or to book an event contact the Simon & Schuster Speakers Bureau at 1-866-248-3049 or visit our website at www.simonspeakers.com.

Designed by Kyoko Watanabe

Manufactured in the United States of America

10 9 8 7 6 5 4 3 2 1

Library of Congress Cataloging-in-Publication Data

Graeme-Evans, Posie.
    The dressmaker : a novel / by Posie Graeme-Evans.—1st Atria Books pbk. ed.
       p. cm.
    1. Women fashion designers—England—London—Fiction.   2. London (England)—Social life and customs—19th century—Fiction.   I. Title.
    PR9619.4.G73D74 2010
    823'.92—dc22   2010013435

ISBN 978-0-7432-9442-3
ISBN 978-1-4391-9034-0 (ebook)

*For Emma Read
with my love and affection.
Fate decided I would have two daughters
with the same name.
I'm very grateful to Fate.*

The Dressmaker

PROLOGUE

I T WAS the season of Advent and the night was blade sharp. Ground-glass white was the frost, and the eyes and noses of London were bright with cold.

It had become late. The market streets of that great metropolis, that city of cities, were emptying as lanterns and lights were staunched without and within the shops and houses. Drays and carts and private carriages rattled away, the harsh crash and grind of iron on stone, and as their noise departed, so too did the wash of human voices. London, heaving with trade and plenty and paucity, would settle soon into the freezing, star-strewn dark and sleep without protest in promise of the Christmas to come.

In a fashionable part of town a little removed from the rowdy vigor of commerce, a hired carriage waited outside of 38 Berkeley Square. A tall and elegant building, number 38 stood among a row of similar mansions. As with its neighbors, stone steps mounted to a black-lacquered door as glossy as pitch or tar. But a brass plate beside the bellpull—so small as to be almost a label—distinguished this establishment from its companions. Engraved upon it were the words:

CHEZ MISS CONSTANCE

MADAME ELLEN GOWAN

MODISTE & MANTUA MAKER

Number 38, then, was a place of trade and not a family dwelling, a singularity in a handsome square such as this.

The carriage horse snuffled. Her master rubbed the mare's ears and said, "Not so very much longer." Theirs had been a cold wait. The driver, a Kentishman, could smell the frost descending; soon the cobbles would wear a silver coat.

A slant of light splashed gold to the man's feet. A visitor was departing from a house close by. Voices carried in that unmoving air.

"Compliments of the Season. Good night, good night!"

The coachman sniffed. He muttered, "Indeed it is. For some." He would have liked to be as pink and happy and fat as that cheerful gentleman. The cold of this night might be tolerable with so much lard beneath the waistcoat.

"To you also!" This from the host and his lady—he in tartan trews of red and green, she in velvet of a violent, unflattering purple. The first notes of a polka began in the upstairs drawing room as the butler closed the door, restoring the night to its proper place outside his master's house. Music and laughter were contained within once more, and the square decently returned to dense, cold quiet.

The horse coughed. She lipped at the coachman's nose and stamped, breathing a chaff-smelling cloud above her old friend's head. This exhalation of the beast, at least, was warm. The man laughed at his companion's attentions. He might not be a fine, portly gentleman but still, there was much to be grateful for—compared to some. His coat was thick and he had a low-crowned hat crammed upon his head and a muffler about his throat. When driving around these winter streets, it was important to have a warm head. His boots were serviceable, too, unlike the shoeless wretches who would sleep on the streets and in the doorways of the city tonight. Their naked feet would be pinched white in this cruel weather. So many were destitute, even in wealthy London. The children affected him most. But what could he do, one man among so many?

The coachman shivered. But the truth past the philosophizing was this: He and the mare had been waiting for two quarters of an hour past the time he had been instructed to return.

The bells at the Abbey had just sounded the half. Soon it would be midnight. The horse snuffled her master's coat. Was there just one more treat hidden in those capacious pockets? The man shook his head. "Sorry, lass. Not even a morsel's left."

The wrenching of frozen hinges announced the door of number 38 had opened. A tall man stood out upon the steps. His face was shadowed but his words, a freight for silver breath, carried to the coachman. "Madame, it remains only to wish you the very best of good nights." The well-dressed gentleman spoke in English but with a bold French accent. "After this most delightful of evenings, be sure I shall count the moments until I may return. All felicitations of the season. Adieu." An elegant bow, a flourish of the hat, and the Frenchman made his departure. He moved with the grace of a dancer. Few men walked as elegantly as he. Perhaps he was conscious of the fact.

Having pulled down the carriage step, the coachman stared respectfully ahead until his passenger, in a flurry of coat skirts, climbed inside. The equipage rocked and settled upon its straps. Knocking the head of his cane against the roof, the man called out, "The business is concluded. For now. Remove me, driver."

"Certainly, Sir." All cabbies are trained to discretion, but privately the coachman wondered about the man's half laugh as he spoke, his not-quite-pleasant tone. He clambered to his seat and gathered the reins in fingers stiff with cold.

"Around we go, lass." He turned the carriage gingerly on the glassy roadway. A movement caught his eye. The door of number 38 had been closed and the outside lantern staunched, but a lady's hand was at the curtain in an upstairs window. A prickle at the nape of his neck told him they were being watched.

The cabbie touched the mare's shoulder with his whip's thong and sharp echoes bounced back from the dwellings on either side as they rolled away. He was convinced that if he were to look back, the lady in the upstairs room would be staring after them still. The man shivered, and it was not because of the cold.

௧

Ellen Gowan turned from the window. The soft net fell to its place with a sigh, a film against the obsidian pane. There was no light in the room, no fire or candle, but Ellen could see her image well enough. It was reflected in the dressing glass on her table. Why was her appearance unchanged? Tonight her carefully constructed world had been taken apart, remorselessly torn into small and then smaller fragments. And yet she looked as she always did. She found that odd. And suddenly it was too much.

"Oriana. Can you hear me? Help me, I beg of you! Oh, please." The wail of a lost child. Hearing herself, Ellen almost broke—she who had not cried since . . . "No!" Hand-heels ground against bone yet these, her eye-sockets, were strong enough. Dams to hold back grief. "I will *not*!" She would push the tears behind the orbs of her eyes, hold them inside her body. She would not cry.

Polly knocked softly. "You need not be alone." Standing in the passage outside Ellen's room, Polly's candle outlined the shape of the door. Like water, light, once introduced, will not be denied.

Ellen did not immediately reply. Her throat constricted even as she said, "Go to bed, Polly."

On any other night, Ellen might have opened the door to her friend. There is solace in an orderly life, chatting amiably while plaiting one's hair for sleep. But not tonight.

Polly's silent shuffle was eloquent. Ellen could hear her breathing. "I know how upset you are. That man . . ."

"No!" Ellen modified her tone. "I cannot talk of—" She stopped. And then, "Sleep well, dearest Polly."

"We will come through this, Ellen. We always have before."

A pause and the footfalls departed. Distantly, Polly's door creaked open and closed with its accustomed *click*.

In her room, Ellen's eyes adjusted to the dark. Slowly, as if emerging from water, she made out her reflection in the looking glass again. The white part of her eye glittered briefly as she moved close to the dressing table. She saw her face as a painter might— the shapes and volumes and planes, the suggestion of color to the mouth and eyes. Was she pretty? He had said she was, tonight. No, he had said, *exquisite* and *beautiful*. Such compliments were abuse from *his* mouth.

"Enough!" At last, rage made its appearance and Ellen rejoiced. Scarlet fury brought a rushing tide of energy, one that rode high in her chest and shortened her breath. But this was from strength, not dumb misery.

Ellen fumbled over to the mantelpiece and found the vestas and the silver candlestick with its honey-smelling, country-smelling, garden-of-her-childhood-smelling candle. This was the first brave luxury she had allowed herself as things improved. Beeswax instead of tallow, even in the bedrooms. The vigorous *click-scritch* as she struck light to the wick was just as it should be, a normal sound on this most abnormal of nights. She touched the flame to the ready-laid fire, a further act of defiance.

Ellen Gowan would *not* cringe and cry in the dark. She would be warm for *she* had earned the money so to be. Let there be fire! Let there be candles, not one but several!

And as the coals caught from the wood shavings artfully placed among them, Ellen stood in the very center of her gracious room, a branch of candles in her hand. Slowly she turned and allowed the pliant flame to illuminate all those things that she, and she alone, had placed there. The gilt-framed paintings, the bound books in their presses, the splendor of the carpet beneath her handmade shoes.

She was the famous, some might say the notorious, Madame Ellen Gowan, creator of gowns and all manner of finery to the ladies of the most prominent families of England, the Great Six Hundred. She had *worked* for her renown, sacrificed so much, and she would *not* allow him to destroy her work, or her life. Not again.

Distantly, the hour began to chime. Ellen stood at her window and stared out at the sky, spangled with stars. *One, two, three . . .*

"He shall not take what he wants. Do you hear me, Oriana? I shall not let him take it." *Four, five, six* . . . "I shall send him back to the past." *Seven, eight* . . . "He belongs there." *Nine* . . . "Mine is the future." *Ten* . . . "I shall claim the future. As you wanted me to." *Eleven* . . . "And I shall not be afraid." *Twelve.* Midnight.

Ellen pushed up the heavy window sash and leaned out. The moon rode high above Berkeley Square and its light found diamonds in the flagstones, turning the world to silver. In that transformation was magic. Or sorcery.

But there was power in this glinting world ruled by the moon, and mystery in its shadows. Ellen was not afraid of the London night, it had proved a friend in the past.

And yet nothing on that frozen midnight was as it seemed. Least of all Madame Ellen Gowan.

Part One

CHAPTER 1

THERE IS a proverb that the salt air of the Fen country breeds folk who are constitutionally hardy. Those that it does not kill. On the first of August 1843, Lammas Day, Ellen Gowan's thirteenth birthday had at last arrived. And today, though she did not know it, the saying would play out in her own life.

As light lifted in the village of Wintermast within distant sight of the Norfolk Broads, pink dawn faded to a haze of gold and pearl. The reapers had been busy all the preceding week in the fields, and the sap of fresh-cut meadow grasses sweetened the air.

Ellen woke as the walls of her white bedroom flushed to rose. She pulled back the window lace and sighed with a happiness so profound, her chest ached. Finally, it was here—it had begun! For, as well as her birthday, this was the final day of term for her father's pupils—the day scholars that the Reverend Edwin Gowan, Curate of Wintermast, taught in the front room of their rectory. In the coming autumn, five of the seven boys would leave for their grown-up schools. And Connie, Ellen's mother, with the willing assistance of her daughter (and their servant Polly's bossier interference) had prepared a feast to celebrate both these great events. Downstairs, beneath a covering of muslin, all the treats were laid out in the pantry ready to be displayed to their guests. Every dish, every bowl and platter they possessed was mounded high with delicacies.

Ellen had a new dress, too, though she was not supposed to know. Her mama had made it for her. She had seen it as she climbed the stairs to her room one evening. A glimmering shape, it had lain partly finished across her mother's bed. That glimpse was enough to show that the dress was too small to be Connie's.

It now hung in her parents' armoire among their own few clothes, for there was nowhere else to hide a surprise of such magnitude in their small cottage. Perhaps, when Ellen put it on, her mother's dressing mirror would help her see if the hue suited her. She was particular about such things. She knew that each person looked good in some colors and not at all in others.

Thirteen. It seemed a great age. Ellen sighed with the responsibility. And then she giggled. Serious thoughts at the beginning of this glorious day? No!

A soft tap came at her bedroom door. Edwin and Constance Gowan were considerate parents.

"Ellen?" This was her mother's gentle voice "Are you awake? We have something for you."

Ellen lifted the latch to greet her smiling mother and father. "Certainly, Mama!"

"Happy birthday, dearest child. Salutations!" As he entered the room, Edwin Gowan leaned down from his substantial height, careful not to knock his brow against the roof beam of the low room.

"How *splendid* you look, Papa!"

Ellen's handsome, if gaunt, father had dressed for today's celebrations with particular care. Over his usual suit of black canonicals—well brushed and sponged by Connie—he wore his doctoral gown from Cambridge. The silk had faded from its original scarlet, and yet the wide sleeves and cloaklike fall of the garment lent the Reverend Doctor Gowan a startling glamour.

Ellen lifted her face to be kissed. Edwin hesitated. His daughter *was* a child still, yet she was changing. Morning light declared the truth. Something swept his heart. Wistfulness? Regret?

"He does look splendid. I do agree." With eyes only for her daughter, Connie had not seen Edwin's expression change. "But you, also, must look all you should on your birthday, Ellen." Stepping forward, Connie Gowan displayed their gift. Across her arms lay a mass of flower-sprigged silk, jade green and pink on an ivory ground. This was not a dress. It was a gown. The first that their daughter had ever been given. For Ellen, all the promise of that one quick glance so many nights ago was here fulfilled.

"Oh, *Mama*." The child was awed. She did not know that the gift had been created from the last dress remaining in her mother's trousseau. That gown had been packed away in lavender years ago for just such a time, and Connie's nimble fingers and many evenings working by lamplight had wrought the transformation.

"And, a lady must have dancing slippers." From behind his back Edwin proffered the shoes with a flourish. Fashioned from scraps of the same silk, he had cut and stitched the soles himself.

Ellen could not know that these would be her father's last loving gift.

A kiss for each of her parents and Ellen ran to the window to inspect her presents. She was oblivious of her nightgown and bare feet. "Oh, this is *so* delightful. How lucky I am. Lucky, lucky, lucky!"

Edwin grinned at his daughter's exuberance, and Connie's breath caught as she looked at him. The yearning, the intensity of the passion she had felt at their first meeting remained in her still. Feeling her glance, he turned and smiled warmly. "Well, wife, we may safely say Ellen delights in your work."

"And yours, dearest husband."

Edwin slipped an arm around Connie's waist. They stood close watching their daughter with pleasure as she twirled and posed, until Connie, with a start, said, "Edwin, please ask Polly to bring up a can of water. We must dress."

"Alas, a gentleman has no place in a lady's dressing chamber. I shall do your bidding, Madame, with dispatch." Edwin bowed and backed away as if in the presence of a queen. Considering the lowness of the door frame and a floor distinguished by its uneven surface and little else other than a rag rug, Edwin managed a graceful departure.

"Come, Ellen, we must dress your hair. By its current state, you might have slept in a hedge. The tangles!"

But Connie Gowan was only pretending severity. Especially when her pretty daughter burrowed into her arms declaring, "I do love you, Mama. And Papa, too. This is the best day of my life!"

The washing took a little time and dressing the hair rather more. And all because Ellen could not sit still. The girl's glance continually strayed to the dress laid out across her parents' bed, and where her eyes went, her body twisted to follow.

"There. It is done." Connie stepped back to survey her work. Ellen's hair (*Storm dark,* she thought, *magnificent!*) was naturally abundant. And wild. But Connie had restrained the curls with pins and pomade, weaving them into a shining plaited corona. Ellen bore the unfamiliar weight well, since the carriage of her shoulders was naturally, gracefully proud. True, Ellen *was* rather young to put up her hair, but today's party was as grand as the Gowans could manage. Where would be the harm in permitting the child to feel just a little grown up on such a special day?

"Can I put the gown on now, Mama? Oh please. Please!"

"Very well. But the silk is delicate. It will tear if roughly handled."

Ellen colored. "I am careful with all my clothes. You have taught me to be!"

Connie hugged her outraged daughter. She raised one of Ellen's hands to her cheek. "Do not be insulted, dear one. The silk is precious to me." She did not say why, as she turned her daughter toward the window. "Now stand in the light. Let me see if I have judged your form well enough." Perhaps the fabric whispered of the past as Connie picked up the gown for she was smiling. "Raise your arms, child." Ellen did as instructed though it was hard not to fidget.

"Can I see, Mama?"

"In a moment." Connie stood with her head to one side. She

was pleased. The cut of the gown was simple, and that had been the correct instinct. Youth needs little adornment. Sleeves of puffed, white voile had been attached to a tight bodice descending in a point to the voluminous skirt. The silk was light enough, however, to move pleasingly with its wearer, and a single flounce at the hem, finished with silk cord of deep rose, was decorative without being fussy.

As Connie laced her impatient daughter, she privately reflected that a girl of thirteen was sometimes a curious object. Soon the child must be supplanted by the woman, and yet the round, high brow, the soft cheeks, and bright color of childhood lingered still in Ellen's face. For those who did not wish to acknowledge the passing of time, perhaps that was a comfort—and Connie knew that Edwin was among that number. But for those with eyes to see—for a mother—each day past thirteen the child walked further away as the woman-to-be stepped a little closer. As Connie tied the sash of ivory ribbon tight, she was both sad and proud to observe the changes in her daughter.

In this last year, Ellen had begun to grow—the deep hem on the skirt acknowledged that fact. Soon, perhaps, she would be taller than her mother. Ellen's shoulders, too, were wider than Connie's had ever been, and extra room had been allowed in the bodice of the gown. As yet, there were only the smallest of swellings upon Ellen's upper ribs, and if her daughter seemed oblivious to the promise of this changed contour, Connie was not.

"No one will ever guess, will they, Mama?"

Connie startled from her reverie. "What, child?"

"That you fashioned this lovely thing? It does not look at all homemade." Ellen twirled away and picked up one edge of the skirt, as if to display a train. "Only from Paris, my dear, might we expect such excellence of cut. The work is too fine by far to come from *English* hands." The girl caught the glacial superiority of a society lady all too well.

Lady Greatorex to perfection, thought Connie Gowan. "Perhaps they will think you made the gown, Ellen. Your skill with the needle has much improved."

It was true. A fair woman, Connie knew that Ellen's abilities had begun to approach her own. Sewing was an indispensible art in any household—especially a poor one—but she had been delighted for more than practical reasons to watch Ellen's talents fulfill their early promise in this last year.

When Ellen had sewn her first sampler at age five, it had been clear that her skills were precocious. For Connie's daughter there were none of the badly set stitches, no knotting and twisting of the yarn that distinguishes the work of a novice. The back of that first piece had been as neat as the front. And by her seventh birthday, Ellen had drawn and cut out the pattern of a dress by herself, and sewn the garment together with almost no assistance. Her choice of fabric, too, demonstrated an instinct for color and an appreciation of style that Connie privately believed to be inborn. Such things could only be encouraged, they could not be taught. Clever and kind was Ellen. What mother could be more blessed?

Why then, when she gazed at her daughter's happiness, did Connie feel such dread? She tried to tell herself that these were natural fears, the concerns any fond parent might feel as her child approached womanhood. But in her heart she knew the truth. Each week that passed showed that Ellen would grow into a beauty that she herself had never quite attained. Yet, if not guarded by wealth and position, that same grace could prove a blight for those upon whom fate bestowed its most capricious gift.

As Ellen turned this way and that, trying, without success, to see how the whole of the dress appeared in the looking glass, she caught her mother's eye. "Is something wrong, Mama? Does the gown not look well?"

Connie stood behind her daughter's shoulder. It was hard to express what she felt. "Do not fear, child. Your appearance is delightful." She reached for Ellen's hand, and mother and daughter gazed at each other in the mirror. And smiled.

"Mother! The bells!" On the far side of Wintermast's green, the clock in Edwin's church tower was striking the hour. Soon their guests would arrive.

"We must see that all is in readiness. Immediately! Where is your father . . . ?"

Connie hurried to the door, and Ellen, with one last glance at her surprisingly elegant appearance, ran after her. She was glad they were so happy today. It was not always so.

CHAPTER 2

URING TERM time, when Edwin tutored his pupils, the largest of the rooms in their cottage became a school. It was furnished with two long tables and backless benches for the boys to sit on. Ellen's earliest memories were of playing with her peg dolls in the window seat, listening as her father's scholars chanted declensions of Latin verbs.

As she grew older, Edwin had included his daughter in the lessons, teaching her Latin, Greek, and Hebrew just as he did the boys. The gentry who sent their sons to Reverend Gowan would have been confounded indeed if they had known that he made his small library—one of the last relics of his time at Cambridge—available to Ellen as soon as she could fluently read. He delighted in her progress—she had his ear for languages and an excellent memory. He gloried, too, in his daughter's inquisitive mind and quietly, but stubbornly, insisted on his right to teach his child among the other pupils.

But Ellen's inclusion gradually became a scandal. Many said it was not right that the sexes should mix in this way. And knowledge of such kind—masculine learning—was widely considered unsuitable for the weaker female mind. Concerned parents removed their boys and the number of pupils dwindled.

But today, on Ellen's birthday, such concerns were forgotten and the schoolroom was a different place. Scoured with sea sand by Connie and Polly, the oak floor had been lightened from dark to honey. And, to clear a space for dancing later, the tables had been pushed back against the walls. Damask roses—scarlet and white, yellow and cream—had been brought in from the garden and made into long garlands twined with wild woodbine. Draped along the sills and around the great window, the flowers had begun to wilt, until Ellen sprinkled each one with water from the well.

The room was drowsily warm, and dust motes jigged in the light. Ellen paused and closed her eyes. Each floral scent was clear, as distinct as the notes Connie played on her old-fashioned spinet. A counterpoint to the melody of fresh-cut meadow grass, the flowers sang a green song that described summer in Ellen's mind.

Connie hurried in with a platter of little butter buns and an apron for her daughter. "Child, your dress! Put this on. We must set out the food."

For days before this, in preparation for the party and as a way of bringing hope to their straitened lives, the house had been filled with a tempest of washing and ironing, baking and churning, and, least pleasant of all, the reek of calves' feet boiling up for the jellies. For Ellen, watching that pot was the task she hated the most. But the liquid she had skimmed all of one long, hot day had been colored and flavored and left to set in the stillroom. And now the magic would be revealed; the glory that allowed the heat of the fire, the stink, and the labor to be endured without complaint.

"When I give the signal, child, and not before." This was the critical moment and Connie's anxiety was merited, for disaster stood close. Ellen, at Connie's nod, slid the plate beneath the mold with steady hands. It required real skill to turn out the garnet and emerald castles from the copper molds (Connie's most valuable kitchen possession) but mother and daughter worked in concert, and Ellen, by her concentration, earned her mother's proud smile.

"There! How nice they look."

Ellen beamed. The jellies glowed in a slant of sun, a worthy centerpiece for the tables of the feast. But then Connie frowned. "Polly, *where* is the marchpane? I do not see it here."

"On the top shelf in the pantry, mam. Where I said they was."

Polly Calstock, the Gowans' maid of all work, called out from the kitchen. Fifteen and sturdy, the previously awkward village girl had lately disappeared into a sullen almost-woman who daily grew more insolent to her mistress, if not her master. And all because she'd been brought a bonnet from London by her brother and with it, inflated tales of his life as an ostler's boy at a coaching inn there.

Mrs. Gowan had never previously worked Polly too hard for fear the girl should give her notice and leave. But now she was looking forward to that day, since trials of will between mistress and servant had become wearingly familiar. She called out again. "Thank you, Polly. When you have finished hulling the strawberries, Ellen will help carry the bowls to the tables."

A loud put-upon sigh was the only response, but there was too much to do for Connie to begin a confrontation. Mother and daughter hurried to the pantry.

"Be careful, Mama!" Connie had quickly climbed up on a three-legged stool to reach the top shelves. Ellen tried to steady it—one leg was shorter than the others—as her mother handed down two pretty china baskets filled with sweets made from almond paste in the form of apples and peaches.

For the principal meat dish, being watched as it warmed by their affronted maid, Connie had sacrificed two of their older hens and three cockerels for a mess of chicken fricassee in the French style. This was to be accompanied by a cold pie of eels in aspic (more calves' feet!). Ellen was not fond of eating eel. To her, the creatures were much better alive and twining together in the marsh. But Edwin had set a trap two nights ago, and yesterday he'd gathered enough for the heroic raised pie that lay on the kitchen table.

Connie prowled the length of the schoolroom, inspecting each offering. To Ellen's eyes, all seemed complete. And perfect.

"Polly! Where are the fresh cheeses?"

"I have them here, mam. You asked me twice before." Polly stood in the doorway. In her hands was the family's one silver salver and upon that, white porcelain bowls of curds. Her mutinous expression declared she would not step forward unless specifically requested.

Connie swallowed a sharp retort at the tone of injured pride. "Yes, girl, arrange the bowls there, beside the bread. That will look nice." The mounds of buns were still faintly warm. Ellen's mouth watered at the thought of salt cheese curd slathered over fresh bread.

"Edwin! There you are. Do you have the cooling tub?"

Edwin nodded patiently at his wife. He took no offense at her sharp tone, it was the result of nerves—and the natural anxiety of any hostess.

"I shall pump some water to fill it presently." He presented Connie with ten stone bottles of elderberry champagne. It was the Reverend Gowan's job each autumn to brew the wine from the bushes in the garden. He stored it in his potting shed, where the liquid fermented in the bottles. Such humble nectar must have darkness and silence, he declared, to attain its proper flavor and sparkle.

"The angelica!" It was a moment of emergency but the candied green angelica, lavishly sticky, was located in its dish on the kitchen dresser. And now, all *was* finally ready for their guests.

"Polly, please wash your hands and put on a clean apron." The girl departed with a sniff. She thought such things fussy.

Connie turned to her daughter. "And, Ellen, you may remove yours. Let me help you."

"Wife?"

"Edwin, *please* to fill the tub?" Connie was distracted as she retied Ellen's sash in a more becoming bow.

"I shall. But first come here, Mrs. Gowan. Your daughter looks very well. And so do you—a pair of most elegant ladies and a credit to our family. Cease to fret. All is prepared, or it never will be now." Edwin opened his arms, smiling. First his daughter, and then his wife hurried to shelter within that loving circle.

"Never forget this day. Our daughter is nearly grown and we have each other. Sometimes our lives are hard but we three remain." Lovingly Edwin Gowan bent down to kiss Connie first, and then Ellen. "There! Let the festivities begin. Our Lord always loved a party—he will not grudge us this small celebration!"

"William, you will be sick!" Ellen watched with awe as the Honorable William Greatorex's jaws closed around another piece of strawberry shortcake. His cheeks, stretched tight, shone as he chewed with remorseless vigor. The boy laughed. Ellen drew back sharply to protect her gown as little flecks of cream flew about.

William did not understand the importance of Ellen's birthday dress. In this world, girls had more than one pretty thing to wear.

"I shall not you know." Or that is what Ellen *thought* he said. It was hard to understand actual words through the wall of cake that stopped up William's mouth.

Since this boy was the most important of Edwin's pupils, he had been seated beside Ellen at the head of one of the tables. The celebratory feast was now well advanced, and William, who existed in a state of near permanent hunger, had emptied the contents of all the dishes within reach of his hands. His companions, some of whom had better manners, watched in astonishment at the bold way he appropriated so much without apology.

"Polly, perhaps you might serve the other table?" Connie plucked the fricassee from William's grasp. For once the maid did not demur. William was the rudest of Edwin's pupils. He treated Polly as if she were a thing rather than a living person. Besides, he had called her fat once and she had not forgiven him.

"Certainly, mam."

Removing the dish from Connie's hands, Polly swung so sharply, her skirts swayed, exposing her ankles. "Polly, you are bold! I saw your stockings!" William's guffaw caught the attention of the boys and soon all were laughing and pointing at the Gowans' blushing servant.

Edwin clapped his hands sharply. "Scholars! Since this birth-

day feast and celebration of term's ending is almost concluded"—
he directed an embracing smile at his wife and the discomforted
Polly—"and since, too, the ladies of this house have toiled cease-
lessly for your pleasure, I think it fit we thank God, and them, for
this bounty."

William, a clumsy boy, chose just that moment to drop his glass
of watered elderberry wine. It shattered upon the floor in shards
and stars. Connie paled. William had been given one of the four
precious glasses that remained in the Gowan household. And now
there were three. There would never be four again. Glass was too
expensive to replace.

The room was silent after the crash. Into that breathing pause
Edwin quickly intoned the familiar words, "Let us pray."

The boys stood in their places and, though restless, closed
their eyes. But William stared boldly about. He was impatient
with prayers. And yet some part of Ellen's distress on Connie's
behalf worked past his self-absorption. As if for the first time, he
saw, really saw, Ellen. A girl, not a child. And a very pretty one.
Her flushed face and trembling lip touched him, which he did not
expect.

William Greatorex colored also as an unwelcome clarity showed
him that the unhappiness of his friend—he was surprised that he
should think of Ellen as his friend—was *his* fault. He had broken
the glass, and such a thing must be important to the Gowans.

Now, expectations of a very high order had been placed upon the
increasingly meaty shoulders of the Honorable William Greatorex.
As such, his days swung between haunted guilt—in the presence of
his parents—and the enthusiasm of relief when freed from, in particular, his mother's disapproving eye. Attending Edwin Gowan's
day school had been an irksome distraction from all the things
that William liked best to do: riding, shooting rabbits and rooks
and hawks, eating, sleeping, and gossiping with the grooms in his
parents' stables. But today the boy finally understood. An important time in his life was ending. A time during which he had been

fairly and kindly treated. The uncertainties of his Great school lay ahead and he was frightened of the change. In all these years past, Doctor Gowan had been patient with him, and encouraging. And Ellen had made him laugh, which had lessened the shame when book learning defeated such scattered powers of concentration as he had. William flushed a deeper scarlet, the skin of his neck all aprickle, when he remembered Ellen's kind eyes and cheerful good humor even when he had been rude to her.

No, he had not understood the gifts he had been given in this place. And now it was all nearly gone. He might never see Ellen Gowan again. Certainly so, if his mother had her wish.

Lady Greatorex did not like Ellen, though William had never questioned why that might be so. Now it was Master Greatorex's turn to feel the sting of tears. He blinked them away and wiped his nose on his shirtsleeve.

". . . and, Heavenly Father, for those of our company who will leave this place today, we thank you for all we have shared together in this room. All the laughter, the joy of learning given and received, the companionship of our friends. For this, and for the feast of celebration in which we have participated, we are truly grateful. Your bounty, Lord God, is without end. Amen."

Ellen whispered the final word with great intensity and opened her eyes to find William staring at her. His own were red and watering and even smaller than usual. At first she was alarmed, but then he smiled. Something had changed. She would never have described his expression as *soft* before, but that was the closest word she could come up with for the compassion and, yes, sweetness in his glance. Strange words to associate with William Greatorex.

The boy's voice was oddly strangled when he said, "Will you come outside to play, Ellen? My parents will be here soon, and I should like to remember . . ." Remember what?

In later years, when the succeeding scenes of this day played out in William's mind, as they often did, he could never put a meaning to that illusive little word. In any case, it was not *what* but *who*. It was a person he did not wish to forget. Ellen. Yet this, for a time, was easy to deny to himself. And that was because of his mother.

Lord Greatorex, a short but massively fat man with a high voice was, though a little remote, always pleasant to Connie Gowan when he brought his boy to Edwin at the beginning of each term. He ignored Ellen, though not unkindly, since she was only the curate's daughter.

Lady Evelyn, William's mother, however—as bony as her husband was fat, with a sharp nose and a similar manner—was frigid rather than distant. Though necessarily civil to the Reverend Gowan as her son's teacher—since he was a gentleman and a university man—she would only rarely acknowledge Connie with anything more than a nod. Or if she spoke at all, it was most usually to complain.

This disdain caused much distress to Ellen's parents. They rightly assessed such treatment as a marker of how far in the world they had fallen. They felt the helplessness of their situation keenly, for they needed each one of their pupils and could not afford to offend the children's parents. The penury of a declining stipend was eased by the fees brought to the household each Quarter Day by the boys. Without them, utter poverty would result, since each year there were fewer villagers to support the parson, and those who remained were poor.

Yet there were worse things than Connie's continual humiliation. For if Lady Greatorex rarely acknowledged Mrs. Gowan, she reserved positive contempt for Ellen. From the time the child was about ten years old, and on every occasion that she visited the curate's house, Lady Greatorex would make loud announcements within Ellen's hearing such as, "Can it be that Miss Gowan is taller *still*? I am quite astonished." And, "Large eyes? I find them vulgar. They call attention to the face. That may be construed as common."

But here, on this sun-dazzled afternoon when the feast was done, William Greatorex, flown a little with Edwin's elderberry wine, hurried after Ellen as she ran toward the garden and there caught and kissed her. And this was just as his mother's carriage drew up at the end of the path.

The scandal was instant. Hurrying from her carriage even before the steps were properly down, Evelyn Greatorex arrived beside William in a cloud of agitated green poplin (a poor color for skin as sallow as hers). Snatching at the boy, she caused Ellen to stumble. And in saving herself from falling, the frail silk of Ellen's pretty gown tore, exposing an arm to the shoulder.

"Wretched girl!" Lady Greatorex's indignation was very great, and her voice loud. Edwin and Connie arrived at a run, followed by Polly and the rest of the boys, big eyed. In frigid tones Lady Greatorex declaimed, "Reverend Gowan, how do you explain *this*, Sir?"

Edwin paled at the venom but he was confused. Why was Ellen's gown torn? "Explain?" He hurried to his daughter and placed an arm around her shoulders. He felt her tremble.

Evelyn Greatorex stared with narrowed eyes at the pair. "Yes, Sir. I said *explain*. Your daughter. My son. Oh, I knew this day would come. I warned of it—and now you see the result of your so-called *education* of both sexes." She pointed at the pair. "Loss of innocence!"

William and Ellen stared at that accusing finger. Time ceased. All that existed, all that *could* exist, was the agony of that moment. They had been playing. That was all. And though Ellen could feel the impression of William's lips—dry and rather hard—on her own, still there was no feeling in that contact for her. Her emotions for him came closest to what she felt for her two brothers, dead as infants, nothing more. That is why she tried to help him when he struggled in class. As if in helping him, she reached out to them.

Yet the heat of Evelyn Greatorex's words was scalding. Each disdainful syllable burned Ellen as surely as lemon juice or salt on a wound. And the world—the sky, the trees—reeled and blurred as the girl's eyes filled up and overran, the tears spotting the stuff of her bodice irrevocably. She was mortified by the laughter of her father's other pupils. Why were they suddenly so cruel? Did they hate her, too?

William sprang back. Wiping his mouth, he hurried to stand beside Lady Greatorex and would not look at Ellen.

Her daughter's shame and distress were too much for Connie. She ran to her child. With freezing dignity, she said, "Lady Greatorex, I must ask that you remove your son from this house. He has most grievously offended our daughter."

Evelyn Greatorex had never before been spoken to in this manner and gasped into a pink-faced silence. Connie caught her breath and continued. "But we are Christians here, Lady Greatorex, and my husband and I will always wish William success with his future studies and his life. We have a great fondness for him from the time he has spent beneath this roof. We shall strive to remember only what is good in your son and will not detain you further. Good day to you both. Come, Ellen."

Ellen raised her head and managed a curtsy without even the hint of a wobble. Her expression was polite but distant as she retreated, straight backed, into the house behind her mother. Her deportment could not be faulted even if, once indoors, tears dropped upon cheeks that burned as if slapped. The Gowans, mother and daughter, collapsed into each other's arms. Connie held Ellen up as she bravely conquered her sobs.

"Why, Mama? Why was William's mother so hateful?"

Connie's eyes darkened. "She thinks you too pretty, Ellen. And worries for her son. He is fond of you."

"We have always been friends. But why should that concern his mother?"

Poor Connie. How could she tell her daughter that Lady Greatorex had been right to fear Ellen's influence over her dullard son? Childhood partialities are long lasting.

"I have asked them all to leave." Edwin Gowan entered the schoolroom quietly from the bright day outside.

All around, as if to mock their distress, lay the scraps and remnants of the birthday feast. Wearily, he removed his scholar's gown and threw it carelessly down. It trailed to the floor over one of the benches. This upset Connie almost most of all, for Edwin was very particular with his clothes, especially his doctor's gown. She hurried to pick it up, but he stopped her with a look.

"Leave it where it lies, wife. It is no more use to me. Or to this family. Today's disaster will see no more boys being taught here—at least not while Ellen is part of the lessons. Lady Greatorex will get her way."

Ellen shivered at her father's despairing tone. She had not understood the considerable cost in him continuing her education among the boys.

Connie's voice trembled. "You cannot mean that, Edwin. Allow me at least to . . ." She bent down again but Edwin snatched her hand away.

In a low voice he said, "I forbid you to touch it. Remember your vows to me, Mrs. Gowan. Obey."

Connie's face drained white and the cords in her neck sprang tight as hawsers.

Fearfully, Ellen gazed from face to face. She had caused this. The day that had begun with such hope had ended in misery—and now her father had spoken harshly to her mother. She had never before heard such words between her parents.

Staring at Edwin with huge, wounded eyes, Connie said, "I would never willingly disobey you, husband. This I think you know."

But she dropped her gaze. "I shall rest for an hour and then Ellen and Polly and I will clear away."

Connie left the room without one backward glance. Ellen heard her mother's footfall as she climbed the stair to their room—it was slow and heavy and the old treads groaned. A noise so familiar and yet, today, so poignant.

"Father?"

Edwin turned. He had been blindly staring through the casements. "Yes, child?"

"I am truly sorry. For everything."

His expression softened from the severe mask of a moment before, and Ellen saw something she had never seen before. Hopelessness. "No fault of yours, Ellen, has caused the events of today."

"What will happen now?"

Edwin Gowan looked at the doorway and toward the stair beyond. He half-started toward it, then stopped. "What will happen now?" He shook his head. "I do not know. I must pray. For guidance. When your mother wakes, tell her that I . . ."

Edwin ceased to speak, his face working as if he would say more. But he held the words back. In his heart.

"What shall I say to Mama?"

Edwin kissed his child's raised face. Gently he stroked a wayward curl, twisted it about his finger—glossy, so alive that when he let it go, it sprung away as if glad to be free. "Let her know that I have gone to the church."

Edwin paused and then, with a sigh, bent to pick up his gown from where it lay half-sprawled on the dusty floor. He shook it carefully, and brushed the nap of the material with one hand. But he did not put it on. Instead, he placed it on a hook behind the door. With one last glance at his pretty daughter, he left the schoolroom and walked out of the house.

CHAPTER 3

Ellen, left alone in the schoolroom among the wreckage of the feast, was oppressed by the heat of the afternoon. The house was quiet. Even Polly was silent. This was unusual, since often, when feeling ill used, she created noise: clogs slapping and clacking back and forth, plates thumped down, the crash of doors left to slam as she passed. But there was none of this.

The pretty gown was an annoyance now, the tight bodice a constriction that Ellen could no longer bear.

"You have been ruined, poor thing."

Ellen did not know that she had said the words aloud. And then she wondered. Was it the boning in the dress or the scandal that caused her chest to ache? Beyond, in the village, the poison of this day would spread as gossip ran, contagion fast, from house to house and through the district.

"Mama?"

Ellen walked up the stairs and peered into her parents' bedroom. Connie was sleeping, one hand cuddled to her cheek. The girl sighed. It would be selfish to wake her mother after all the hard work and the upsets of the day. Soundlessly, Ellen pulled the door closed and tiptoed to her own warm room, where she unlaced the gown with some difficulty.

Hanging on a hook behind the door there waited her everyday dress of cotton gingham. Ellen wriggled into the shapeless garment with more pleasure than usual. The cloth was old and soft and familiar. Familiar things were good. And then she hesitated. Hanging on another hook was the sunbonnet that her mother insisted she wear outside the house. Ellen felt like a baby when forced to wear the faded thing, but she heard Connie's earnest voice as she gazed at the flopping brim and the annoying long strings. *The skin is much damaged from even the lightest exposure to the sun. One has only to see the village women. Even the girls too soon resemble their mothers' weathered faces from working in the fields. A lady is known by the fineness of her skin. You will thank me when you are grown, Ellen.*

On another day, Ellen might have smiled, remembering Connie's admonition. Not today though. Today there were tears, as she buttoned the back of her dress and tied on her apron and the much-despised bonnet. She would not disobey her mother today, not even in thought.

Downstairs, Ellen found Polly sitting at the kitchen table. The smell of mint tea was pleasant, its source the steam rising from a cup in Polly's hand.

"Do not disturb yourself." Ellen waved for Polly to sit though she had barely stirred, and had certainly not risen. This was just the child of the house, and not her mistress.

"When Mama wakes, let her know I have gone to the church? Only for a little while. I'll not forget to return and help."

The maid sipped loudly, then said toward Ellen's departing back, "Too much work for one, and *that's* a certainty."

Edwin Gowan was upon his knees. They were sore, as was his head from thinking too much. And not praying. And from despair at that fact.

He knelt alone at the steps leading to the altar of St. Michael the Archangel as he had so many times before. His was a Norman church built upon Saxon foundations, the most ancient building in Wintermast. He had great fondness for its honest plainness, so like that of the people he served and sought to comfort. But now he was a man unsupported by even a skeleton of belief. For if he had had doubts about his faith before, after this morning something profound had shifted within his heart. Now he truly saw the injustice of the world and the powerlessness of most people within it. And he did so without any sense that his God—formerly a presence, a voice, an *other*—was anything but vast silence. Certainty had fled, and with it hope.

"Why?"

It was the only word he had. He whispered it, head bowed. Then he looked up and asked, "Why have these things happened to my family?"

Gazing at the crucifix above the altar, he saw the familiar object for what it was. A thing of wood eaten by worms. *A carving.* Nothing more. He had faithfully given his life to serving the myth that this object represented. Nothing had dissuaded him. The years of study, the poverty, not even his wife's increasingly poor health or the deaths of their first four babies in the harsh marsh winters had taken him from the path. Once, he had been sure the price paid was supportable. That God would make all things well in the end, if he was patient and faithful, like Job.

Edwin coughed, his breath caught in shock. He saw now with terrible clarity that he had been deluded.

"Dear Lord." It was a last, fearful plea against nothingness.

"Lord? Speak to me?"

Ellen kicked up dust as she crossed the common land. It lay in the center of the village and was the shortest way to her father's church. On a hot day the green shade here was pleasant, for there was a copse of lime trees and a thicket of blackberries prized by the village people for the fruit in the autumn and the rabbits who made their warrens among its roots.

St. Michael's lay a little way in the distance. Its dauntless, squat tower claimed the sky just as the Normans had once seized the lands and waters of the Fens from the Saxons. As familiar as their cottage, St. Michael's was almost another home for the Gowans.

Ellen stopped in the cool shadows of the porch. She peered around the half-open door. Her father was kneeling before the altar. Praying was very important to him, she knew, but if she could not speak with her mother, perhaps he could help her resolve the pull and pang of all that she felt? Should she be completely candid? William's kiss meant nothing, but something unsettling had been in his eyes at the last. What was it?

Ellen dawdled forward a step or two. Her back prickled as she recalled the moment before the catastrophe. William's expression had gone from sweetness to . . . what? Covertness. Could she tell her father that? What would he say?

She gazed at Edwin's still figure. His hands were pressed together and his head bowed. A man absorbed by devotion. No. She would not interrupt him to speak of such uncomfortable feelings. Not today.

Easing the door closed, Ellen left the cool porch for the glare of the high, hot sun. Unconsciously, her feet found the path around the church that led toward a particular part of the graveyard. She often walked there, especially with Connie. The four small graves. Here they were. Eliza and Mary, her sisters. And Tom and Edward, her brothers. She sat on the seat that her father had built so that Connie might be comfortable when she visited their children.

She had never heard their voices, and it was hard for Ellen to imagine that the babies buried there were all older than she was— and would be taller and more grown up if they had only survived. Her oldest sister, Eliza, would be nineteen now. Perhaps she would have talked with Ellen about William Greatorex?

Ellen closed her eyes. If she tried really hard, she could almost see Eliza's face. They were sitting on the side of Ellen's bed and her sister was laughing. Her hair was straight, not curly as Ellen's was, and she had leaf green eyes, their father's eyes. But she was a merry, happy person—Ellen felt certain of that.

She asked, earnestly, "What would you have done, Eliza? Was it my fault?" Ellen pressed her hands to her suddenly hot cheeks.

"Our poor parents. I do not know what will become of us. Do you know? Can you see the future where you are, Eliza?"

The earth answered. Like a snake beneath the turf, a tremor ran across the ground toward her. It passed under Ellen's boots and on toward the church, and the lime trees tossed their branches as if in a storm. But the air was still.

That astonishment was not enough. Now came the sound of something enormous being torn apart, ripped like cloth, followed by a tremendous charge of noise. An invisible force flung Ellen to the ground. Coughing, she struggled upward and saw . . . the tower was falling. The church gaped open like a shocked mouth as the bells fell down and she heard her father scream out Connie's name.

"Papa!"

Removed from the sky as if it had never been, white dust rose from the site of the tower into a serene blue sky.

Villagers ran out into the street in the tumult, as the old building came down and their own cottages shook. Shouting and pointing, the women clutched their children and screamed as the chimneys on their houses rocked and the windows fell from their frames.

"Papa! Oh, help him. Please!"

Ellen stumbled across the mound of stone that had been the tower, weeping and coughing. She could only breathe in gasps.

The ground was still moving as men ran to Ellen. Young and old together, they scrabbled and shoved and pushed, trying to prise the masonry aside. The children watched, shocked into silence. The oldest among them remembered the great storms of five winters ago, the lightning that had split the tallest oak in the village, but this was different. No one living had seen destruction of this kind before.

Perhaps it was only minutes, perhaps it was an hour, but they found him. Lying, open eyed, at the base of the altar steps, his face was undamaged though white as a statue from plaster pulverized to flour.

But Edwin Gowan's chest and legs had been crushed by the bells.

"Do not look, child."

"Nod" Noddington, a large, kind man and a friend to the Gowan family, knelt beside the sobbing girl and tried to turn her head. She shook his gentle hand away.

"Can you hear me, Papa?" Ellen raised her father's unbloodied head in her arms, cradling him as he had her, once. "Look, Nod! He's breathing. See? There! We must ride for the doctor in Holcroft." He was alive! But Nod and the others, the Gowans' neighbors for so many years, saw the truth. Edwin Gowan had died with his church.

As gently as he could, Nod detached Ellen's arms, holding her as she struggled. "There's nothing more we can do for your daddy, child."

"But he breathes!"

"We shall look out for him, now."

"No!" Ellen's voice rose as Nod lifted her up and bodily carried her away. But then she ceased to fight. The silence of the children and the sorrowful expressions of all who had helped confirmed what she could not, would not, accept. Her father was dead.

"Put me down."

The man stopped on the roadway in front of the church, among the chaos of fallen branches and masonry. "You are certain?"

Ellen nodded. He placed her down as if she were a thing as fragile as glass.

"I will come with you, Miss Ellen. You shall not go home by yourself."

Ellen knew what he meant. Nod thought to tell her mother, but she knew where her duty lay. She alone had caused this tragedy. Her behavior, her sin—William's kiss—had brought God's wrath down upon her father's head. Literally. He had died calling out her mother's name but now they would forever be estranged. It was for her to atone. If she could.

"I shall tell my mother."

Nod eyed their curate's daughter doubtfully. She was white and bloodied, her clothing torn from the search. A double shock for her gentle mother.

"This is an unfair burden, child. And not yours to carry."

Ellen gazed patiently at the man. "You do not understand."

Nod watched Ellen Gowan as she resolutely turned away from the church and all that lay behind her. Her small figure diminished as she crossed the common toward her undamaged home.

He shook his head sorrowfully. So much trouble visited upon this poor family, and all in the space of but a day. How could God allow such things to be?

Nod sighed and turned away. His neighbors were huddled together in the street, too frightened to go back inside their houses. What was best to be done first among the chaos of the village? Account for the living, and pick up the broken pieces of their lives.

Wintermast had been sacked and burned more than once in the bad old days of his fathers and his fathers' fathers, but the church had always survived, Nod thought. Not today.

What would happen to them now?

CHAPTER 4

EXHAUSTED BY the day and all that had gone before it, Connie had slept deeply until distant tumult invaded her dream. Lady Evelyn was suddenly screaming at her, shouting and crying. Unaccountably, they were on a ship together. It pitched so violently that Connie clutched at the railing, trying to steady herself and escape as the boat rocked more wildly still. What if she should fall into the water? She could not swim. But then she was deep, deep in a cold sea. She could see the surface above, but could not reach it no matter how she tried. She would drown! Terrified, Connie woke with a jolt. Somewhere, someone was crying. Ellen? No. This was a very young child, surely.

Connie pushed back the covers, blinking the last of the dream away. She must find Edwin. They quarreled so rarely. Her first duty now was to offer comfort and an apology for her pride. Then they would face what must be faced, together. They had managed in the past and they would again.

The door silently opened.

"Is that you, child?"

Pale and bloody-handed, Ellen stared at her mother from the landing.

Connie frowned, confused. Her daughter *was* crying. Was she dreaming still? But her heart caught in a vise as Ellen tried to speak. This was real. She held out her arms. "Tell me."

Tears carved silver lines on Ellen's face as she ran to her mother. She clung to Connie, drowning in the truth. The world she had known all her life was gone.

"He. He is . . ." The image of her father's face was all she saw.

Connie's arms convulsed around her daughter. There was a hammer in her chest beating at the bones. She struggled to breathe.

"Papa. In the church. He . . ."

Polly, waiting fearfully at the bottom of the stairs, heard her mistress scream. From some ancient memory she crossed herself as Connie wailed like a soul in Hell's fires.

"Stop! Mother, please. Polly!"

The maid took the stairs at a run, and stopped in horror at the open bedroom door. Connie Gowan, Polly's controlled and gentle mistress, had clawed her face in bloody streaks.

"Mistress!"

The two girls were stronger, just, than the crazed woman. One on either side, both weeping, they forced Connie back to the bed. There she collapsed. Silent, suddenly rigid.

Polly and Ellen stared at each other fearfully. Was Connie dying also? Polly rallied first.

"She is cold with the shock. Best we get Mrs. Gowan warm." Ellen, trembling, did as Polly instructed. They covered Connie with the counterpane as she lay inert as a log beneath their hands, though open eyed. Drawing the curtains closed against the glare of late afternoon, they left her to rest. If she could.

The night after Edwin Gowan's death passed slowly. If Ellen slept, it was as if on stones. Then as first light rose, she sat up with relief and lit her bedroom candle. All was well—the loss of her father, the confrontation with Lady Greatorex, these were parts of some savage dream brought on by the heat of the previous day. Ellen ran quickly to her parents' room, seeking their comfort as she always did after a nightmare. But there was the truth.

Her mother lay alone, still dressed in her best clothes. She had not moved though her eyes were closed.

"Mother?"

The candle, held high, cast Ellen's shadow across the wall, and as she moved closer to the bed, it grew larger until it lay across her mother's heart.

"Let me bring you something, Mama. You have not eaten or drunk since . . ." Not by the turn of her head or the flicker of an eye did Connie Gowan indicate that she had heard her daughter.

"Mama. Please. Cannot you speak to me? It is I, Ellen. Only me."

The shadow of the little girl holding the candle trembled. But Edwin Gowan's widow did not stir.

Polly was busy at the hearth when Ellen, washed and properly gowned in a clean, black housedress, descended to the kitchen at dawn. Polly, too, had contrived mourning garments, though her skirt did not match her bodice.

Preoccupied, Ellen went to the pantry for a heel of bread only to smell the ripe odors of all that remained there from the celebration. Flies had made a meal of the ruins of the jellies, for they had been left uncovered. The syllabubs, too, had soured and corrupted in the heat.

"Polly!"

The maid hurried in. Ellen glared at her.

"The food should have been covered. It's all spoiled!" Ellen was immensely angry at the waste of such precious foodstuffs—and the labor that had made them.

Polly gulped, her face an unbecoming scarlet. "I am so sorry, Miss Ellen. I am, really, but . . ." She mopped her eyes with the edge of her apron.

Grief smothered Ellen's fury. But she would not cry. Not now when there was so much to do.

"I accept your apology, but it shall not happen again. Please clean out the pantry and give what can no longer be eaten to the pig. After you have finished, we shall discuss the day. My mother will be hungry when she wakes. I shall prepare a posset."

Polly's eyes widened. The child had found an authority that the mother had never entirely achieved.

"But you must eat also, Miss?" She removed the bread from Ellen's hands and quickly laid it on a plate. Hurrying to the kitchen table, she placed a knife correctly beside it with the butter dish next to a bowl of damson jam and a clean napkin ready for Ellen's lap. Bobbing a curtsy, Polly straightened her cap and pulled back a chair.

Once, Ellen might have stifled a giggle at Polly's earnest expression. Now she did not notice, for she sat without ceremony. Lifting the lid on the butter dish, she sighed. And replaced it. She had thought herself hungry but food, now, seemed offensive.

A little later, Polly watched Ellen stir a bread posset over the remade fire. "Should you use the sugar, Miss Ellen? Mrs. Gowan would find it strengthening."

Ellen shook her head. "My mother has often said she prefers our honey. That we have in plenty. I have not skimmed the milk, though. She will relish the cream." Loaf sugar was expensive.

Polly cleared her throat nervously, then she said, "I forgot to say something before. I put the linen from the party to bucking earlier. Should have been done, by rights, yesterday, but . . ." She did not finish the sentence. What was not spoken lay like a lump between them.

Ellen forced the words from her constricted throat. "I do not suppose the stains will have set so very badly. There is still the schoolroom to be tidied, however."

Polly, knowing well that her duties included clearing up after the party when others in the house were so plainly unable to do what was required, hurried to gather the dishes that had remained untouched since the feast. Yesterday she would have wheedled Ellen's help with a task she loathed.

Polly's clogs were noisy as she clumped back and forth from the schoolroom, and Ellen closed her eyes against the pain in her head. After a moment, she ladled the posset into a small bowl. Sprigged with blue flowers it was only earthenware, though pretty. Perhaps it would give her mother some small pleasure, some reminder of normal existence?

The staircase to the second floor was steep. It was no easy task for Ellen to balance the tray so that nothing spilled. At her mother's door she knocked softly. "Mama? Are you awake?"

There was no response. Ellen lifted the latch with one hand and pushed the door in with her shoulder, saying brightly, "You must be hungry. I hope you like your breakfast." The room was sunlit, and it was a radiant, sweet-smelling morning, just as yesterday's had been.

"Mama?"

Her mother's face was in shadow and Ellen caught her breath. Connie lay so still! Panic propelled Ellen forward and she nearly dropped the tray. But her mother's breathing was even and deep. She did not stir.

Putting the food to one side, Ellen stroked Connie's hair back from her brow. "I wish you could hear me. I wish . . ."

After a time, Ellen sighed. "I shall leave the tray here for you." She covered the food with a napkin and lingered a moment, then another, by the door.

But there was a pressing task to accomplish, one that could be put off no longer.

Ellen retrieved the inkwell from the windowsill in the kitchen. It was pewter with a lid of horn. She raised the lid gently. Edwin had made it himself when the original cover had broken, and this was something that, until yesterday, her father had used each day of his life. Holding this humble object, it was almost as if she touched his hand with her own. Ellen gasped back a sob. *I will not cry!*

On the table, a single rose spilled, wilted, from its vase. The flower had been placed there by Connie a few days before—

something pretty to look at as she worked in the kitchen. Now, many of the petals had fallen and lay scattered, winding sheets for two dead flies. Connie would be distressed if she saw this small disorder. Ellen scooped the rubbish into one hand, but as she glanced about to see if there was more that should be done, she wondered why she had never before truly seen how shabby their kitchen was.

The curtains at the casement had been sewn by her mother and their pretty drape spoke of taste, but calico was the cheapest fabric that might be purchased, and even this was patched. Edwin himself had made the dresser in which was kept the everyday crockery and, over the years, he'd carefully repaired each of the kitchen chairs. Everywhere Ellen looked there was evidence of her parents' thrift and ingenuity. And their pride. For if the Gowan family did not have many of this world's goods, Connie always said they should cherish what they had and be grateful for each other. Ellen swallowed. *Grateful for each other?* They were two now, not three. Yet she, too, had pride. She was Connie and Edwin's daughter. By her actions she must prove herself worthy of her parents. This was her responsibility after the events of yesterday.

But it was hard. Her eyes blurred.

If only she had known what William had been about to do.

If only she had spoken with her father in the church. She might have drawn him outside into the sun and then . . .

She would not! She would not think of what had happened and what might have been. All she had was the present and what must be done. The tabletop, for instance. It must be scoured, for no spot of grease, no morsel of dirt could be permitted to defile her current task.

Thus, after scrubbing the already white wood and washing her hands, Ellen took a single sheet of paper from her father's study and placed it beside the inkwell. Sitting at the table, she dipped a quill and glanced upward. "Help me, Mama."

2nd of August, AD 1843
Archdeacon, the Very Reverend Virgil Anstruther
Park House
Middle Harrow
Near Norwich

Dear Sir,

It is with great sorrow that I respectfully write to you today. My melancholy duty, however, is clear. Since my mother is presently unwell, it falls to me to inform you that my father, the Reverend Doctor Edwin Gowan, your curate in Wintermast, was yesterday the unfortunate victim of an accident. His life was

She could not do it. She could not write the word lost. *Lost* meant her father would never call out her name again. *Lost* meant he would never return home from church. *Lost* meant her mother's anguish and her own. *All* was lost in his death, perhaps even their home for her father must be buried. Would they then lose the right to this house?

Ellen's breath caught in painful gasps. Something was tearing a hole in her chest from the inside. A living thing with power and talons and no mercy at all. Sorrow was too tame a creature to cause such pain. This was anguish. Ellen dropped the quill. Ink defaced the page in blots and dribbles.

"Oh, Miss Ellen."

Polly's arms encircled Ellen's body, but she did not feel that warm embrace. Yet as the gale of feeling blew away, she returned to the surprise of another person's compassion. And the certainty that she must complete her task. Her mother was helpless, she was not. And when Archdeacon Anstruther read what she had written, help would surely be forthcoming.

After a frugal lunch of salad from the garden and boiled eggs, Ellen went to her mother's room with Polly. Between them they propped Connie up against a bolster and as many pillows as could be found in the house, including Ellen's own.

Connie was awake but silently shook her head as Ellen tried to spoon food into her mouth.

"But I made the posset with honey, Mama. Just the way you like it."

Polly nodded encouragingly. "It does look delicious, mam." The maid swallowed a lump larger than an egg as she spoke. Connie's face had sharpened. Her eyes were sunk in dark pits and the bones of her cheeks and nose stood painfully proud. Polly had seen her granny die last winter. Mrs. Gowan had that same pitiable look. The maid had not known before that grief could kill a person.

"Please? Just for me?" Ellen tried to cajole her mother as she would a stubborn child.

Connie, unspeaking, moved her head away. No.

"Perhaps your mam will drink then, Miss Ellen?"

Ellen offered the beaker of milk with both hands. Their tremor was pronounced. "New this morning, Mama."

But Connie would not drink.

Despair roughened Ellen's voice. "Mama, do not die. Do not leave me, I beg you. Please. Just a little sip."

The evil cloud that enclosed Connie Gowan dispersed a little with Ellen's misery. She reached out a hand to touch the tears that dripped from her daughter's eyes, and struggled to sit straighter so as to swallow a little of the milk. But the dark returned. Too quickly.

Prone upon her bed, Connie stared at the ceiling, unblinking. She began to cry, slowly at first, and then more violently until sobs shook her body in the way a dog will shake a rat to kill it. And nothing that her poor unhappy daughter could do was enough to stem the flow. Until, at last, Connie Gowan slept.

CHAPTER 5

I T WAS the evening of the third day after Edwin Gowan's death and Ellen was in her father's vegetable patch. She was digging potatoes for dinner and had hitched her housedress up to mid-shin so that it would not get dirty. Sweating from the work, she was unaware that dirt was smeared across her face. But physical labor was an antidote to despair, and there was some satisfaction to see new cream tubers filling up the bucket by her side. Soon there would be sufficient for several days' worth.

"The Reverend Mr. Wyleford is here, Miss Ellen." Polly's anxiety cut the soft evening into *before* and *after*.

"What? Who?" Ellen was just as startled as their maid. "Mr. Wyleford! Sir, I did not expect, that is . . ." Wiping her hands upon her apron, Ellen hoped the gloaming would be her friend and disguise the action. "Will you step inside? Polly, perhaps you might conduct . . ."

And then Ellen remembered. Her dress. *Her legs!* A hot blush mounted the girl's neck.

Mr. Wyleford, a similarly disappointed curate to Edwin Gowan—he, too, managed an impoverished living for an absentee vicar while hopes of advancement withered—spoke over Ellen. "I have come to see your mother, Miss Gowan."

He frowned as he inspected the girl before him. There was just enough light to see that the daughter of the house was filthy. *What is her mother thinking?*

Intimidated by the man's glance, Ellen faltered. "Sir, I am sorry indeed to tell you—"

"Tell me what, child? Speak plain!" Very tall and very thin—painfully bony, as if food was an enemy, not a friend—the cleric loomed down out of the evening, a black crow with a nose quite sharp enough for a beak.

The girl shrank back, saying, "Mama continues ill. Sir."

The parson opened his mouth, but violently coughed when no words emerged. His father had tried to banish a stammer by putting his son's head beneath the pump each time he could not say a word. The cough remained to remind him.

Inspecting the gaudy sunset as if it gave him personal offense, the man stared over Ellen's head before enunciating with diligent care, "I had expected to interview Mrs. Gowan to ascertain her wishes. I am to conduct the service therefore, regrettably, speak to her I must and shall."

Ellen pulled at her skirt. She was relieved when it fell around her ankles. At last. Decency. Belatedly she understood the sense of what he had said. "Did you say, the service, Sir?"

The man replied testily. "Of course the *service*, child. Did you think your father, a Christian and a cleric, might be buried without one?" From a pocket he extracted a letter and waved it. "My instructions are clear. This came from the archdeacon today."

"Archdeacon?" repeated Ellen, faintly. Why had the Reverend Anstruther not written to her? He must have had her letter by now. "Sir, as I said, she is too ill. It is not possible for you to speak with my mother. But you and I may discuss what must be done."

Her visitor mumbled, apparently to himself. "This is most irregular. Edwin cannot have meant that I should." His tone was so aggrieved, Ellen could only stare.

Her impatient visitor continued, "Your father must be brought here in the morning. I shall arrange it. I believe he lies in his vestry?"

Ellen nodded. Polly had told her where Edwin was, assuring her that Nod had made certain Edwin was respectably disposed, laid out in his Sunday canonicals. Anguish and guilt had kept Ellen from her father's side. He must be so lonely, without even one member of his family beside him. Her eyes filled up and over-flowed.

Alas, the Reverend Wyleford hated women's tears. They embarrassed him, though he could not have named the actual emotion. Eyes and mouth contracting with distaste, he hurried on. "The Archdeacon has devolved full authority upon me, and my duty is explicit. I shall assume control." Ellen swallowed hard. The man's imperious tone made her face hot. Yet she must control herself, for her parents' sake. She tried to sound grateful. "Sir, I thank you for this care of my family, however—"

The cleric cut her off with a loud sniff and slapped his hat on his head, the old-fashioned wig beneath giving out little spurts of dust. "I shall return in the morning. Early." A parting glance, sharp as an awl, left Ellen in no doubt that her visitor disapproved utterly of the Gowans and their irregular way of life. Most of all, he disapproved of Ellen herself.

The following morning, Edwin's coffin was carried into the parlor by Nod and three of Polly's younger brothers.

"Put the trestles there." Elias Wyleford pointed to the end of the room. It was the only dark place in the parlor, and that distressed Ellen.

"Please, Sir, do you think we might place my father near the bow window? The prospect of the garden is charming from there." Edwin had loved to gaze out at the trees as he taught his pupils.

The parson ignored her. A dead man does not care about the view. "Here, I say. Carefully, man!"

Distracted by the sorrowful child, Nod stumbled against the dais. The parson and the girl started forward, but there was no need. The vicar's coffin would not be dropped. Nod said, "Lay him down softly, boys."

The parson peered at the box in which his colleague would rest until the last trump. It was very plain. But a further duty must be observed, though he did not approve. "The casket shall be opened, Mr. Noddington. Those who visit will wish to see Reverend Gowan. Miss Gowan, we shall leave the men to their work. There is much to do and I will not have them distracted."

Elias Wyleford grasped Ellen's hand and towed the girl behind him as he left the parlor. His fingers were cold and hers, warm. Perhaps he meant comfort, but Ellen could not be brought to see it as she later sat with Polly in the kitchen.

"But he will not listen. And my mother does not stir even though I have told her . . . how things stand."

What to say to Connie about the impending funeral had exercised Ellen's mind even as, one by one and in family groups, Edwin's parishioners visited their house in a steady flow all day.

"The reverend has your good at his heart, Miss Ellen. And your ma's also. His task is hard. If he does not feel it seemly that—"

"Seemly? He does not have a heart. *That* is not seemly in a man of God."

It had been Ellen's most fervent wish to sit with her father through the night before his burial. But the minister judged it unsuitable that a girl, an underage daughter, should be the principal mourner of the Gowan family. Thus, on the evening of Edwin's last night aboveground, the schoolroom door had been locked. Only the living pastor and the dead man in his box would pass the funeral eve together. Through the keyhole he had said, "You will thank me one day, Miss Gowan."

In the kitchen, Polly patted Ellen's hand. "He seeks to spare you, that is all."

"But I will not see my father again. And neither will my mother." Ellen was numb. No tears left to cry.

CHAPTER 6

THE STORM woke her. Ellen felt no surprise at the violent weather. God was surely present in this turn from summer to winter on the funeral morning. Perhaps it was His way of mourning the death of His servant. If that were so, He was too late. But today, Ellen must first deal with practical matters. Her clothing. The black housedress would not do—she would not shame her father with a garment so old and faded. Light struggled to rise faster than the punishing wind. It keened, and Ellen could not, but she found the will and strength from somewhere to do what must be done.

In her mother's room, Ellen chatted to the silent Connie as if all was well while she searched the clothes press.

"Mother, I hope you do not mind, but I should like to wear your black straw bonnet today. And the long jacket also—the one with the frogging and the jet buttons. The skirt that goes with it, too, if you please." And gloves. Where were they? She found a pair laid away in lavender, but Connie's best bonnet had disappeared. Until Ellen remembered. The *top* of the clothes press.

"Here it is!"

The hatbox was carefully brought down. Ellen had coveted it all her life for it was a pretty thing—even frivolous. Rose and black stripes, rather faded, adorned the outside where a pasted label declared MLLE. DUPAIRE. BESPOKE MILLINER. LITTLE HAMMER LANE. LONDON. A reminder that her mother had once been young and that her father had actually bought a fashionable hat as a present for his bride in their hopeful early days.

Bespoke Milliner. To Ellen the words conjured magic even if the box now contained only a mourning bonnet swagged in dull veiling.

"Thank you, Mama. Reverend Wyleford will look for me soon, and I must be ready."

Shivering, Ellen stripped off her housedress and pulled the black skirt over her undershift. Turning the waistband over and over into a neat roll, she secured it with pins once the skirt was a suitable length. Ellen tried to move carefully. If she forgot, the thicket of barbs would rake her skin. The jacket proved less difficult. A plaited belt of Russian leather, another relic, was tied twice around the waist to draw the jacket in.

Ellen began to feel some confidence in this hasty creation. If, frustratingly, she could see little detail of her appearance in Connie's dressing mirror, the general shape seemed suitable when covered with her own black shawl.

The last challenge was the hat. Ellen gathered and twisted her hair into a tight hank. This she wound around her head and anchored with long pins. The bonnet, too big if her hair was down, sat neatly over the mass and more hat pins held it there. The wind was high, but she would not scandalize the congregation by losing the bonnet as she walked to church behind her father's coffin.

That stark image punctured Ellen's disassociation from the day and what its function would be. Giddy, she swayed before her own reflection. Bending her head until the vertigo passed, she pulled down the veil so that her swollen eyes could not be seen and walked down the stairs to wait patiently and alone for the Reverend Wyleford.

The parson unlocked the parlor door to find Miss Gowan standing, immobile, before him.

"I shall walk behind my father's coffin, Mr. Wyleford. On behalf of my family." This was a statement. And something in that still, black figure was intimidating. Veiled, properly dressed, Ellen seemed far from the distressed child of the previous evening.

The parson was depressed by the long vigil spent beside Edwin Gowan's coffin. Elias Wyleford was accustomed to death, but he could not deny that an uncomfortable presentiment of his own future had lain before him last night. It was the cheapness of Edwin's coffin that distressed him the most. That, and the certainty that he would not be mourned in the extravagant way of the Gowan women. Passion had never informed his own marital relationship, and it was difficult to imagine his acid-tongued wife driven to madness by his loss. That knowledge made him unaccountably sad. An unfamiliar emotion.

"Very well, Miss Gowan." He spoke softly, and the vulnerability in his eyes startled Ellen.

"Thank you, Sir." Impulsively, the girl stepped forward a pace. For one alarmed moment, Elias Wyleford thought she might kiss his cheek.

"H-h-hot water, if you please. I must wash."

"Polly has a kettle on the hob." Ellen hesitated then said, "It would honor my mother and my father, Sir, if you would walk beside me to the service."

The request caught the priest off guard. Dignified was not a word Elias Wyleford would formerly have applied to Ellen Gowan. "I, too, would be honored, Miss Gowan. Honored."

The people of Wintermast overflowed the ruined church. Those who could not find a place inside thronged the churchyard seeking shelter against a glass-sharp wind off the Wash. It cried like a woman and flung sleet against their raw faces.

Conducting Edwin's service in what remained of St. Michael Archangel made the Reverend Wyleford very nervous. True, the bulk of the building still stood and the wooden ceiling of the nave seemed sound. But if the damaged walls should fall while they were all gathered together, a far greater tragedy would result than the death of just one man, no matter how beloved. And yet the church, shattered though it was, still contained the largest of Wintermast's interior spaces. (The taproom of the George Inn was large also, and had been only slightly damaged, but was scarcely suitable to the circumstances.) The cleric made his decision. The service would proceed in Edwin's church. God must want it so, for it was His storm that had driven them inside.

I am the Resurrection and the Life, saith the Lord. He that believeth in me, though he were dead, yet shall he live. . . .

Ellen seemed to see through the walls of the coffin to the man who lay inside. *Are you there, Father? Can you hear me? Can you see us?*

Whosoever liveth and believeth in me shall never die. For I know that my Redeemer liveth and he shall stand at the latter Day upon the earth. . . .

It was so simple, the oak box in which her father slept. There was no ornament, not even his name carved on the surface. A card and a bunch of violets, from their own garden, were the only adornments. The scent of the flowers was a grace note upon this bitter day. Ellen had lettered the card herself.

> The Reverend Dr. Edwin Gowan, late curate of the parish of Wintermast. Much loved and dearly missed by his sorrowing wife and daughter, and by his parishioners. We are left inconsolable by this untimely passing.

A cruel, cold rain soaked the best clothes of those in the churchyard as they strained to hear. Even the children were silent, half-hidden among their mothers' skirts. The youngest did not understand, but the adults did. Times were hard and now they would be harder still. It was unlikely that Wintermast would ever see a kinder man than their late vicar. And who would rebuild his church and repair their houses? The damage to the village and Edwin Gowan's cruel death were symbols of their lives. The rain wept for them all.

☙

That evening, as she tidied her mother's bedroom, making work for herself, Ellen described the events of the day. Was Connie listening?

"You would have been so proud, Mama." Ellen smoothed the coverlet. How she yearned for love and reassurance. Did her mother know? "More than a hundred souls came to Father's service. Many from beyond the village." Ellen spoke lightly. None of Edwin Gowan's former pupils had attended, nor the Greatorex family.

Sudden thunder burst overhead and Ellen flinched. The last of the storm was heading out toward the Wash. She cupped her candle against the draft. Each precious stub must be guarded now.

Ellen picked up her mother's limp hand and pressed it to her cheek. Connie's skin was cold. "Many kind people have brought us gifts of food, Mama. Papa would have been touched. So generous, especially now when so much has been destroyed in the village."

Half-lifting Connie with some effort, Ellen turned the topmost pillow. "Now, if you are quite comfortable, I shall leave you to rest." The voice of the wind was eerie, as if it said what Connie could not. Ellen was not especially upset tonight as she kissed her mother's brow. Emotion was stored up in some distant place. She knew where it was but had no need to go there.

Closing the bedroom door, Ellen's shadow preceded her down the stairs and into her father's room. He had called it his library. There his desk waited and all his papers. Edwin Gowan had been an orderly man. The walnut desk had three large drawers in its lower part, and above the slanted work surface, a series of small partitions contained his most used books on theology—those he consulted when writing sermons. The drawers, Ellen knew, held household accounts. These went back to the Gowans' earliest years in Wintermast and were written in Connie's hand. Her mother saw to the day-to-day running of the house and she had faithfully noted each small expense, each tiny amount made from the sale of eggs, butter, or milk. The shelves above the desk, however, were where Edwin kept his personal papers. It was these documents that Ellen knew she must now examine.

The candle flame danced. Ellen's hand was shaking. Standing before her father's desk, unwilling to sit in his chair, she said, "Please forgive, Papa, that I see no other course of action."

Of all the things that she had had to do in these last days, this seemed the greatest intrusion into the hidden part of her family's existence. The part that had been her parents' sole domain.

Fearful things are best done quickly, Ellen.

Edwin's voice was so clear, Ellen swung around, expecting to see her father. But he was not there. That empty space was shocking.

"Oh, Papa, if you are here, help me now." Was there comfort in the empty air?

Placing the candleholder on a shelf conveniently provided by her father—from where the light would shine directly on the desk—Ellen sat and extracted the nearest sheaf of documents. As she read, her fears were confirmed. There was no money. None at all. The fees received from the parents of Edwin's pupils last Quarter Day had already been banked and immediately used. True, a three-month portion of her father's stipend—paid in arrears—was to be paid on the first of September, but that was nearly three weeks away. Meantime, because he was not there to conduct the Sunday services, there would be no weekly contribution from the parish, meager though that had been of late (too many trouser buttons in the collection plate, not enough coins).

The food in the house was perishable and would be consumed in a few days—if it could be made to stretch that long. They had nothing.

CHAPTER 7

THE NEXT morning, Ellen sat swollen-eyed at the kitchen table. A small bowl of salted porridge was placed before her.

"I did not know we had oats still, Polly?"

Polly nodded, though she blushed. "There was one crock in the pantry." She busied herself swabbing the dresser shelves, hoping that Ellen would not ask more about this miraculous appearance. *Charity* from the Calstocks was different from the villagers' gifts of cakes and such. Polly's mother had stressed that when she'd arrived that morning with the oats. *"Do not tell her where you got this. She has enough to contend with, Polly."* Of course she had, poor child.

Polly cast a glance over her shoulder. "There is something else I think you should read, Miss Ellen. You will feel better if you do."

Ellen stirred the porridge in the bowl. Polly was kind, but food seemed an irrelevance today. "There are more of my father's papers to be gone through. There is much to assess and I have no time to read for pleasure."

"But these might have a bearing upon the same. Your family's situation, I mean."

With that, Polly hurried to the pantry and extracted a packet of letters from a jar hidden on a high shelf. There were twenty or thirty at least, bundled up and tied with a riband of watered silk.

"And this is only some of 'em. Your mam swore me to keep this secret close. Even from your pa. The letters is from your aunt, and Mrs. Edwin told me he would not have liked to know that they was writing to each other. Mrs. Edwin trusted me to take her replies to

Norwich when I could, and also to bring the letters to her from the post, first, before the reverend could see them. Many times I had to skip to the kitchen just a whisker afore he caught me. We laughed, your mam and me, 'bout that, I can tell you."

Poor Polly. She gulped back tears at the thought of happier days. "It seems so strange, still. Him never coming home. But your aunt, now, she knew what was going on here, the troubles with money."

Polly blushed scarlet at this impetuous remark, and Ellen was discomforted. It was one thing to properly grasp the serious nature of her family circumstances and quite another to find that it had been commonly understood by a girl not much older than she was. How many others in the village were privy to the knowledge?

Polly clasped one of Ellen's hands, saying gently, "Do not be upsetting yourself. Your family's business stays within the walls of this house. Many things you might think me, but do not brand me a gossip, Miss Ellen. Besides, your mam trained me. I may not be the best or most handy girl about the house, and we have our ups and downs, but your mother has trusted me and I would not betray that."

Ellen was shaken. All this time she had thought Polly a heedless creature. The maid patted Ellen's hand. "You read. Go on. You'll feel better."

Wiping her eyes and nose on her sleeve and not even noticing the lapse of good manners, Ellen picked up the first of the letters and was shortly both glad and sorrowful to discover her mother's secrets.

Connie's older sister, her aunt Marguerite, had indeed been generous to their family in the past. Daisy, as she signed herself— though she was the wife of a baronet—had continuously provided small sums of money when circumstances had been particularly bad for the Gowans. And that had been often. Connie had not ever told Ellen of the subterfuge—nor even hinted at the fact.

How strange it was to find a whole river of mystery had flowed beneath the surface of their life for all their time in Wintermast. There it was on paper. Only acute desperation could have brought her mother to beg such favors, since she was a proud person. To explain away the miraculous money, Connie had been forced into further deception. She had allowed Edwin to believe it was earned from the sale of eggs, cream, or even preserves from their orchard fruit. Connie would have hated each one of those lies, but the provision of charity from a member of her estranged family would have been bitter indeed to Edwin Gowan if he had known, and so the lies continued.

Ellen had always loved the story of how her parents first met and fell in love. Now the letters told her a less-gilded version of the truth.

Her father had once been a chaplain and tutor at Peterhouse College, Cambridge, one of the youngest Doctors of Divinity ever seen in that ancient place. *That* Ellen knew, since Connie was so proud of Edwin's scholarship. And her mother had often laughed when she said that the Reverend Doctor Gowan might have been living at the University still, an unmarried don, if a single, fateful event had not occurred one shining day around bud-burst in the spring of 1821.

It was then that the Reverend Doctor Edwin Gowan had first been introduced to Miss Constance Elizabeth Lightfoot. Then seventeen, she and Ellen's grandmother were at Peterhouse to take tea with Septimus, Connie's older brother, who was a scholar there.

It was at this point in the story that Ellen always interrupted, asking, "But what were you wearing, Mama?"

Connie, who pretended not to care for clothes (having few, as a married woman), would say, vaguely, "Oh, pink, I think. A round gown with a flounce or two. And a velvet pelisse."

As part of the ritual, Ellen would coax, "And the bonnet?"

"White straw, lined with swansdown. Silver ribbons."

Inevitably, if Edwin was within hearing distance, he would say, "And as pretty now as then, my dearest one."

The little girl would clamor, "But what happened then?"

Connie would reply that her mother, requiring directions,

sought guidance from a handsome gentleman just then sauntering through the quad in his academic gown, who had replied, "Perhaps you are Mrs. Lightfoot? I am Doctor Gowan, your son's tutor. Septimus has told me of your visit."

With a certain irony, Connie always declared that a life of antiquarian study in a place so perfect it was nearly devoid of women for most purposes, had left the young don's heart perilously undefended. But that when her eyes met his, the course of both their lives was determined.

Ellen frowned now, staring at the text before her. She knew that her mother had been expected to marry well and that when an exchange of letters between the couple had been discovered, the Lightfoots had been displeased. But she had not known the depths of that displeasure nor understood, fully, its consequences.

Edwin had been orphaned young and entered Cambridge on a scholarship. And as a university teacher without family and only a small stipend, he would not do as a suitor for the younger daughter of the Lightfoot family. And yet none of the extensive threats from Connie's father, nor the anguished entreaties of her mother, could deflect the couple from their purpose. They loved each other. There was nothing more to be said.

Therefore, as soon after Connie came of age, a quiet wedding was reluctantly arranged. And on that day, the radiant Miss Constance Lightfoot became Mrs. Edwin Gowan without regret. This had been the end of the story that Ellen knew. Now she learned more.

After the wedding, Connie's family had turned away from their disobedient child, settling only a very small sum upon her as a marriage portion. From the letters, it was obvious that Ellen's grandfather had been an unforgiving, self-righteous man, who had only timidly been opposed by his grieving wife. *If thine eye offend thee, pluck it out* was his philosophy. From her wedding day on, Connie was considered as dead by her father. And his wife, son, and elder daughter Marguerite were forbidden any contact.

But there was worse to come.

On taking a wife, a college don was expected to resign his post, and this must have had serious consequences for the young couple since Connie's small dowry was rapidly consumed in maintaining a semblance of gentility in rented accommodation. Fortunately, just as the money ran out, a kind college friend provided an introduction to the absentee owner of a living in the small village of Wintermast in the county of Norfolk.

The Very Reverend Virgil Anstruther interviewed Doctor Gowan and an offer of the Assistant Curacy of Souls was subsequently made. And there, beside a wide coast of mist and mere, of whispering reed beds and wild seas, the newly married Gowans arrived to make their home. And the family had never left because no further preferment came in all the years that Edwin struggled to support his wife and child as the gentry around the village enclosed the land for sheep, and drove his parishioners to London looking for work.

Ellen had never met her mother's wealthy sister but now, having read Daisy Cleat's words, she gathered a sense of the person from the pages—generous, loving, and concerned to assist her beloved sister while preserving Connie's pride. Ellen liked her aunt for this delicacy of feeling, and for the good sense exhibited in wise advice.

Ellen sighed as she folded the last of the letters. It had been sent only a day or two before her birthday and contained the fond hope that she might enjoy that significant day very much. Thoughtfully, Ellen picked up a pen and began to write.

> 6th of August, AD 1843
> Lady Cleat
> Shene House
> Near Richmond
>
> Dear Aunt Marguerite,
>
> It is my sad duty to inform you . . .

This time, Ellen did not cry as she recounted the tragic events of the last days. In fact, as the letter grew longer and longer, her face brightened.

She had an idea.

Toward evening, Polly found Ellen in the garden gathering windfalls from the largest of the apple trees. In Ellen's sometimes lonely childhood, the branches had been a refuge when she was unhappy. Today, gathering fruit provided practical solace of another kind.

"Good news, I hope, Miss Ellen. Nod brought it earlier."

It was a letter. Her mother's name was written on the front and on the back was scrawled, *Anstruther.* Ellen's frown lifted. "This must be from the archdeacon. I shall take it to Mama immediately!"

Ellen hurried into her mother's bedroom brandishing the letter. "Look what I have here, Mama. Reverend Anstruther has replied at last. Shall I read it for you?" Ellen allowed herself to pretend her mother's silence was consent. Quickly sitting on Connie's bed, she broke the seal and began to read.

> Mrs. Edwin Gowan
> The Rectory
> Church Street
> Wintermast
> 5th of August, AD 1843
>
> Dear Madame,
>
> Please to know that my wife, Mrs. Virgil Anstruther, and I extend our joint and most heartfelt commiserations upon this, your recent unfortunate loss.
>
> Not being informed in a more timely fashion of what has transpired,

Ellen frowned. What did the archdeacon mean? She had written as soon as she could.

> nonetheless we would wish to register, with deep regret, the impossibility of our attendance at your late husband's obsequies. We had been summoned to Norwich, to the bishop's palace there, to discuss the alarming events in Wintermast and other villages in the parish. Only this, the most pressing business imaginable, could have prevented our presence at so sad an occasion to condole with you and Miss Gowan.
>
> I am certain indeed that my appointed deputy, the Reverend Elias Wyleford, did all that was proper and Christian in my place to comfort the parishioners of Wintermast in their double loss—the kind services of your husband and the grievous damage sustained in the earthquake. As a man of belief, you will understand I am sure, that I can only see God's hand at work in both these calamities. Signs such as these are very clear. As ye sow, so shall ye reap.

Ellen faltered. Was the archdeacon saying her father was somehow to blame for both catastrophes? She glanced at her mother. Connie's eyes were open. She was staring at the window through which there once had been a view of the church tower. Ellen cleared her throat.

> The Reverend Doctor Edwin Gowan, your most estimable husband, was an educated man and yet an humble servant of the greater cause in which I am still privileged to labor. He has now, I am convinced, gone to his just reward at the right hand of our mutual Savior.
>
> As I write to you, I hold before me the recent letter from your daughter announcing this most tragic news.

Perhaps, since Miss Gowan will, quite rightly, have been suffering from a wholly natural depression of the spirits, we shall pass over the matter of uncertain spelling and ill use of grammar to observe, merely, that I am grateful for the information contained therein.

Ellen flushed pink. This was unjust! As Edwin's daughter, she had taken such care with every word. "Shall I continue, Mama?" Connie said nothing. "I think I must." Ellen spoke to herself. She was upset, but made an effort to control her feelings for Connie's sake. Clearing her throat, she continued.

Understanding also from Miss Gowan's communication, Madame, that the sad events of the last days have rendered you unwell—for which I am very sorry to hear, the same as is my wife—your daughter has asked that I consider granting a lengthy period during which you may continue to reside in the Grace-and-Favor dwelling that you currently occupy while your affairs are put in order.

Madame, it would give me the very greatest pleasure to accede to this request. However, I find myself embarrassed in this matter. It is my first duty, as vicar incumbent of the parish, to place the spiritual needs of my parishioners at the forefront of my concerns. To that end, I am certain you will understand the necessity of another curate being appointed to Wintermast with all speed since I, myself, am unfortunately not able to oversee this important task. The house attached to the living will therefore be required for a new servant of the Lord.

Ellen's voice trailed away. She swallowed. Holding the page closer, she stared at the individual words. Bland white paper, clear black letters. There was no mistake. The archdeacon was asking them to leave.

"Continue, child." From weakness, and disuse, Connie's voice was a whispering thread.

Ellen almost dropped the letter. "Mama!"

Connie's eyes were sunk deep in shadow, but a spark burned there. One thin hand clasped Ellen's. "Read on."

The child continued. Each word was the blow of a hammer, a well-disguised hammer, but one wielded with precision.

> However, dear lady, as I understand your situation to be precarious, I am pleased indeed to offer you the sanctuary in which you reside for a further two weeks from the date of this letter. After that time has elapsed however, I would ask that you vacate the premises, together with all the goods and chattels you presently possess (and excluding, of course, those that were in situ when your husband took up his post some years ago, and for which I include, with this, an inventory).

Ellen gasped. Did their landlord expect that they would abscond with the furniture?

Connie took the letter from her daughter's hands. "This implied distrust is most wounding of all." The page shook as she read the final phrases out loud.

> Therefore, dear sister-in-Christ, I wish you God speed in your onward journey. May He keep you in the hollow of His hand. And please to know that you have a good friend in the person of this, your correspondent. One who wishes, respectfully, to remain,

> > Your servant in Christ,
> > Virgil Anstruther

> PS: An acknowledgment of this letter will be appreciated.

Fury did what grief could not. It removed Connie Gowan from her own living death. With strength that was surprising, she crumpled the letter and threw it to the floor. Embracing Ellen with arms thinner than sticks, she said, "I am disgusted. *Disgusted!* Bring me a pen. This must and shall be responded to!"

Ellen was seriously alarmed at Connie's hectic color. She said, soothingly, "The letter does not deserve a reply, Mama."

"No. But *he* deserves condemnation. And exposure. I shall write to the bishop. That man's treatment of us, and most particularly *you*, is disgraceful. A child, alone and defenseless!" A hand pressed against her chest, Connie's pallor was now extreme.

Ellen hurried to the nightstand and poured water into a cup. "He is not worth your distress, Mama."

Like a child, Connie held the cup in both hands and drank. At last she was able to speak. "To think *that* man, whom your father did his best to respect and honor, preaches the word of Christ." She shuddered.

"Oh, Mama . . ." Exhausted, Ellen lay down beside her mother. Connie stroked her daughter's pretty hair. The action calmed her. She whispered, over and over again, "I am sorry, child. So sorry."

Ellen said, drowsily, "So am I, Mama. For everything."

She did not know when, finally, she slept, but it was a deep slumber without dreams, for the first time since her father's death.

CHAPTER 8

THE NEXT morning, summer returned, warm and glorious. Ellen brought a breakfast tray to her mother's room and was delighted to find Connie sitting in her chair beside the window. Neatly dressed in an old mourning gown, she had contrived a widow's cap from a piece of black lace to which she had sewn ribbons of the same color. These were tied beneath her chin in a modest bow.

"Mama! You seem so much better." Perhaps it was true. Connie's gaunt face *was* a little brighter than it had been, and her eyes were restored to their accustomed fresh blue.

"I am hungry." Connie seemed surprised. "Do you know, I think I might eat something."

Ellen laughed, though tremulously, as she placed the dish of coddled eggs at her mother's hand. The hens, at least, continued to lay. "It is good, therefore, that Polly cooked these especially, Mama. And I made bread." Ellen did not say that she had used up the last siftings of flour—enough for one small loaf. "I am anxious to know if you like it."

"The smell of baking woke me. A comforting thing, is it not, in a house?"

Ellen did not reply as she arranged a napkin in her mother's lap. Her father had enjoyed the scent of fresh bread. *Christ's gift to a Christian home,* he had called it.

"Thank you, my dear, for all your care of me."

Connie reached up to her daughter, with tears in her eyes, and caught one of her hands. "You have had much to bear."

Ellen knelt beside the chair. How comforting it was to lay her head in Connie's lap. "I have managed, with Polly's help, Mama. She has been very kind."

The hand stroking Ellen's hair paused. Connie said, "I am very glad for it."

Ellen sat up, smiling. She was determined to change her mother's wistful mood. "But now, you must eat, and while you do, I shall tell you of an idea I have had."

Obediently, her mother took a little food from the offered bowl. She could sense that Ellen was nervous.

"Delicious! Please compliment Polly. The eggs are just as I like them. And the bread is . . ." Connie took a bite, and then another. "Excellent. Most accomplished. And very grown-up."

Ellen was warmed by her mother's approval, but after so many days without food, Connie could eat only a little and soon the dish was put aside. "Finish it for me"—she smiled at Ellen—"and Polly shall not tax me for wastefulness." She watched with pleasure as Ellen quickly swallowed what was left, wiping the bowl quite clean with crusts.

Connie sighed. "And so, child, what is this grand stratagem? It must be considerable. I have rarely seen you look so serious."

Ellen stood. "I have something to show you, Mother."

She stepped quickly from the room, and a moment later returned with her aunt's letters. Kneeling beside Connie, she said, hesitantly, "Mama, I have been thinking about our situation. These are yours, I think?" She held up the bound letters.

Puzzled, Connie nodded. "They are, certainly."

Ellen placed the bundle in Connie's lap. "I must tell you something. I have read them."

Connie flushed a brilliant pink, and as quickly the color fled, leaving her face stark and very severe. "You have read my private correspondence?"

"Oh, Mama, please do not be angry. Please! I had to do something and Polly told me about Aunt Daisy. How she has helped us all these years. I read the letters because I could not speak to you directly."

"Then *I* shall speak to that girl. This is disgraceful! The breach of the confidence that was placed in her is—"

"Mother, no! Polly has shown me what needed to be done. Or, the letters have, rather. I have not known how to tell you, but now we have so little time. I *had* to make decisions for us both."

And then it all came out. Ellen tried to explain their parlous circumstances, the need for immediate action. And she spoke, too, about the funeral and what had preceded it. The destruction of the church, and the fact that Edwin had died calling out for his wife.

The ocean of their shared sorrow seemed not to have a shore. But at last, as Connie wiped her aching eyes, Ellen said, "We must go to London. To Richmond. I think we have no other choice, Mama. I have written to Aunt Daisy asking for refuge. She will have received my letter by now. Or so I pray."

Connie finally properly understood the fortitude with which Ellen had faced these last terrible days without her protection. She said, gently, "I am humbled by all you have accomplished, Ellen. Tell me, therefore, what must be done for we shall do it together. Your father would be so proud of your courage since his . . . since he left us."

She held out her arms—and that loving embrace between the Gowan women was all that was required to seal the course of action.

"But, Mama, there is one puzzle I cannot solve, though I have tried."

"And what is that, dear one? When all the other difficulties have been managed so well by you, surely this must be a small thing."

"I am sorry to speak bluntly, but we must have money. And there does not seem to be any in this house, not even a penny piece, that I could find."

Connie smiled. "Well then, if that is what we must have, go to my dressing table. What do you see there?"

Ellen pulled back the small curtain that disguised the plain deal shelves behind. "Your underlinen, Mama. And one or two other things."

"Is there the rosewood box?"

After a moment, Ellen nodded. She had not seen it since it was partly covered by an old Indian shawl. "And there should be another, also. Covered in green leather but smaller. Bring them to me."

The first, inlaid with the initials CG in brass, was deposited in Connie's lap, and she slid a small hook from its keeper to lift the lid. In a nest of sapphire velvet there rested a silver-backed dressing set. A hand mirror, hairbrushes, a pin tray, and an ivory comb with a worked silver handle.

"These your father gave to me. A gift on the day of your birth." With one finger, Connie traced the worked silver, the delicate repoussé work. Ellen nodded. She had always loved the pretty things, so brightly polished and so rarely used. A family treasure.

Distracted by images from the past, Connie's hand strayed to the locket that was around her neck. This, too, was precious. She said, bravely, "Perhaps Edwin would not mind so very much if we sell this as well?"

"Mama! No. You cannot." Ellen was aghast. The locket contained tiny portraits of Edwin and of Connie. He on the right and she on the left of the two halves when opened. Connie herself had painted both likenesses with a tiny sable brush. Each was exquisite. And when the locket was closed, their faces were concealed within a heart of gold.

Her daughter's distress touched Connie. She was grateful for its reason. Reaching out, she kissed Ellen's cheek. "Very well. We shall not sell it. But this, perhaps, must be considered." Connie opened the green box and Ellen gasped.

"Oh, Mama! How lovely." A brooch of rubies lay upon black silk. In the form of a rose, the stones were the size of the nail of Ellen's smallest finger, and at its center was a pearl greater than a very fat pea.

"This is from your grandmother, Ellen, given to me to wear upon my marriage day. It was her mother's also. I had thought to give it to you, when you married. I have never worn it because there was sorrow in the giving, and some in the receiving, as you must now know from the letters. It is the only thing I have of my mother now." She held the brooch to the light. Heart red, blood bright. "But it shall be sold." Said with determination, Connie's eyes were wistful.

Ellen understood. "Something as lovely as this will fetch a fine price, Mama. If you are sure?"

Connie nodded, replacing the jewel in its resting place and handing the boxes to her daughter. "You must go to Norwich with Mr. Noddington. Today. There is a jeweler there. A good man. He will not cheat us of fair price if you say you are my daughter. It may be that he recalls our meeting in the past." Connie coughed, and hurried on before Ellen could respond. "Mr. Eldershaw has his shop in Goldpenny Lane behind the market square. Anyone will know of it."

Norwich, with its crowds and noise and pressed-together houses, was always an assault, and the reek of animal dung and tannery waste was worse on that hot day than Ellen remembered.

The jeweler's shop, however, when they found it, presented an elegant appearance to the street—with white-painted columns and shining windows.

"Nod, will you wait here?"

The carter nodded. He'd never been inside such a place in his life and could only think of his dirty boots. "I shall not stray. But you call if you need me, Miss Ellen."

"I shall. Thank you."

Ellen slipped down from the pillion saddle and walked to the door with seeming confidence. A bell sounded as she entered, high and sweet. Ellen gulped. Silver bells and gilded French chairs were intimidating, but she waved through the window to Nod to reassure them both.

A moment later, an old man in a wig, last fashionable fifty years before, appeared behind the counter from the back of the shop. He was a little taller than Ellen, and his expression seemed kind. Outside, Nod relaxed as he saw the child being courteously invited to a chair.

Time passed, and the morning grew hot in the narrow street. Nimrod, the reliable old cob they'd ridden to town, was hungry. He whickered for his nose bag.

"Much longer and you shall have your lunch, my lad." Nod patted the gelding's thick neck just as the shop door opened. He leaned an arm down. "Up you come, Miss Ellen." He did not like the girl's looks. She was very pale.

"What did the merchant give you?" Perhaps, after all, he must enter the shop to extract a better price for Mrs. Gowan's goods.

Twice Ellen tried to say it. Twenty-eight. *Twenty-eight guineas!* But she choked each time. She passed the little drawstring bag to her companion. Nod whistled when he looked inside, then handed it back to her.

Triumph restored Ellen's voice. "We have enough to travel to London! Much more than enough."

Then her eyes clouded. Twenty-eight guineas was a small value to set on her parents' life in Wintermast. And yet, it was *something*, a significant something, to have saved from the wreckage. She brightened.

The little velvet bag contained hope. At last.

But one more task remained to be accomplished. Connie had asked Ellen to buy new black clothes for them both. The Gowans would wear mourning for a full twelve months, and this was a severe trial. Ellen must find clothes that could be adapted to four distinct seasons. But where were such things to be found?

"You there. Out of the way!"

Though he did not like the man's tone, Nod pulled the gelding to the side of the lane as a river of black-faced sheep flowed by, driven on by their bad-tempered shepherd.

Ellen brightened. "Quickly, Nod, we must follow the sheep!" She pointed toward the market square. "It's market day. And look."

Nod squinted. In the farthest corner of the market square, near the cathedral, a woman had clothing of many colors displayed on the tail of a cart.

"That lady has blacks!" Ellen stared anxiously at her companion. "Perhaps they're just slops, though?" Nod shrugged. Ellen sighed. "Oh well. Nothing ventured . . ."

She began to wriggle from Nimrod's back, but Nod stopped her. "No, Miss Ellen."

"But luck is with us!"

"And yet, child, you must not hurry there nor look too glad to inspect the goods."

Ellen protested, "I have money." She shook the little bag.

Nod frowned, saying quietly, "Do *not* be showing that so freely about. Do you wish to be robbed? Besides, the cart-wife will take you for wealthy, and you'll pay more than you should."

Ellen stared at Nod. "Wealthy? How could she think that?"

The carter pointed at her Sunday clothes, sewn so carefully by Connie, and at her polished boots. He said, patiently, "Well, you don't look as she does, do you? No. First, we shall buy a pie and I shall give Nim his lunch."

He gathered the reins and nudged the flanks of the horse who started forward with a grunt.

"But, Nod!" Anxiously, Ellen tugged at his sleeve. "Someone will buy the clothes while we eat."

The savory aroma of steak and kidney, just then passing by on the breeze, caused Ellen's belly to contract. Breakfast had been long ago and far away. She scanned the stalls, sniffing like a hound.

Nod gazed about no less keenly. "If you are kind enough to buy for us both, well then, we'll break at least one of those bright coins into pence and a sixpence or so along with the shillings. That is the kind of money you must offer. Small coin, rare silver, certainly not gold. She'll not attract much custom while we eat. This is not a market for clothes. Too many farmers selling stock and too few wives."

Ellen went to protest. But instead she stared toward the distant cart and did not dismount as Nod found a baker's stall and tied Nim to a post with his nose bag in place. Later, with a freight of beef pie aboard—a warming burden in the solar plexus—the conspirators planned their campaign.

"Now, Miss Ellen, you must walk past the cart all indifferent. Then turn back, look at what is offered, and sneer."

Ellen gulped. "Sneer?"

Nod said firmly, "It must be done. And no matter what blandishments that old woman offers, you shall walk away."

Ellen lowered her voice and looked anxiously about. She was unaccustomed to conspiracies. "And then?"

"Well, *then*, you shall watch a master at his work." He winked. "Remember, now. Sneer. Think of someone you dislike."

Lady Greatorex! Ellen retied her bonnet ribbons with resolve. To her surprise, as she dawdled through the press of the market, a haughty expression upon her face (or so she hoped), people fell back and allowed her to pass. Near to the cart she paused, as if extremely bored. And that, as planned, allowed the cart-wife an opening.

"Fine wares here, Miss."

Ellen yawned and gazed vacantly at the cart's cargo. Piled up to twice her height were dresses, skirts, and blouses, mantles and shawls and coats. Some garments had also been hung out on poles. Propped against the sides of the vehicle, these fluttering husks of another's life might have seemed pathetic to one in less need. But Ellen's eyes sharpened at the sight.

"I see you looking at the black bombazine, Miss. These clothes formerly were the property of Mrs. Percival Weigland. I use the lady's good name only to speak to their quality. An old family, all their goods first class. Sadly, the lady died on Tuesday last.

"Her daughter, being distraught, declared all her mother's clothes must be sold, so as not to be reminded of her loss."

Ellen stared across the busy market, saying nothing. Was it right to be the beneficiary of another's sorrow?

"I know what you are thinking, Miss."

Startled, Ellen said, "You do?"

The woman, small but vigorous, pressed close. She nodded, tapping one finger to her nose. "You be thinking your own dear mama would look very fine in this." With a flourish she brought down a pole and waved the gown at its end like Regimental colors.

Made of watered black silk, jet beads had been sewn in a key pattern around the neckline, and lace filled the décolletage. A fine garment, expensively made, if a little passé in style.

Ellen raised her brows. "The black is somewhat faded, however?"

"Oh no, Miss." The seller anxiously spread the skirt. The hue of the silk was even and dense, and from the folds of the fabric the ghost of lavender wavered upon the air.

A brief glance, and Ellen turned away, hoping the woman had not seen the avarice in her eyes.

"Wait, Miss! I have more."

Muttering, the cart-wife briskly picked through her stock. Standing behind, Ellen saw two other dresses that would suit Connie or even herself, if the waists were drawn in with a belt and the skirts tacked up. One, a night gray jersey, the other, black merino wool so fine that it, too, might have been silk. And there were also skirts and bodices, separate pieces in dark colors that might look well upon either mother or daughter.

"And here is the very best I have."

The woman dragged two garments from a pile. "The cloak is French. The other, all the way from Calicutt, was made for a dusky princess, as I was assured."

A caped cloak of indigo blue gabardine, so dark that it was three quarters sister to black, and lined with charcoal silk. The other was a large shawl intricately embroidered black on black, with small beads of gold attached along its edges. Ellen knew that Connie could use such a garment to transform even the plainest gown.

The seller, in the frenzy of her search, had also cast aside a promising sleeved mantle of black velvet with frogging in the military style. It lay beside a mass of other garments, orphaned from its rightful place upon a rich woman's back. From the bottom of the pile, two pairs of kid boots, both black, had also emerged, and now lay abandoned beside the cartwheels as if just kicked off by their owner.

With reserve bordering on hauteur, Ellen said, "I see nothing that I like. Good day." She turned away.

"Miss? You have not seen all!"

But Ellen strolled on, playing the part of a spoiled Miss with bad manners as if born to the role.

Some minutes later, after trying to understand all that Ellen wanted him to buy, Nod ambled toward the cart and allowed himself to be caught in similar fashion.

Ellen, hiding behind Nim, watched breathlessly as once again the game of inspecting and selecting, and inspecting again—with much scandalized shaking of the head on Nod's part—was played to the finish, and a price discussed with animation. Returning with five extremely large brown-paper parcels, Nod shrugged when Ellen exclaimed at his success. And at how little money he had spent.

"Do not feel you have cheated that lady. She got those clothes for nothing. What daughter, grieving for her mother, sells the clothes she does not want to keep?"

"But five shillings and eight pence, Nod, *with* the second pair of boots thrown in? That cannot be fair."

Nod grinned. "We have paid less than we might have if the cart-wife had waited for a better market. She was greedy, but now has five shillings and eight pence she did not have before. Do not feel sorry for her trouble—she would not for yours!"

Riding home to Wintermast, Ellen considered what Nod had said. How complicated life was—the surface so different from what lay beneath. With what remained of the money, and their rich new clothes, she and Connie would now not have to arrive in Richmond seeming bereft of a place in the polite world.

Perhaps, if they could only grasp it, a future might be found outside Wintermast.

CHAPTER 9

THE FOLLOWING days passed rapidly, each moment over-filled. But Ellen could not sleep on their final night in Wintermast. Below, the old clock in the hall ground out the tenth, eleventh, and, finally, twelfth stroke of midnight.

Shivering, she sat up. What would her next bed be like? This one was too short for her lengthening body. She had to sleep curled up like an infant, yet its lumps and bumps were a warm refuge on a cold night when the rain fell on the thatch, or a place of retreat when in distress.

What if there was no similar haven to be had in London?

Two weeks had passed since Ellen had written to her aunt and if there was no post tomorrow, they would leave Wintermast not knowing if a welcome awaited them in Richmond. Would her aunt's family take them in, or would they be turned from the door? Ellen winced at that dark thought.

Kicking back the covers, Ellen felt for the flint that lay beside the candlestick. *Click-scritch!* Why were all noises at night so loud? And again, *click-scratt!* A breathed hiss, and light bloomed beneath her fingers as the wick caught.

So worried was Ellen, she did not notice the tallow's reek, or that her hands shone luminous with the flame behind them, something she had always found magical.

Light peopled her room with shadowed objects. Beneath the window lay a wooden trunk. In it were the few things that she and Connie would take to London. Packing its contents had been the final task of last evening, though it was not yet corded-up in case they should remember something in the morning.

"Are you there, Father?"

Taking her candle to the window, Ellen drew back the pale curtains and gazed out toward that part of the sky where once the church tower had stood.

"Do we have your blessing to leave Wintermast?" *To leave you?* That is what she meant but could not say.

Nothing, no sound, no shift of wind, answered Ellen Gowan. The starless night was silent.

At first light, Ellen found her mother standing before the small looking glass in her bedroom. Some strands were loose about Connie's shoulders as she pinned up her hair, and there was white now among the nut brown. In the reflection, the mother sought her daughter's eyes.

"There is one final thing before we leave."

Ellen was dismayed. She had thought her mother's spirit and body were mending, but this morning Connie's frailty was clear.

"You must rest before the journey. I can do what is required, Mama."

But Connie held out her hand. "Will you come with me to say good-bye?"

Peace, soft and deep, suffused the air of Wintermast's burial ground. Gravestones leaned together, old friends with time. They alone knew who lay beneath the turf, since the winters of a thousand years had washed away their ancient inscriptions. And it was there in the green quiet among the yew trees that Connie and Ellen had their final conversations with those they loved so much. Ellen's brothers and sisters and now, her father, too.

Connie held the hand of her last living child very tightly. This was the first time she had seen where Edwin lay.

"It is a comfort that Mr. Noddington will place your father's memorial here soon. He is a kind and good soul." She paused at the head of Edwin's grave. "The storms of winter will not touch your brothers and sisters here. They have each other. And now, your dearest father will protect the little ones as he did you."

One by one, Connie placed a posy of meadow flowers upon each of her children's graves, but the roses from her garden she saved for their father. Ellen ached for what was lost as her mother laid the flowers upon the rich earth.

And then Connie knelt and spread wide her arms as if to embrace Edwin beneath the clay. That was too much.

Ellen crumpled and they mourned together, grains of soil clinging to their clothes.

Until the end of her life, Connie would keep a little of what she brushed from her skirts that morning. That tiny packet she placed beneath her bodice, tight against her heart.

It was the last link that remained to Wintermast, and to him.

Later in the morning, Nod pulled up his dray at the parsonage, calling out cheerily.

"Anyone here for Norwich? What about you, fair lady?" He touched his shapeless hat. Connie smiled at the little compliment.

"Certainly, Mr. Noddington. Today is the very day."

Mrs. Edwin Gowan stood at the front door with a straight back. Ellen, red eyed now that the moment had come, was not so strong.

"Climb up, child."

Nod reached down to help Ellen, and as Connie joined them on the cart seat, she settled her new traveling cloak with a practiced twitch. Poor she might be but she was certainly not without some small vanities.

"There is but one box between us. Some few others of our

possessions are to be sent on, and Polly has kindly agreed to see to that, but she will need your help, Mr. Noddington. We shall make appropriate payment, of course."

Connie spoke with calm and scrupulous courtesy as if this journey, so fraught with uncertainty, an ending and a beginning, was a course she had chosen and not a thing forced upon them by fate.

"Polly, come here, child."

Poor Polly. Standing in the doorway and watching, she tried hard to stifle the sobs that racked her. Leaning down, Connie drew the girl into her arms and kissed her.

"May yours be a long and happy life, Polly. We shall think of you often. A kind heart such as yours is rare treasure indeed."

Ellen looked on in wonderment. How strange it was now to remember that these two had once found every day spent together a trial.

The girl swallowed, then said, "Good-bye, Mrs. Gowan. May your journey be fortunate, too, with a warm welcome at its ending. And, will you write to me with your busy fingers, Miss Ellen? It would please me to know how you are getting on?" She tried to smile.

Ellen, too, embraced the girl who was now her friend. Her grief was sharp as a wound. They really were leaving. Polly's brimming eyes told her so.

Having loaded the luggage, Nod thought it a kindness to urge Nim through the ruined village as quickly as he could. A final wave to Polly, and the Gowan women set their faces toward the road. They did not look back at the parsonage or the figure weeping at the front door of what had been their home.

But as the cart rolled along the hard summer track, faces appeared at doorways and windows, and voices called out, "God speed you, Mrs. Gowan. And you, too, Miss Ellen. A happy future to you both."

Ellen tried not to cry with those they passed, but her longest glance was reserved for the churchyard. She twisted around and watched until, at last, the broken building disappeared behind a bend.

"Rest, my dearest ones. I shall return to lie among you." Connie whispered the words so soft, she had not expected that Ellen might hear her. But she did.

It was well past the dinner hour when the Norwich coach rolled into the yard of an inn in Cheapside, after a journey of two days. Less dusty than the highway but noisier and just as busy, the White Hart Inn accommodated two hundred horses in its stables, and the many-storied black and white house provided lodgings for almost as many travelers.

Among the shouting and bustle, as their horses were uncoupled and a fresh team led to the traces, Connie stretched out a hand to her daughter. "I feel so strange, child. Dizzy and weak."

Ellen, less affected by the sudden difference from motion to no-motion, helped Connie down and escorted her to a long bench. More than one of their companions was resting there, white faced after being rocked about for so long.

"I shall find our trunk, Mama. And then, when you feel well, we will make our way to Richmond."

But securing their luggage was difficult. Ellen was confronted with a mound of boxes, bags, and sacks, their trunk being at the very bottom of the pile.

"Sir? Sir, may I ask for your assistance?"

An ostler's boy turned toward Ellen. His expression remained hard, though he saw, of course, that the girl was pretty, if very young.

Fingering the coins in her reticule, Ellen said, "If you would convey this box to that lady, there will be a penny when she and I are safely on our way."

Muttering half curses from the weight of his burden, the youth dropped the trunk at Connie's feet and held out his hand for the money. It was then that Ellen decided upon a daring course of action.

Ellen said, "Mother, we shall hire a wherry."

"All the way to Richmond? The expense, Ellen, is . . ."

"Less than observing you collapse. You are not well and we surely can*not* walk to my aunt's house carrying our trunk!"

Connie began to protest, but as she stared at the eddying throng in the courtyard, she saw no kind response in any face. None would catch her eye or even smile. That, more than all things, convinced her of what must be done. She would not risk her daughter to the uncertainties of London's streets.

"Very well. We shall take the river to our family." It had a fine brave sound, *family*.

CHAPTER 10

THE TIDE was rising on the Thames as the Gowan women descended the public water-stairs. On Connie's insistence, they held fast to each other's hands. She was fearful that Ellen might be lost among the crush of people.

"Room, Sir!" The stable-hand had been persuaded, for another penny, to transport their box in a barrow from the inn. He had a loud, harsh voice, and the Gowans hurried close behind as he bumped his burden from step to step. Connie smiled nervously at the affronted strangers in their champion's wake, but Ellen did not. She was staring at the women's clothes.

"Ellen! Your skirts!" Connie urgently demonstrated lifting the hem of her gown. Enough so that it did not drag in the grime, but not so high as to expose the ankles.

"Young man, there seem many boats to choose from."

A mass of craft jostled and rocked just beyond the shore, each occupied by a waterman shouting out his own particular service. Connie raised her voice against the human din.

"What should we expect to pay to Richmond?"

The boy was brusque. Soon he would be missed at the inn. "Two shillings even."

Connie's shock was considerable but before she could balk, Ellen said loudly, "For so much, my mother will expect an excellent vessel and good service."

Their youth grunted but cast the girl an alert look. "That red hull. Over there." He pointed at a wherry that was dirt brown rather than red at the outer edge of the congregation of boats. He cupped his hands and bellowed.

"Lady and daughter here. For Richmond." A wave from one of the watermen in the chosen vessel acknowledged the request. But the vigor of the objections hurled at the outsiders intimidated Connie, as the other boatmen, only reluctantly, allowed passage to their chosen vessel.

"Should we not take one of the nearer vessels, Sir?"

The boy shrugged. "Not if you want good service. They're friends of mine and will see you right." He nodded at the boat as it bumped against the wharf, and winked at Ellen but held out his hand for the penny just the same.

Once out upon the river's face and away from the arches of the bridge, their chosen watermen pulled hard against the flow. In the dazzle of the afternoon, the wherry made steady progress as a breeze blew the river's stench away toward the distant, unseen ocean.

Above and below the bridge, the river was busy with life. Ships and skiffs of all sorts and sizes were abroad, some bound for the East India docks and London's pool with sails half-yarded, or heeling over toward the many wharves and private moorings that jagged out into the river's stream.

At length the noise and babble of the city lessened, and the warmth, the slap of the water against the hull, the rhythmic pull of the blades eased Ellen's passage toward sleep. She leaned against her mother.

Untying the ribbons of her daughter's bonnet, Connie said, "Rest, child, we shall be there soon enough."

"Tell me about Richmond, Mama. Does my aunt live in a very grand house?"

Connie did not immediately respond. Then she said, "My sister does indeed have a fine home. Your uncle is a prosperous man."

Ellen settled against Connie's shoulder. "But what does he do, Mama?"

"He is a lawyer, child."

Ellen yawned. It was hard to absorb this new world when sleep reached out with misted fingers.

"I shall see it all, properly, next time. The river, I mean." Did Ellen think the words, or say them?

Ellen slept, and when she opened her eyes, the sky was half dark. A banner of scarlet was flung across the horizon where land met sky, and here and there, moving shafts of gold poured through rents in the evening cloud. In the east, the first stars could be seen, silver dots in the mazy evening.

"Wake now, Ellen." Her mother's voice was stronger, more purposeful. "We are here." They had arrived at the edge of a town.

Above, on the riverbank, warm light streamed from the windows of an inn, and only a step or two away a cluster of single-horse carriages waited for last custom. Ellen heard the drivers talking. Someone laughed and her spirits lifted. It was good to hear laughter.

Their arrival at Richmond was speedily accomplished. Negotiating the gap between the boat and the landing cautiously, the watermen assisted the Gowans to the shore. A carriage was quickly chosen and their box strapped on, as Connie and Ellen climbed inside the dark interior. The smell of sweat and mold were pungent reminders of previous passengers and time itself. The cabbie climbed upon his box and called down, "Madame, where would you have me take you?"

Connie clutched Ellen's hand tightly.

"Shene House, if you please. It is a mile or so beyond the town upstream. The estate is on the river. Perhaps you know it, driver?"

A moment of silence and then, "I know it, Madame. Everyone around Richmond knows Shene House." The man's tone was odd, but he wheeled the cab about without further remark and, clucking to the horse, set Connie and Ellen upon the course that Edwin Gowan's death had decreed.

It was close to full night as their carriage rattled to a stop outside a lodge on the walled perimeter of an estate. The gates that spanned the drive were fast closed.

Ellen's eyes strained to penetrate the gloom. A confused impression of towers and buttresses could be made out in the distance, specter gray against black, with ranges of many windows piled one upon the other. But all were dark. Perhaps the family was not at home?

The driver called out, "Gate. Gate ho!"

Nothing stirred. Muttering, the driver clambered down, puffing with the effort for he was very fat. A moment later, he beat upon the lodge door with a cushioned fist. "Gate! I have visitors for your master and mistress."

Silence.

Wind moved through the trees, a great breath, as branches tossed, creaking, toward the now-invisible stars. Ellen shrank close to her mother's side. They were both too anxious to speak.

Again, the driver addressed the blank door and called out impatiently. This had been a long and tiresome day and he wanted his own fireside, ale, food, and a pipe, in that order.

"Gate! Come, man!" After a moment he turned and shrugged. "Ladies, what would you have me do?" Connie gasped but said nothing. Her worst fears had been realized.

The man began a weary trudge back to the carriage when, suddenly, the door of the lodge was wrenched wide and a wash of light displayed a narrow-faced man with a napkin tucked into his neck band.

They had disturbed the gatekeeper at his dinner and he was not pleased. He held his lantern high, waving it toward the house.

"No one said to expect visitors." His tone was rough. Unannounced females in a shabby carriage could not be of importance.

In glacial tones Connie addressed the man from inside the vehicle.

"I imagine that my sister, Lady Cleat, will be greatly displeased by your insolence. Open this gate. Immediately."

The man's bravado hissed out of him, punctured like a bladder. He pulled the napkin from his neck and, bowing, hurried to obey. Hauling first one gate and then the other back to their full extent, an aperture formed that was far wider than their small carriage required. Assumed authority had created this servility. Ellen would remember that.

The hackney rocked and bucked as the driver clambered back to his seat. He gathered the reins and flapped them, and the Gowans bowled through the opening, leaving the lodge keeper in their dust.

A half-moon was rising and in the torn light, the ribbon of a white drive unfurled before them as Shene House, turreted and partly hidden by trees, loomed ever closer, the silver river at its feet. Was it possible that this vast building would become their home?

Ellen saw her aunt's house stood upon a low mound of higher ground, the better to survey the river. But the trees of its park crowded close to a set of outer walls, the fortifications perhaps of earlier days. Later she would learn that these parapets enclosed the gardens around the main buildings, but to her eyes, their frowning height at first suggested a prison.

The cabbie slowed his horse as the drive opened upon an entry court between a pair of towers. Each was topped by a chain-draped griffin clutching an escutcheoned shield. Their expressions were not friendly, as if they resented the impertinence of these approaching strangers. As they passed beneath that ferocious gaze Ellen shivered. She had a sudden image of the hansom seen from their height. It must seem about as small as a beetle!

The carriage rolled across the empty forecourt between two long wings of the house. Closer and closer, the central range of rooms presented a broad, flat face three stories high and many windows wide. This part of the house was surmounted by a pediment in the Greek style, and a flight of wide, shallow steps led up to a pillared portico on the scale of a small temple. Beneath that, two great doors, each three times the height of any normal man and bound in bronze, were closed against the world.

"Mama, there! Do you see?"

An orb of silver was moving from room to room behind the windows. One solitary lamp. No other light spilled from the rest of that vast, dark building.

"Yes, child. I expect they will have heard our approach."

Connie straightened Ellen's bonnet and quickly retied the ribbons of her own. Her fingers were clumsy. It was hard to see the true state of their clothes. Perhaps that was a blessing, for though Connie had tried to brush off the accumulated journey dust before entering the hackney, it was only later that she saw how truly filthy she and Ellen were.

Gravel crunched as the carriage stopped, and the driver, puffing, clambered down once more. The Gowans, educated now, braced against the sealike swaying. Panting, he wrenched the door open and pulled down the steps, even holding up a hand to assist Connie.

Their boots made a brave sound as they walked across the graveled court toward the steps. The pebbles were spread so thick, their feet left barely a mark upon its moon white surface. Behind them, the driver trod heavily, breathing hard under the weight of the box. The effort carved channels of sweat upon his veined cheeks, which was clear to see when one of the two doors beneath the portico opened and light shone down.

"What do you want?"

This unfriendly greeting issued from the mouth of a giant—an *ebony* giant. Ellen had never before seen a person with dark skin and gaped from shock, for which she received an unfriendly stare.

The man did not address the visitors further. He glared at the driver.

"Well? Who are these people?"

The cabbie gulped. Claret-faced and shapeless with his own lard, he looked a lesser form of life when measured against their magnificent interrogator.

Having come so far to reach this door, Connie was determined they should be admitted. Placing a hand upon Ellen's shoulder, she spoke clearly and calmly, as if she might not be understood.

"I am Mrs. Edwin Gowan. My sister, Lady Cleat, will know to expect us. This is Miss Gowan, my daughter. Please to inform your mistress that her sister and niece are without."

Would the man stare her down? Would he slam that great door upon their hopes? A long, insolent glare attempted the contest, but at last the giant stood aside. That was all the invitation the Gowans ever received to enter Shene House. And the man made sure they understood his authority. Staring at the cabbie, one thick arm described a half circle.

"The tradesmen's entrance is at the back of the house. Take the luggage there. You will be paid for your services. Go."

The door crashed closed upon the driver's affronted face. Mother and daughter both heard him shuffle away with a disgruntled *hhnmpff!* and then came the snap of his boot heels as he descended the stairs to the forecourt, wheezing.

The noise of the door being bolted was as loud as the report of a gun. Ellen jumped with fright, though Connie did not, for she had armored herself, mentally, against this contemptuous man.

Inside the house it was colder than the open night. But there came, then, the click of a flint as a candle was lit. Four more in sconces on either side of a tall mirror were kindled, and the glass doubled the lights, but the silvering was old and as mottled as a map. The reflection of their faces wavered strangely when they moved, as if Connie and Ellen were wraiths, conjured from another realm.

Peering out from behind her mother, Ellen observed all that could be seen by candlelight. They were in a hall-like room of vast proportions, and the ceiling, far above their heads, was lost in shadow, though she could just make out that it was painted with what appeared to be a riot of allegorical figures. Gods? Saints? Impossible to tell.

The walls were wainscoted to half height in matched, colored marble. Above, there were rows and rows of portraits. All those eyes staring down from the gloom were intimidating.

"Wait here."

The man of shadows (for such he seemed) pointed to a wooden settle. It was richly carved but hard and uninviting. One by one, doors opened and closed as his footsteps, and the light he carried, receded deeper and deeper into that otherwise silent house.

CHAPTER 11

ONNIE GOWAN sagged. She would have fallen except Ellen caught her and half-carried her mother to the settle. As she sat, Connie covered her face with her hands. She fought not to cough.

"Mama?" Ellen spoke hopefully, though her voice trembled. Her mother was still so frail, and the journey had taxed her. "We have arrived. And soon we shall sleep between clean sheets, and then tomorrow . . ." The brave words faltered.

Connie dropped her hands. Her face was drained though she gazed about, trying, as her daughter had, to absorb the form of this place.

"Mama? All will be well, will it not?" Ellen asked only what all children ask for: certainty in an uncertain world.

Connie sat straighter. Holding out her arms, she summoned a smile for her daughter. "Come here, my darling."

The girl huddled close to Connie's side. She would have liked to hide her eyes in her mother's shoulder, so unfriendly was the feeling of that cold room.

Connie removed Ellen's bonnet gently. "Whatever shall happen, we have each other. That will always be. I shall never abandon you. Not while I live." Just then footsteps could be heard, returning from the same quarter. The heavy tread of the man and a lighter footfall, almost running. Connie fell silent.

"Sister!"

The door opened and a slight, pretty woman darted toward them, arms wide in a welcoming embrace.

"Oh, I had quite given you up, Connie. And this must be my dearest niece?" Ellen curtsied and was drawn into a warm embrace. "Let me but look at you, dear child!"

Kissing Ellen's brow, Daisy Cleat continued at impetuous speed. "I wrote to Wintermast immediately when I received your letter, Ellen, saying that it was my dearest wish you should come to us, but there was no reply."

Connie blinked. "This is very strange. We did not receive your letter."

The sisters, hands joined, peered at each other, puzzled but smiling. Daisy laughed, though Ellen thought her aunt oddly nervous.

"Oh, there will be an explanation, sister, and we shall find it. Do not fear. But I am so sorry for this dark homecoming. Isidore does not like to light unused parts of the house. Yet if I had known of your arrival, every window would have been ablaze to welcome you to Shene."

Connie smiled warmly. "You have not changed, dearest sister. Always generous."

"Oh, Connie, step closer to the light. To think that you were eighteen when last we saw each other."

Daisy's voice faltered. Perhaps it was the emotion of the moment, but her sister's face, seen beside her own in the eerie surface of the old mirror, seemed so much more haggard. A stranger, viewing them thus together, might think Connie the older of the two.

Connie rallied, "And you but twenty, if memory serves."

"And yet *you* were the first to be married. I was quite left upon the shelf!" Daisy Cleat turned toward Ellen, beckoning the girl to join them.

Connie laughed—actually giggled, Ellen thought in wonderment. "No shelf for you, dearest sister, for I know that marriage beckoned very soon." A moment's pause. And what was not spoken hovered, light as feathers. Ellen looked from one to the other. There were secrets here. "A flower you were named for, Marguerite, and a flower you still remain. Bright and pretty and fresh as the daisy you are."

"And to speak of pretty! Ellen is a beauty even so young. Ah, she and Oriana will be such fast friends. My dearest child has always longed for a sister." A shadow passed across Daisy Cleat's face, quickly banished.

Forgotten by the women, the manservant coughed. Daisy addressed the man over her shoulder.

"Yes, Warwick. Shortly."

Her tone was constrained. Another might not have sensed it, but the sisters, it seemed to Ellen, resembled each other in more than their features. She could always tell when her mother was anxious and Daisy was no different, though she smiled brightly when she said, "I can see how tired you are from your journey, and surely you must be famished. Warwick, conduct Mrs. Gowan and my niece to my rooms. Jane is to be sent to them there. Their luggage, too, is to be brought upstairs."

She hesitated and then made a dismissing motion with her hand, as if she expected her order to be countermanded.

"Jane is my maid, Connie. She will assist you to dress. We have not yet dined. Isidore travels very frequently to the city and often he will stay at his club. His profession is a most demanding one, of course. We had not expected that he should return to us tonight but it is fortunate indeed that his plans were altered."

Daisy turned to her niece. "And, dearest Ellen, your cousin Oriana will be delighted for you to join her a little later for a children's supper in the nursery. Now, I must apprise my husband that you are safely arrived. He will be so pleased. Come, Warwick, about this happy business, and with dispatch!"

These last words were joyously pronounced, but Daisy's voice trembled a little. In that moment, a cold, phantom hand became a fist beneath the waistband of Ellen's dress. Something was not right.

After kissing Connie and Ellen and commending them once

more to Warwick's ministrations, Daisy Cleat hurried away. Ellen found that strange. Why did her aunt not conduct them herself?

Worse, the man himself stood beside the inner door with no indication from his expression that he intended to obey his mistress.

Connie folded one of Ellen's hands through the crook of her arm. "How delightful it will be to meet your cousin and my niece, at last." She did not name her sister's husband and Ellen wondered about it. "Now, Warwick, we are ready. Conduct us, please, if you will be so kind."

The man, so addressed, bowed without expression. He threw back the door with a graceful movement, a lamp held high to light the way, the pattern of a model servant.

Connie said, brightly, "I confess I shall be pleased to change out of these clothes. And the prospect of rest in a good bed is enticing indeed."

The door closed behind the little party, and Warwick led them at a measured pace toward the back of the house through a chain of increasingly illuminated rooms. Few were smaller than a good-size barn, thought Ellen, and none of them cozy.

At last they entered a grand central chamber and blinked in the dazzle of a many-branched candelabra. Immediately before them, a noble staircase of white marble ascended in two broad, unsupported curves to where floor upon floor disappeared into darkness.

"Madame, I shall see that Jane is brought to you upon the instant." Warwick's bow was deep. Greatly condescending, he even addressed a courteous inclination of the head to Ellen. However, the pair had little time to reflect upon the magnitude of the change before he swiftly departed through a baize-covered door beneath the nearer part of the divided stairway.

Connie quivered. Ellen could feel the energy of desperation drain away in a flow as real as breath.

"Just a little longer, Mama." Her hand was beneath her mother's arm, and she stood as close beside her as she could. There were violet circles beneath Connie's eyes.

"You are my kind and loving support, child. And I am ashamed. Again. This is not right."

Ellen whispered, "We are each other's strength, Mama."

"Mrs. Gowan? Miss Gowan? I am Jane, Lady Cleat's maid."

A plain woman of something close to thirty with a wide face and the luminous eyes of the very shortsighted bobbed a curtsy. Without apparent humor, Jane's air was grave, but honesty and kindness were there to be observed by those with the wit to see.

"Please to follow me, Ma'am. And you, Miss. You must both be fair exhausted."

The maid's voice was pleasant with a warm west-country burr. Her accent brought to mind the low fizz of bees, busy in the blossom of Ellen's favorite apple tree at Wintermast.

"And, here we are."

Some domestic sorcerer had set a hip bath filled with hot, scented water before a fire in the cheerful room they now entered. All its appointments were opulent. Gilded mirrors hung upon every wall, and the windows were all covered in a fall of red silk. To call these adornments *curtains* was too mean a word.

"This is my mistress's dressing room, Mrs. Gowan."

"A bath!" Connie brightened visibly.

The maid smiled. "There are screens in the corner, Mrs. Gowan. Perhaps I may help you to undress there while Miss Gowan rests? I shall attend to you, Miss, a little later."

Jane pointed and Ellen saw that an armchair had been drawn up close to the fire. A worked velvet rug had been flung over one arm and a cheerful little cushion provided for her head. The child required no second urging. Two days of bone-jolting travel upon hard benches and the moldy cushions of the hackney, and now here was a plush-covered chair with feather cushions, deeper than any bed, into which she might sink.

Too soft, too deep. Moments later, Ellen fell asleep, and woke only when a gentle hand, which she had thought, in her dream, to be her mother's, recalled her to the firelight-flickering, candle-illumined world they now inhabited.

"Miss Ellen? Miss? Should you like to wash?"

Connie smiled at her daughter from the mirror of an ebony dressing table as Ellen scrambled from the embrace of the chair. Dressed in the black silk gown from Norwich, Connie made a pleasing sight. The dress was creased from packing, but she had paired it with the black and gold cashmere shawl. She looked just as Ellen had hoped she would—like a well-clothed and genteel person.

But Ellen was suddenly anxious. Her only suitable gown for evening was dark gray, and that would more properly suit half mourning after Christmas. Now, its lighter hue could be seen as lacking respect for her father's memory.

Connie understood the dilemma. "Your aunt has a surprise for you, Ellen. Do show her, Jane!"

"Very well, Madame." Jane opened an armoire and extracted something from it. Returning, a gown could be seen laid across her arms. Fine black lace over an underskirt of ink-dark peau de soie.

"This was Miss Oriana's. It was made for her last year when her grandmother died. The old Lady Cleat, that was, her father's mother. Miss Oriana is taller since that time and this dress was hardly worn before she began to grow."

Jane displayed the garment for Ellen, who said, hesitantly, "It is beautiful." She was afraid to touch the lace. It was finer than a web. "And very valuable. I should be frightened of damaging it."

"But your aunt asks if you would consider wearing it as a particular favor to her. First, however, you must bathe and we shall brush the dust from your hair."

Connie's eyes were brilliant and happy at last. She knew how well this elegant garment would suit her daughter.

Jane had summoned more cans of hot water from the kitchen as

Ellen slept, and the bliss of sliding deep into steaming water was profound.

Grit begone, Ellen thought. *Smuts and filth float away and trouble me no more!*

Gazing down, her arms and legs appeared distorted by the water, but in that state of hazy enjoyment, Ellen pursued a critical assessment of each part of her person. *Toes ten, straight; knees two, rounded; thighs two, thin; belly one, a little rounded; chest . . .*

There she stopped. Her body, that comfortable, flexible thing that had carried her through the world without complaint, was now different. Changes had happened, and very suddenly. And since Ellen now saw these differences in her person, so, too, must her mother. And Jane. A stranger.

Ellen's skin flushed deep scarlet. She cringed down beneath the clear water, trying to hide.

Sensitive Jane understood. She said, softly, "I believe there is a draft. Miss Gowan, I should not like you to catch cold. Allow me to pull the screens around, and I shall leave you a bath sheet."

Connie called out, "Hurry, child, I should not like to keep your aunt and uncle waiting."

Behind the screens, Ellen left the bath with confused regret, and did not look again at any part of her body as she clambered over the side and wrapped herself in the bath sheet. In fact, she turned her head away lest a glimpse of any unfamiliar aspect of her person confused her further.

Soon clothed in the prettiest gown she had yet worn (though black, this garment eclipsed even the birthday dress), Ellen delighted in the elegance of its cut. She was thrilled to find, also, that the drape of the lavish material from which it was made provided the suggestion of a train to arrange over one's arm.

But later, descending the staircase beside her mother, dread captured Ellen Gowan again. She was grateful, certainly, to be clean and warm and well-dressed (even if the gown was borrowed), and with the expectation of a dinner to fill their empty stomachs. Yet

Sir Isidore Cleat held their fate in his hands, not yet touched in kinship.

Would he be kind to them, as Aunt Daisy had been?

"There you are!"

Ellen's aunt was seated behind a large embroidery frame in a room even more elaborate than the one Connie and Ellen had just left. She was engaged in matching strands of silk thread for color as her sister and niece entered, and half-stood to welcome them.

"Marguerite, do not disturb yourself." These might have been the words of a kind husband to his delicate wife, but the tone was distant.

A tall man with a sharp face and narrow shoulders, Sir Isidore Cleat stood upon a hearth rug of oriental splendor. Behind him was a richly carved mantelpiece of Carrara marble.

He must certainly be rich, thought Ellen, *if that carpet can be risked to a spitting fire!*

"Sister-in-law, I welcome you to my house." Eyes of a chilling gray inspected Connie as he spoke, and then transferred their attention to her daughter. Isidore's face, however, an uneven collection of sharp lines and angled planes with a pale, straight mouth, displayed no movement.

Connie Gowan paused in the doorway. Ellen sensed her mother's sudden discouragement.

"Brother-in-law, Ellen and I are most deeply in your debt. This kindness, the shelter of your house having lost my husband and Ellen's father, is a most Christian act." Her heart was in her eyes.

A pause stretched into silence. Daisy remained obediently seated but she held out her hand toward the visitors to cover the lack of response from her husband.

"Come, Connie, it is much warmer here." She patted the Sheraton sofa beside her own chair and smiled brightly. "And, Ellen, how well you look in that dress. I am delighted!"

At a signal from Connie, Ellen went to her aunt. Daisy held Ellen's fingers tightly but her gaze was fixed on her husband.

"It is the happy duty of a family to offer succor to its own, is it not, dear Isidore?" The hopeful upward lilt caused another frown from its object. Once more Isidore Cleat gazed at Connie and Ellen and said nothing.

And just when it seemed clear that this second intimidating silence meant he disagreed with his wife's sentiments, Isidore's features rearranged themselves by a series of small stretches and twitches. The company recognized at last that he was smiling. All was not lost!

"Hello. You must be Ellen. I am Oriana."

Ellen turned to find a thin, shy girl smiling from the doorway. Oriana had Daisy's kind eyes but her father's high shoulders and long arms.

The younger girl stood up quickly to greet the elder, so quickly that she might have fallen, for the borrowed dress was a little long. But Oriana caught her cousin. The strength of those slender arms was surprising. To cover the confusion of the moment, Oriana said, "Mourning suits you, Ellen. You *are* lucky."

Poor Oriana. Horrified by what she had said, her skin fired crimson. She stuttered on, imploring forgiveness with her eyes. "I meant to say, that dress looks very much better on you than ever it did on me. You must keep it, Ellen. Please, I should count it a *great* favor. You look so pretty." The words were wistful but not envious.

Daisy filled the sudden silence. "And, daughter, here is your aunt, my dearest sister, Constance. Come, make yourself properly known."

Oriana hurried to Connie and bent down awkwardly to kiss her aunt's cheek. That was the occasion of laughter from them all. Even Isidore obliged with a wintry smile, for when Connie rose to embrace her sister's child, it was seen that Oriana was a head and more taller.

"Tomorrow there will be so much to discuss. Oh, *so* many delightful things to consider for the future. That will be most exciting." Daisy spoke as if the presence of the Gowans at Shene House was natural and entirely settled. But a fugitive glance at her husband betrayed her.

Would Isidore Cleat signify his final approval that Connie and Ellen might live underneath this roof? A nod, just one, would indicate his agreement. After a pause, it was given by a slow inclination of the head. Tension departed in a joint exhalation of breath from all four females in the room.

Daisy, with an embracing smile, said, "And now, Ellen, here is Oriana's governess to take you both to the nursery for supper. You will share your cousin's bedroom, it is certainly large enough. Eat your fill and sleep happily and well after your long journey home to Shene House."

The governess was a tightly corseted young woman of unremarkable appearance. She wore a plain blue gown and beckoned the girls from the open doorway, since she was not introduced by name nor invited to meet Connie or her daughter personally. A brief glance addressed to the visitors had an unsettling intensity, but then a pleasant smile was offered, almost as a garnish.

Following her cousin's lead, Ellen curtsied first to her uncle then to her aunt and, lastly, to her mother. She would have kissed Connie for her mama's comfort and her own, but she sensed Isidore's impatience that the girls depart to realms that he, most likely, never saw.

And yet, before the doors to the withdrawing room were closed by the silent Warwick, who had been standing in the shadows of the hall all along, an indelible picture was fixed in Ellen's mind.

There, legs apart before the fire and chin thrust forward, unquestioned lord of his domain, stood her uncle. And almost at his feet sat her aunt and mother. The former, gazing at her husband as if to drink up each precious word he might utter. The latter, smoothing the silk of her skirt, her glance fixed on the carpet.

It seemed to Ellen that the two women had the posture of sup-plicants. This was troubling, and though Oriana did all that could be expected to make her cousin feel welcome in her new home, chattering brightly of all they would do in the coming days, and how much they would enjoy their lessons together, it was not enough to quiet the anxiety in Ellen's heart.

CHAPTER 12

"AWAKE, SLEEPYHEAD!"

Ellen sat up in the dazzle of morning, her head heavy from . . . something. A nightmare with no form.

"Good morning, Oriana. Am I very late?"

Standing in her shift at the washstand, Oriana said, kindly, "No. Not yet. That is why I woke you. I hope you do not mind?"

It had been more than a month since Ellen and Connie's arrival at Shene, and as the cousins became acquainted, the affection between them quickly deepened.

Energetically, Ellen kicked back her coverlets. She would banish the odd oppression she felt. "Of course I do not. Thank you!"

Oriana offered a sponge. "The water is warm but perhaps you should hurry a little."

Oriana's domain was on the third floor of Shene House. The nursery, bedroom, sitting room (where the girls also took their meals), and schoolroom faced the forecourt, and from this aerie the girls were the first to see visitors arrive, and inhabitants of Shene depart.

This morning, as she dressed, Ellen saw one of her uncle's carriages draw up to the portico below. A moment later, Warwick escorted Sir Isidore through the front door.

"Father is going to town again. Mama told me he will be away for some days."

Oriana's tone lifted. Ellen, absorbed with the scene as it played out—the manservant bowing, his oblivious master ignoring both the courtesy and the man as he climbed into the brougham— fumbled with the laces of her dress.

Oriana laughed. "Half-asleep still, I see. Here, let me or we shall never eat."

Holding the back of a solid chair, Ellen breathed in as her cousin pulled the bodice tighter and tied off the lacing. Ellen was hungry, of course, but she was not looking forward to what would come after breakfast. Mathematics.

"And therefore, as you see, Pi remains a constant."

The governess wrote the formula on the board with chalk that squeaked and then broke. "Continue with page thirty-six, children. I shall return."

Miss Wellings went in search of more chalk, and Oriana, always sensitive, whispered, "Is there something you do not understand, cousin?"

"Oh, no. That is, I do not wish to offend your governess, but perhaps Miss Wellings has the formula wrong?"

Oriana smiled, teasingly. "Really?"

Ellen blushed. "It is just that the value of the formula is—"

"Did you speak, Ellen?" The governess had returned.

Ellen half-stood from her chair. "I do apologize, Miss Wellings."

The governess smiled kindly. "In my schoolroom, pupils do not address one another unless given permission. However, as yet you are a stranger to our ways. You will know that in future. To return to Pi. It is my expectation that you will understand all its properties when I conduct our mathematics examination in three weeks." She looked quizzically at Ellen. "Miss Gowan, is there something that distresses you?"

Ellen, most uncomfortable, said nothing.

"I give you permission to speak."

Relieved, Ellen blurted, "Thank you, Miss Wellings, but I was always taught the ratio of Pi was 3.1416, not 3.5416."

Silence grew until, with an uneasy laugh, the woman said, "Of course! A simple error. Thank you indeed for pointing out that oversight, Miss Gowan."

Miss Wellings turned back to the board as Oriana surreptitiously mouthed to her cousin, "There. She is not so bad." But as Oriana became absorbed in her work, the governess looked back.

Ellen, glancing up, caught her eye. The woman's expression was hostile.

Ellen squirmed, but as the chalk squeaked on, a small rebellion grew in her heart. She did not want to embarrass Miss Wellings, but Edwin Gowan's daughter would not dishonor her father's teachings.

Shene House was always happier in the absence of Ellen's uncle. With Isidore in town, Connie and Daisy would happily stroll in the gardens as they cut flowers, or ride out in the park together, chattering with the ease of childhood companionship renewed. Their daughters, after their lessons, would run through the endless rooms and grounds shrieking from the joy of being alive and having found each other. Even Warwick was seen to smile from time to time as the girls fled past in happy career.

But as the days became short and grew colder, Isidore spent increasing time at home. Shene House grew silent again as Daisy encouraged the girls to keep to their own part of the house unless their company was requested. Furtive glances and whispered conversations between the sisters became more noticeable, and, in so far as she could tell, Ellen began to suspect that not only was Daisy frightened of her husband but Oriana, too, avoided Isidore's presence whenever she could.

It was very difficult to understand what caused such tension, since Shene was an orderly place where little that was unexpected took place. Each day, according to the season, there was a timetable of happenings laid down by Sir Isidore and administered by Daisy, as the mistress of Shene.

This unvarying routine was controlled by a gong that Warwick struck before the principal meals and at other times, and was designed primarily for the comfort of Isidore Cleat. Ellen knew that many grand households revolved around the master first, and his family second. And so, in the beginning, this did not seem strange.

The succeeding months passed quickly until spring was signaled by the white and green of snowbells pushing through the crust of diminishing snow. If it was still cold outside, indoors it was warm and comfortable. And to Ellen's delight in her older cousin's companionship was added the pleasure of an abundance of pretty clothes for the first time in her life. Oriana's wardrobe was extensive, and she was generous to her cousin with outgrown gowns and shoes and hats.

And in the spring, Oriana insisted that Ellen be taught to ride. That was a happy distraction. The younger girl soon learned from watching the older one's fearlessness on her Irish hunter, and it was only a month or so before Ellen, too, was confident enough to jump hedgerows in pursuit of Oriana's horse. Her Welsh pony was considerably more stolid, however, and not nearly so fast.

Sketching lessons, too, were especially enjoyed since they were taught by a charming old man from Richmond. Mr. Nosworthy's proud boast was that he had been an Artist Resident at the Brighton Pavilion for the late prince regent until that gentleman's untimely demise (but perhaps to the country's relief).

Whatever the truth of Mr. Nosworthy's many stories of court life and his exalted former patron, the park, as spring gave way to warmer weather, was inspiration enough for any nascent artist. And as the afternoons lengthened, the girls spent many happy hours sketching, while their tutor exhorted them to ever greater efforts. Ellen, in particular, improved her style quickly under his tutelage.

One afternoon, sketching together on the terrace outside Daisy's sitting room, rain speckled the flagstones. As fast as his elderly but gallant knees would allow, Mr. Nosworthy hurried to assist as the girls packed up their easels and the trio rushed inside in a scatter of giggles. Daisy's smile was welcoming.

"Have these two taxed you very much, Mr. Nosworthy, with all their silliness?" Secretly she delighted in seeing Oriana so happy. She turned to her sister, asking merrily, "Connie, what do you say? Perhaps our daughters are not sufficiently serious about their studies?"

The puckish old gentleman bowed. "Ladies, I must protest! Though we enjoy our work, the company of such talented young artists is inspiring indeed. And it is my experience that pleasure is the nurse of all skill."

Oriana laughed. "My skill is not very great at all. Come, Sir, confess. I am not in the least offended by the truth."

She danced to Daisy and kissed her. Turning, bright eyed, Oriana's tone changed. She became serious. "However, my cousin has real ability, does she not, Mr. Nosworthy?"

Diplomatically, their tutor smiled at both girls. "Each of you has a unique sensibility. That is all I shall say."

But Oriana grabbed Ellen's hand and drew her forward.

"Cousin? Have you even shown Aunt Connie the work you have been doing?"

Pink-faced, Ellen shook her head. Mr. Nosworthy brightened. He approved of Ellen's modesty, but was also proud of the improvement in his younger pupil's skill, for which he would be pleased to claim credit. Another course of lessons would certainly be forthcoming if her work was advantageously displayed. "Come, Miss Gowan, in this instance, I do agree with your cousin's assessment. The watercolors of this last week are, in my professional judgment, excellent, if you are brave enough to show them. Do you have them close by?"

Daisy invited the tutor to sit. "Tea, Mr. Nosworthy? It will refresh you while my niece finds her work. Ellen, there is excellent seed cake. A piece will await your return." She nodded encouragingly.

Ellen bobbed a curtsy to her aunt. She did not want to seem churlish or falsely modest, besides, she relished the pleasure that painting had brought to her life. The sensation was still a new one but she forgot time, and much else, too, when she worked with her brush.

With thickening rain, the day had darkened inside the house. Daisy's retreat was some distance from the back staircase that led to the nursery rooms, and even after all these months, the house was confusing to Ellen. Somewhere among the dim lengths of endless corridors, she took a wrong turn. No staircase—or not where she had expected it to be. Perplexed, she turned back. Oh for a path of crumbs to follow, or a woolen thread to trace to its source!

Ahead, light shone through a partly opened door. Ellen hurried toward it, convinced she had found the correct direction. As she got closer, she saw she was mistaken.

But there was something here—an aroma that drew her on. She closed her eyes and sniffed. Old leather, old paper, old ink. Rich and spicy and dry with a tang of acid. The scent summoned the past. Ellen peered around the door and into the space beyond. And gasped.

Her father had talked of his books as a library, but this, *this* dignified the name.

Ellen entered the vast room as reverently as if it were a cathedral. It was lined with shelves that climbed toward a decorated ceiling where Apollo drove his chariot through an improbable bower of pink and silver clouds.

So many volumes. Tiers and tiers—thousands! Ellen allowed her fingers to trail across the bindings of the shelves nearest to the door. *Ah, Father, how much you would have gloried in this place.*

Tears stung and she closed her eyes against them. Perhaps, for one moment, she could pretend that he was here. That if she reached out her hand, Edwin Gowan would take it and they would stroll among the books together, happy in each other's company.

But blunt truth would not be denied. Her father was gone. And this place was not Edwin's library. It belonged to Isidore Cleat.

With rushing horror, Ellen came to herself. What if she were discovered!

So great was her haste to leave that Ellen stumbled when the toe of one shoe caught in her skirt. She saved herself from falling by clutching to an eagle-headed lectern. It rocked and righted itself before she fled its outraged glare. Later, when she found the correct staircase and then the safety of the nursery, Ellen wondered why she had been so frightened.

The answer came unbidden. Isidore. She had trespassed in his sanctum. What if he knew?

That evening, after their nursery dinner, the cousins were summoned to the drawing room. Ellen was so plainly nervous, Oriana stared a little. Normally, it was she who was reluctant to join her parents.

"There you are! How delightful a picture you make. Do they not, Isidore? The girls, I mean?" Daisy spoke breathlessly, as if she had been running.

Isidore, as was his habit, said nothing, though Ellen felt, rather than saw, his eyes slide toward them as they curtsied. She would not look at him.

"Good evening, Father." Oriana glanced at her cousin.

Ellen faintly echoed, "Good evening, Uncle." Isidore nodded. This was acknowledgment at least.

Daisy rallied. "Oriana, Papa has something to say to you." She smiled brilliantly at her husband. "Isidore?"

Isidore Cleat cleared his throat. A harsh sound. "As your mother says, Oriana. We must speak of your sixteenth birthday. There will be a party this year. A children's ball."

Oriana flung Daisy a panicked glance. "But, Mama, had we not decided on a small celebration?" She stared at her cousin. *Help me!*

Ellen heard the words as if Oriana had spoken them. She hesitated.

"Does the thought of a ball for children displease you, Ellen?"

Isidore Cleat so rarely addressed his niece, she jumped.

"No. That is, I mean, yes, Sir. It would be delightful, certainly. However, for my part, I dance indifferently. And . . ." She cast a wild glance at Oriana who caught up the refrain.

"And I dance not at all well either, Papa. Miss Wellings has quite given me up in disgust. And I should really so much prefer—"

"You will do as I say!"

The chandelier quaked in that percussive roar as silence shivered and spread. After a moment, Isidore said, more moderately, "This will be a gathering for our neighbors. And our close friends. I shall not tolerate selfishness in the matter."

Close friends? Ellen had seen little evidence of such. The Cleats seemed to pursue a private existence behind the walls of the estate. "Important clients of my practice in the city will, naturally, be invited also."

Ellen knew without looking that Oriana was distressed, but could not smother a small frisson of excitement. A ball? Even if it was for children, she had never seen or been to such a thing.

But Connie had stiffened, and Ellen, glancing at her aunt, saw that she was similarly rigid. As if in a wax display, her hand was unmovingly poised above the embroidery. She said, abruptly, "Very well. We shall discuss the party in the morning, children. Good night."

Daisy's tone was pleasant but her glance was direct. *Leave.*

Ellen took the hint, relieved to avoid further exchanges with Isidore. Pulling her cousin's arm through her own, she curtsied, compelling Oriana to do the same. And then, since she took the lead, both girls quickly left the room.

Later that evening the cousins lay in bed, talking softly.

"You see, Ellen, fine clothes and fashionable people frighten me. I do not like to feel foolish, or for strangers to stare."

Ellen reached across the space that divided them and caught her cousin's hand. "If you attract notice it is because you are far prettier than you know, Oriana. That in itself is attractive."

Ellen was sincere, for she had seen her quiet cousin change over the last months. Oriana had grown taller and her waist had narrowed. Her shoulders were now well formed, when she remembered to lower them, and her neck was long and graceful. Her hands, too, were particularly lovely. The fingers were delicate, with oval nails of a natural pink. And if her face was narrow and more pointed than was commonly considered beautiful, well-defined cheekbones and a serene brow provided a frame for large eyes. Her hair, too, an abundant cascade of amber brown, was an ornament to the gentle face beneath.

"I am certain," Ellen said, "that you will enjoy dancing with the boys at the ball. And they with you. Your program will be filled in an instant!"

Oriana said passionately, "I shall hate it. All of it!"

Ellen squeezed her cousin's hand. "But it is all about to begin, is it not? This ball is a prelude to your first Season in London."

Oriana said broodingly, "The marriage market. Yes. But I think Papa will never approve of anyone as a suitor unless he has expressly chosen that person for his wealth and position. Mama thinks so, too. Did you see her face when he mentioned his clients from the city?" She shivered. "Old men. But whatever my father thinks, Mama is determined that I shall meet people of my own age. At the ball she, in particular, will expect that I make meaningless conversation with boys I hardly know. And dance with them as if it is the most delightful thing in the world."

"Perhaps it will be. Delightful, that is. Perhaps, no matter what you believe or fear, someone whom you least expect will be there and—"

"No! I shall never marry. I shall *not* give my life into another person's hands." Oriana's voice had risen. Her agitation was painful.

Ellen was not sure how to comfort her cousin. She said, hesitantly, "But a good marriage is possible. My parents loved each other very much."

"They were fortunate." Oriana snuffed the candle abruptly. She turned her head on the pillow and said, "Good night, dearest cousin. I have kept you talking too long."

For some time the younger girl lay musing as Oriana's breathing slowed and deepened into sleep.

Would she, one day, marry? And if she did, what kind of person would her husband be?

Papa, what had you hoped for me? A quiet marriage to a good man whom I can cherish, and who will cherish me as you did Mama? Or did you desire worldly success for your daughter? A glittering triumph out in the great world?

Ellen smiled in the dark. She did not have to ask that question. She knew what Edwin would have wanted for her.

Happiness. And love.

But Ellen Gowan liked the thought of glittering triumph, too.

CHAPTER 13

O NE MORNING, Connie made a visit to the schoolroom before Miss Wellings or Oriana had arrived. She came upon her daughter gazing toward the river. "Is something wrong, child?"

Ellen started. "Nothing at all, Mama. Oriana and I will shortly be *most* agreeably engaged in studying the agricultural pursuits of the people of the Deccan. I have been anticipating that happy fact for two days."

The irony made Connie laugh but she tried again. "I know that look. What worries you?"

Where to start? Ellen hesitated, and then said, "A gown, Mama. For the ball. And shoes. I know they cannot be thought of."

Connie attempted to speak, but Ellen cut her off cheerfully. "Even *you* could not contrive a cut down ball gown from the clothes we have, let alone me. I shall watch from the stairs with Miss Wellings." The smile wilted.

Her mother said, mildly, "This is your decision?"

Ellen nodded. There was a sheen to her eyes, which she blinked away as Connie said, "Well, since you have the thing so clearly settled, you may not wish to hear my news." She turned to leave.

"Wait, Mama! News? What news?"

"Madame Angelique, how delighted I am to see you here. We are all looking forward to the gowns you will make for us. Warwick, tea is to be brought for our visitor."

Daisy's smile continued bright even though Warwick closed the doors with unusual force. Dressmakers as guests? He did not approve. She ignored him.

"Madame, I believe you know my daughter?"

Oriana curtsied, graciously acknowledged by the visitor.

"But you will not yet have met my sister, Mrs. Edwin Gowan, or my niece, Miss Gowan?"

Bows were exchanged as the vivacious Frenchwoman exclaimed, "*Mais,* Madame Gowan, *c'est* han *honneur* to make your acquaintance. And that of the so charming Miss Gowan!"

Attired in a walking-out costume of a peplummed slate gray jacket, fastened daringly with large red buttons, over a skirt of cream worsted and trimmed with black at the hem, the dressmaker made an elegant picture. Curls of an improbable wheat blond clustered beneath a straw bonnet, *à la paysanne*. This confection was adorned with artificial cherries that bobbed about as she expressed delight in all she saw. "But, zis *chambre*! So exquisite, chère Lady Cleat. *Et,* the prospect of the *parc* you have here, *c'est noble. Formidable!*"

If asked how old her visitor was, Daisy Cleat might have said Madame Angelique had seen her thirtieth birthday but not yet her fortieth. She would have been wrong, and by around five years, but the appearance of well-counterfeited youth was part of the success of the lady's business. Madame was also possessed of a breathy giggle that was amusing in itself. Clients liked to laugh as they gossiped in their fittings, and she so obligingly set that tone.

Thus began a morning of unexpected delight that even Oriana, so shy about the public celebration of her birthday, eventually allowed herself to relish. And all these pleasures began with the mysterious contents of Madame Angelique's very, very large reticule.

This embroidered velvet bag was evidently heavy. Pulling open the tasseled drawstring, Madame dipped one gloved hand inside as if investigating the depths of a cornucopia. "*Alors, dans ma sac* I have delights for all. Let us examine *Les Images de Couture. Comme ça!*"

With a conjuror's flourish, Madame withdrew a number of illustrated Ladies' papers. These were an expensive novelty, since the best were printed in Paris and difficult to obtain in England. Connie and Ellen sighed with guilty bliss.

With tiny steps, Madame ran to each of the sisters dispensing largesse and then to Ellen, her skirts whirling as if in a waltz. Their animated visitor advanced last upon Oriana, who, alarmed, drew back in her chair.

"*Mais,* please to stand up, Mademoiselle. Allow me see you, I beg, so that I may render best service. Eet is *votre anniversaire natale.* You shall indeed be the belle of zis ball. I shall see to zat."

Oriana reluctantly stood as the fractured French poured over her head like syrup. Ellen ached for her cousin. In another person, a blush might have been a comely thing, but Oriana's face was ember red and shiny.

Madame, however, was tact itself. "Now to turn, if you please, Miss Oriana. *Eh bien, charmante!* The carriage of the head, alone, it is exquisite! You are to be congratulated on your daughter, Lady Cleat. And so slender a waist! Such wonderful hair!"

Taking Oriana by the hand, the enthusiastic modiste drew the girl to a conveniently placed sofa and encouraged her to sit. "*Immédiatement,* I see ze image, the picture of what we must make for you, Miss Cleat. Allow zat I show you."

The lady now withdrew from her *"sac"* a stick of charcoal and some sheets of thick paper. Ellen approached, eager to watch.

In only a moment, a figure emerged upon the page as the dressmaker traced a graceful form with the head carried proudly.

And as the likeness of Oriana grew beneath her fingers, Madame said, "Zis gown, do you see? *Vraiment* appealing yet youthful, as it must be. And light so zat, as you dance, the skirt will float like a cloud. Delicate *mais vrai jolie!*" The busy fingers flew on.

"Oh, Madame. So beautiful." Oriana surrendered to the possible. The tight-waisted bodice descended to an Elizabethan point from which sprang a skirt of several, ever-wider tiers created in a gauzy fabric bound with ribbon. Each tier was caught up in broad scallops by bows. The neck, modestly high, was decorated with the same, although the sleeves were tight and plain and ended just below the elbow in a narrow ruffle.

"Pink and white, I think, Mademoiselle. Adorable!" A swatch of deliciously pale velvet, pink as fondant, was produced from the capacious bag. "For the bodice dis velvet and the pink, also, for the bows. *Naturellement*. But in satin. The skirt and the sleeves of the gown shall be voile, white and soft as snow. And pure. Also, there must be little pink slippers with white velvet roses at the toe. Very suitable." Madame smiled at the smitten Oriana.

Daisy clapped her hands. "Perfect, Madame. Sister? Do you not agree?"

Connie happily assented. "Charming indeed."

Oriana stuttered her thanks. "Oh, Madame, I think what you have drawn is very lovely." She offered a shy, sweet smile.

"*Et pour vous*, Mademoiselle Gowan? Have you seen, perhaps, a plate of the fashion from Paris that pleases you?"

Ellen was confused. Her aunt must be considered next in precedence and then her mother, surely? She was the youngest and least important person in the room.

"Alas, I am not as tall as my cousin, Madame. She has the height to carry many of these lovely garments, whereas I might do best in something simpler. A flowing line, I think, but the color must be somber. Gray, mostly, and with little trimming."

Ellen tried not to sigh. Late spring had softened the air and the sun was bright on many days. Her father was never far from her thoughts, but increasing light had leavened the dark of winter in more than the natural world.

On impulse, she said, "Might something be done by contrast of light and dark materials? That could have an elegant effect." Ellen began to imagine a gown that had echoes of earlier times, with a higher waist and longer, wider sleeves than were commonly seen, as suggested by the saints' statues on their church in Wintermast. Her father had always loved *his* saints.

Madame Angelique smiled at Ellen but her brows rose. "Describe to me more of this gown, Mademoiselle?"

Ellen swallowed nervously. "Well, perhaps an overdress of gray silk, and beneath it, a skirt of pearl-colored satin?"

Madame Angelique inclined her head in a listening pose, one finger to her chin as if to play the part of Ellen's muse.

"And, I think, quite voluminous sleeves, also gray. They should be satin for the drape. But only a plain bodice with black ribbon at the waist, and black binding on the margins of the sleeves. And a fichu of white voile at the neck? Gray and white and black. Very simple."

Madame Angelique proffered charcoal and a sheet of paper. She said, respectfully, "Can you draw what you see, Miss Gowan?"

Ellen was intimidated. After the skillful demonstration of the Frenchwoman, how could she hope to follow without seeming foolish?

Mercurial energy, however, carried Madame Angelique to a place on the sofa between the sisters. "And while our little *artiste* works, perhaps we shall discuss the gowns for Mrs. Gowan and yourself, Lady Cleat?"

Three heads were soon bent to the illustrated magazines, as Ellen stared down at the blank page she had been given. She was expected to render her "vision," as Madame Angelique had called it, but where to begin?

"Start with the head, Ellen," Oriana murmured. "Begin at the beginning."

Something seized that black stick, for assuredly it was not Ellen herself, or so she thought. And that *something* made a bold mark on the paper. A swirl that became a head and neck and shoulders. Oriana was unenvious. She liked to see her clever cousin shine.

"Yes! Just as Madame instructed. Draw what you see in your mind."

Heart running at a giddy speed, Ellen closed her eyes. She longed to impress the dressmaker but there was something more in this, she knew, though just why the sketch mattered as much as it did she could not tell.

"But this is excellent. Professional. And clever." The girl looked up to find Madame Angelique staring at the finished sketch. She spoke with no trace of accent.

Ellen was elated. "You are very kind, Madame." The dress-maker twitched the illustration from her hands. She peered at it, muttering. "Not kind. Never kind to talent, for such must be developed and that is a long, hard road. But"—she gazed into Ellen's face—"it is sad to find ability in the hands of one who will never use it to real effect."

Ellen shrank back. Madame Angelique's eyes were severe. What could she mean? "But, I like to draw."

"You like to draw? Many like to draw, but few *can* draw. Yet girls such as you, Miss Gowan"—the dressmaker's eyes flicked about the gracious salon—"with all that this world provides, do not have the need, or the hunger, to pursue such talent. God grant that remains the case." Madame broke off and her face was haunted. Ellen yearned to make a riposte, to say that all this seeming prosperity was insubstantial as a fog, but Madame Angelique suddenly held her drawing aloft, declaring, "But see, an illustration *excellente! Charmante! Prodigieuse!*" She caught Ellen's hand with a laugh that tinkled like a French clock's chime. "Come, Miss Gowan, show to your mama and your dear aunt dis triumph."

With strong fingers encircling her wrist, Ellen could not resist. And yet, she was confused. If she had caused Madame grief in some way, she was sorry for it. But what did *she* want? Ellen would not have been comfortable with mere compliments and would not have believed them. Madame had offered sincere recognition of something that Ellen had not known she possessed, but Madame also seemed to consider an ability to sketch a curse. How strange this exchange had been!

CHAPTER 14

A T SHENE House, preparations for the ball began as a whirl, which increased to a blur as the days passed. It was as if the building, breathing deep, began to fill up with life the way a bucket does when held beneath the pump.

Ellen had been told that Shene was considered one of the finest gentleman's dwellings outside London, but she liked some parts of the building more than others. Close to the river, Shene seemed more like a castle than a house since it had crenellations and tiny windows, buttresses, and towers with thick walls.

The "new" part, however, built more than seventy years earlier, before old King George became quite mad, had origins that were classically Palladian, and, to Ellen, that symmetry was cold in its rational perfection. And because the mansion was very large, and the Cleats a small family, much of the older part was left shut up with the furniture, the pictures, and even the carpets swathed in calico. Room after room of unmoving, shrouded shapes that made Ellen shiver.

The ballroom lay in that part of the mansion normally uninhabited. This vast chamber was the folly of a seventeenth-century Cleat, a close friend of that lazy rake Charles II. The former had visited Versailles in the train of the latter when Charles had lived in exile. While there, the companion of the British prince fell ruinously in love. For the rest of his life, twin passions for that great palace *and* a demanding French aristocrat almost beggared his family.

This particular Cleat had thought that his inamorata was an heiress but found the opposite to be the case on their wedding night (she, in turn, had been told he was a wealthy "milord" and fallen "in love" accordingly).

In time, Charles Stuart was restored to his throne, but not all his faithful supporters found success when they returned to England. Legend had it that the lovelorn husband, disillusioned by his beloved's lack of affection when he brought her to the ruin that Shene House had become, built the ballroom as consolation for a cold bed. He, with a passion for dance ignited in France, delighted in providing lavish entertainments for his master and the court.

Alas, balls and ballrooms are expensive, and he, an impractical if amusing man, ran through his revenues far too fast for anyone's comfort, not least that of his expensive wife. The fortunes of the Cleats steeply declined until another ancestor bought shares, fortuitously, in the East India Company in the following century. Hence the new wing that had been grafted upon that otherwise ancient building.

Ellen had never before been behind the locked doors of the ballroom. She and Oriana watched together as the parquet floors were polished and the covers taken down from the paintings and the mirrors.

Six precious chandeliers, with chains of silver leaves and lusters of Murano crystal, were lowered one by one. Teams of four men were required, so great was the weight and value of these chandeliers. Washed by hand and polished with silk, the lusters seemed on fire when the sun struck through the long windows.

The day before the ball, flowers began to arrive by barge from London. And a stream of drays brought ice, boxed and packed in straw, and all manner of delicacies that the overworked kitchens and gardens of Shene could not supply. Caviar from Russia, salmon from Scotland (though it was not the season), and plover eggs by the many-score.

☙

As the sun began its journey down an inflamed sky on the night of the ball, light flared from the ballroom sconces for the first time in more than a hundred years. And flame found its own reflection in the eerie depths of those great mirrors, as the first squeaks of the oboes and the saw and scrape of violins being tuned brought the room to life.

Oriana and Ellen had been dressed for at least an hour, and both were fidgeting. They were waiting for their parents in the same hall where Connie and Ellen had first arrived, desperate not to crease their new finery.

"You look very nice, cousin. Delicious!" Ellen's naughty whisper was sincere. Faint pink was the perfect color for Oriana.

The older girl beamed. "Do you really think so?" Privately she thought Ellen looked far more elegant. And prettier, too.

Ellen giggled. "Of course I do. Goose!" She paused then said with a grin, "I know you know."

Oriana's glance was alarmed. "What?"

"Not what. Who. Do not lie to me, cousin. You are looking forward to the dancing. All those young men. You've been humming for days!"

Oriana held up a fan to hide the blush. Now the night had arrived, it was hard to pretend she was not excited. "But I do not feel at all confident. Oh, look. There is Mama, and my aunt. At last!" And Isidore, too. But he was scowling. Something, as usual, had displeased him.

A quick curtsy to her father, and Oriana went to stand beside Daisy, for iron-shod wheels were rolling across the graveled forecourt. At a signal from Warwick, footmen in scarlet coats and white wigs pulled back the bronze-bound doors, and as the guests advanced toward their hosts, the butler intoned the first of many illustrious names that night.

"Ivor, Lord Bellstone and the Lady Bellstone. The Honorable Master Peter Bellstone. Sir Manderville Urquart and Lady Urquart. Miss Arrabella Urquart."

The Gowans had withdrawn a little toward the back of the entrance hall. If Ellen was daunted by the poise of the children who passed by, she did not show it. Yet on seeing her, one or two of the boys smiled. But as another youth noticed her discreetly to his friend, Ellen swallowed. *They are laughing at me!*

Connie squeezed her daughter's hand. "Those young gentlemen admire you, my darling." She tipped her fan in the direction of the boys.

Ellen paled. She said loudly, "Shall we go in, Mama? I feel conspicuous, standing here."

"Certainly. You must have dancing partners." Connie smiled encouragingly at another boy, just then passing.

Alarmed in case Connie should accost the stranger, Ellen linked her arm through her mother's and towed her forward. Together, they joined the slow-moving throng happily converging on the doors to the ballroom.

Inside, something of a maelstrom had developed as young gentlemen roamed the ballroom with only one intention. The prettiest girls had to be persuaded to write their names on dance cards attached to the program before the orchestra leader picked up his violin bow—a signal that the music would shortly begin.

The partner-picking anxiety was elevated a notch as the orchestra rose and the conductor took his place upon the rostrum. This was an energetic young man with wild locks of glittering black. He turned to the assembled guests and bowed with an embracing sweep of his arm. To the dismay of all the young men present, a visible ripple ran through the young ladies when they saw how very handsome he was. Those teeth! His eyes! That glinting smile!

Oblivious to the attention, this was a children's ball after all, the maestro tapped his baton on the music stand. He raised his arms and . . .

"Do you not wish to dance, child?" Ellen had deliberately hung back and now had almost missed securing any partners. "There, you see, that young man over there. He's smiling at you again. Perhaps he has a sister you might like to meet?"

"I am quite content to watch, Mama. There is so much to see!" Ellen looked anywhere but in the direction of her would-be suitor—a youth with disastrous skin and very red hair that grew low on his brow. Her last encounter with an amorous boy had led to disgrace. She was not eager to repeat the experiment.

Connie squeezed Ellen's hand. She thought she understood her daughter's natural reticence, but tonight was an opportunity for her child to meet others her own age. Connie was so worried about the future. Ellen was far, far too young to think of marriage, but if she were able to stay at other suitable houses from time to time, her world might expand beyond the oppressive atmosphere of Shene.

"There is Oriana. She does look pretty!" Connie was delighted for her niece.

But Ellen knew her cousin better. "She is not happy, Mama. Oh, dear . . ."

As the music began, Oriana had led the dancers to the floor since this was her party. Fate, however, had partnered her with an eager boy who was half a head shorter than her, and though confident, clumsy.

Pretty gown or not, from the smile that congealed on Oriana's face it was clear to Ellen that her cousin found this first waltz a torment. Her partner, less schooled at hiding his feelings, appeared more and more dismayed each time he stumbled. The more uncomfortable he became, the more he stepped on the hem of the lovely pink gown.

Connie winced. "Poor Oriana! She is trying so hard to be gracious!"

As the couple swept by, Ellen smiled encouragingly. But the waltz, at last, ended. As soon as Oriana had curtsied to her partner, she hurried across the ballroom to Connie and Ellen, fanning herself to dissipate the heat of embarrassment.

"I thought it would never be over! Oh, Ellen, he had the largest feet and hands. I could feel the sweat, even through his gloves. The top of his head tickled my chin!" Oriana's strangled whisper was delivered from behind her pink-feathered fan.

The girls tried not to giggle, and quaked with the effort of suppression. Connie frowned at them reprovingly. "But, where is your next partner, niece? He will be looking for you."

"I believe that the dance is mine?"

Startled, both girls looked up. Ellen stared into a boy's face not inches from her own. *Brown eyes.* Mute, she gazed at the tall stranger. He smiled. Ellen could find nothing to say. Her throat was dry as ash.

The first bars of a polka jaunted out. The stranger held out his hand. Ellen swallowed. And smiled.

"Oh, yes! Here it is." Oriana blushed, winsomely! "Connor, is it not? Moncrieff. My writing. So disordered!"

The spell was broken.

Ellen saw the truth. The boy stared at Oriana and she at him, as if both had been woken, dazed, by a bright light.

"Shall we?"

Connor Moncrieff took Oriana's hand as if it was the most precious of objects and led her away. And as they began to dance, Ellen heard him say, "You write as you dance, Miss Cleat. Divinely." But it was *his* skill that made Oriana sway with a dryad's grace.

He did not see me. I am invisible.

"Daughter?" Connie's anxiety penetrated the suffocating fog that muffled the music. Ellen straightened her spine.

"The dancing is delightful, is it not? So many pretty dresses! The ball is a success already. And the music is certainly all it should be."

The babble flowed on as if some other person used her lips to speak these bright inanities, while the entire time the real Ellen Gowan was helplessly battered by a power she had not thought real. The yearning that filled her, that caught and squeezed her chest, had a tidal force, a most terrible pull as she watched Oriana blossom with joy in the arms of Connor Moncrieff.

I do not exist.

And all that evening as she watched her cousin dance, dance after dance, with Connor Moncrieff, an inner voice wailed, in utter desolation, *It should be me. Why isn't it me?*

There was a rapid *tap-tap-tap* of heels in the corridor outside the schoolroom before the door was flung open, extravagantly wide. Ellen jumped. She had been expecting Miss Wellings and dreading the moment since, distracted after the ball a few days before, she worried that her Latin homework was not fully mastered. "Oriana! You look different."

Oriana giggled, her eyes shining. "Do I? Perhaps *that* is because I have a secret." Her cousin danced, twirling, into the room. She was clutching something to her chest.

Ellen tried to smile but her face was suddenly stiff. She could see what it was. A note.

"Well, aren't you going to ask me what it is?" Oriana stopped, dizzy from her exertions.

"Let me guess. Your homework. You have written a list of the verbs we must recite."

"Wrong! Guess again."

"Well then, all the dates of the kings and queens of England."

"No!" Oriana held out her hand. In its palm lay a piece of paper, quite small and folded over at least twice. There had been a wax seal, but it was broken. She hurried to the window seat. "Come and look. Quickly. I can hardly breathe."

Nodding at the door, Ellen said, warningly, "Miss Wellings."

"Never mind that! Can you guess who wrote this?"

Oriana opened the note with great care, as if what she touched was holy. "*He* did."

Ellen swallowed. "He?" The cliché was correct. Envy *was* green. Bile green.

"Connor. Mama has given it to me." Oriana offered the paper to Ellen. "Do you see?" She pointed. "Here, and here. He has asked Mama if he might pay a visit to personally thank us for inviting him to the ball. Today. At teatime! What shall I *wear*? Oh, Ellen, you must help me. You are so good with clothes and I never know. Say you will help me?"

"Of course. Of course I will." Ellen coughed. Her chest hurt. She must be generous, she *must,* even if her heart was peeled and squeezed dry with grief. She was losing her only friend to the boy who should have been *hers.*

"Girls. Why are you not at your desks?"

Miss Wellings rounded the open door at speed. She seemed more irritable than usual. Perhaps the ball had affected her. She had not been invited.

"The declensions I asked that you memorize. You may begin, Miss Gowan."

Ellen stood behind her desk. The first misery supplanted by a second. Latin. "The verb to love, present indicative, active singular. *Amo, amas, amat.*"

Halfway through the recitation, Ellen's anxiety began to diminish, and as she finished, she allowed a small but definite flourish into the pronunciation of the last conjugations.

"To wash. *Lavo, lovare, lavi.*"

But this faultless performance had not pleased Miss Wellings. "The list of conjugations is incomplete, Miss Gowan."

Ellen opened her mouth to protest but the governess spoke over her pupil. "You have been remiss." She turned to the board, and began to write more verbs than had been recited.

Oriana stared at her cousin and slowly shook her head, mouthing *Unfair!* Ellen flushed. "But, Miss Wellings, I have the list here. I noted them down." She began to scrabble through her desk.

"Miss Gowan!" Miss Wellings was staring at Ellen. The pupils of her eyes had contracted to black dots. "I have taught not one but many children. You are the first who has dared to contradict me in this insufferable manner. Lady Cleat shall, of course, be informed." She turned back to the board, saying over her shoulder, "I had planned to give you five hundred lines at your first impertinence. That number now will be increased to two thousand. And the sentence will be, 'I am uncivil and lazy and must learn that false pride in my supposed abilities is the greatest sin of all in children.'"

After the continuingly painful hours of Latin that succeeded luncheon, it had been a scramble to dress in time for tea.

Oriana was therefore deprived of the opportunity to change her clothes more than three times. A blessing in its way, reflected Ellen. And now, in the drawing room, Daisy presided over tea *en famille,* with only Warwick to wait upon them. Small cucumber sandwiches and five varieties of cake, besides pikelets, scones, and tiny pastries, had been supplied by the cook. Enough food for a squad of hungry people.

"And tell me, Mr. Moncrieff, do you have plans now that your studies at Winchester are complete?"

Connor replied, "That rather depends, Lady Cleat. My father says he would prefer I go on to Cambridge since it is near our home, but the outdoors life satisfies me. Truthfully, he and I are never happier than when thinking of improvements for the estate. Clairmallon lies in Norfolk, as you may know, though we have our house in London, of course. I shall stay there for at least the next month or so." Ellen felt, rather than saw, Oriana tremble. *He will be close by!* "But the country is my future. I am content to work our lands. Papa has taught me so much."

Daisy smiled. She approved of practical people, and this specific practical person was the heir and only child of a wealthy, elderly widower, a longtime client of Isidore's, who showed no inclination of marrying again. "I should be glad indeed to have a son such as you, Mr. Moncrieff. Your father must be proud. You must both come to dinner very soon."

Connor cast Oriana a soft glance from beneath his lashes. Oriana glowed with such intensity that Ellen, quite deprived of appetite, put down her plate of little cakes.

"Warwick, more hot water, please." And as the man left the room, Connie, with a shrewd glance at the young couple, asked, "But what of worldly ambition, Mr. Moncrieff? Or travel, for instance. Does that hold no appeal?"

Connor said, lightly, "Why travel when one's heaven resides at home?" This time he dared to glance openly at Oriana, though quickly. She, struck dumb, paused with a jam tart half in and half out of her mouth.

Daisy was the first to recover from this remarkable statement. She peered at their visitor quite sharply. "More cake, Mr. Moncrieff?"

Connor stood gracefully. He bowed to his hostess. "Perhaps I might hand these delightful refreshments?"

Daisy waved her assent and beamed. Such good manners! Better and better.

"Miss Ellen, may I tempt you to another of the sandwiches?" He was smiling at her. Really at *her,* this time.

Ellen found sufficient control to reply (though, a little strangled), "I thank you, Sir. Perhaps one."

Connor bent down until they were six inches apart. A point of light deep in his eyes lent brilliance to his gaze. How did Ellen's hand not shake as she removed one of the tiny triangles to her plate?

"For you, Miss Cleat?" Connor transferred his attention to Oriana.

Loneliness, *aloneness,* swept Ellen's being as her cousin leaned forward and her fingers briefly touched Connor's as they gazed at each other. Ellen was shaken. It was plain that the feeling between the pair was considerably advanced. Soon, Oriana would be lost to her, as would Connor. Which was worse?

Unseen by the younger people, Daisy and Connie exchanged a significant glance. Oriana, suddenly, was not to be considered a child. And neither was Connor, since he was a young man about to leave school. This situation was a serious one and must be carefully managed if the credit of both parties was to be preserved and neither hurt or shamed.

Absorbed in the situation of the older girl, neither Daisy nor Connie observed the effect on Ellen of Connor's presence. She, after all, *was* merely a child, still.

But Ellen Gowan had ceased to be a child the day her father died. And she had fallen in love as deeply as Oriana. What was she to do?

CHAPTER 15

Ellen had always relished summer, but as a procession of warm, ever-lengthening days succeeded one another, her spirits sank. With the exception of their shared sleep and lessons, she and Oriana were less and less together. But that was not so much the cause of Ellen's low spirits, as the knowledge that her absent cousin was more often with Connor Moncrieff than she ever could be. Oriana for the first time in her life was interested in clothes, and increasingly, when Madame Angelique visited Shene House she did so exclusively for Miss Cleat. Miss Gowan, meanwhile, served as a silent witness, except on those rare occasions when her opinion was kindly sought.

Oriana, at last, was happy. First love subsumed her, and in these warm days she, with Daisy as chaperone, was often away from Shene on picnics with new friends. Young people of a similar station and around her own age to whom Connor introduced her.

Less and less was it presumed that Ellen would accompany her cousin. Thirteen was different from sixteen. Thirteen, in fact, did not seem to be wanted or needed by sixteen. That hurt Ellen very much.

"Wait, Ellen! Stop! I have something to show you. A secret."

It was evening and the cousins were running through the kitchen gardens toward the orchard. Ellen, for the sheer joy of escaping the tedium of the day, was twenty yards ahead of her cousin. But Ellen noticed that Oriana seemed unusually agitated when she allowed her to catch up.

"What kind of secret?"

Ellen wondered, did something, some slight thing—a feather— touch the back of her neck.

"This. I am not quite sure what I should say in response. And you write so well." Oriana dropped her eyes.

Ellen took a small white note from her cousin's hand and opened up the folded page, smothering a gasp.

Miss Oriana Cleat
Shene House
Near Richmond

Dear Miss Cleat,

For some time I have pondered the wisdom of writing to you. Now, summoning what little courage I possess, I have at last set pen to paper.

To say it plain. Since the occasion of your birthday ball, it seems to me we have become firm friends. But, of course, when together, we always find ourselves among others of our acquaintance.

This note, therefore, is to ask—no, to implore—if, from the kindness of your sweet heart, you might consider meeting with your correspondent in a more private fashion? The riverbank, at some convenient place and time, would provide an agreeable rendezvous, if this request has not offended you?

Please understand that though profound respect has made me hesitate to offer this invitation before, I now have matters of great seriousness to discuss. Therefore, I beg your understanding and acceptance of the same.

In anticipation of a favorable response,
I sincerely wish to remain

Your servant, always,
Connor Moncrieff

With a calm that came to her as a gift, Ellen carefully folded up the little letter and gave it back to her cousin.

Oriana, made anxious by her silence, asked, "Do you think me very bad for wishing to write in return?"

Ellen's face stretched to a smile. "Not at all. I can see that you love him already. I, too, find him a charming person."

Oriana glimmered with happiness. "You have guessed! Oh, I am so glad. It is such a relief to be plain about my feelings." She hugged Ellen, who suffered the embrace but did not return it. "I do not dare to think what he might have to say to me but to know that you, also, have regard for Connor gives me courage. I should have been so sad if you thought less of him than I."

Uncoupling Oriana's hands from her own, Ellen ran down the last few steps to the orchard. Time. She must have time to compose herself. But Oriana hurried on behind.

"I slept with the note under my pillow last night, thinking of—oh, everything! Each moment, every glance, all the precious seconds we have spent in each other's company."

Ellen stumbled but did not pause. Once, Oriana and she had had no secrets. Had she now been supplanted by this boy that they both loved, so that, in time, she would be cast away like a neglected toy? A soft, sad wind began to blow through her being, the lonely wind off the marshes on the edge of night.

"Ellen, wait."

Oriana was a pace or so behind. Her tone was anxious. "We might write a reply together? I should hate him to think I do not care by being tardy in response." They had reached ancient walls of red brick where the peach trees displayed their fruit, gilded in the evening light. As the heat of the day faded, the peaches gave up their scent to the air, a faint blessing but no consolation.

Ellen glanced at her cousin. Rapture had softened Oriana's eyes to mist.

"I should be so grateful if you would come with me to meet Connor, cousin. For propriety's sake? I could not go alone. That would be wrong."

"For propriety's sake. Yes. I quite see that."

Why did the ache of envy and grief not go away? Why must it be renewed each time she saw the joy in Oriana's eyes?

"You are so generous and kind, Ellen, and so solicitous of my happiness. My dear, true friend. How lucky I am that fate brought you to Shene. And to me. What would I do without you?"

Shadows advanced across the grass, longer and longer. Soon the gong would sound for their dinner. "I must change. Miss Wellings will not approve of afternoon clothes at our table. Will you come, cousin?" Oriana held out her hand, but Ellen shook her head.

"Shortly. I should like to watch as the sun sets."

Oriana said, warmly, "Of course. A perfect evening. The effect of the light is delightful."

Ellen said nothing. She did not care about the light. She did not care about changing for dinner.

Oriana chewed her lip. She was almost certain that her cousin was unhappy but she did not know why. Helplessly, she said, "Well, if you are sure?" Ellen nodded. But as Oriana hurried away toward the house, Ellen half-watched until the girl's slight figure was lost inside the immensity of Shene.

All at once a longing came over her: Isidore's library. He was away in London and need never know.

The house was quiet as Ellen ran to the mahogany door. It was closed. Was it locked? Since her first visit, she had asked Oriana about her father's library and been told how valuable the collection was and that Isidore considered it his private sanctum. Heart beating a tattoo, Ellen's fingers closed softly over the handle and turned it. The mechanism clicked and the door opened. Ellen caught her breath. Evening filled the room, embalming the books in honeyed light.

One step became two, became ten, and Ellen paused beside the lectern. The eagle's glance was hard. Was it her imagination that his head, with its slashing, cruel beak, had turned toward her? But if he was the guardian here, could he not sense that she belonged among these treasures?

Ellen refused to be intimidated by that oak stare. She walked slowly along the lower shelves and paused from time to time. A set of library stairs led upward to a narrow gallery fifteen feet above her head. Would she climb those iron treads to see what was in the higher shelves? Dare she? As she set one foot upon the bottom rung the gong distantly sounded. Dinner! Very soon she would be missed.

Ellen quickly opened the door and ran. She did not see Miss Wellings. The governess, too, was hurrying to the nursery wing. She paused, surprised, as she saw Ellen slip from the library. Had the girl been given permission to enter, or was this a privilege she had taken to herself?

Miss Wellings silently counted to ten. And then to five. Enough time to allow Ellen to reach the back stairs.

The spirits of the governess grew lighter. It was not often that she had the advantage of the presumptuous Miss Gowan, and, as with so many things, knowledge was power.

CHAPTER 16

I T WAS Ellen's birthday. As the house lay sleeping, she slipped from the nursery and stole into her mother's darkened room. Climbing into Connie's high bed, she huddled against her back. Ellen had thought her mother asleep but Connie whispered, "My dearest child. May today be a wonderful anniversary of your birth."

"Oh, Mama."

Ellen wriggled into her mother's arms and they clung together. Connie had been crying. A year, a whole year, had passed since that terrible day, and the tragedy of Edwin's death was too raw, still, for pretense of joy. Yet if there was some comfort in their sorrow, it was that mother and child were together.

At length, Connie said, gently, "You must go back to your bedroom. I shall see you at breakfast." She kissed away her daughter's tears.

Ellen, her head light from weeping, did her mother's bidding. But crying is a release, and in her bed again she slept a little, and opened her eyes smiling when Oriana said, "Time to wake, keep-a-bed."

Ellen sat up with a start. "Are we very late?"

Oriana laughed. "Late enough. Happy birthday, dearest cousin. I have this for you. I hope you like it."

A brown-paper parcel was shyly extended. Oriana had decorated it herself with sketches of flowers and birds, charming for their naïve sincerity.

As Ellen untied the large bow that bound it up, she said, warmly,

"The wrapping has cost you a great deal of time, and I never saw you do it. You clever thing!"

Oriana giggled, but then grew serious as her cousin uncovered a tiny velvet-covered box.

"I asked Mama, and she agreed. Our grandmother gave it to me as a Christmas gift. But you are the only child of her youngest daughter and I think you should have it." She did not say, *Because you have so few mementos of our family*, but that is what she meant.

With trembling hands, Ellen opened the exquisite little object. In a dimple on pearl-hued velvet was a cameo brooch. On it, the coupled profiles of two young girls, the likeness of each quite clear. "Is this . . . ?"

Oriana nodded. "Yes. My mama and yours. It was made when they were each around our own ages."

Ellen hugged the brooch to her heart. "You are more than kind to me." To feel such unguarded affection after days of misery was a relief. Perhaps all would yet be well.

And Oriana, normally so controlled, embraced her cousin tenderly, saying, "But you are easy to love, dearest Ellen. And I want you to be happy today." Tact would not allow her to speak of Edwin Gowan.

Ellen threw back her bedclothes. "Well then! We had better get up or your mother and mine will not be pleased, and then I really *will* be sad!"

"That is very pretty, Connie. You have such taste!"

Daisy sighed with pleasure as her sister placed the nosegay of roses upon her daughter's plate. The buds, cream flushed with softest pink, were only just open and there were drops of water upon the sage green leaves.

Connie touched one finger to a pearl of dew. It trembled but adhered there. "One day, Ellen will see her birthday as more than the memorial of tragedy. I wanted to remind her that life continues. And that beauty remains, always. That can be her consolation, if she will permit it to be so."

"And she is your consolation." The sisters stood quietly, hands lovingly joined until Daisy said, "For all the sadness of this day, you were very lucky in your marriage. You and Ellen were greatly loved. And if Edwin has gone from your lives, at least there is that to remember."

"Oh, Mama. How lovely!"

Connie matched her daughter's valiant spirits as she and Oriana whirled into the breakfast room.

"Happy birthday! And here are yet more treats." A white napkin had been spread over an uneven little hillock lying before Ellen's place. It was intriguingly shaped, that mound.

"Would you like to open your presents before or after breakfast, dearest niece?" Daisy caught Connie's eye, and nodded brightly. *Sadness begone! There is no chair at this table for you today.*

With the healthy avarice of any fourteen-year-old, Ellen said, fervently, "Presents!"

"Very well."

Connie smilingly removed the napkin to reveal a straw bonnet with green ribbons and roses of pale-yellow silk. There was a pair of matching fingerless gloves also. Connie had trimmed the hat herself and crocheted the gloves over many laborious evenings. From Daisy there was a shawl with a pattern of swirling gold on a cream ground fringed with silver tassels. Ellen draped the lovely thing around her shoulders, and ran to a mirror.

"How smart I feel!" She turned back to the room, laughing and flushed. The three at the table said nothing for a moment. Daisy was the first to speak. "And you *look* very smart, too, dearest niece." She caught her sister's eye again and smiled.

Oriana said, with transparent honesty, "And how grown up you are!"

Impulsively, Ellen hurried to her cousin and kissed her. Side by side, the truth was clear. Happiness had transformed Oriana, that was certain. She was pretty, but Ellen was beautiful.

The breakfast passed pleasantly with much laughter, but toward the end of the meal Ellen grew quiet, and Connie saw that she had eaten very little. Edwin Gowan was an unacknowledged presence in the room.

"What would you like to do today, dearest cousin? It must be your choice."

Ellen smiled warmly at Oriana, but reached out a hand to Connie. "Do you know, I should so like Mama to show me where she picked the roses. The garden in the morning is my special delight."

"Do not be sad, Ellen. He would not want that." Mother and daughter were slowly walking down the herbaceous borders of Shene's gardens. Ellen was considerate of her mother. A year might have passed but Connie's health continued to be frail. Also, the tension of living at Shene took a toll on her rest, leaving her hollow-eyed and a prey to exhaustion.

"Not sad, Mama. Not now. Merely reflective."

Connie said, lightly, "Too much thinking is bad for children. Nod used to say that."

Ellen stopped and asked quietly, "Am I still a child, Mama?"

Connie did not know what to say. The image of her daughter before the mirror, only an hour earlier, could not be denied. She took Ellen's face between her hands and said tenderly, "You will always be my child. My rosebud."

Ellen said, solemnly, "Mama, if I tell you something, something very important, will you promise the knowledge will remain between us?"

Connie replied, uneasily, "I should hope that I can."

That was not enough for Ellen. She walked on a little way.

"Ellen?" Connie hurried to catch up. She arrived at Ellen's side, breathing raggedly, a hand to her chest.

"Is this where you picked the flowers, Mama?"

Near the riverbank Ellen was standing before a climbing rose. It was very old, the trunk as thick as a good-size tree, and its branches rioted along the length of a wall supported by lattice. Everywhere was a profusion of cream and pink blooms. Some were still tightly furled, some open and almost blown, the prey of plundering bees gathering stores for winter. The insects gave the rose tree a voice like the hiss of a distant sea.

"What did you want to say to me, Ellen?"

"Mother, I cannot tell you unless you give me your word." Ellen was polite but certain.

Connie paused then said, reluctantly, "Very well. Since it is your birthday. Whatever you say shall remain in my confidence."

They both watched as a bumble bee, many times larger and slower than the common workers, exited from the heart of an opened flower, a creature of gold dust.

Ellen touched her mother's wrist. She could feel Connie's pulse racing and that alarmed her. "Shall we sit, Mama?"

Secretly grateful, Connie allowed herself to be persuaded to a stone bench placed beside the roses. "And so, child?"

Ellen sighed. "Connor Moncrieff has written to Oriana. He has asked her to meet him secretly so that he can declare his feelings. She loves him, too, Mama. I think he means to propose."

Connie paled. "But this is not to be thought of! Oriana is far too young."

Ellen said, solemnly, "Love does not need age to be real, Mama. Oriana is only a little younger than you were when you first met Papa. You told me yourself that your love for my father was kept from his parents and yours until, by accident, they found out."

Connie tried to speak, but could not. She turned away. Clandestine love had been the origin of the Gowan family tragedy when she was cast out of her family.

"Are you unhappy for Oriana and Connor, Mama?"

Connie shook her head. "No. Not unhappy. But young affection does not often last. We were very lucky, your papa and I, that ours was lifelong. This is not what I would wish for Oriana or for you, Ellen."

"But you loved Papa. You still do."

Emotion seared Connie Gowan. "Ah, child." She held out her arms and Ellen sheltered there.

The morning was warm and drowsy. The Gowans sat in companionable silence together watching as a flotilla of swans glided past, parents and their half-grown cygnets from the previous spring. "Will Aunt Daisy miss Oriana? Should Connor and she marry, I mean?"

Connie gazed at her daughter. After a moment she said, "And now it is my turn. If I say what is in my heart, this will be *our* special understanding?"

"Our secret, Mama. Just yours and mine."

"Very well then." Connie paused, then continued, "I do not think my sister will be displeased should this affection deepen to a lasting love. She desires, above all, that Oriana be cherished by a good man. Isidore, however, will do all he can to prevent such a match."

"But why? Connor will be wealthy. This would be a most advantageous alliance. Is that not the point of marriage among grand families?"

Connie glanced at her daughter, surprised at Ellen's pragmatism. "Perhaps. But your uncle has other plans. He will wish Oriana's marriage to create financial advantage, certainly, but he expects much from their daughter's London season. A duke's son perhaps, or that of an earl, will be encouraged. Even a titled widower if his rank is high enough." Ellen recalled Oriana's distrust of the *old men* her father knew. "A plain Mister, no matter how wealthy, will not do for your cousin."

Ellen stared at the river as it slipped past below. "And yet, money and love seem rarely to be related. In fact, perhaps the one drives the other away? My aunt, for instance, does not seem happy."

Perhaps it was emotion that made Connie catch her breath. She began to cough, and it took some time for the spasm to die away. Eventually, she continued, "Since we are speaking of such serious things, I must tell you that what you sense here is my fault." She colored seeing Ellen's startled glance. "You know that your grandfather was very angry at my marriage to your father. I had thrown myself away for love, he said. A word he despised. And since I had chosen a penniless scholar, he believed I had shamed the family. But I would not be dissuaded, and in acting so willfully"—Connie shook her head, tears standing in her eyes—"I sealed my poor sister's fate. There would be no *love* permitted for Daisy. Her marriage to Isidore was arranged for mutual family advantage between our father and Isidore's. That is common enough as you say, but often, in such a situation, the families will try to match the couple well enough so that love may grow in time. This was not considered important in my sister's marriage.

"Your aunt has her place in the world and wealth, too, though it is her husband's money, not hers. She has been a loyal wife and a loving mother, but I believe Isidore thinks of my sister as a thing. A suitable possession, an adornment to his position. He values her, as he does his furniture, or Shene's pictures, or the books in his library, but he does not love her. The word would not make sense to him. And Daisy, my poor, sweet sister, is trapped. He has come to have a power over her, and her actions, that she seems not able to resist. Her life is tolerable when she does not cross him, but . . ."

Connie faltered. Ellen said nothing. She had never heard her mother speak in this blunt way before.

"I have said too much, child. It would be a kindness for you to speak with Oriana. If she feels as you say she does, she *must* inform her mother of the seriousness of the situation. They will need to prepare, for when Isidore finds out . . ." She shook her head. "Oh, I do not trust that man. We are all flies to him, creatures to be squashed without thought if we become inconvenient.

But while we live here, Ellen, you must be careful. Do not test him."

The thought hovered, unspoken, *Because we have nowhere else to go.*

Ellen said, slowly, "And me, Mama? When the time comes, shall I make a successful marriage?"

How much it hurt Connie, but perhaps it was best to face the truth.

"You are years away from your wedding, but meeting a suitable young gentleman while we live on Isidore's charity may be difficult. Oriana is his focus, his *project*, not you." A bleak little laugh followed. "However, my wish for you is that, one day, a respectable person whom you are able to like will make you as happy as Papa and I once were." She tried not to sound sad.

Ellen was downcast. Respectable? What of love?

Connie understood. She rallied. "But you are clever, Ellen. You will make something of your life. I am convinced of that. I am so proud of you. You have become a talented artist. Perhaps, if we were not at Shene, we might live from the work of your pen and brushes. And I can sew. There now, two professions we have between us. London is the place for people like us. Or, since you are a scholar, thanks to your father, we could find other employment together. Me as a housekeeper, you as the governess of the household. We need only wait a year or two, until you are a little more grown. Patience is all that is required."

Ellen had a sudden vision of Miss Wellings. Her unhappy eyes. Unwillingly, she felt some compassion for the governess and her two dresses—one brown, one blue. She had not been told the young woman's history, but something had deprived Miss Wellings of any other choice than teaching the children of the wealthy. Soon she would be too old, and too unattractive, to marry. How lonely she must be and how bleak her future.

Ellen resolved that she would try to be kinder to their teacher, but here, on her fourteenth birthday, she issued a challenge to fate.

She might be a girl, she might be young, she might—at this point—seem helpless against the adult world, but no power she knew of would force her to become a governess. Ever.

She *would* make her own way. And the river that was life would carry her to where she wanted to go.

CHAPTER 17

Sir Isidore returned from London two days after Ellen's birthday. She was reading in the window seat of the nursery bedroom when the Shene barouche rolled up to the front portico and her uncle stepped down. Even from a distance he seemed angry, but since his expression was often pained, she thought little of it.

As Warwick closed the great doors, Ellen turned the page, absorbed in the story. Minutes later she read no further. Rapid footsteps were approaching along the corridor. Oriana.

"My father has returned."

Her cousin was framed in the open door.

Ellen nodded. "I saw the carriage." She closed the book regretfully as Oriana hurried toward her. She had rarely seemed so agitated.

"Mama has sent a message. Papa wishes to hear me play the pianoforte this evening." Oriana clenched her hands in a painful knot.

Ellen forgot to feel sorry for herself. She said, gently, "You play delightfully, Oriana. He will be very pleased with your progress. I can turn the pages, if you like."

"No! You must perform also. Please, cousin."

Ellen said soothingly, "If that is your wish. A four-handed duet?"

Oriana brightened. "Yes! It will be unexpected."

This last was half-muttered as the older girl flung up the lid on the piano stool and riffled through the sheet music stored there. "We must practice. Note perfect, nothing less."

Oriana propped a manuscript on the nursery piano and the two sat down. While her cousin flexed her fingers above the keys, Ellen ventured, "You seem distressed." She actually meant, *Has anything happened with Connor?*

Oriana shook her head. Then said, hesitatingly, "Only that I have thought constantly of a certain person since you and I wrote the letter."

Ellen shrank from the thought. *Something has changed.* "You may speak freely to me."

Oriana swiveled to her cousin. "You cannot know how grateful I am, dearest Ellen, for your kindness." Her voice trailed off. She stared at the ivory keys as if uncertain what they signified. "However, I have been very troubled. I do not like to deceive my mother. And Mr. Moncrieff has written me another note. He asks that we meet tomorrow but I have not replied. Not yet. I have been meaning to tell you." She looked at Ellen imploringly. "What should I do?"

Ellen turned the pages until she found a piece of music they both knew. "This one?"

Oriana nodded and placed her hands on the keys, but Ellen paused. "Aunt Daisy is a most understanding person. I think if you spoke with her, shared your feelings about Mr. Moncrieff"—she swallowed. It was hard to be generous, sometimes—"you would feel less burdened."

Oriana nodded. "Excellent advice."

Ellen smiled, a poultice plastered over wounds. "Very well then, let us play. And one, and two, and . . ."

The night was cold even though it was August, and a fire spat softly on its hearth. Connie and Daisy sat together on the sofa, and Isidore was in his usual place on the hearth rug as the girls arrived in the drawing room. After arranging the sheets of manuscript on the German piano, Oriana nervously stepped forward to introduce the piece she and Ellen had selected to play.

"Father and Mother, and you, Aunt Connie, you may like to know that we have chosen a duet by Beethoven. It is for four hands. We hope you like it." Oriana curtsied formally to her parents and her aunt, and Ellen did the same.

"Delightful. And ambitious!" Daisy gazed intently at her daughter though she smiled encouragingly. "Playing together, Isidore. How novel this is."

Isidore said nothing.

"Begin when you are ready, girls." Daisy linked her fingers through her sister's. Her voice was rather high and she spoke quickly.

Oriana, under her breath, counted them in, "One, two, three, and . . ." Both sets of hands came down on the keys at the same moment and the opening chords were flawless. Synchrony and harmony.

Now Ellen took the lead with her right hand, an arpeggio, then another, into which Oriana chimed with her left. The polyphony built and built—question and response—until Oriana dared to cast a delighted glance at her cousin.

Ellen smiled as the music flowed back and forth between them. She was astonished at how well they seemed to be playing. *The whole* is *greater than the sum of the parts,* she thought happily.

It was then that she became aware that Isidore had moved. He was now standing directly behind his daughter.

Sensing her father's presence, Oriana faltered. She missed an entry, and that confused Ellen. By the time the younger girl had thought to repeat the phrase, the energy of attack had been lost. Some moments of disjointed playing followed until Oriana took her hands off the keys. Ellen continued for a moment before she, too, hesitated and stopped.

"I am sorry, Papa. It was entirely my fault. I became distracted. We can begin again, if you would like us to." Her voice was unsteady.

"You were both playing delightfully." Connie had hurried over and put an arm around each girl. "I should like to hear more. Should you not, Daisy?"

But Isidore's voice was cold as lake ice. "It is plain to me that Oriana has not been diligent in practice. You said you were distracted, daughter. How can that be so?"

Oriana was silent, caught in the snare of her father's glance. Ellen said, quickly, "I can assure you, Uncle, that we both practice."

"You can assure me of nothing. I was speaking to my daughter. Come. Confess, Oriana. Or must I name the *person* who is the cause of such negligent behavior." A silent gasp from both girls. Ellen felt her mother's hand clench on her shoulder.

Isidore swung to face his wife. "And you, Madame, have been derelict in your duty also. Mr. Connor Moncrieff is not welcome in this house. He is not to speak with Oriana or communicate with her in any other way. That is my instruction to you." A moment later, the door of the drawing room closed behind the master of Shene.

Daisy sat, pale and contained, on the sofa. "I do agree with Connie, children. Your performance tonight was excellent. But now, I think, it is time for bed."

"Mother, I wanted to speak with you." Oriana had risen. Her voice quavered. "There are things I should have said."

Daisy raised one hand. Her face was drained. "In the morning. Good night, children."

Oriana capitulated. Quickly gathering the sheets of music, she took Ellen by the hand. It was only when they were in the nursery bedroom that she said, in agonized tones, "How can he know? Who has told him?" Falling on her bed, her sobs were wrenching.

Ellen stroked her cousin's brow. Oriana's distress upset her greatly. "Perhaps it will be for the best? There will be no more need for deception."

Oriana looked up, her face ravaged. In a horrified whisper she said, "The best? My poor mother. I have hurt her grievously, and not just by my silence. She will pay for this. If only I had told her." Oriana wept as one bereft of hope.

∽

The next morning, the sun rose into a world darkened by rain. Oriana and Ellen were immured in the schoolroom in a state of high tension. Expecting to be summoned to her father at any moment, Oriana visibly sagged when Jane arrived with a message from Daisy. Isidore would be working in his library all day, and was not to be disturbed by anyone, for any purpose.

Miss Wellings, too, was especially liverish as lessons began. Since the incident of the Latin verbs, the governess had inflicted increasing petty tyrannies upon her younger pupil, and today her persecution included physical punishment. Freely applying the edge of her ruler to Ellen's hands during French conversation, her student's palms were very soon crossed with burning scarlet lines. It seemed that nothing Ellen said, or did or wrote, would satisfy their teacher today.

"May I be excused, Miss? A call of nature." The governess waved assent to Oriana as she tapped the blackboard impatiently. Her nails were inordinately long. The sound was unpleasant.

"Miss Gowan, pay attention. Read aloud what I have written here."

Ellen stood beside her desk. She was wary. For the last hour Miss Wellings had paced up and down the schoolroom, her lips compressed to rigid white lines.

"Avec mes amies, nous sont faires les jeux au bord de la mer."

"Non! This pronunciation is execrable! Intolerable!"

Miss Wellings wrenched a hank of Ellen's hair. The pain was vicious and Ellen screamed. The woman slapped her. "Stupid, lazy girl! You waste my time with inattentive idiocy!"

And that was enough. Ellen hit Miss Wellings's cheek with an open hand. The crack was audible. Months of resentment lent strength to that blow, and a red mark spread across the face of the governess just as Oriana returned.

For one terrified moment, tutor and pupil stared at each other.

Then the governess sank down as if stabbed or shot. Before either girl could reach out a hand, Miss Wellings scrambled up and ran from the schoolroom, wailing. The door clapped shut. The cousins were mute with shock.

Oriana took Ellen in her arms. Both were trembling. "Alas. I shall speak with her."

"Oriana, I swear I had done nothing! She has been so horrible to me lately. You have seen it."

Oriana nodded. Miss Wellings was always nice to her, of course. "Something has upset her today."

Ellen shook her head. "I agree, but when you were out of the room, she tore at my hair and hit me." She touched her forehead and her fingers came away bloody. "I did slap her. I did not mean to but . . ."

Oriana rocked the younger girl. "She is unfair to you. I see it. But Papa must never hear of this. She is a favorite of his, though Mama distrusts her." Oriana pressed her frightened cousin close. "Hush, little one. Hush, all will be well, I shall see to it."

"Why does she treat me in this way, Oriana?"

The older girl looked sad. "You are pretty, Ellen. And young and clever. Better educated, too. She sees that and it makes her resentful. And frightened for her position, I think. Yours is a life filled with more promise than hers has ever had. These are your only crimes." She wiped Ellen's eyes and kissed her. "Miss Wellings is not a bad woman, merely unhappy. Stay here. I shall see if I may mend this sad situation. Envy. So difficult."

Ellen was never to forget the compassion in Oriana's eyes. How could she have allowed herself to be jealous over something of such little account as the affections of a boy? But worse was yet to come.

That evening, as the cousins descended the great stair to make their adieus for the night, they heard a woman cry out. A short, anguished scream.

Ellen paled. "Mama!" And then came another cry. This was Daisy. Silence followed. And sobbing, quickly muffled.

Gathering her skirts, Ellen ran down the last steps, Oriana at her heels.

"Wait!" Oriana caught her cousin's hand. "We must be careful. Please, Ellen."

Panting, the younger girl paused. "But something terrible has happened!"

"Papa will not like it if we fuss." Oriana held her cousin back. The younger girl strained to run to the door, where shadows massed between pools of feeble illumination.

"Miss Oriana, Miss Ellen." Warwick. They had not seen him.

He bowed and said, "A little tardy tonight, young ladies, but no need to hurry. You are expected." His tone was pleasant. Ellen stared at the man. Had he not heard?

"Miss Oriana and Miss Gowan, Sir, and Ladies." The girls were greeted by the usual scene. Daisy at her embroidery frame, Isidore standing before the fireplace frowning at his newspaper, and Connie with an opened book upon her lap.

Daisy said, brightly, "Hello, girls. How nice you both look this evening. Delightful. Do you not agree, Isidore?"

Her husband looked up from his paper. "What? Yes, a charming picture." His glance, abstracted and a little cold, was a contradiction to the conventional sentiments expressed.

Connie Gowan said nothing. Her face was in shadow as she peered down at her book. The branch of candles beside her chair cast light upon the page but not the person.

Ellen hurried to sit beside her mother on a footstool. She murmured, "Are you quite well, Mother?" It was all she could think to say.

Connie said nothing. She moved slightly in her chair and the light touched one cheek. Ellen saw a red mark there, very close to the eye.

"Your face!" She reached to touch the swelling.

Connie grasped her daughter's hand. "The merest trifle. I slipped while dressing." Connie Gowan stared at Ellen. *Say nothing.*

Daisy broke in, "I shall shortly ring for arnica, Ellen, and a pound of steak to be applied to the bruise. Your mother has been very brave." This was pronounced with feeling.

The silence that grew from that remark was thick with things unsaid. Isidore Cleat turned over a leaf of the *Times* and Ellen jumped at the rattle. She moved closer to Connie's side. How shocking it was not to speak, especially since her mother's breathing was ragged and shallow and she struggled not to cough.

Seated beside Daisy, Oriana was rapidly sorting embroidery silks, red with rose, yellow with gold, sapphire and turquoise with indigo. She did not look up.

Ellen burned and froze. Fury, fear, helplessness. With each passing moment it became more and more impossible to say or do anything. Isidore Cleat cleared his throat. Unwillingly, Ellen looked at her uncle. He was staring at her over the top of his paper. She flinched as his face moved. He was smiling.

Ellen knew what that smile meant. Power. The mark on her mother's face, Oriana's silence, Daisy's industrious concentration all confirmed the actuality of that word. And he was looking at her. She tried to meet his glance, but could not. And hated herself. Her despair amused Isidore. He went back to his paper with a jovial sniff.

Connie Gowan touched her daughter's hand. *Please,* she mouthed. Ellen sagged. They were trapped. All of them.

CHAPTER 18

A LITTLE BEFORE dawn on the following morning, Ellen crept downstairs in her nightgown and wrap.

She tapped softly at Connie's door. Speaking directly into the keyhole, she whispered, "Are you awake, Mama?"

There was no response.

Behind Ellen, a corridor of closed doors ran toward a long, uncovered window. It was getting lighter with each passing moment.

More urgently she asked, "Can you hear me, Mama?"

A faint voice replied, "Yes, child. Come in."

Ellen eased the door open and slipped through into the dim space beyond. Her mother was not in bed but sitting at her dressing table. The triple mirror reflected her face from all sides.

Ellen ran to Connie. "Did he hurt you very much?" How dreadful to ask such a question.

Connie shook her head, but her left eye was half-closed and the flesh over one cheekbone puffed and swollen. The mirror displayed the injury in cruel detail.

"He was angry with us both. He blames your aunt for Oriana and Connor Moncrieff's friendship and believes that you and I are complicit. There are spies in this house." Connie's eyes darkened. "And when I tried to tell him that Daisy had not known that Oriana planned to meet clandestinely with Connor Moncrieff, he hit me. I was very shocked but then, when he hit her also . . ." Connie shook her bowed head. "I have seen Isidore upbraid Daisy before, but never raise his hand to her in my presence." Hot, shamed tears ran down Ellen's face.

Connie said, gently, "You did what you thought was right, child. We both did. This is not your fault."

"He must be brought to account!" Ellen almost shouted the words.

Connie pressed a finger against her daughter's lips. In heart-thudding silence they listened. Nothing stirred beyond the door.

Ellen whispered, "Shall we leave this place?"

Connie exhaled a long sigh. "Ah, child. Love and duty keep us here. If we go, I should desert Daisy again, as I did long ago. And Oriana, too."

"Oriana? Do you mean that he . . . ?"

Connie shook her head. "*No*, child. No. So far as I know, he does not abuse his daughter as he does his wife. But Isidore controls my sister through their child and what he *might* do. I trust and pray that Oriana knows only a little of what transpires between her parents."

Ellen might have said, *Do not be so sure,* but did not.

Despairing, she asked, "How can he do as he does, Mama?"

Connie did not immediately answer. She rose and went to her window, pulling the curtains back. But for the vivid bruise, her face was pale as the voile.

"Some men feel it is their right to be obeyed in all things. As I grew up, I slowly became aware that my father controlled my mother in every way, and through her, us children. That was the hold he had over her. And when I married your father, because I had opposed your grandfather's will, my punishment was to be cast out of the family. Isidore Cleat is cut from similar cloth. Perhaps this is why my sister cannot challenge his behavior. He is too much like Papa."

"What can be done, Mama? *Something* must be possible."

Connie hurried to her door and locked it. In a soft whisper she said, "I have asked myself often, over these last months, what course of action will be best. Not just for my sister but for you and me, and Oriana also." She grimaced. "All that you see around you, my sister's jewels and clothes, the very food we eat, belong to Isidore. If Daisy left him, or if he cast her out, she would be homeless and penniless. He has told her so, and I do not doubt it. Oriana, of course, would remain with her father since she is not of age. As the wronged party—deserted by his wife, in the eyes of the law—Isidore would have even more power to determine her future. Do not forget he is a lawyer. The contest would be most unequal. My sister would lose any action she might try to bring in Parliament—for that is the only place a divorce may be obtained. The scandal, too, would be immense. She will not inflict such shame upon your cousin."

"So they are condemned to a life of fear? And we also, while we live beneath this roof? Mama, this cannot be tolerated." Ellen's whisper was fierce.

Connie smiled faintly. "I begin to see my daughter is a lion, and not a girl at all." Her voice faltered. "I had so hoped that Shene would prove a refuge for us both, but principally for you. Here there is shelter and, when Isidore is away, a happy existence. And you have Oriana. I delight in your affection for each other. You are a support to her, just as I am to my poor sister. Without me, without us, I fear for what Daisy might do. Also, it seems to me that *he* is a little kinder to her in my presence. Except for last night." Her eyes darkened.

Ellen was troubled. "Happy? How can we be happy, knowing what we do?"

"We must put our own feelings aside. Oh, I must think! Think what to do! Edwin, if you can see us, give me your counsel. Please." The stricken appeal was consumed in coughing.

Ellen held her mother as the paroxysm subsided. "There will be a way. We shall find it together." She wiped Connie's eyes tenderly, avoiding the bruises as much as she could.

Connie clung to her daughter, and then released her. "You must go, my dearest. The servants will be about soon and it is Isidore's habit to rise early also. His rooms are close by." She led Ellen to the door.

"Avoid your uncle, for a solution to this evil will take time. Do not provoke him. We must give him no further excuse to persecute my sister or your cousin."

Ellen nodded. What other choice was there?

Connie kissed her child tenderly. "We will survive. And we must help Oriana and Daisy do the same. I shall pray for guidance."

Later that morning, Ellen's hands were sweating as she turned the knob of the nursery door. The governess and Oriana sat silently at the breakfast table. Miss Wellings did not acknowledge her younger pupil as she joined them. Ellen sat down to a bowl of rapidly cooling porridge just as a large, plain teapot was deposited by Kitty, the nursery maid. It landed on the table with a jolt and a quantity of scalding liquid belched from the spout.

"Oh! Sorry 'bout that. I did not scald you, did I, Miss Ellen?" The tea had, in fact, very nearly splashed Miss Wellings.

In freezing tones, the governess said, "That will be quite enough. Be about your work."

Favoring the room with a toss of the head, Kitty clattered to the nursery door. "I was only asking, Miss."

Miss Wellings flushed a pained scarlet. Oriana caught Ellen's eye and grimaced unseen by her governess. None of the servants offered respect to the woman. That was an ongoing humiliation.

"Eat quickly. We have much to do." Miss Wellings forced the congealing slurry into her mouth, as did Ellen. Oriana ate nothing at all.

Not then, nor in the following hours, was the incident of the previous day raised. Instead, a frigid precision entered the discourse, such as it was, between Miss Wellings and Ellen. Icy politeness from the former, as few words as possible from the latter. Drearily the girls pursued their studies as the governess marched back and forth, back and forth, drilling Oriana and Ellen until a crisp rap on the door announced Jane.

"Miss Wellings, I am to dress Miss Gowan. She is to be brought downstairs. Sir Isidore's special request."

If Miss Wellings had thought to object, Jane's pleasant smile and hard eye would have dissuaded her, so she did not. And before the governess waved dismissal, something unsettling occurred. She stared at Ellen, and deliberately smiled.

Ellen, with a panicked curtsy, hurried from the room. Normally even Isidore was to be preferred to Miss Wellings in this mood. But not now. Not after that smile.

Ellen's belly contracted against her spine.

Isidore Cleat sat behind an austere desk in his library. A palm-size unremarkable book lay before him. But when Isidore opened it, Ellen, who had not been invited to sit, saw what was upon the page and gasped. Isidore's gaze sharpened.

"Something upsets you, Ellen?"

"No, Sir. That is, I am not upset. Merely surprised."

"And why might that be so?"

Ellen's courage held. Just. "I believe I may have seen a book similar to this before."

The sneer that had marked Isidore's face changed. After a pause, he replied, "A child such as you will *of course* be familiar with hand-lettered manuscripts of such antiquity."

Thrusting the book close to Ellen's face, he said, "Tell me what you see." He would not permit her to hold it.

Ellen replied with care, "This is Greek, Sir. The ancient Koine."

Isidore had collected himself. With no emphasis, he asked, "Can you read it?" Ellen nodded, and her uncle gestured to the page. Ellen traced out the words with difficulty since the brown letters were faint.

"*If someone does evil to you, you should do good to him, so that by your good work you may drive out his malice.*" She faltered.

"That will do." Isidore stared at Ellen consideringly. "What else can you tell me?"

"From the style and the content, I believe this may be a copy of the *Patrologia Graeca*. A collection of the sayings of the early Desert Fathers. Koine fell out of use in the third century, so this is likely to be very ancient." Ellen stopped.

Isidore was smiling at her. He said, "You did not learn your Greek from Miss Wellings."

Ellen hesitated. "My father, Sir, had a library also. In all the ancient languages. I was permitted to read the works he had collected."

Isidore leaned forward and stared into her eyes. Ellen was rigid with the effort not to look away. He said, softly, "Whatever your late father may have sanctioned for his own property, the same does not hold for Shene. These are my books. This is one of the most important collections in England. And the most valuable. I am its custodian." He knew that he had frightened her. And she knew her fear pleased him, for he smiled again, more broadly.

"You entered my library without permission and you stole this book. That is why you seemed surprised when I showed it to you. In this house, you alone knew its value."

Ellen blinked, too astonished to do more than stutter, "S-steal? No!"

Isidore picked up a silver bell and shook it, its tone was sweet and cold.

The library door opened and there came the rustle of a woman's skirt. Someone was approaching. Ellen started as Miss Wellings arrived at her side. Her profile was rigid and her hands clamped in a bony ball at her waist.

"Miss Wellings, recount what occurred this morning. Consider your words carefully."

"Very well, Sir." The governess humbly cast down her eyes. "It was a little before breakfast. I was concerned that neither Miss

Cleat nor Miss Gowan was at the table, so I went to their bedroom."
She hesitated. Isidore Cleat was staring at Ellen.

"Continue, Miss Wellings."

"I observed that Miss Gowan's bed was in disarray, and stooped
to tidy it. She is often careless, of course."

Hurt by the slight, Ellen went to speak but the governess hurried on, "And I saw that object." She gestured to the book.

"Let us be clear, Miss Wellings. You found this volume in the
bed of my niece?" One long finger touched the leather binding.
"You are certain?"

"Oh, Sir, would that I were not! But I had observed Miss Gowan
leaving your library once before, when you were away. From her
furtive manner, I was certain that she had no leave to be here." The
glance she gave Ellen, awl sharp, was payment for yesterday. "As I
say, the manuscript was concealed beneath her pillow."

Ellen swallowed. "Uncle? Please allow me to speak."

"You may not. Miss Wellings, what is your opinion in this
matter?"

"Sir, I have none. Unless . . ." The governess raised stricken eyes
to her employer's face.

Sir Isidore nodded. "Continue."

"Unless, sir, Miss Gowan had taken the book without your
permission."

Ellen gaped. "No!"

"For what end, I do not know, of course." Miss Wellings finished smoothly, but the rising cadence, the sorrowful shake of the
head, suggested suspicions that she was too kind, too scrupulous
to express.

"Thank you."

"But, Uncle, please, none of this is true! I did not take your
book."

Isidore ignored his niece. "Miss Wellings, a final question. Your
face is marked. From what cause?"

The governess closed her eyes. A brave heroine. She said, brokenly, "I regret, Sir, to speak of this. Miss Gowan hit me. With her open hand."

Ellen attempted to answer, "But you pulled my hair and . . ."

Miss Wellings spoke quickly. "You see how it is, Sir Isidore. Miss Gowan seeks to prevaricate, to deny the culpability of her actions." Interlacing her fingers again, Miss Wellings said, "Yet, another person witnessed what passed between your niece and me. Later, she kindly attempted to speak on Miss Gowan's behalf, to ask me to forgive the unforgivable." The governess shook her head. A well-managed pause then, haltingly, "My witness, as you must have guessed, Sir, is your daughter, Miss Oriana."

Isidore Cleat cast Ellen a grave look. "What you have told me is shocking, Miss Wellings. Very shocking indeed. It compounds the wickedness of theft to a far greater degree. And though I should prefer my daughter to not be involved in any part of this sordid affair, I see little choice but to test the truth of this last statement. Warwick!"

The governess bowed her head as the library door opened. There stood Oriana. Isidore pointed at Ellen.

"Stand here." As Oriana arrived beside her, Isidore said, "Miss Wellings, you may ask my daughter one question. Nothing more shall I permit."

Miss Wellings, her eyes brimming, passionately declared, "Sir Isidore, my single aim is to preserve your daughter from pernicious influence." With tears upon her lashes, she turned to Oriana. "Miss Cleat, did you enter the schoolroom yesterday just as your cousin struck me? Here, this mark . . ." Her voice trembled.

Oriana glanced helplessly at Ellen. Her father frowned. "Daughter? We are waiting."

Haltingly, Oriana said, "I did not precisely see the action as described, Father."

"Do not fence with me. To the best of your understanding, do you believe your cousin attacked Miss Wellings, leaving the bruise we see here today?"

Wretchedly, Oriana whispered, "Yes, but, Papa, there is much you do not . . ."

Miss Wellings seemed shocked. Her chin quivered as she said, "Miss Oriana, I am surprised. Since you were a little girl we have confided in each other." This was genuine hurt.

"Allegra, I do not know why you have brought this dispute to my father, but . . ." Oriana's voice had a desperate edge.

Isidore spoke harshly. "Because it is her duty. That is what she is paid for. And I will not have you taken advantage of by paupers who seek to exploit your trust." Ellen's eyes widened at the contempt. "You have been betrayed, as have I. Your cousin stole this book. Perhaps to sell."

Oriana's mouth dropped open. Ellen cried out, "No! Oriana, Miss Wellings is lying. I do not know why but . . ."

Isidore turned away. "Enough. I have heard enough. Miss Wellings, please escort Miss Cleat to her mother." He waved his daughter away.

"But, Father, let me tell you why—oh, please, you must listen." Hurried away by her governess, Oriana's final words were cut as the door closed behind the pair.

The silence in the library grew heavy and more terrible. At length, Isidore dropped his hand from his eyes and glared at Ellen. "What grieves me most is that a member of my own family should have repaid my generosity in this treacherous, this appalling manner."

"Uncle, I did not steal the book. I did not." Ellen's eyes filled with tears as she whispered, "Please believe me. Please."

"Did you enter my library without permission? Did you hit your governess?" He was standing over her now.

Mired in despair, Ellen forced herself to speak. "Uncle, I would not steal from you. I could not do such a thing."

Isidore spoke over Ellen. "Avoidance condemns you. It is shameful that your actions were necessarily exposed by a courageous woman who cared only for your welfare. You and your mother will leave this house. Today." The bell was rung again.

The library door eased open. "Sir?"

"Warwick, escort Miss Gowan to her mother. Neither is to speak with my wife or my daughter before leaving Shene."

Warwick murmured, "Certainly, Sir."

Severe as a judge, Isidore stood behind his desk. "You are fortunate, Ellen, that I am merciful. Children are transported to Australia for thefts many times more minor than yours. Go."

The door closed. Ellen, automaton-like, paced the long corridor behind Warwick and then the even longer staircase to the upper levels of the house.

What would she tell her mother?

CHAPTER 19

"I WOULD COME with you if I could."

Daisy had quietly opened the bedroom door. The sisters ran to each other. "I am so sorry, Connie darling. So sorry. And that your *daughter* should be treated thus, used in this way as a warning to *me*."

Connie Gowan did not shed a single tear, though Daisy could scarce breathe for sobbing.

"Do not regret that we are leaving, sister. Regret, rather, what is left behind. You must think of how you can escape this man. When Ellen and I find somewhere suitable to live, you and Oriana must join us there. Isidore's influence upon you both is malign."

"Escape?" Daisy's face was gray.

"Sister! You must listen to me. This helplessness comes from brutal treatment. This is not right. At least we shall breathe free air together, away from this place. And him."

Daisy Cleat shook her head. Her eyes were dull. "Right? There is no right in this house nor ever has been."

Below, a gong was beaten. Luncheon had been announced. The routines of existence at Shene were set in adamant. "He will question my absence. You must go. Take this. Sell it." Daisy unfastened her necklace and pressed it into Connie's palm: a single strand of pearls and small rubies. "I will hide its loss somehow. And I will always help you, if I can." She shivered. "Write to me? Please."

Miserably, Connie nodded. Daisy grasped her sister's hands. "Go to Richmond. To Madame Angelique. She will shelter you tonight. I have sent her a note. Jane knows where she lives. Promise me you will leave immediately. It will not be safe if you stay a moment longer than you must."

For whom? wondered Connie, as she embraced her sister fiercely. And then Daisy fled.

"We shall take nothing with us but what is ours."

Connie hauled their old trunk from beneath her borrowed bed with Ellen's help. She was possessed by the strength of those who have nothing to lose.

Ellen was frightened by her mother's fixed expression and said, "Let me do it, Mother. Please." But Connie did not listen. Pulling up the lid, she sought the garments Ellen had bought in Norwich.

"Help me to dress, child. And you must change also." Ellen did as she was bidden though her mother was too agitated to stand still.

"Mrs. Gowan?" It was Jane. From distress, her eyes and nose were rabbit pink. Closing the door, the maid wrung her white apron to a creased mass. "Madame has sent me to help. I am so very sorry. We all are."

With the exception of Daisy and Oriana, Connie did not trust any of the inhabitants of Shene House. She turned her back to the maid and, stiff fingered, fumbled at the placket of her morning gown. The dress had been a present from Daisy. "Ellen, your assistance if you please."

Nervously, Jane drew closer. "Let me, Ma'am. Please, I beg. How can I abide you and Miss Ellen leaving if there is nothing, no service I can render, to make this departure kinder?" Jane's face crumpled.

Connie's suspicion drained away. She dropped her hands, helpless. "What a coil is this, Jane? My poor sister. And Oriana. Perhaps Ellen and I have the best of it." Weary words, and so sad. She stared at the open doorway where she had last seen Daisy. "We shall soon be done. There is not so very much to take." Connie understood what Jane risked. In helping them, she courted disaster.

"But Oriana. Mother, I must say good-bye. Please!"

Connie steeled herself against Jane's anxious glance. "Very well. You have moments only, Ellen."

"Ellen!"

"Dearest cousin, I could not go from Shene without . . ." Ellen's careful courage faltered.

"Oh, Ellen. What will you do? Where will you go?" Despairing, Oriana drew her cousin to their favorite window seat.

"I will write as soon as we are settled." Ellen did not acknowledge her fear or Oriana's.

"Yes, send your letters to Jane. I shall be watched now, but she will hide them for me. Allegra Wellings has much to answer for and answer she shall, you may depend on it." That gentle face had never seemed so grim. Or so determined. "Among everything else, I believe it was she who told Papa about Connor."

Ellen shrugged. "Miss Wellings is a pawn. Her spite toward me, and the manuscript, were conveniences to my uncle. A means to an end. He wishes us gone since we have observed his treatment of my aunt. And of you." She hugged her friend fiercely. "Be happy. You love Connor so much, and he will be good to you. Ask for his help." She stood quickly, breaking Oriana's embrace.

"But we shall always be friends?"

Ellen paused in the open doorway. She smiled at her beloved cousin. "Always."

The girls gazed long at each other, eyes bright with tears.

"Good-bye." Oriana had no words, no heart, for anything else.

"Until we meet again." And then Ellen Gowan was gone.

At the last moment, as Connie and Ellen scrambled to board the wherry at the Shene water-stairs, Jane pressed a piece of paper into Connie's hand. Though it was unsigned, she recognized her sister's writing. *You will find Madame Angelique beside the Eagle and Child. Hers is a tall and crooked house. She knows to expect you. Written in haste.*

And so the Gowans set out once more, trusting themselves to fate and that old river, the Thames.

Part Two

CHAPTER 20

MADAME ANGELIQUE'S house was one of the most curious in Richmond. Narrow and crooked as described, its small windows winked at the sun as if they were party to a private joke. And, twisted to one side, the building leaned against the Eagle and Child as a lover does. Behind the house, a long, thin garden led down to the river's edge where water lapped among reeds.

Ellen rapped the door knocker sharply against the plate. The crash echoed in the void behind the door. No footfall approached, no voice called out. Waiting, Ellen tried to smooth the skirt of her maid's uniform and retied the strings of her cap. Her old clothes and boots had been too small, so Jane had purloined a kitchen maid's dress, with a shawl, a cap, and clogs. Connie had been reluctant, but there'd been no other choice. Not if she wished to avoid her daughter walking bare-legged up Richmond high street.

Ellen lifted the ring again but before it could strike, the door was wrenched inward. "Yes?"

An angry youth of eighteen or so stood there. He glared down, nostrils pinched white. Common serving girls, it seemed, offended him.

"No!" Ellen forced a clog between the jamb and the door as he began, rudely, to close it.

Narrow-eyed the youth said, "What do you want?"

"Please, Sir"—a concession to appearances—"Madame Angelique expects us."

"I was not told. And who might be *us*?" He stared above Ellen's head, seeking this impertinent servant's companion.

"Raoul! You forget what few manners you possess. Miss Gowan, I am delighted to see you here." Madame Angelique had emerged from the interior. She spoke with only the smallest trace of accent. "But where is your dear mama?" As she addressed Ellen, Madame Angelique's brows slowly ascended. Ellen blushed. The servant's dress was well-used, even the cap was darned. How different her appearance was from the last time they had met at Shene.

"I left Mama at the water-stairs. I wanted to be sure, that is . . ." She coughed, embarrassed.

Madame Angelique said, smoothly, "*Naturellement*. You were uncertain of your reception. A dutiful and thoughtful child." The lady turned to glare at the youth beside her. He hunched.

"It is hardly my fault, Mother. I was not told to expect our guests." The sneer needed no words. Ellen blushed a hotter scarlet.

Madame Angelique scowled at her son. "*You* are most welcome in this house, Miss Gowan. As is your mother. Raoul! Make your address."

The young man sniffed, and when he bowed, the incline of his head was slight. "Charmed to make your acquaintance, Miss Gowan."

The flat tone displeased his mother. "Monsieur de Valentin, you make our guest uncomfortable. You were not born to be a clod, Sir!" Resentfully, the youth glowered as his mother continued. "You will go with this young lady and conduct her mama to us as you should. Immediately. Do you hear me?"

Ellen scuffed her clogs against the cobbles. Raised voices frightened her. She said, humbly, "Mr. de Valentin, I would be most grateful if you could accompany me. There is a trunk, you see, and it is hard for us to carry it alone."

This was the wrong thing to say. The contemptuous curl of the upper lip returned.

Mortified, Madame Angelique spoke harshly to her son. "You

will carry it back, my boy, and with good grace. None in this house is too grand or too proud to work. Go!"

Bobbing a panicked curtsy, Ellen hurried away not daring to look back, and Raoul followed her. She could hear his footsteps.

Connie Gowan stood alone upon the landing stage. She was staring along the river toward Shene. Ellen called out, "Mama!"

"Ellen! I had quite given you up."

Picking up her skirts, Ellen ran down the steps.

Connie patted her hand. "And who is this gentleman, child?"

"Mother, this is Mr. Raoul." Ellen paused. She had forgotten his last name!

The youth spoke with hauteur. "Raoul de Valentin, at your service, Madame Gowan." Sweeping off his hat, the bow was all it should have been.

Connie gracefully curtsied. She was bemused by this young exquisite, for Raoul sported a swallow-tailed coat of sober blue over a high-collared shirt and fawn trousers set off by braided seams. A bow of good linen completed a picture not often seen in a country town. Ellen wondered if his mother's clever fingers had made those garments, or if Raoul patronized a London tailor. Perhaps the de Valentin household was wealthier than it seemed.

"Madame de Valentin, my mother, has sent me to render assistance." He gave a supercilious glance at the Gowans' humble trunk.

Ellen scowled. Raoul's contempt annoyed her now, especially when her embarrassed mother colored. "This is very good of you, Mr. de Valentin. I hope it will not be a trouble."

Raoul, overconfident, bent to raise the trunk. Ellen enjoyed his surprised grunt when he tried to lift it. But poor Connie was horrified.

"Is it too heavy, Sir? Ellen, we must assist Mr. de Valentin!"

Raoul reared up with the trunk on his back. "Madame, I would not think of it. The box is a trifle. Lighter than a trifle."

Panting, he mounted the first stair and then the next. Half-turning, he said, "You see, it weighs so little I might run, should I choose." Sadly, the following step was slimed, and in that moment of bravado, Raoul's foot slipped and he fell. Rolling, he knocked his head upon the box as he dropped it.

"Oh! Mr. de Valentin!"

Horrified, Connie covered her mouth with her hand, but Ellen had to turn away. She choked back unkind laughter as the boy leaped up, brushing his trousers. Their pristine fawn was now fatally smeared with green.

"No! That is to say, not at all, I thank you, Mrs. Gowan." He glared at Ellen (he had heard the snort), and at the innocent box. The cause of this disaster, however, was sturdy and therefore undamaged.

"I *insist* that we find some assistance, Mr. de Valentin. The trunk is considerably too heavy for you. Oh, I blame myself for this. Kindness itself, and this is your reward! It is my most fervent hope that the marks on your handsome clothing will wash out with care and time." But Connie knew, and he knew, too, that the stain of slime was only rarely successfully removed.

"All will be well, Mrs. Gowan. Do not fear." Raoul clamped his hat upon his head, after extracting it from a puddle, where, unfortunately, it had rolled. This time, bent hook-shape, he took each step with care.

Connie and Ellen followed behind. Some anxious minutes passed before Ellen was able to say, with relief, "Here is the house, Mother." Waiting at the open door was the dressmaker.

"Madame Angelique. How kind you are to receive us." Connie's posture, rigid as a small tree, stiffened, and the lift of her chin betrayed her. A gentle person will sometimes pretend to strength she does not own.

"Mrs. Gowan." Angelique curtsied. "Raoul, take the box inside." The dressmaker stood to one side. She ignored the state of her son's clothing, as if such things were commonplace.

"I fear we have already inconvenienced your son, but we hope our arrival is not an imposition, Madame?"

Angelique said, warmly, "Not at all, Mrs. Gowan. Please to come inside."

Raoul, panting, rejoined his mother. Side by side, the resemblance between the two was remarkable. And Ellen, against her will, saw how very good-looking Raoul de Valentin was, as she walked past him into River Cottage.

Connie and Ellen were ushered by their hostess to an elegant parlor.

"Please, Mrs. Gowan, take this fauteuil." A comfortable armchair stood before a long window. "I believe you will enjoy the view of the river from here. Water, I find, is calming to the soul." She rang a small bell and a pleasantly shy girl answered the summons. "Tea for our guests, Peg."

As the maid curtsied and departed, Connie hesitated. "How kind you are, dear Madame Angelique. Considerate indeed since our circumstances are . . ." Her face worked. Without comment, the dressmaker encouraged her guest to sit. A modiste hears much, and the best are discreet as priests.

Peg returned with a laden tray from which she set out Sèvres cups and saucers and a matching sugar bowl along with crested silver spoons, a gold-chased strainer, and a pretty creamer. The elaborate teapot had a table all to itself within reach of Madame's hand.

As the door closed behind the maid, Angelique began to pour with singular grace. She relished the small ceremonies of civilization. At a glance from her mother, Ellen rose. "May I assist you, Madame?"

"You, Miss Gowan, are a dutiful child, as I so quickly saw." Angelique handed Connie's cup to Ellen. "I only hope that you and your dear mama can forgive my son's behavior."

Connie ignored the amused quirk of Ellen's eyebrows as her daughter handed her the teacup. She murmured, "Mr. de Valentin was most gallant, Madame."

Angelique de Valentin sighed. "Raoul is not a bad son, but young people today are accustomed to more freedom than you and I experienced, Mrs. Gowan. And I was forced to spend much of his childhood working to support us both." She shrugged a little helplessly. "I believe it is guilt that caused me to indulge his eccentricities more than I should have, but he lacked a father's steadying hand, you see." Sadness darkened those expressive eyes. "He is a clever boy, however, and has a good heart. And natural good taste. An advantage, should he go into this business."

Connie tried not to look startled at such confidences from a person she did not know well. There was a moment's silence as Madame poured her own cup of tea. Then, "Mrs. Gowan, I think you are aware of the unfortunate history of my family?"

Connie set down her cup. Blushing a little, she nodded. Daisy had told her something of Angelique's background. "Therefore, you will understand perhaps that my son has an illustrious lineage. However, Raoul's grandfather, the marquis, lost all his lands and possessions when the family fled France in the Revolutionary years. Like so many others of the Noblesse, they found a home, of a kind, in England. But that way of life, all they had known, all they had been bred to, was gone. Others live now on the de Valentin estates and in the houses of Raoul's ancestors." Madame sighed again. "I knew this when I married Raoul's father—my family, too, were émigrés—and I knew, too, after my poor husband died and we were alone in the world, that I must work or we would not eat. Philippe was so tragically young, God rest his kind soul." Her eyes brimmed, and Connie leaned forward to clasp Angelique's hand. The dressmaker whispered, "Please forgive me. To remember is to mourn afresh."

Naturally kind, Connie was touched by Madame Angelique's suffering. "Dear Madame, you have been very brave. There is nothing to forgive. I, too, lost my husband, Ellen's adored father, and our circumstances are similar for we, too, must earn our bread. We lived at Shene because my sister took us in when we lost our home.

We were grateful for that shelter, but the world changes. Now we must move on and we are not too proud to begin again." She did not mention Isidore Cleat.

Angelique sighed. "Alas, Mrs. Gowan, the world can be an unkind place. When they left France, Raoul's grandmother, Madame la Marquise, was at first reduced to taking in washing. That shame killed his grandfather, and continuing sacrifice broke his son, my husband, also. However, the women in this family have proved resilient. I learned from my mother-in-law. With hard work, and an ability to sew, I have created a business that supports Raoul and me. And Lady Cleat has been one of my most loyal customers. Without her patronage and her friendship, you would not have found us here in this comfortable house. When I first arrived in Richmond, Raoul was a tiny baby and I was unknown. Your sister brought me to the notice of the first families here, and I became established." Angelique cleared her throat, clearly touched by the memory. "Mrs. Gowan, I have presumed to explain our history only so you may understand why Lady Cleat has turned to me. I would be proud indeed if you felt able to accept shelter beneath this roof. A gift, you understand, from my family to yours. Offered in gratitude."

Connie stirred her tea. "So kind an offer cannot, in good conscience, be refused. However, I am not accustomed to idleness and neither is Ellen. Perhaps, in some small way, Madame Angelique, we may repay your compassion. In kind if not in coin?"

The dressmaker stared thoughtfully at the river. After a moment she clasped Connie's hand and said, impulsively, "Lady Cleat has so often praised the beauty of your embroidery, Mrs. Gowan. And I understand that Miss Gowan, too, has talent with the needle among her many accomplishments." A radiant smile embraced Ellen. "And such is the demand for my services as the winter season approaches, I cannot satisfy all those who would commission me." She put down her pretty cup and the sun caught its gilded rim. It occurred to Ellen that perhaps not quite all had been left behind when the de Valentins fled France. "In short, Mrs. Gowan, I should be very glad of your help at the present moment. I can offer room and board and a small stipend. Such will be my honor and pleasure."

Ellen was delighted to see her mother smile. "Madame, I cannot sufficiently explain how much this means to Ellen and to me. For too long, we have existed on the charity of my sister and such is not our way. We shall be most pleased to assist in your salon in any way you think good, until we can make further arrangements. There is much to decide, and my sister must be consulted." Perhaps the uncertain future frightened Connie, for she caught her breath and coughed, and could not stop.

Ellen took the cup from her mother's hands. "Let me help you drink a little, Mama. You will feel better."

The tea was indeed a panacea, and eventually Connie continued in a stronger voice. "It will not be easy, Madame Angelique, but I am convinced that prosperity awaits us in London and God will provide us with a home. If my dear husband were here, he would say we must have faith. His was so strong. He would have known what to do."

Connie faltered, the courage visibly running away like sand as the realization sank in: There was no going back to Shene, and without the kindness of her sister's dressmaker, she and Ellen would truly be without shelter in an indifferent world.

Perhaps Madame Angelique understood more than they knew. She smilingly placed her hand on Connie's. "Until London, then. But for now, Ladies, there is work to do!"

CHAPTER 21

O N THE afternoon of their arrival, Connie and Ellen were given an airy attic room in which to sleep and work. It lay beneath the sharpest point of the roof of Angelique's house, and the steep pitch dictated the odd shape of the space beneath. There was something of the feeling of Wintermast in the leaded casements, the lime-washed walls, and the rag rugs scattered across the board floor. Having once been a winter storeroom, their bedroom was scented by the ghosts of long-ago apples, which was a cheerful thing.

In one corner was a large bed, big enough for both Connie and Ellen to sleep in. A deal chest of drawers stood in a niche beside the fireplace, and there was also a cupboard with a curtain instead of a door. Here they could hang their few clothes. Their other personal possessions remained in the trunk, the lid of which served as a dressing table.

As the last days of summer and all of autumn quickly passed, the dark memories of Shene began to lose their hold on the Gowans. This was a new, sunlit world, and Ellen was delighted to see the growing collaboration between her mother and Madame Angelique deepen to friendship as the busy weeks slipped by.

In most respects the two women were a foil for each other. Connie's quiet good humor and gentility were the perfect contrast to Angelique's vivacity and impulsiveness. Laughter was a natural companion to the serious business of fashion at River Cottage, for Madame excelled at setting a lighthearted mood among her ladies, with her outrageous French accent and her charm (the first was mostly abandoned when the door of the salon closed for the night; the second, fortunately, survived). And if Connie was the more serious of the two, her eye for color and form could not be faulted, a quality that quickly came to be appreciated by Madame's clients.

With Angelique's encouragement, Connie began to blossom. Slowly, she acquired confidence in her own judgment, and her creativity, long smothered by poverty, was ignited. She began to advise on color and materials, then sketched designs and, at last, actually fitted some of Angelique's ladies in garments that she herself had cut and pieced together.

To make herself useful, and to assist her mother, Ellen volunteered for a number of tasks, including making the salon's clients comfortable while they waited, and taking appointments. Peg was thus freed to ferry trays of tea and refreshments from the basement kitchen, and very soon the two were happily working as a team. In the evenings, Ellen sat with her mother and Madame in the companionable kitchen and sewed. And, all the while, she watched and listened. And learned. And became a little happier. Perhaps this was also because an unlikely friendship had begun to grow between Ellen and Raoul de Valentin.

Ellen had made it her task to draw water for the household before the working day began. It was no hardship, as she relished the soft air and the quiet of the late-summer mornings, but the first time she hurried, half-awake, to the well in the kitchen courtyard, she was brought up short.

Raoul was standing beside the well. He had stripped off his shirt and was sluicing water over his head and naked torso.

"Mr. de Valentin!"

Startled, the youth looked around and caught Ellen staring.

"Miss Gowan! I do apologize." Raoul quickly covered himself, as Ellen, blushing, dropped her eyes. Sincerely contrite, he said, "It was an irresistible thought to wash outside on this bright morning. I hope you are not offended."

Shaking her head, Ellen walked past him, but as she did so,

Raoul's hand touched hers, holding the handle of the pail. "Please. Allow me. It is the least I can do. Besides, the bucket will be too heavy for you to lift."

The two collided, however, when Ellen tried to step back as he bowed. She tried not to giggle. The formality of his gesture was spoiled by billows of damp linen clinging to his chest.

"Shall we begin again? Do give me the bucket, Miss Gowan. I promise you, I am quite strong enough to lift it." Raoul smiled teasingly. He was apologizing for more than today's unlikely meeting.

The radiant morning somehow expanded as Ellen handed Raoul the pail. She stammered, "B-be assured that I am grateful, Sir. For this kind service."

"Miss Ellen?" Peg was calling.

"Coming, Peg." Ellen hurried past but Raoul put out a hand to stop her. "How is it with you in this house?"

Ellen paused. She responded, cautiously, "Mama and I are very happily settled, Sir."

Raoul moved closer. "And yet my mother can be a demanding task mistress. She works so hard, she expects all beneath this roof to do the same." His expression darkened. But then he said, lightly, "If ever you should need a friend, you have one in me. I hope you will remember that, Miss Gowan." His touch was light on her arm.

"Miss?" Peg called again.

Ellen glanced at Raoul's hand. The youth stepped back. He carried the pail to the door, and Ellen, with a nod of thanks, hurried inside. Had she misjudged him? The sullen boy she had first met seemed like a different being now.

On the succeeding morning, Ellen was not entirely surprised to find Raoul at the well yet again. Another brief conversation took place between them, and the following day also. And as the season slowly turned to winter, Ellen began to anticipate seeing Raoul each morning with keen pleasure, though she was careful never to linger for more than a moment. But those moments, like a string of diamonds, glimmered in Ellen's mind when she thought about

Raoul de Valentin during her busy days. In those encounters, she learned that he longed to leave Richmond and set up in business for himself, rather than work for his mother.

Raoul was passionate. And impatient. And proud. In this and in so many other things, she and he seemed alike. That was exciting. Ellen loved to hear him talk of his dreams, for she had aspirations to share also. She told Raoul of her secret wish to be an artist. A fashionable portraitist, perhaps. Or if not that immediately, then starting a modest dressmaking business could become a means to that end. She and her mother would run it together. Madame Angelique's salon was an excellent model, for the fundamentals of such an enterprise seemed, at their heart, to be simple things. Once the clients were found, quality of work and imagination were required, along with charm. Ellen was convinced that between her and Connie, they shared all the characteristics that were needed.

"I do agree, Miss Gowan. I find you very charming indeed. How could the fashionable ladies of London resist where I cannot?"

Of course Ellen giggled at nonsense such as this, but one morning Raoul went further. "You will need friends, if you are determined to set up in London. I can be one. A friend to your business and to you. If you will have me?"

Ellen blinked at his serious tone. After a pause she said, "I shall always be glad of your friendship, Sir." But why, staring into Raoul's bright eyes did she suddenly see Connor's face? Connor had receded from her mind those last weeks, along with all that had happened at Shene. Perhaps that had been a deliberate choice. Ellen frowned and tied her shawl tighter against the chill. And her thoughts.

"You are cold. How inconsiderate I am." The youth peeled off his jacket and slung it gallantly around her shoulders.

"Only a little, Sir," Ellen said, shyly.

She knew she should not have accepted Raoul's offer. But she liked the rasp of the tweed against the skin of her neck. And his smell was on the cloth. Ellen had to force herself not to stroke the velvet collar.

On that frozen morning, it had taken extra time to fill the bucket, for ice had first to be broken in the well, and as Raoul hauled up the dripping pail, he said, thoughtfully, "Well, if your plans advance to a greater degree, there is a person whom you should meet. Mrs. Carolina Wilkes. She lives in London. Her mother and mine worked together in the past, before we came to Richmond. And they were friends then, though there was a falling out later. For what cause I do not know. Carolina and I have continued the connection, however. I see her sometimes, when Mama sends me to town for materials. Mrs. Wilkes would appreciate your skill with the needle."

Ellen said, lightly, "It is not I who am skillful, Sir. I merely assist your mother, and Mama, with their work."

He looked at her thoughtfully. "You are too modest, Miss Gowan. You have what my mother calls the *touch*. She sees it, and so do I. I am something of a judge, you know. In this, at least, Mama has taught me well."

Arriving at the back door, Ellen wondered why Madame Angelique and Carolina Wilkes's mother were no longer friends. But the warmth of Raoul's fingers as the pail was transferred between their hands drove away all such reasonable inquiries.

Yet, two shadows lurked within Ellen's growing happiness. The first was that Connie was working too hard. Fitting Angelique's clients by day, she continued to design and cut and sew late into the night, even after Ellen had gone to bed. She had always been frail, but now she was thinner than split willow and increasingly troubled by the cough that had first afflicted her at Shene. Her discomfort increased as the days grew short and cold, and Ellen observed that she ate less and less. Ellen told Raoul of her worries and was touched indeed when, one frosty morning, he presented her with a syrup of figs, honey, and cloves in a blue glass bottle. He'd had the Richmond apothecary make it up, and for a time the mixture seemed to help Connie.

The second shadow was that though her mother regularly wrote to Daisy, as Ellen did to Oriana, nothing was ever received in return from Shene.

"It is my belief that your dear sister is too frightened to write, or even to give me a message." Angelique was making tea before bed, while Ellen and her mother were sewing at the kitchen table. "As you know, I have always contrived to give your letters directly into her hands, or to Jane. But Lady Cleat is very closely watched. Warwick, for instance, is now always present when we meet. That is a new development."

The dressmaker hesitated, but then withdrew a small packet of letters from her bag. "As you see, this week has not been a fortunate one. I shall try again when I take the finished dress to Lady Cleat on Monday next." She bent to inspect Ellen's work. The girl had almost finished hemming her aunt's new gown. "But this is excellent work, Ellen. I should not be surprised by your nimble fingers, of course." She smiled encouragingly. Ellen beamed.

Advent arrived, and then came Christmas. This was a happy celebration, with small presents exchanged among them all at breakfast before they went to church.

Ellen looked up to find Connie's eyes on her as she smilingly unwrapped Raoul's gift, two lengths of ribbon, prettily embroidered. "How kind of you, Mr. de Valentin. These are charming indeed."

Later, as she and her mother walked behind the de Valentins through the snowy streets, Connie said, "Ellen, we must be careful not to trespass on the generosity of Madame Angelique and Mr. de Valentin. Too much obligation on our part will be the result."

Ellen glanced at her mother. "I am not sure what you mean, Mama."

Connie stopped. With a gentle hand, she brushed the snow crystals from Ellen's bonnet. "When the weather is warmer, we shall move to London. In that city we can support ourselves, independent of kind friends."

"But we are happy here and our work is useful. You have said so yourself, Mama. And we cannot just abandon Aunt Daisy and Oriana." There was a desperate edge to Ellen's voice.

Connie gazed sadly at her daughter. "I have almost given up thinking I shall hear from Daisy. I must find another way to reach her. And useful work or not, Richmond is a refuge only. It is not our home. Now we must hurry, or we shall be late for the service."

Ellen continued to plead with Connie as they approached the church. "But Madame Angelique's business is even more successful, thanks to you. She will feel your absence particularly."

"I do not say we shall go immediately. That would not be fair to our kind friend, as you say. But go we shall, and there is an end to the matter."

It was unlike Connie to express such determination, and Ellen could extract nothing further as she was shepherded through the doors of the church. Raoul and Angelique were seated together in a box pew. Connie entered first and sat between Ellen and Raoul.

And this was Connie's own shadow.

Ellen's mother had become worried that the friendship between her impressionable child and the more worldly Raoul de Valentin was far too close. For, though she had developed great fondness for the mother, she did not trust the son.

CHAPTER 22

"MY MOTHER has decided. We are to leave for London."
It was warm again and, with the lengthening days, drawing water was a pleasant task once more.

"But why, Miss Gowan?" In his agitation, Raoul pulled too strongly at the windlass and the pail tipped, losing its contents down the well shaft.

So great was her misery, Ellen hardly noticed. "As you know, Mama has become increasingly unwell. She feels we are a burden to your mother and the time has come for us to secure an independent future." She shrugged helplessly. "She will not be dissuaded, though it does not seem sensible to me that we should leave when she is in this state. To be honest, Mr. de Valentin, I think there is something more. Something she will not speak of. To me, at least."

Winding up the bucket again, Raoul frowned. It was true that Mrs. Gowan had been less able to work lately, and though Ellen had tried all she could to take on Connie's tasks, there was only so much that was possible. Perhaps Mrs. Gowan was right. The salon, after all, was not a charity. But then his gaze softened.

Ellen sat on a mounting block. Her head was bent and he could not see her pretty face. He would miss her very much. As if of its own volition, his hand hovered above her shoulder. Did he dare to offer comfort? But then Ellen moved and his hand dropped. He said, hastily, "Of course, your mother will obtain superior medical advice in London, and I'm sure that is part of her intention. Try not to be anxious. All may yet be well. You have so many exciting plans."

The girl shrugged. Her voice was dull. "You are right. And we have some money saved. Not much, but a little. Your mother has been generous."

"Ah yes, Madame de Valentin is famous for her generosity. To others, at least." Raoul's tone was surly.

Ellen was puzzled. She knew that mother and son clashed, but she had never understood why Raoul opposed Angelique so often.

Raoul unhooked the bucket, then said, "You are certain Mrs. Gowan will not change her mind?"

Ellen shook her head. "Mama has told me she will shortly speak with Madame. We are to leave this morning."

"Today? Then there is much to do. Come." Picking up the pail, Raoul strode to the kitchen door, Ellen hurrying behind.

"But, Mr. de Valentin!" If he walked directly into the kitchen carrying the bucket, the genteel little charade of these months past would be exposed, at least to Peg. And she might be quiet, but she liked to gossip.

"No time for prevarication, Miss Gowan. We must help your mother see where her best advantage lies."

Neither one saw Connie Gowan. She had been descending the stair from the bedroom, and through a window had observed the pair by the well. When Raoul leaned down as if to touch her daughter, Connie flinched. Her instinct had been right! Ellen's reputation would inevitably be damaged if they continued to live at River Cottage.

She had failed her daughter in the past, but now she would protect Ellen, whatever the cost. That was her duty.

Madame Angelique could not change Connie's mind. From the open front door, she watched with great sadness as her son escorted the Gowans toward the London end of the road. The dressmaker had tried very hard to dissuade her friend from leaving. During the miserably cold spring just past, Connie had begun to cough blood into her handkerchief, and whatever reasons she now gave for their sudden departure Angelique saw it as plain madness to be traveling while being so ill. She would have nursed Connie with her own hands, if she'd been permitted to.

There was one small comfort, however. Raoul, for once, had offered every assistance to help the Gowans on their way. Madame Angelique was not to know the irony inherent in that gesture.

Now, as the trio walked along the high street, each step was an effort for Connie, though she feigned excitement. "I have not seen London in an age. But where are you taking us, Mr. de Valentin? Is it far?"

"Not at all. Do you see that field there? On the bank, a little beyond the mill." Raoul pointed to a large raspberry plot.

"Yes, Sir, I do."

"Well then, Mrs. Gowan, I invite you to enter that gate with me." A mysterious wink. Ellen smiled mistily. She would miss his droll ways. She could not think that Raoul had brought them this distance for no purpose, and yet, a raspberry field? As the white road curved closer to the water, however, she saw a landing stage at the river's edge. A barge was moored there and a small team of men and boys was quickly loading the vessel with trays of small baskets lined with green leaves. The sun turned the fruit to rubies, and cast gold across the water. A common magic. Against her will, Ellen was enchanted.

"The *Nancy Deere* will take you smoothly downriver, Mrs. Gowan. Will she not, Mr. Hartigan?"

"Soft as a pillow, Ma'am." The barger was a kind man, Ellen thought. He helped Raoul assist Connie to a seat near his wheel, even placing sacks on the planks.

Now it was Ellen's turn. Raoul held up his hand. She hesitated. Except for the accident with the pail, she had never deliberately touched Raoul de Valentin in all the days that they lived beneath his mother's roof. But light flashing off the water, bright as cut crystal, was no more brilliant than his eyes. She trusted him. Yet as

Ellen stepped down, he stumbled and she almost fell. Raoul caught her, and in that moment his body measured hers. Her cheek, where his whiskers had grazed, stung with confusing fire.

"Ellen?" Connie half-rose with alarm. The sooner they were gone from the place, the safer her child would be. "Sit beside me."

"Yes, Mama."

Ellen scrambled forward ungracefully. If the wings of her bonnet obstructed a clear view, they also hid her embarrassment. Connie, however, met Raoul's eyes with a very sharp glance indeed.

The youth called out breezily, "I almost forgot. I have something for your mother, Miss Gowan." Ellen stopped. And turned. And sobbed a breath. In the silver morning, Raoul's face had the clean beauty of a Greek kouros, the sun god Apollo.

Raoul held out a piece of paper folded in half, and Ellen made her way back to him before Connie could prevent her. He said, urgently, "I have written an address here. It is in Spitalfields. My friend Mrs. Carolina Wilkes lives there. She will be delighted to know you when she reads what I have said." Ellen nodded. She did not trust herself to speak. What if she should never, ever see Raoul de Valentin again?

"Ellen?" Connie was calling her. Effort made her voice crack.

"I thank you, Sir, for your many kindnesses to us." How hard it was to turn and go.

"*Au revoir*, Miss Gowan. I shall not say good-bye."

Ellen did not reply as she joined her anxious mother in the stern.

Raoul stood high above them as the *Nancy Deere* turned out into the stream, a black shape against the light. And when he raised an arm and waved, Ellen did so also, holding it there longer than she should have.

Connie breathed a ragged sigh. She did not like to see Ellen so unhappy at this parting, but she was pleased that the dangerous Mr. de Valentin had now departed from their lives. Or so she most fervently hoped.

᭶

Longer than a tall house was high, wider than a narrow road, the *Nancy* quietly made way on the silver water as it was pulled along, at first, by two horses on the towpath. Then, as they got near the broader part of the river, Amos Hartigan hoisted a sail above their heads with the help of his barge boy. In that instant, the sky turned from pearl to blue and all around them the reaches of the river displayed their splendor.

On either side, trees in high-summer dress slid past as grand houses with shining windows and lawns to the water's edge slipped away to stern. There were hay wains waiting in the fields beside the river, too, as teams of women stooped and cut and bound the sheaves now that the dew was off the meadow crops.

Before them in the barge, summer's plenty was piled up high. There were all manner of foodstuffs here. Peas in their pods and long beans, so fresh they snapped with a *pop*. Cherries, red currants, and raspberries were packed among leaves to keep them cool. All sweet, all fragrant. All delicious. Ellen's belly grumbled.

"Go to, Miss. Eat! They'll not notice what you take." Amos had heard Ellen's stomach complain. Her smile was reward enough.

"Mama?" Ellen offered scarlet cherries to her mother, but Connie said, faintly, "Mr. Hartigan is very kind. You have them, child. I am not hungry." She tried to smile but pain was a dark presence in her eyes.

To be polite, the barger asked, "And where shall you be bound for when we dock at St. Katherine's, Mrs. Gowan, if I may ask?"

Ellen responded politely for them both. "We have friends to go to, Mr. Hartigan. In Spitalfields." Connie caught Ellen's eye and shook her head. It was her daughter's nature to be too confiding, but Amos did not see the byplay and cheerfully said, "Spitalfields? Now that is convenient, for my cargo goes to the market there. What street do they inhabit, these friends?"

"I do not know. Mr. de Valentin did not tell us. We just have a name and an address."

"Mr. Hartigan," Connie managed to speak over Ellen, "your cherries are so very red, Sir, perhaps I shall manage a few."

"Look! Oh, look, Mama!" An elegant heron stalked the bank—a sight to remind Ellen of the Fens. "Only see how handsome he is?"

The bird speared a fish with its beak and the poor creature was rapidly swallowed, progressing down the heron's feathered throat as a helpless, convulsing lump. Ellen's eyes misted. How cruel life was. Amos Hartigan observed her distress. "A quick death, Miss. Not much time to think on what's happened—if a fish thinks at all. Now a cat with a mouse: Drawn-out is that, and filled with terror for the little thing." Absently, the barger stared at Connie, but he looked away when Ellen noticed.

Connie sat up as their craft came around a long bend in the river. With an effort, she pointed. "There, child. London at last. Adventure awaits!" In that moment, Ellen believed her mother.

Like Dick Whittington, they would swiftly make their fortune. She would rapidly become a famous artist, selling only to people she liked, and, from the river of guineas that would flow into her hands, Connie would be dressed in silk. Her mother would read and rest as much as she liked, and her only occupations would be to embroider and play the piano that Ellen would buy for her. Delicious and strengthening foods would be served, and soon Connie's skin would be rosy again, all the shadowed hollows banished. And there would be a garden in their pretty house beside the Thames. That was her dream: long life, success, and happiness for them both.

CHAPTER 23

As the barge pushed downriver toward St. Katherine's dock, a booming hum, restless as the sea, occupied the air. The city had woken for the day.

The closer they came to the shore, the more London clamored for their notice. Ellen breathed its reek and felt its energy so that, soon, the very air seemed to tell of opportunity and strange fortune. But the streets running down to the river were narrow and dark and mysterious and old. This was the other truth of London.

Ellen had been told by her father that fields once surrounded the old walled town, long, long ago. Now they must lie somewhere deep beneath the broken pavement and all the centuries of filth. That was the nature of an ancient city: It consumed itself eternally. St. Katherine's dock, however, was modern and heaved with carters and porters, all loading for the market at Spitalfields in a roiling mass. Tempers were short and time had wings. London must be fed!

"Mama, we cannot take our trunk." Ellen was staring at the wharf as Amos Hartigan brought his barge closer to the quay side.

Distressed, Connie began to gasp for breath. "But it contains all we have in the world." Ellen grasped her mother's hand. "We cannot carry it through the streets without help. There is just you and me to do it." *And you have no strength,* Ellen thought, but did not say. Connie's condition had worsened during the hours of their journey, and now this was one of the many reasons Ellen regretted leaving Richmond. Her only hope at that moment was to secure lodgings with Mrs. Wilkes and quickly find a doctor for her mother.

Amos saw the problem, and the size of the box. "The landlord knows me at the Rabbit and Grapes." The black and white inn was set above the dock. "He'll stow it if I give him the word. Birtles is his name."

Nancy Deere bumped up against a mass of other barges. And there was much pushing and jockeying as each captain fought to bring his craft to the quay side so that *his* cargo might be unloaded sooner than the rest. The teeming foreshore there resembled a disturbed nest of ants, as baskets of fruit and flowers and trays of vegetables were plucked up on all sides and carried away by a mass of waiting men.

"There he is." Ellen jumped as Amos cupped his hands and shouted, "Master Nelligern! This way, Sir! Here, if you please."

A red-faced man with a purple nose, thick shoulders, and long arms was wind-milling a path to the river. Hearing the bargers' bellow, he raised a hand and lumbered about. Tacking through the crowd, sweating and cursing as he came, his flapping suit of black was a dark hole on that bright day. His clothes—capes about the shoulders, pockets big as bags, and two watch chains straining at the bow of his belly—were of another time, as was his hat—a tricorn the size of a tea tray. "I see you, Amos Hartigan. Late. Again!"

Following close behind this colossus came a string of lesser men. Nimble as crickets, these porters jumped down to the barge as Amos brought the *Nancy* to shore farther along the quay.

A face as round as the risen moon loomed out of the sky.

"What's this?" One rolling eye inspected Connie and her daughter. The other was scarred and permanently closed (a sword the cause, when the silk weavers had rioted thirty years earlier).

"Too thin, the both of them. Throw 'em back, Amos!" His gust of laughter was echoed by the porters, busy at their loading. But for all the huff and bluster, that single eye was not unkind. "Nelligern, I am, Mistress, and Daniel is my name, same as my father and his father before. Daniel Nelligern. Vegetable and fruit merchant, and general purveyor of quality comestibles. Though like to be a *former* merchant if this does not go *faster!*"

"Mr. Nelligern, I am pleased to make your acquaintance." Connie's voice was almost too soft to hear, with a pause between each word. "I am Mrs. Edwin Gowan. My daughter, Sir, Miss Gowan. Mr. Hartigan has been most kind."

"Kind? Who gave you leave to be *kind* when you bin so werry late, Amos? The owner of these fine fruits will not be pleased with *kind.* His cherries and raspberries will spoil because of your delay."

That growling rumble spurred the porters, who scrambled, threw, packed, and carried faster at the ominous sound. It was well that they did, for the line of barges behind the *Nancy* was long, and opinions freely offered on their slowness. Amos gestured imperturbably toward Connie. "Daniel, you might assist this lady and her daughter if you had a mind to."

"Assist, you say?" The red-faced man, his one eye narrowed, reared back for a better view. "Assisting is your gaff, Amos. Come, my lads." The contents of the barge had vanished as the porters filed away from the wharf, each with a tower of baskets higher than seemed logical or possible on their heads.

Amos shouted, "You might take them with you to the market. They will need to walk, otherwise."

Daniel paused, and turned. He gazed at Connie for a moment, expressionless. Then, bellowing, he said, "And if I do . . ."—the women huddled together—"*If* I do, they shall not be a trouble to me?"

Ellen blurted, "Never, Mr. Nelligern. I am quick and strong. I can carry things, too."

Gazing at Ellen, Mr. Nelligern laughed so immoderately, a tear eased down that vast face and his hat bobbed about as he made his way back toward them.

"Come along, then." He leaned down and plucked Connie from the barge just as she struggled to stand. His actions astonished Ellen's mother into unprotesting silence, as he restored her to her feet on the quay. No man's hand had touched Connie Gowan since Edwin's, except for the brutal Isidore's. Ellen gulped back giggles at her mama's expression: outrage, relief, confused gratitude. There was even a little color in Connie's face.

Ellen said, fervently, to Amos, "*Thank you,* Mr. Hartigan. You have been so kind. And the box. I shall remember the name. Birtles, you said." This last was flung over a shoulder as Ellen linked an arm through Connie's and half-carried her mother away, behind their unlikely champion.

The first sight the Gowans had of Spitalfields was from the front seat of a market wagon, pressed tightly between the wagoner, a small man with a squint and broken teeth, and the mountainous Daniel Nelligern.

Connie was discomforted by the close proximity of two strange men, and kept a tight hold of Ellen's hand. But her daughter was interested in all that she saw. Every face, every doorway, every shop was unlike any other in her experience. And though she had never before seen a filthier or more crowded place, that teeming, odorous mass had force and power. To breathe that air, with the reek of sewage and putrid meat, the scent of flowers and tang of spices, was to sense that life held possibilities undreamed of.

Once away from the river's side, a tangle of streets led toward Whitechapel High Street and on to Commercial Street, where the Spitalfields markets lay.

"Would you tell me about this place, Mr. Nelligern?" Connie nipped Ellen's arm, a feeble pinch. It was unseemly to be so forward.

But Ellen's temerity amused the merchant. "Well now. I should say there's been a market here for a hundred years and more. Without us, London might not get her apples or her roses, her potatoes and raspberries."

Mr. Nelligern spoke proudly, as his dray swayed its slow way up from the river, but the traffic of wagons and people and carts was much impeded by choked streets and broken paving. Men yelled, straining to be heard as whips snapped above the heads of the horses. These beasts would have willingly moved faster if they could have, but the press of animals and people was indescribably great, especially as the dray got closer to the market buildings.

Ellen asked, wondering, "Does the whole world come to Spitalfields, Mr. Nelligern?"

"Pretty close, child. The silk weavers are long gone, but their grandchildren remain, so you will still hear French spoken. The Russian tongue is that of the Jews. And there's Irish—the Gaelic, they speak—flood here, too, looking for work. And Chinee. Only the Lord knows what they mean when they gabble."

They had arrived, at last, in a great cobbled yard. Mr. Nelligern addressed Connie. "Now, Mrs. Gowan, you and your daughter must stay just where you are." He climbed down from the cart as the dance began again. Porters loading and hurrying away and returning to their drays against the swell and tide of hundreds engaged in the same task. Connie began to cough. Ellen held her mother close as the violence of the attack diminished. Exhausted, she leaned against Ellen's shoulder, but her thin chest still heaved, and scarlet drops and clots daubed the front of her gown. The black silk took up the blood quickly, but Ellen was horrified at its quantity.

Mopping her mother's face with her handkerchief, Ellen said, "I shall find water." Despairing, it was all she could think to offer. But Connie whispered, "Stay with me, child."

Ellen embraced those frail shoulders longing for something, anything, to change their luck. The bones were brittle and small beneath her hands. "Just until you feel better, Mama."

Leaning against her daughter, the pair sat quietly together as the chaos of the market swirled around the wagon. After a time, Connie straightened her spine, though she was sweating and very pale. "Can you find Mr. de Valentin's note, child?"

Ellen had put the paper in Connie's reticule. On it was written *Mrs. Carolina Wilkes, Minories Court off Fournier St.* Ellen
scanned the lines he had written beneath the address and blushed
slightly. Raoul had referred to her as *Mrs. Gowan's beautiful and
talented daughter.* She cleared her throat. "He has been very kind.
He confirms that Mrs. Wilkes has rooms to let out. We are to say
that he has sent us, Mama, and ask that we be accommodated until
we are settled in our new business."

Connie silently nodded, one hand pressed to her chest. Ellen
gathered courage. She could see no other course. "But you are too
weak to walk, Mama. I shall find this place and return with assistance." Ellen scrambled from the wagon.

"Come back!" Connie called out, just as tears started running
from Ellen's eyes. Suddenly looming, there was Mr. Nelligern.
Wiping her cheeks, Ellen ran to the surprised merchant. "Sir, I
beg you. Is Fournier Street close by? My mother is very ill. I must
find help."

His expression softened. "There it is, child." He waved at the
roadway that crossed the street upon which they had arrived.
Through smoke-thickened air, Ellen thought she saw a run of noble
houses with high gables. Did Mrs. Wilkes live in one of those?

"Ellen, please. Return to me."

The girl wavered. She called out, "I shall, Mother, as swiftly as
I can." Urgently, she asked, "Sir, will you permit my mother to rest
here until I return?"

Their champion cast a shrewd look at Connie, her white, thin
face, and slowly nodded.

"You shall find your mother where she is, but the wagon will be
over there." He pointed to a shaded spot, out of the sun. And then
he strode away, bellowing, "Where's my peas!"

Ellen had expected the noise to lessen, but as she ran to Fournier
Street, it was no less full of people.

Irish girls with plaid shawls sauntered by in pairs. They stared rudely at Ellen's clothes. As she passed the wagon of an Italian street vendor, he called out in a loud voice, "Fruita, strawberry and-a raspberry . . ." On the other side of the roadway, Jews with long side locks sold clothes from small stalls. Their stock hung above Ellen's head on pegs rammed between the bricks. "Clean! New! Fashion from Paris!" sang the merchants. But these were sorry garments, patched and faded. And where was Minories Court?

"You have arrived. Now, this is excellent!" Ellen swung around and gaped as Raoul de Valentin stepped out from among the crowd, grinning. He shone in this world of dirty strangers, for he was clean and elegantly dressed.

"Oh, Mr. de Valentin, I did not expect that we should see you so soon." Shock that he had so boldly followed them, and joy that he was *there*, made it hard to speak—at least, rationally.

"You did not? But how could I, in good conscience, loose you upon London and not prepare my friends?" Laughing and audacious, he tipped his hat.

It was as if the sun had risen in that grimy place. Ellen was dazzled.

"*And* you have found the Minories. Clever soul!" Raoul pointed to a building close by.

It was a slum.

The day's sparkle fizzed away. What would Connie say when she saw this place?

The entrance to Minories Court, an arch of broken stone, was soot black. Behind it was a courtyard where washing hung out on sticks under tiers of smeared, blind windows. There was a little piece of sky above but smoke obscured the blue even as Ellen looked up.

Raoul was not insensitive. He said, defensively, "It is not so bad as it first appears, Miss Gowan. The house is very commodious. When you have settled and found work, we can look to somewhere else. A cottage with a nice garden where you can paint as your mother recovers. I know you like flowers."

His words echoed Ellen's dreams, as he knew they would. Hope softened the shape of squalor. Ellen curtsied as gracefully as she could among the throng. "Sir, I am grateful for your kind offer. Most truly but—"

"This is she?" A handsome woman in her mid-twenties had emerged from the courtyard. She was staring at Ellen intently, but speaking to Raoul. Ellen's nose twitched. The stranger smelled pungently of warm earth after rain or the musk of the stable overlaid by violets. Her eyes, so dark as to be almost black, were brighter than a jackdaw's and as curious.

Raoul said, lightly, "Mrs. Wilkes, my dear, you are correct." Ellen's eyes widened. Mrs. Wilkes was young. Somehow, she'd imagined an older woman.

With an embracing sweep of his arm, Raoul continued. "May I present to you Miss Ellen Gowan, late of Shene House and niece of Lady Isidore Cleat. Her father, as you may not be aware, was that very distinguished biblical scholar and Fellow of Peterhouse, the Reverend Doctor Edwin Gowan of the parish of Wintermast. Now sadly deceased."

"Sorry indeed to hear of your loss, Miss Gowan." The words, if not the expression, were compassionate.

"Just so." Raoul bowed in Ellen's direction. "And, Miss Gowan, I am delighted to make known to you Mrs. Carolina Wilkes, Chandler of Fashionable Stuffs. A very good friend to my family, and to me."

"And shortly to be yours, I am sure, Miss Gowan. How is your talented mama? Mr. de Valentin told me she has not been well?"

Ellen glanced at Raoul uneasily. Her mother would not like a stranger knowing so much. She started. Mother!

"Mr. de Valentin, I must go." Picking up her skirts, Ellen ran down Fournier Street heedless of all in her way. There was the market, the yard was close.

"Stop. Wait." Raoul's hand shot forth and grasped her wrist. He had run after her and caught up. Ellen struggled to break free but Raoul was stronger. "Allow me to assist you. You cannot do this alone."

"I . . . yes, thank you, but I must . . ."

Half words matched incoherent thoughts. Ellen twisted her hand free. Lifting her skirts from the filth, she hurried on again.

"Mama!"

In the shade of the only tree in the yard, Connie lay unmoving. She was stretched the length of the wagon seat and someone had partly covered her body with sacking. Connie's eyes were closed and her face was at peace.

Ellen ran to the cart.

"Mama, speak to me. Please! It is I, Ellen." She scrambled up, ripping a flounce and barking her knees. She heeded neither. Anguish seared as if she had been flung on a fire. This was her fault!

Sobbing, she took Connie in her arms. "Please, please, please." *Do not go away, do not leave me.* Ellen was in Wintermast again, locked in those black nights of sorrow. She rocked that narrow body as if she were the mother, Connie the child.

Connie stirred. "Ellen?"

Her mother's struggle for breath was Ellen's struggle, too. As long as she lived, she would carry this burden. "Dearest Mama, I am here."

"Mrs. Gowan, you shall be brought to your bed, there to recover. All will yet be well." Raoul meant each hopeful word. Ellen stared at him, helpless and blind with grief, her tears dripping on Connie's face.

Raoul said, urgently, "I shall seek immediate assistance."

Ellen nodded. Dazed, she watched him go. He was all she had.

It took three of Daniel Nelligern's men to carry Connie from the market to Minories Court. One at her shoulders, another with an arm beneath her back, and a third to support her legs. In this manner she was borne up the staircase inside Minories Court, with Mrs. Wilkes at the head lighting the way. Her oil lamp cast only feeble radiance, and smoked. Raoul walked behind the men with Ellen. If he had not held her up, she would have fallen.

Mrs. Wilkes unlocked a low door on the third floor of the building. An effect of the age of the house was that the corridor's floor sloped down to one side, as if the world itself had tilted.

"One of my best rooms for your dear mother, Miss Gowan."

Connie's eyes were closed as she was placed on the bed. She seemed asleep as Mrs. Wilkes drew the covers up. As she was leaving, she gave Raoul a significant glance. "Come to me when she is . . . when you and Miss Gowan are finished here."

The oil lamp was taken away, and what little light the uncurtained casement provided was enough to show a comfortless, low-ceilinged room with a single bedstead. The chest at its foot and a frail wooden chair comprised the remaining furniture. A piece of mirror was propped on the mantel of the fireplace, and the board floor's only covering was a rug worn colorless with time.

Oblivious to all this, Ellen knelt beside her mother, her face close as if waiting for a kiss. "Mama?" she whispered. "Can you hear me?" But Connie lay still. Her brow was cold, as were her poor hands. "Mama!"

Raoul placed his hand upon the girl's shoulder. Softly, he said, "Ellen, your mama has gone to a more peaceful place. Let her rest."

Connie's chest moved beneath her daughter's hand. A tiny rise.

"Help me!" Ellen struggled to raise her mother. "Please, Mama. Do not leave me. Please." Raoul lifted Connie higher against the pillows as her eyes wearily opened. "Child. So sorry."

With much effort, she raised her hand to touch Ellen's face. But then her expression changed. She had seen Raoul behind her daughter's shoulder.

"But . . ." She began to cough.

In despair, Ellen held Connie closer. "Hush, Mama. Do not speak if it hurts you."

Connie's expression was desperate. Ellen leaned down to hear at least one of the words her mother was trying to say. "I am here, Mama." She swallowed. Tears were useless now.

"Him. Be . . . Do not . . . I beg . . ." Connie's whisper was a rasp. She stared accusingly at Raoul. He could not meet that burning glance.

"What do you mean, Mama? Tell me." Ellen rocked her mother, to soothe her. To soothe herself. Connie's eyes closed in a long sigh.

If Ellen could have breathed life into Connie, she would have. Raoul leaned down. He tried, gently, to remove Connie from Ellen's arms.

"No. No! Not yet."

Perhaps Connie heard her daughter. She turned her head and a smile transformed her face. She was staring at a point beyond the bed.

"Edwin." Connie tried to raise her arms as if to embrace a person standing there.

Ellen's nape prickled as Connie said, a piteous catch in her voice, "I knew you would come. And see, here is our child. So lovely."

And that was all. A long breath and Connie Gowan died.

CHAPTER 24

WHEN LATER, Ellen Gowan tried to recall the days after her mother's death, there was only confusion. Raoul urging her to eat or to sleep she remembered, and only because these occupations seemed unrelated to her state of being and therefore strange.

But time turned dark and slow, and it was as if she had a caul about her, an enclosing membrane that protected her against all human feeling, all human need.

Mrs. Wilkes, and all her intrusions, these, too, Ellen remembered. She had still been holding Connie when the young woman arrived with bowls and sponges, and a ragged bath sheet. Putting down a can of water and unbuttoning her sleeves, Mrs. Wilkes briskly said, "The poor lady. I've laid out more than a few and I should think you have had no experience in the matter. Give her to me, child."

"No. I thank you."

Taking the things from Carolina Wilkes, Ellen closed the bedroom door. Ellen did not see the offense she had caused. She saw little as she began to undress her mother's cooling body, until she found the tiny drawstring bag. Then the world became painfully vivid. Ellen stroked the soft blue velvet. Connie had sewn this, her fingers had set these stitches, and this delicate thing had lain over her mother's heart and against her skin for all this time. Gently, Ellen undid the string. Inside there was dust, soft and dry and fine. She knew what it was. This was from their last day in Wintermast. It was soil from her father's grave. The room blurred but Ellen would not allow herself to cry. There was work to be done.

Connie's appearance almost destroyed her resolve. Shrunken by illness, her body was pitifully small. Yet Ellen felt her mother's presence in the room. If Connie's remains were empty of her spirit, the air was not.

Ellen stood very still and closed her eyes. *Are you here with me?* Did she imagine the voice that breathed, *Always*.

"I shall sponge you first, Mama. That will be best."

The sweat of Connie's last day had soured on her skin. Perhaps there would be consolation in washing away the grime. Yet Ellen found it hard to lift each unresponsive arm or to press the sponge against the rib cage and watch as the water ran away between ridges of bone, so close beneath the skin. Connie's feet were particularly touching. So small, Ellen could hold each one in her hand as she tenderly washed it.

"And now, Mama, your hair." Ellen worked patiently, wincing only when, once or twice, the comb snagged in the tangles. She did not want to hurt her mother.

Time was suspended as she worked. She did not know if hours had passed, or minutes, but when the task was done, Ellen covered her mother's body with a blanket. She knew Connie was dead, but she could not leave her to the indifference of cold air.

Ellen stood beside her mother's body with this small comfort at last. Connie was decently clean. Her colorless face was unlined and still young. She might have been one of Ellen's own lost sisters, and not her mother at all.

It was not possible for Connie's coffin to be carried upstairs in Minories Court, since the stairs were too narrow. Raoul arranged that Connie therefore be wrapped in a winding sheet and brought down to Mrs. Wilkes's front parlor, a room that had little natural light and the cinnamon smell of rot. There, trestles had been placed before the empty fireplace and a pine coffin, cheap and thin-sided, lay upon them.

Ellen did not know the men who carried her mother down. She did not notice their faces. All she saw were their hands, as they awkwardly laid Connie in the wooden box. A calico shroud had been wound around her mother's head and tied under her chin in a large bow to prevent the jaw from falling open. The face was covered by a coarse napkin.

Raoul picked up a hammer to secure the lid of the coffin.

"Stop. Please! One last time, I beg you. Let me look at her." The youth stood back. Ellen hesitated. This was her mother. She had washed Connie's body and dressed her. She was not frightened of seeing her in a coffin, was she?

Raoul understood. "Shall I remove the cloth?" Ellen shook her head. She lifted the napkin. There were the pennies she had placed on Connie's eyelids; money to pay the ferryman. Her father would have called this archaic superstition but he had understood, too, the power of ancient symbols. So did his daughter.

Ellen picked up the first coin and then the next so she could see her mother's entire face. The metal was cold. She knelt beside the head of the coffin. Connie's hands were crossed over her breasts, and Ellen had placed the little bag of soil beneath them.

"Dearest Mama." Ellen tried to commit each feature of Connie's face to her mind and heart and soul. "I hope you understand my decision. You will rest here in London with me. We shall be close, and I can come and visit you. As we did them. At home." Wintermast. One day, Connie must be returned to her husband and her children but not now. Ellen could not face that now. She could not bear to be all alone.

Suddenly it was real. The force of loss, at last, was heavier than a blow. Dizzy, she bent to kiss her mother's mouth. Cold and pale and soft. Her tears fell on Connie's eyes. They ran down her mother's cheeks and soaked into the unbleached cloth above her heart.

"Is there a pen? I must have a pen. And ink."

Raoul had replaced the coffin lid and the first nail was driven home quickly. He asked, confused, "For what purpose? We have little time."

"I would not have my mother go to her grave, unnamed."

Raoul shrugged helplessly. "The parish will keep the records, Ellen. You will know where she lies." But he looked about the room just the same, until he found a pewter inkwell and a quill beside it. With some trouble, Ellen wrote on the raw wood, *Mrs. Edwin Gowan of Wintermast, Norfolk. Beloved wife of the Reverend Doctor Edwin Gowan. Mother of many, missed by all who knew and loved her.*

The ink soaked into the unvarnished wood. The stain would hold. Connie would not go unknown to God.

In the courtyard outside, a cart was waiting, an ancient, patient horse between the shafts. The vehicle was too small for Connie's coffin. The foot hung out a little way beyond the tail and there was no room for Ellen to ride beside it. She and Raoul would walk behind the cart to the graveyard of Christ's Church, nearby. The small savings Connie had put aside from their work with Madame Angelique had been enough to pay for the service, the coffin, and the winding sheet, but that was all. Ellen had to find work if there was to be a memorial stone.

A thin, soaking rain began, gathering and sliding down their backs as they set out. Soon, Ellen's dress clung to her skin, and her skirts, heavier and heavier, made it hard to walk.

No flowers, no mourners, no bell. After the quickly spoken service, Ellen knelt beside the open grave in the mud. She could not pray. She could only gaze at her mother's coffin until the clods of wet clay, thrown down by the gravediggers, covered the top and the words that were written there.

The morning following the funeral, Ellen woke stiff and cold. She was lying on the bed where Connie had died. She had no memory of how she came to be there, but it seemed that she had lain on top of the covers all night dressed in her dirty black gown.

And though she was weak from hunger, Ellen came to a decision. Today—this very day—she would leave Minories Court. She would not stay in this place of dreadful memories. She must wash and eat, and then . . .

Her head ached with a truth that she could not face. She did not know where to go, or what to do. Eventually, she would start a business as she and Connie had planned to do. Her mother had wanted her to seize fate with both hands, but those same hands found it hard to undress without help, and Ellen was close to tears as she unhooked the bodice of the black dress at last. It had been Connie's.

There was water remaining in the can that Mrs. Wilkes had brought upstairs some days earlier. Stripping away her shift and draws, Ellen washed as fastidiously as she could and combed out her hair before winding it into a bun. She felt older, and putting her hair up, as a woman would do, anchored that feeling.

Naked, Ellen shook out the black gown and brushed the folds as vigorously as she could, even slapping the bottom of the skirt against the bed end. The exercise warmed her and the silk withstood the assault, as the mud was dislodged satisfactorily. And though it was a pagan act to dress without undergarments, she would *not* wear the underlinen another day.

Clothed again, at least on the surface, Ellen pondered her next act. She must eat and she must write to her aunt. Perhaps Isidore would confiscate the letter, but she must try. Not another day could be allowed to pass without Daisy hearing of the death of her beloved sister.

Ellen descended to the lower floor, placing each foot carefully on the stair treads. She knew there were people behind each one of the doors she passed—Mrs. Wilkes's unseen lodgers, coughing themselves awake—and she did not wish to be seen or heard.

The door to the front parlor was unlocked, the room dim and sour behind it, but the ink pot and the quill were just as she had left them. Was there paper? In Ellen's fragile state, despair was her dark companion. It gathered power as she weakened, for there was no scrap of paper to be seen. Yet as she slumped against the door-jamb, hope struggled upright in her soul.

There were books in this room. Several shelves of unread novels in cloth bindings, their pages still uncut. Even cheap books had blank front pages before the text. It was against all the reverence for the printed word that Ellen had been taught, but the act of tearing out the untouched front papers of *The Castle of Otranto* forced Ellen's chill companion into the shadows as she began, with great sadness, to write.

Afterward, Ellen blew on the ink to dry her tragic news. If Raoul remained in this house, she must find him so that her letter might be posted. Easing the door open, she stared along the unlighted passage. In the distance, someone was talking—male or female, she could not tell.

As she crept closer to the sound, she began to make out words. "... and nothing, not one thruppence, nor even a penny piece or a farthing have I had. It cannot go on, my brave, and it shall not."

Mrs. Wilkes. Ellen stopped, suddenly cautious. Light outlined a partly opened door.

A man spoke. "Her mother has just died, Carolina. Would you put a price on even this?"

Raoul. Ellen drew back against the damp wall. They were talking about her. Should she stay, or go?

"*That* I have already paid, my chick, in the loss that room has given me. *And* in the food your doxy has taken here."

Raoul spoke reasonably. "Ellen is not my doxy. Have a little compassion. As I told you some time ago, an opportunity exists here. I did not count on the mother dying, but . . ."

Mrs. Wilkes's voice rose over his. "*Compassion?* How would you describe the quality of the water I carried to her with my own hands? That was compassion for you. *And* I offered to lay the woman out, much thanks I got. Let us not forget *also* the services of my men in carrying the mother down to her coffin to my parlor. Some would call that bad luck, willingly courted. And all for nothing!"

"Sweet Carolina, she will pay you. Ellen is a good girl, a hard worker. You will see."

The woman laughed derisively, but her tone changed as her shadow crossed the light. "How much of a 'good girl' is she? They do say all women are sisters under the skin. Shall we put that to the test with your little country mouse?"

Raoul laughed. It seemed to Ellen that he was nervous. "I told you in my letter, Miss Gowan has other talents. She can sew. That is how the money will be returned to you. I will help her set up in business."

"*Miss* Gowan is it? Pah. We want no haughty dressmakers here. No money in sewing—or girls who think too highly of themselves, neither."

"But, Carolina, I have a plan. You will not be sorry."

Carolina laughed, low and breathy. "Ah, such a one for a plan as you are, Mr. de Valentin. But *my* plan would be to put a price on that scarce commodity Miss Gowan still owns. The one she sits on."

Ellen gasped. She did not wait to hear more.

Ellen ran to her room and locked the door. There was little enough to pack, and she made a bundle of linen in a pillowcase, which took but a few moments.

"Ellen?" A soft knock. Raoul.

Ellen stared at the door. She was truly shocked by his conversation with Mrs. Wilkes. *Chandler of Fashionable Stuffs,* indeed. Raoul must have known all along how Mrs. Wilkes earned her living and what her *lodgers* did. *Is that what you were trying to say, Mama?*

"Go away. I never want to see you again."

"Please, Ellen. Let me in. There's a good girl." He was pleading.

Ellen was angry. "I am not your good girl. Nor anyone's. We trusted you." Her voice wobbled.

"Unlock the door, I beg you. Your situation here is very grave." Ellen closed her eyes. She would not be swayed.

"My *situation*, Sir, is my own concern. Your services are no longer required. My mother saw you for what you are and tried to warn me. In my foolishness I have let her down." An image of Allegra Wellings came to her from somewhere deep. Must she become a governess after all? "When I have secured a suitable position, Mrs. Wilkes shall be paid for the use of this room. Every penny." Ellen leaned against the doorjamb. Tears spilled down her face. She tried not to sniff.

Raoul spoke softly into the keyhole. "No. You are not a child. It is of that I wish to speak. I am so sorry to have brought you here. I, too, have been let down. Now I must protect you, for assuredly you cannot protect yourself. Your mother, no matter what she thought of me in life, would understand now that I am sincere. There is nothing else to be done. We must marry, Ellen."

CHAPTER 25

THE POUNDING in Ellen's head ceased from sheer astonishment. She hiccupped. "Why?"

Raoul sounded hurt. "Because I love you. Do you not know that?"

Love. Ellen saw the actual word float toward her out of the dark. It seemed a foreign thing, as if no meaning was contained within the letters. "I do not believe you. You were flirting with that woman. I heard you."

Raoul spoke earnestly. "But we were children together. She is like the older sister I never had, that is all." Ellen opened her eyes. He sounded sincere. "Ellen, I loved you from the first moment I saw you standing on our step."

That was too much. "You did not! You were rude. And horrible."

Raoul responded urgently, "That was pride. I was angry with my mother. She humiliated me and I behaved badly. But we became friends, did we not?" Raoul paused.

In that small silence, Ellen remembered his arms around her, his rough cheek against hers when she nearly fell at the barge. Could that sensation, that dizzy buzzing, be called love? It was different from what she had felt for Connor Moncrieff.

Perhaps her body had more purpose than her mind. Perhaps she was merely exhausted and starving, but Ellen watched as her hand—with a steadiness she could only admire—placed the key in the lock and turned it. And there he was. So handsome. Smiling. And yet with anxious eyes.

That touched Ellen. She had thought herself numb. She went

to the window and opened it. There was little air from the enclosed courtyard below and the room was hot. *She* was hot.

"How can we marry? I am not of age."

"But, Ellen, you *are*. With a special license a girl can marry at fifteen. Today is your birthday. Had you forgotten?"

She stared at him. "My birthday? How do you know?"

"I know many things. And, see, I have presents." Raoul had been hiding something behind his back. "These are for you." He placed two striped bandboxes on the bed and stepped back. One was large, one smaller. "Happy birthday." Why did the sentiment not seem ironic?

Curiosity nudged Ellen the few feet from the window. She raised the lid of the first and gasped. Raoul, the dressmaker's son, had chosen well. He smiled, delighted. "You like it?"

Ellen drew out the gown from its nest of tissue. Of purest white silk, the dress had seed pearls set in a band around the neck, and a fall of silver lace at the elbow of each sleeve. In that dark room, the dress shone. There were soft kid boots, too, the color of best cream, with silver buttons. She arranged the dress on the bed, smoothing its folds with one hand. It was perfect.

Raoul cleared his throat. "There is a bonnet in the other box." He retreated to the door. "I will wait outside, my darling, until you call me. And then I have the best surprise of all." The door closed softly behind him.

There was indeed a bonnet. Pearl satin with a high-poked front to which was fixed a short veil of delicate lace. A plume of ostrich feathers lay beside it in the box. A filigree keeper was secured to one side of the crown of the bonnet, and Ellen slid the feathers into place. They were bound together with silver wire, and swayed bravely above her head when she put the bonnet on and pulled the veiling down.

From the mirror, a girl in a dirty black dress and a white bonnet stared back. Ellen turned to look at the gown lying across Connie's bed. Her mother was dead. She should be in mourning. But the gown was so beguiling, and there was a side placket with hooks and eyes. Ellen might dress without help. If she chose.

She moved closer to the bed and picked up the dress. The fabric, for all its volume, was light, for it was wedding ring silk—so fine that it would flow through a gold band. The cut was gracefully simple, and the boots were perfect, too. White stockings had been rolled up inside the toes, along with pale blue garters to hold them up, above her knees. *Something blue . . .*

Mama, forgive me.

In a fever, Ellen undid the stained black dress and kicked it away. It lay, a pool of reproachful shadow, on the floor. Naked, she pulled up the stockings and the garters and stepped into the white gown. Now only the boots remained.

Ellen unlocked the door. "You may enter. If you like."

Feeling shy, she did not look at Raoul. But then his face was behind hers in the glass. Staring, he said, "You are very beautiful." His voice was almost rough.

Ellen felt the movement of her heart as it began to speed. She pressed her joined hands against her ribs, thinking, confusedly, to slow its beat. Raoul did not touch her, but his eyes made her giddy. Heat rose to her face behind the veil.

Ellen shook her head. These feelings frightened her.

"You are kind. But I cannot marry you. We are both too young. I hope you can understand." But she knew, as she said the words, that she wanted nothing *more* than to be Raoul de Valentin's wife. The feeling was intoxicating. And absurd!

Raoul laughed, as if she had said the most amusing thing. Then he grew serious, his gaze beseeching. "Stand before the altar with me, Ellen, be what you are meant to be. My bride."

He withdrew a piece of paper from an inner pocket. SPECIAL LICENSE was printed upon it, with black writing beneath. He held it up. "We *can* be married. This afternoon. All the arrangements have been made. This is my surprise. Oh, Ellen. Say yes. And we shall leave this place, together."

Impulsively, he knelt upon the dusty boards, to the peril of his pale woolen trousers.

Consider! You know so little of this man. Mama did not trust him. And what of Mrs. Wilkes? Something is not right. Think! An inner voice fought against the dizzy tide of feeling. And lost.

"But, Raoul, what shall we live on? I have so very little, and you are dependent on your mother."

"But this is the best news of all, for I am here with Mama's generous support. For once. Who do you think made the dress?" Leaping up, he clasped Ellen's hands joyfully. "For you, my darling, I shall conjure magic out of the air. We shall want for nothing." Gently, as if he had a rope, he reeled her closer, laughing, until she stood before him, his hands upon her shoulders.

And then she remembered. The trunk. It was at the inn beside St. Katherine's dock. It contained her aunt's necklace. His eyes changed as her own brightened. "What are you thinking of?"

Ellen allowed herself to rest against Raoul at last. He sneezed, the feathers tickling his nose. "I am not, in the end, without a dowry." Excitedly, she told him what remained from Shene. "Mother had been planning to sell it so that we might set up our business. And bring my aunt Daisy and Oriana to London. If I sell it, Mama shall have her headstone and I . . ."

Raoul whirled her in a giddy, happy circle. "*We* shall sell it. Immediately! It shall be I who will set us up in business. And when we are a success, and we shall be, our house will be big enough for your aunt and cousin, too. Oh, I have such plans."

Ellen was shocked that Raoul spoke of disposing of Daisy's present as if he had a right to it. But he had flung back the veil and was kissing her—darting little kisses, all over her face. Ellen was shaking so much, he pressed her closer—just to help her stand. "I will bring in the custom and you shall sew, and embroider, and run the workshop. Mother spoke to me often of your talent. With me to guide you, we shall see it flower!"

Could life change so easily? Ellen's surprised soul answered

Yes. Her father had died and instant disaster had been the result. Her mother, too, had gone, and she had thought the future black as night. But dawn succeeded darkness and, it seemed, misery could be supplanted just as quickly. By happiness.

They heard boots mount the stairs and a voice called out. "Mr. de Valentin, are you there?" Carolina.

Raoul quietly locked the door. Taking Ellen's hand, he drew her to the darkest corner of the room, a finger to his lips.

The landlady knocked. "Miss Gowan? Mr. de Valentin?" Raoul put his hand over Ellen's mouth, but his eyes were very bright. Rigid, Ellen watched as the doorknob turned.

"Mr. de Valentin, I suspect you are within. I will not have locked doors in my house!" The knock turned from polite to thunderous.

Raoul's face was very close to Ellen's. One arm slipped around her waist, and then the other. The whisper tickled her ear. "Steady, my beloved." She shivered in his arms.

"Ellen Gowan! If you are with that man, you are more foolish than I thought you!"

Slowly Raoul's mouth descended upon hers, and Ellen found that she could not breathe; did not *want* to breathe.

"This door shall be broken down. For which you shall pay!" Perhaps they heard her step receding, perhaps they did not.

"Come with me, Ellen." He kissed her lingeringly. "Marry me."

"Yes." The word whispered itself.

Ellen blinked. Suddenly it all seemed simple. "Yes, I shall marry you, Raoul. Of course."

St. Olave's Church in Crutched Friars near the Tower was an ancient place. It had stood for more than nine hundred years and was a pretty building with a neat, squat tower, however, the condition of the exterior was better than the interior, which seemed neglected. The tiles were unswept and dust lay in the corners. Too many dead flowers were among the living ones in the altar vases. And yet, when Raoul took Ellen's hand and they walked together down the short aisle, she thought only of all the brides who had come before her to this place. Ellen was carrying a posy of white roses, and as she breathed in their scent, the garden at Wintermast seemed to embrace her. She saw the child she had once been, hiding in the fork of her favorite apple tree clotted with spring blossom.

But how had that little girl found herself here, on her wedding day, without even one member of her family, or Raoul's, to see them married? Ellen paused, a step or two from the altar. Her heart was racing. Soon, there would be no turning back. *Mama, Oriana, tell me I am right to do this. Please.*

Raoul tightened his grip on Ellen's hand. He said, softly, "Courage, my dearest. I am here." But Ellen seemed unable to move forward.

"Are you sure, Raoul?"

The veil obscured Ellen's face but he heard the catch in her voice. "Trust me. Believe in our love. That is all you need do."

Believe in our love? Once, she had thought she loved someone else. What would have happened if Connor had chosen her at the children's ball? She might still be living at Shene. He might have written to *her* and not Oriana. But that was not what had happened. . . .

"Ellen?" Raoul was drawing Ellen closer to the altar rails. She did not oppose his will. This, at least, was real. With Raoul, she had a future, and he wanted her: She saw that in his eyes. Connor was a long-ago dream, and he had fallen in love with Oriana. That was the truth.

And Raoul had done as he had promised. He had rescued her from Minories Court, for a carriage had been waiting in the street outside. That had been a wise provision, for murder would have been committed by the lady of the house if she had caught them leaving.

It had all happened very quickly.

When Carolina had clattered away in a fury, they locked the

door behind them and ran to an empty bedroom close by. They had hidden there as the woman returned, accompanied by a man with a hammer. As he assaulted the door, the din was tremendous. One by one, doors creaked open all along the corridor and tousled heads peered out to observe the show. Many were gentlemen, but many more were ladies. Of a particular kind. She saw the truth. Without Raoul, this would have become Ellen's life, too.

With a crack, the lock was pried from the wood. In that moment, when Mrs. Wilkes plunged through to the room beyond, Raoul and Ellen had run for the staircase and were down the first flight before the landlady saw that she had been duped.

Ellen and Raoul heard her fury—the whole establishment heard it—as they hurtled down the stairs with the landlady only a landing behind. As the avenging virago charged on, she screamed adjectives that Ellen had never heard in her life, but she was too late.

The front door slammed behind them, and holding hands, the pair flung themselves into the waiting carriage.

"For you. No bride without flowers!" A posy of thornless white roses was thrust into Ellen's hands as Raoul thumped the roof. "St. Olave's. Crutched Friars. Quickly, man!"

Now, in the empty quiet of the cold, old church, Ellen, after prompting, repeated the words for the priest and for the sake of the man she was marrying.

"I, Ellen Elisabeth Gowan, take thee, Raoul Villiers de Valentin, to be my lawful husband. To love, honor, and obey. In sickness and in health. From this day forth and for evermore, until death do us part." She faltered. There had been a great deal of death. But Raoul had tight hold of her hand. He would be her life now.

"And now, Mr. de Valentin, the ring. Upon your bride's finger— yes, that is the way." Ellen's eyes were glazed with tears as Raoul slid the slender gold circle along her finger. How she longed for Connie and Edwin's presence. Or that of her cousin.

"And say after me: With this ring, I thee wed."

Raoul's voice shook. "With this ring, I thee wed."

"With my body, I thee worship."

His hands gripped hers. "With my body, I thee worship."

"And with all my worldly goods, I thee endow. So help me God. Amen."

"And with all my worldly goods I thee endow. So help me God. Amen."

"You may kiss your bride, Mr. de Valentin."

Raoul lifted the lace hiding Ellen's face and encircled her with both his arms. She tensed. He kissed her, but she was too nervous to respond.

"Mr. de Valentin, you and your wife must complete the formalities in the vestry. If Mrs. de Valentin cannot write, she may make her mark."

Mrs. de Valentin. It was strange to hear how easily her new identity was accepted in the world. "But I *can* write. I am the daughter of a scholar." Ellen was proud to be able to say that today, as Raoul conducted her to a small table in the vestry.

Once there, the parson plucked Raoul's sleeve, drawing him away. After a moment, her new husband returned.

"Dearest Ellen, there is a slight change in our plans. The parish registry has been damaged and our marriage cannot be recorded in it today." The parson nodded soberly. His expression was grave. "There was a fire, you see."

Ellen was bewildered. "But, I thought all marriages . . ."

Raoul said, quickly, "The Reverend Lydgate"—he bowed to the parson, who responded in kind—"has, however, supplied us with this." He was holding a sheet of paper. "We are to write our names here and the date. The parish sexton will be our witness."

They heard a discreet cough and Ellen turned to find a respectable-looking man in a fustian coat waiting inside the vestry door.

The parson cleared his throat. "I do assure you, Mrs. de Valentin, that the details of your marriage will be included in the registry of St. Olave's as soon as we have it returned to the church."

Raoul put the document upon the table and the sexton hurried forward with an ink pot and quill. "I shall sign first." He scrawled his name with a flourish beside the word *Groom*. "And now it is your turn. Mrs. de Valentin. Here, where it says *Bride*. My own darling wife." He spoke softly, for her alone.

And so Ellen Gowan signed, for the first time, *Ellen de Valentin* where he pointed.

The future had begun.

CHAPTER 26

WITH BOTH hands around her waist, Raoul lifted Ellen from the step of the hackney as it stopped beside St. Katherine's dock.

"We shall celebrate, my darling. I want the whole world to know of our happiness."

He walked his new wife to the door of the Rabbit and Grapes, her hand resting on his arm. As they entered the taproom, Ellen wished she had dropped her veil, since the conversation of the patrons ceased as they entered, quickly succeeded by a babble of comment.

"Felicitations!" called out one of the drinkers, and another said, "Lucky man." There was an explosion of good-natured laughter, in which Raoul happily joined, though Ellen fixed her eyes to the sanded floor. They were all looking at *her*.

"Welcome, Sir and Madame, to the Rabbit and Grapes. My name is Birtles."

The publican, hearing the uproar, had joined the throng. He understood instantly that the shy, freshly minted bride found his patrons intimidating.

"Mr. Birtles?!" Ellen was so grateful to have found someone she knew, even if only by name. "My friend, Mr. Amos Hartigan, deposited a large box with you some days ago? From Richmond. I am its owner. Mrs. de Valentin now." Ellen glanced shyly at Raoul. "Before my marriage today, my name was Gowan."

Raoul spoke quickly. "Certainly, but we can discuss this shortly. For now, Mr. Birtles, champagne! We must celebrate this happy day!"

"Certainly, Sir. And Madame. Whatever your desires may be, we shall endeavor to serve you. The private parlor is this way."

The publican led the couple through the crowd of wharf navvies, clearing a path for Ellen, though he and Raoul could not shield the girl entirely from the admiration of the crowd. Some whistled, some stood on chairs to see Ellen pass, and there were eager offers to toast the couple, provided the bride would share the loving cup with her new friends.

On the riverside of the inn, the private parlor was quiet once the door was closed on the noise. It was a large, comfortably furnished room with red squab cushions on a window seat and a fine, if distorted, view of the Thames through leaded casements. The strange sea green glass was old and mottled, and it changed the color of the river and the sky. For Ellen, gazing across the Thames, it appeared as if London had lately drowned. A curious effect.

But the day turned rainy as she watched, and she was grateful for the sea-coals burning in the grate. The material of her dress was diaphanous. Glorious in sunshine, less glorious beneath gray skies. Ellen's spirits, too, after the dramas of the morning, sank suddenly from bright to dark. *How strange,* she thought, *the room is moving.*

"Ellen!" Raoul caught her as she slumped.

"Madame!" The publican rushed to assist, but Raoul brushed the man aside, placing Ellen on a sofa hurriedly drawn up before the fire.

"It is the excitement." Raoul chaffed Ellen's hands. "Champagne, Mr. Birtles. The great restorative!"

"Upon the instant, Sir!" The publican hurried away. Noise from the taproom flowed in as the door opened, and was staunched as quickly when the door closed. Now there was only the soft hiss of the fire, the distant glut of the river as it heaved against the dock.

As Ellen tried to sit up, Raoul said, tenderly, "Lean on me, my darling. Do not tire yourself."

"But the room. Why does it swim, Raoul?"

Raoul's brow cleared. "Ellen, when did you last have food?"

She frowned. "I cannot remember. I really cannot."

Raoul quickly untied her bonnet ribbons though Ellen protested. Setting the hat to one side, he undid the placket of her dress though she tried to deflect those busy fingers. "No, sweet Ellen. You must be comfortable."

Ellen's curls escaped their bonds, though not Raoul's notice.

"May I?" he asked. Her breath was a little ragged but she did not think to disagree as he removed the pins one by one. All at once, the mass fell around her shoulders.

"Shake your head." Raoul's voice was low.

Mesmerized, Ellen did as he had bidden. He did not break his glance, but raised her hand and lingeringly kissed the inside of her wrist. And a little higher, beneath the lace. The soft skin in the crook of her elbow was unbearably sensitive to the touch of his lips.

Slowly, moment by moment, inch by inch, Raoul drew Ellen toward waters in which she had never before swum, the deep pool of the senses. Eyes half-closed, she sighed. She could not have named the feelings that possessed her, but she sank deeper and deeper until she felt nothing but his mouth on hers.

A discreet knock propelled Ellen upright with a gasp. Raoul frowned, but when three waiters—all in black, with white aprons down to their feet—bearing laden trays preceded Birtles into the room, his expression changed. Especially since Mr. Birtles himself carried a large silver urn with ice and a dew-covered rehoboam of champagne. "Compliments of the house, Sir and Madame."

Ellen's eyes widened. She had seen such luxury only at Shene.

An anxious thought nudged happiness aside. With the exception of the champagne, who would pay for all this plenty? The wedding breakfast was sumptuous and enormous. Fresh oysters accompanied a consommé of veal with sherry to begin the meal. Next, a galantine of duck was laid on the table beside a hash of chicken simmered in cream. There was also a platter of hot roast beef and cold ham—with side dishes of buttered peas, green beans, salad à la Russe, and potatoes duchesse. Then came trifle, ratafia biscuits, and a baked custard dusted with cinnamon, and three types of cheeses and grapes to finish. And that was just the food.

Champagne, milk stout (*For fortitude's sake, Sir*, whispered the innkeeper), burgundy wine, and port were also supplied.

When the men departed, Raoul ate and drank heartily of all that was offered, but Ellen's appetite was quickly extinguished. She knew that soon they would be shown to the best bedchamber the Rabbit and Grapes possessed. And she had no one to ask for advice.

A wide, canopied bed of black oak dominated the room. Carvings decorated each of its surfaces, a riot of naïve forms. Grapes and apples and peaches among flowers, birds and many fanciful animals, including a unicorn. But it was the repeated motif of a naked couple among the foliage that drew the eye. Ellen had never before seen such a cheerfully frank depiction of people innocent of clothing.

"I see you looking at the bed, Mrs. de Valentin. It was built in this room when the inn was constructed. It is called the Genesis for two reasons. One is obvious, of course," the innkeeper explained.

Raoul caught Ellen's eye. She blushed a fiery pink as the suddenly embarrassed publican hurried on, "As for the other, you will find the story of Adam and Eve if you follow the carvings around from left to right. Everyone knows the sad conclusion to that tale, but you might find a surprise when you see how it ends *this* time. I wish you joy, Madame. And you, Sir, also. May yours be a long and happy life together."

Mr. Birtles bowed and went to the door, where he coughed, then said, "The box, Sir. I had almost forgot. I have it waiting for you."

Though he was impatient to be alone with Ellen, Raoul grinned. "Very well. Bring the damn thing in. It is very important to my wife, for it brought us together." He winked at his bride, who blushed.

"Certainly, Sir. Immediately." The impassive publican stood

to one side as two men, servants of the inn, walked in hefting the wooden trunk to the foot of the bed.

"I thank you, Publican." This time, Raoul left nothing to chance. He escorted Mr. Birtles from the room and closed the door. And locked it.

"And so, wife. Let us test your new-made vows." Raoul leaned his shoulders against the door. His gaze was bright and focused. Ellen tried to swallow but her throat was dry. She hesitated. Softly, he said, "Come here."

Hair unbound, in her white dress, Ellen crossed the room from one kind of life to another. She stood trustingly before her husband.

"Put your arms around my neck." Ellen complied. All her senses were amplified, so that when her bodice brushed against his jacket, the hushing rustle made her jump. He smiled. "Do not move until I say that you may. Whatever I shall do. Do you understand?"

She giggled breathlessly. "Is this a game, husband?"

He laid a finger across her lips. "Hush." Then he kissed her, softly at first. "No. Not a game."

Ellen closed her eyes, and gasped as Raoul's tongue explored her lips, forcing them gently apart. "I said, do not move." His hands slid the length of her side and she shivered. He smiled and kissed her more deeply. If Ellen sensed that Raoul was pulling up her skirts, she did not care. Higher. She gasped again. Fire. And ice. His hands moved again. She had no underclothes!

"Stop!" Ellen tried to unlink her hands but this he would not permit. She was breathing as fast as he, and for a moment they struggled. "Please, Raoul. It is the wine. I am sorry but I feel so . . ." She could not describe what she felt. She did not have the words. "And there is something I must tell you."

Raoul heard the desperate seriousness. He drew back a little. "So my bride harbors secrets?" He did not laugh.

Ellen would not look at him. His cool tone unnerved her. She spoke quickly before her courage fled entirely. "Only one. Before we met, I thought myself in love."

His hands dropped. After a pause, he said, "And did this love express itself?" There was an edge to his voice.

"No!" Ellen was horrified. "Not at all. He did not love me. Oh, Raoul, I want our lives to begin today. That is why I told you. I want to forget the past." Ellen was close to tears. "And I was wrong. I did not love him." She closed her eyes as Raoul's hands returned. This, *this* was love. Proper, adult feeling.

"So. You have broken a vow already. You opposed my wishes a moment ago. I did not expect my wife would be a disobedient woman. I am gravely shocked." But Raoul was laughing. And so was Ellen. Giddy laughter. He held out a hand. "This is strange, I know. But I am glad I have married an honest woman." He seemed amused and she relaxed a little, even giggled, as she allowed him to lead her, coax her, toward the Genesis bed.

"First, wife, there is the undressing. Since we have no maid, allow me to perform this service for you."

"But, Raoul, I shall have nothing at all to wear." At eye level, the naked Eve, offering the apple to her equally unclothed husband (watched by the grinning serpent), seemed to mock Ellen's modesty.

Raoul's reply robbed Ellen of words. "Certainly. But then there are other vows we must test, together. And for these, clothes are not required." He had found the hooks and eyes. They uncoupled as he kissed her, an arm firmly around her back in case she took fright again. With his free hand he eased the dress from Ellen's shoulders and drew her arms from the sleeves, leaving her breasts exposed. She blushed and tried to cover herself.

"No, sweet Ellen." He removed her hands. He was trying to be patient. "This really *is* your duty to me. We are married."

Perhaps she responded to the tone of authority. Perhaps, in her heart, she wanted all that he wanted. This time she did not protest as the dress was drawn off over her head, though she closed her eyes very tight. Raoul tossed the gown over the trunk as he unbuttoned his jacket and stripped it off, quickly followed by his stock and shirt.

They stood together in silence. She naked but for her stockings and garters, he in boots and britches, his chest bare. His breathing was audible.

"Ellen, open your eyes. Please." His voice cracked. They were skin to skin. He cupped her face in his hands. "You are so beautiful. And so brave. I adore you. I shall adore you." A lilt of laughter.

Slowly, she raised her arms and, this time unbidden, linked her fingers behind his head so that her breasts flattened against his chest. Soft against hard.

He groaned when she softly kissed him. "Take off your shoes, Ellen." She kicked them off, turning her back modestly. He said, "Sit on the bed."

Raoul knelt before her. With exquisite slowness he slid the garters over her knees and peeled away her stockings. Now she was utterly unclothed, just as Eve and Adam were. But the room was warm and she did not care.

"What vow do you mean to keep, Raoul?" It was an innocent question. Or not.

"This one." He scooped her up, a tangle of splayed legs and arms, and planted her in the center of the bed. "With my body, I thee worship."

She woke with a start. They had drawn the curtains of the bed late in the night and at last, as the sweat dried on their bodies, slept. Ellen, though her head ached, was smiling. In the dark, in the wilderness of sheets and blankets tossed that way and this, she yawned and sleepily felt across the mattress for her husband.

"Raoul?"

She sat up. He was not there. "Raoul?" Ellen's heart hammered. He had gone!

"My darling is awake." The heavy tapestry drapes separated in a flourish, and morning glared through the gap. Ellen winced and shaded her eyes. "I thought . . ." Helpless distress swept over her, a gale of feeling that blurred her vision with tears.

"You thought I had left you?" He laughed joyously. "On the day after our wedding night?"

Ellen hiccupped as he gathered her in his arms. "My goose. My very own goose." His hand caressed her back. Long, slow, rhythmic strokes. "Such a pretty goose. All mine to consume and not even Christmas."

Ellen gave a watery giggle but responded passionately as he kissed her, until she said, "Raoul, the light hurts my eyes." Raoul laughed as he flicked the curtains closed and rolled back against the bolster. "Let me see. Champagne. At least a third of a very large bottle. Though I drank even more. Then, red wine. And, of course, there was port with the cheese. And you ate only a little."

She said, reproachfully, "But I was nervous. I could not eat."

Raoul propped his head on an arm, grinning. "And why, my darling, were you nervous?"

Pulling up the sheet, Ellen turned her back. "You know very well. It is not gentlemanly to ask such a question." She heard the bed coverings rustle and shift as he moved closer, inch by inch, and she suppressed the urge to giggle.

"Very well, I shall be forced to answer for you." The sheet was whipped away, and Raoul, with a dexterity that a more experienced person might have called suspicious, turned Ellen so that her hips were against his own. "Last night you were a virgin. And I had the very great pleasure of removing you from that irksome state."

"Sir! You are too familiar."

"*I* think I have only just begun to teach you what *familiar* might truly mean." He kissed her, and as if Ellen had no will of her own, her hands gripped his shoulders, and her body rose against his as his hands roamed. "But you are dressed!"

"Perhaps you should remove my clothes then, Mrs. de Valentin? I shall show you how." Lying back in surrender, he said, "The shirt, if you please." Ellen sat up cautiously; if she had felt light-headed earlier, the ache by now had departed.

One by one she undid the buttons of Raoul's shirt and extracted an arm. Ellen felt a stealthy hand caress her breasts. She paused.

"You *are* a fumble-fingers, wife. Continue, if you please."

Freeing his other arm, she protested, "If you do not wish me to fumble, Sir, have a care where you place your hands."

"Oh, I care. Very much. But they have a will of their own." As if to demonstrate, his fingers traveled the length of her spine, and finding the nape of her neck, pulled her down.

Raoul whispered into her mouth, "And now the britches." He kissed her.

Breathless, Ellen said, "But you are beneath me."

"An acute observation." One night with Raoul had taught Ellen much, but not this. She tensed, and hesitated. Raoul raised himself, half-sitting against the bolster. "Kneel over me." He quickly parted her knees and placed his fingers between their bodies, as he unbuttoned his fly, giving her no time to think. He touched her in that secret place and she winced for she was sore, but the feeling changed as heat followed where he led, deep in her body. She was writhing, whimpering when he entered her, but he grasped her hips and helped her settle to the rhythm. And if the rough wool of his britches chafed her inner thighs, Ellen did not care. There was only this, only him. His chest, her breasts. His mouth, and hers . . .

"Did you know?"

"Know what, my darling?" Raoul yawned, and idly played with one of her curls, extending it, watching it spring back. An hour had passed. They were lying together as the late morning sun, now welcome to their bed, gilded both their bodies.

"That I would change. Become different."

He chuckled and stretched languorously. "I thought you might.

They say all women are sisters, under the skin." He grimaced. Those had been Carolina's words. Ellen had heard them, too.

"But even me?" She sat up. "I know so little but I want to please you, Raoul. As your wife, not some doxy."

He heard the hurt in her voice and scrambled to sit beside her. "And I, you. What's this?" He hugged Ellen close, and with one finger wiped the drop of water from her cheek. "We have all our lives to learn to please each other. And we will. Beginning at this very instant!"

He rolled over and slid down the side of the high bed, snatching up his clothes. Ellen looked away, and then looked back. The light of day showed each muscle, each angle and plane of his body. Yes, he was as beautiful as Apollo.

"What are you doing?" She wanted him to return, but did not know how to ask.

"Changing our future! Do you have a key for this?" He meant the box.

Ellen was mortified. "I have left it at Minories Court. Oh, Raoul, what shall we do?"

He had shrugged on his shirt after buttoning his britches. "Extemporize."

Grinning, he strode to the fireplace. Only ash remained from the night before, but there were fire tools. Weighing the poker in his hand, Raoul eyed the hasp and staple. A large padlock had been secured through the loop. "Will you permit?"

Ellen nodded. She would permit him anything.

"Very well!" Raoul raised the poker and brought it down sharply. But the old iron padlock was made from stout stuff. It took several blows to break the lock apart. Inevitably, the box was damaged. Ellen sat in bed hugging her knees, as she watched Raoul. This was her last link with Wintermast. And to her mother. Intent on opening the trunk, Raoul did not see Ellen's wistful expression as the hinges of the lid wailed when he pulled it up. "Where shall I look, wife? Show me."

"I cannot get out of bed naked."

He grinned. "Nakedness is the very best dress for a bride." She laughed. It was good to laugh.

"But you are right. The world would look askance if it could see you. And, besides, there are clothes here."

He held up a plain woolen shawl in black and dark blue, a black dress, a linen shift, and some long cotton drawers. They were all Connie's. He gazed at her with wickedly narrowed eyes. "From what I know of you, these might fit." Ellen blushed.

He strode to the bed, brandishing the underclothes. "I shall not watch as you put them on, I promise. Or, if you prefer, you can stay warming the bed and I shall go buy some new things for you."

Ellen drew the sheet higher, covering her breasts. "I should like to wash but I will wear what we have, for the present."

He nodded. "Then I shall call for water. Would you like the maid to help you dress?"

Emphatic, Ellen shook her head. If she had been stared at in the inn yesterday, it would be worse today. She could just hear the sly questions. "And how was the night, Mrs. de Valentin? We hope you are quite well." *No!* She would dress herself. "A can of hot water is all that I require."

"Very well." Raoul pulled on his knitted short stockings and his boots, and made an effort to tie the stock pleasingly. The linen had been sadly crushed the previous night. His jacket completed the effect: a sober young man about town, a married man with responsibilities. "Just as soon as I have found the necklace, I shall leave you here to dress." He tossed Connie's gown and her shawl over the foot of the bed. They lay beside Ellen's wedding dress, black against white. "Where might it be, Ellen? Do you recall?"

"In a black silk bag."

"Here it is!" Raoul hurried to the window. He pushed open the heavy casement and leaned out into the sun. He whistled. "These rubies are fine stones. The pearls, too, are an excellent size *and* well matched. We must thank Lady Cleat properly one day, for these will fetch a very good price."

Happily humming, he pulled the window closed and restored the necklace to its little bag.

Ellen was nonplussed. They *were* married, it was true. And Raoul had the right to sell her property without consulting her if he chose. So why was she dismayed by his enthusiasm? All he wanted was their joint welfare. Should she not be pleased by his care of her?

"Is something wrong, my darling?" Raoul paused at the door, looking at her curiously.

Ellen summoned a bright smile. "Nothing at all. Hurry back to me."

Scooping up his hat from a bench by the door, Raoul bowed before clapping it to his head. "I shall, dearest Ellen. Every moment I am not by your side will be sweet torture. Sweet because I shall have the anticipation of return!"

The extravagance drew a genuine smile from Ellen, but as Raoul left, she slumped against the pillows. Hesitantly, she leaned forward and picked up the shawl. It smelled faintly of lavender and tansy flowers. The humble scent repellents against moths and fleas conjured Connie's face so clearly that Ellen gasped. "Oh, Mama. Have I done right?"

In the morning dazzle, she half-saw her mother sitting on a chair set before the fireplace. Ellen blinked. And then there was nothing. The chair was empty.

"Be happy for me. Please." Ellen was lost in the waste of the Genesis bed. And very alone.

CHAPTER 27

E LLEN STOOD at the open casement and watched the river flow to the sea. Outside, gulls swooped and called over the gunmetal water as traffic of all kinds moved up-river and down. Wherries brisk as water beetles, sailboats languorous in the light airs.

Bells struck the hour from the city. Twelve strokes. Raoul had been away for more than three hours. To calm herself, Ellen paced the length of the chamber. Up and down, she began to count: *one, two, three, four* . . .

Each time, as she approached the bed, her attention was caught by Eve, and Adam, as they played out the eternal story of the Fall.

Here was God creating the first man—the deity suitably large, Adam much smaller. And there was Eve, stepping neatly from Adam's chest as she was made from his rib. God gave them the Garden, and the happy pair were Lord and Lady of all they surveyed, receiving homage from the animals in Eden, including a very odd elephant (as well as the unicorn; its head lay in Eve's lap, a sign that she was still a virgin, then).

Ellen, intrigued, stopped pacing. She peered more closely. The man and woman were holding hands. In another image they seemed to actually be coupling!

Before last night, Ellen would have looked away, embarrassed. Now she did not. She did not like to be ignorant. Ah, but there, lurking in the canopy of an apple tree, was the serpent. Next, Eve accepts the apple and offers it to Adam. They eat, and see that they are naked. God reappears. Arms outstretched, wreathed in clouds, he dominates the foot of the bed. He is very displeased, for the man and woman know now that they are naked and hold leaves to cover their bodies.

Remembering what the publican said, Ellen pursued the story along the other side of the bed. Here the terrible banishment from the Garden begins. Gates are opened by frowning angels. Animals mock, and horrified trees bend away as the shamed and cowering couple are driven toward the desert beyond Eden. The serpent, triumphant, slides away, its evil work accomplished. And there *is* one last scene, played out on the headboard. Occupied with other things last night, Ellen had not seen it, but now she drew back the bed curtain, and blinked. The naked, miserable Eve had been transformed. Her face was the same, but now she was crowned as a queen and clothed with wide skirts and a fluted ruff around her neck. Seated on a magnificent throne, she held an orb and a scepter in her hand, while Adam knelt below. He was dressed as a courtier.

Ellen peered closer. God, much smaller than the queen, was kneeling on the other side of the throne, apparently worshipping Eve, the woman he had created. Was she a goddess, then? But that was blasphemous, surely?

"She's supposed to be Elizabeth. The Virgin Queen, so called. Birtles told me so."

Ellen swung around. "Raoul! I did not hear you!" He had opened the door very quietly. Her heart leapt at the sight of him. She ran to his open arms, and he kissed her lovingly.

"Apparently, the mayor of London wanted to burn the carver at the stake with his bed, but the old queen herself saved the man. She liked the carvings, apparently. Even came and saw it. Offered her blessing to those who would sleep here, beneath her image. And that includes us." He winked. "If you are not too tired, I have a surprise. Is there a hat to go with that dress? Quickly now."

Connie's everyday bonnet of black straw was found, and a few minutes later, Ellen and Raoul were rattling away from the Rabbit and Grapes in a hansom cab.

"Where are we going, Raoul?"

He would not tell her, but when they stood in front of the little house, she knew. It was in the very new suburb of Hackney. So new, the next street of houses was only partly built on the last parcel of meadow flats that had once been a farm. But Ellen fell in love at once. Fell in love with the bright white paint, the clean windows, and the latticed porch that sheltered the front door. Even with the Gorgon-headed knocker (though the snake-haired monster reminded her of Carolina Wilkes). There were lilac bushes and white roses next to the street, while down a side path, a small green garden could be glimpsed.

"Do you like it, my darling?"

Her heart swelled. "Very much, Raoul." Hand in hand, they gazed at the cottage together.

"Very well then. It is yours. Ours, I should say."

"Do you mean it?" Ellen was so full of happiness, suddenly, she could not remember sorrow.

Raoul held up a key. Opening the black-painted door, he pushed it wide and picked Ellen up in his arms. "The prerogative of all grooms, I believe, is to carry their brides over the first threshold."

Restored to her feet, Ellen gazed around in wonder. She and Raoul were standing in a minuscule hallway, but it was broad enough to contain a small table, a blue armchair, and a half-case clock. A staircase with a cupboard beneath it occupied one wall, ascending to rooms above. It was narrow, but the carpet on the treads was new, and the stair rods of shiny brass.

He said, anxiously, "I took it as it was. With the furniture. I hope you do not mind."

"Mind?" Ellen did not know what else to say. It was all so pretty, and so modern. Excitedly, Raoul drew her through to a parlor. There was a low sofa and two small chairs, and a ladies' writing desk in front of the bow window. Curtains of factory-made lace screened out the street outside.

"My lady." Raoul bowed Ellen to one end of the couch. She curtsied, then giggled and sat.

"We have it for this month plus three quarters more. And there is the right to renew the lease for a further three years at an excellent rental. I have paid eight guineas on the barrelhead."

He was so happy, so sure she was as delighted as he. And she was, but Ellen's elation was shadowed when he talked about money. "But, Raoul, can we afford it?" She gestured at the pretty sofa. It was upholstered in cut velvet, and there was fitted carpet on the floor—a luxury.

Flicking his coattails, Raoul sat beside Ellen. He took her hands in his, and said, "Yes. I obtained a fine price for your aunt's necklace."

"How much?" Did she really want to know?

"Thirty-seven guineas." He looked a little shamefaced. "I thought you might be upset. At selling it, I mean."

Ellen's conscience woke with a pang. How sensitive and kind he was. "Not so much upset as . . ." What was it? Ellen surprised herself, deciding to speak the truth. "You did not ask me. To sell it, I mean." But she was troubled as soon as she uttered the words. They were married. Their goods, such as they were, should be held in common. She felt very ungenerous.

Raoul tenderly drew her close. "I understand. But I have such plans, you see. And my nature is an impatient one. We needed a home. And now I have found it. Can I show you the rest?" He reached out a hand and Ellen took it. He was nervous.

She said, softly, "I should love that."

Enthusiasm restored, Raoul took Ellen on a tour. At the street level there were two front rooms: the parlor on one side of the hall and a dining room on the other side. "This will be perfect for our dressmaking clients, do you see? You can fit one lady in *here,* while another waits *there.*" He gestured to the parlor. "All that is required is a dressing screen and a chair."

The domestic offices of kitchen and scullery were next. In the first, there was a modern coal range and a built-in dresser. Raoul waved as he spoke. "A table, some chairs, and the usual domestic equipment: pots and pans, knives and forks, crockery. There is a weekly market that will give us all we need."

Ellen sighed happily. The kitchen was snug and pretty. It even had checkered cotton curtains at the windows. And the scullery was thoughtfully laid out with a window over the sink. Natural light and a view of the tiny garden behind the house would brighten the everyday chores. And then she saw it: an apple tree. Big and far older than the house. A reminder of home.

"Oh, Raoul! How could you have known?"

Ellen hurried outside to the end of the small plot of land. She embraced the rough trunk as if the tree were a sister.

Sauntering behind, Raoul laughed. "Careful, sweetheart. We cannot have the neighbors thinking my wife is odd!"

Eventually, Raoul coaxed Ellen back to the house, and to the upper rooms. "Two bedrooms, you see? And a box room also." None of these rooms was large, but they were lit by good-sized windows, and in the biggest room there was a wooden bedstead. It had a rolled-up mattress covered in ticking. "I thought this could be ours. And the smaller can be your workroom. It will need a sturdy trestle for cutting. And a cabinet for buttons and trimming and your tools. Dress fabric can be stored there, but also calico for the toiles, buckram for stiffening, and so on." The dressmaker's son waved airily. He might not know how to cut a pattern or hem a seam, but he knew what the business required.

Ellen said nothing, but privately thought that the other bedroom might be put to another use one day. A child? That seemed a remarkable thought.

"Do you approve, Madame de Valentin?"

"Very much, Monsieur de Valentin."

Ellen hugged Raoul. Amused, he returned the embrace. He eyed the bed. "And do you think, wife, that we might christen our little house? Just for good luck?"

The following day, Mr. and Mrs. Raoul de Valentin moved into 19 Carnarvon Avenue by the act of depositing the wooden trunk upstairs in the box room.

It *was* a pretty house, and there was a long row of exactly similar buildings on each side of the street. Ellen particularly liked the warm red brick from which the house was made, and was very proud of their varnished front door. It was a glossy black, as if it belonged to a mansion in the wealthiest part of town. There were even window boxes and Ellen, delighted with all she saw, decided that daffodils must be planted there.

Happy mornings were spent at the local shops or the market. Setting out soon after she had cooked breakfast, Ellen walked almost daily to the Hackney high street carrying a basket. A market was held there each Friday, and Ellen soon found stall prices much cheaper than the shops. She was not afraid to bargain, taking pleasure in paying a penny less here, a farthing more there for goods of superior quality.

But Raoul was not idle either.

"Ellen, do you approve?"

It was during their first week in the house, and Raoul had been out the entire afternoon. This time Ellen had no time to worry about where he might have gone. At first light, she had retrieved her sackcloth apron from the box and scoured the cottage from the ceilings of the bedrooms (cobwebs!) to the cupboards in the scullery (silverfish!). And then she picked a basket of nearly ripe apples, which she placed in the sun all along the windowsills. Tomorrow she would peel, core, and slice them, then make apple butter and apple pie with cinnamon. Raoul had purchased the spice quills and he had paid too much, of course, but they both liked the taste. Sitting at the desk in the parlor, Ellen was intent on writing down what she recalled of her mother's recipe, but had trouble remembering the quantities.

"What did you say, Raoul?"

He sighed. "My wife is distracted! These handbills. And this." He offered Ellen a stiff piece of cream card. Printed on it was: MRS. R. DE VALENTIN. MANTUA MAKER AND MILLINER. THE LATEST FASHIONS FROM PARIS AT REASONABLE PRICES. APPLY WITHIN. The handbills said much the same, though they gave the address.

Ellen was silent.

"You do not like them." Raoul was crushed. But then he saw Ellen's face. She was radiant.

"*Of course* I like them, my darling. They are perfect! But—"

"But no buts!" His pride restored, Raoul happily continued, "I have spoken to all the businesses in the high street. The butcher, the chemist, and the haberdasher will put the bills in their windows, in return for a discount for their wives and daughters. I have set up an account at the haberdasher, too, and ordered various materials. This is an excellent beginning, Mrs. de Valentin!"

Raoul swept Ellen from the chair and danced her about the room, the furniture impeding their progress more than a little. Laughing, out of breath, they collapsed on the sofa.

"But, Raoul!"

"Again? Have I not satisfied your doubts, Madame?" Mock indignation.

"It is only that I worry. You are certain all will be well. For you, to say it is to believe it. And yet my skill and experience are—"

"Extraordinary! I told you. My mother admires your talent, and her judgment is acute."

Madame Angelique. They had not talked of Raoul's mother during these last remarkable days. It occurred to Ellen again how strange it was that Angelique had not been present on their wedding day. "Have you spoken with my mother-in-law?" To think of her thus was odd also. "I should like to write to her and thank her for the dress. And ask her to come and stay with us here."

She so hoped that Madame would approve of their marriage.

Besides, she would enjoy showing off the house, and asking her advice about the business, too.

Raoul frowned. "No," he replied. He dropped her hand and stood. "There is something I should have told you. I am afraid my mother and I have parted on unhappy terms. Money. It is always money with her."

Ellen was puzzled. "But did you not say she had been generous?"

Raoul said, hastily, "She was. But then, of course, she changed her mind. She wrote to me and asked that I repay, immediately, the money she had lent me, and that I pay for the wedding dress, too. The dress that she quite clearly said was to be a gift to you. That is her way, of course, but I have had enough."

Ellen looked upset. She went to speak, but he quickly sat beside her. "This is our life now, Ellen. I will not have our marriage strained by her interference. I worked for nothing for so many years at Richmond, and now, when I ask for just a little help, she treats me, treats *us,* like this. Very well. She has made her bed. I shall not see my mother, ever again."

Ellen was very troubled, and said, hesitantly, "But Madame Angelique was so good to Mama, and to me. And I have learned so much from her." Raoul saw his mother in such a different way from the kind woman that she had known, Ellen was confused.

Raoul drew her close. "You are loyal to her, I know, and that is to your credit. But you only know one side of my mother. I am your husband and I hope you will respect my decision to have no further communication with her." Raoul got up from the couch. His expression was suddenly remote.

Ellen asked, nervously, "Where are you going?"

"The coal cellar. It is cold tonight. A fire will cheer us both." He was right. Rain spattered the windows. Ellen shivered. Of course she would respect Raoul's wishes, but someday, surely, Angelique would be welcomed back into their lives. Money couldn't have been the sole cause of such a definite break. Raoul was a proud person and he had dreams. Perhaps Angelique had failed to see that, had still thought of her son as a boy requiring her guidance.

Ellen made a vow to herself. She was Raoul's wife and Angelique's daughter-in-law. She would find a way to heal the breach between mother and son. It was her duty and she welcomed that.

Raoul returned to the parlor with a full scuttle of coal. He looked unhappy. Ellen said, tenderly, "I am better at setting a fire than you are. Besides, you have dirtied your jacket."

He looked at his sleeve. Ellen was right. The velvet on the cuff had a black smear on it. He grinned, good humor restored at the sight of Ellen on her knees, busily brushing out the hearth. "Such an industrious little housewife I have."

"You do, Sir. And now you must be banished to change for dinner. I shall set the fire and check the roast, and do the same myself."

"Will you now? Perhaps I can help. The changing, that is, not the fire. Soon enough we shall have a maid for that, and the cooking, too." He pulled her up. Ellen yelped, holding her dirty hands away from his clothes. "And then, Madame . . ." Heedless, he kissed away a smudge of soot on Ellen's cheekbone.

"Then, Sir?"

"We shall have more leisure for the important things. Like this." Raoul began to unbutton the bodice of Ellen's gown.

And she forgot all about Angelique.

CHAPTER 28

23rd of November, evening, AD 1845
17 Carnarvon Avenue
Hackney
London

My dearest Oriana,

I hope this letter finds you well. After some months in this
house, all continues happily here. The business is finding
more custom and I enjoy the designing of ladies' clothing
a great deal. All that my mother and Madame Angelique
taught me seems, now, to bear fruit, for I see so clearly
in my mind what I desire to make. It is a real pleasure to
conjure the finished garment from bolts of material and
cards of lace and buttons.

Ellen paused. It *was* engrossing work, for she had an instinct
for making simple designs appear other than what they were. But
though she truthfully enjoyed creating a garment from an idea,
Ellen knew that the third sentence of her letter was a lie. Customers for the business were scarce and becoming fewer each day. She
sighed and continued.

I think I have told you that I am responsible for the
housekeeping and the cooking, for as yet I do not feel we
can afford a maid (though Raoul disagrees). My husband

works diligently with our local merchant community to
interest their wives in our increasing success.

Increasing success? Ellen's vision blurred. She seized the sheet
of letter paper and screwed it up. "How is it I write twice each week
to my cousin and my aunt but still hear nothing in return?"

When Raoul did not reply, Ellen looked over her shoulder. He
was reading the morning's edition of the *Hackney Gazette*. "Do
you think Oriana and Aunt Daisy have cut me off?" She so hoped
Raoul would say that her fears were groundless.

But he frowned. "For your sake, and ours, I pray that they have
not."

"But Jane, I am sure, is loyal? It is to her I send the letters." It
had been more than a year since they left Shene. Perhaps Jane no
longer worked for Daisy. Ellen turned back to the writing desk.

Though I have often said that you and my aunt are
welcome in our house here at Hackney, I hope you
understand the seriousness with which I extend the
invitation.

Our second bedroom is small and it would be necessary
for you to share a bed with your mother. But we are able
to live here only because of the generosity of dearest Aunt
Daisy. We do not forget our debt of gratitude to her. This
roof is your roof. You need not stay at Shene, cousin.

Ellen stole a glance at Raoul. He was silent. If he felt her eyes
upon him, he gave no sign. Though the evening was cold, she had
persuaded her husband that the coal they had should be kept for
when it was truly freezing at night.

Poor Raoul. She longed to comfort him but did not know how.
Perhaps it was a sense of failure that made him so distant. But it
was her duty, and her joy, to support her husband and keep his
spirits up.

"Would you like tea, Raoul? It will only take a moment." Her words trailed away as he rattled the paper and retreated deeper behind its folds. Ellen stood. She would finish the letter tomorrow. She had no heart for it now.

"I shall press your shirt for the morning. Your cream trousers, also." She leaned down to kiss him, but Raoul turned his head away. Ellen colored, hurt. "I shall be in the kitchen."

As Ellen left, Raoul put his paper down in despair. He had reached the opinion that Ellen herself was the problem in their business. He was an effective salesman, and the drawings she made of gowns and mantles and hats were all beguiling, but Ellen was younger than many of the daughters of the high street shopkeepers. Their wives would rarely risk sparing pennies on a stranger, *especially* when the husbands looked so warmly on the young Mrs. de Valentin. And those one or two who did commission a garment expected the work to come at a substantial discount, since Ellen was unproven.

Raoul sighed. He could hear Ellen in the kitchen. She was singing to let him know that she was cheerful despite all. But as he looked around the pretty room, he saw the edges of the illustrated fashion papers he'd obtained from Paris had begun to curl.

Dropping the newspaper to the floor, he stood. He was cold and had had enough. Lighting a wax taper from a flint box, Raoul applied it to the ready-laid fire. The coals began to catch and he watched the flames bloom, one booted foot upon the fender. *Desperation frightens our clients off. They can smell it.* He looked around the room again. *Far too elegant, that's the catch. A grand name, too.* And Ellen's accent was of a different class than that of her clients. Why had he not thought of this before?

"You lit the fire?"

He did not look around. He could feel her gaze on his back. "What of it?"

Ellen said nothing, but a moment later her arms slid around his waist. "I am so glad you did, Raoul." She nestled against his back.

He caught a sob in his throat. Truthfully, he did not deserve her. He swiftly turned in her arms. "My dearest one." Tenderly, he kissed her eyes, her mouth.

"We will come through this, Raoul. I know that we shall." She was kissing him in return, fiercely. Hope flared as they gazed at each other. And he remembered their passion.

"Come to bed."

She giggled. "But the bedroom is cold, husband. Here is warm." He raised his brows. Where was his shy bride now?

"Very well, sweetheart. Very well." His busy fingers loosened her gown as hers unbuttoned his trousers. Just for tonight, he would forget about how few of the sovereigns remained from the sale of Lady Cleat's necklace. And fewer still from his mother's money. Not for the first time, he reproached himself for having taken it. Ellen must never know.

Now as they lay before the fire, shadows dancing on the walls and light gilding their naked bodies, Ellen rejoiced. Raoul was laughing again. He wanted her again.

As Advent tide arrived and colder winds rattled the sashes, Raoul was away from the house for all that remained of daylight day after day.

And then came the evening when he did not return.

That night was frigid. There was the breath of snow in the air and as the temperature dropped, the glass misted as Ellen peered out. She knew that by morning, the windows would be slick with ice inside the house.

As the hours ticked by, signaled by a lone, distant bell, Ellen lay sleepless. She had gone to bed early to save candle ends and coals, and had worn as many shawls and scarves as she had over her nightgown. She'd even put on fingerless gloves. But night is not a friend to hope. Images flared behind her eyes when she closed them. Raoul thrown from a carriage, his blood pooling on the cobbles. Or bailed up by thieves and desperate to escape. They'd find little in his pockets, but might murder him still.

"Is that you?" She must have slept. There was faint color in the sky. "Raoul?"

She smelled him before she saw him. Smoke and beer.

"Bleeding hell!" He stumbled on the stairs. There was a loose rod, and she heard him slide down several of the treads.

Ellen sat up. Anger extinguished terror. "Where have you been? I had thought you dead. And worse!" She heard herself. And cringed. She was a shrew.

"Yes, go on. Rail at a man when he's down. As if you care." This last was muttered as Raoul slumped against the doorjamb.

Where had he gone, the beautiful boy she had married, the man she so loved? "Oh my darling, I have been so frightened. You have left me alone so often these last days. And there is no money. I cannot even buy food." She did not mean to reproach him, but desperation spoke.

"No *My darling* for you. You know how to cut a man."

Ellen froze. The expression on Raoul's red face was coarse, his lips drawn back like a dog's.

All at once, nausea took her. A great wave that would not be denied. Somehow she got from the bed to the window and vomited on the roof of the kitchen below. Shaken, wiping her mouth with one hand, she turned to find Raoul staring at her. The gaze of a drunk, once focused, is terrifying. Ellen moved to the far side of the bed as he gathered himself.

"Sick, is it? Why would that be?" Now she saw he had a valise in his hand. He went to their small clothes press, riffled its contents. Shirts, stocks, linen.

He is taking his clothes. "What do you mean?"

"Happened before, has it?" Raoul hauled out his best jacket, his spare trousers. He was so disdainful, the tone was a slap. But it was true. Over the last days, she had felt unwell often in the mornings but thought it a result of sorrow. He snapped the valise shut. "Meaning to tell me, were you?"

"What? Tell you what?" But she knew. His face told her. She reeled where she stood. She *knew*.

"That you are in pup. Another unwanted mouth." He looked at her with loathing.

Ellen's heart contracted. It was as if she had swallowed salt. Her whole being wailed, but she said, "Perhaps I am carrying our baby. I do not know."

"Not *know?* How could you not *know?!*" He was shouting at her, the sound so great, it knocked around in her head.

"Please, Raoul." She had no other words. Imploring, asking for tenderness, she held out her hands to him. "I love you." She whispered the words.

And understood, immediately, that they were not wanted. That she was unwanted.

"Carolina knew. She knew all along. She warned me. If only I had listened." The self-pity was maudlin.

Ellen stared at her husband. "Carolina Wilkes? Have you spoken with her?"

He shrugged uneasily. Something in her tone pierced Raoul's wall of self-concern. "None of your business, but yes, I have. I've *spoken* with Carolina, if that's what you want to call it."

He hauled down a hatbox, muttering to himself. "All supposed to be so easy. How was I to know the old woman would up and die?"

Raoul stared at Ellen, belligerently unfocused, and said, "I can do nothing for you. And Madame de Valentin, you can do nothing for me."

Ellen sat on the bed. Her knees would not hold. Wrapped in an old shawl, she said, flatly, "We are married. I am your wife. We pledged to see each other through the bad times." *Put the valise down, I beg you, my darling.* But she did not say the words.

He sneered. "So it's money, is it?" Raoul fumbled in his trousers and she heard him mumble, "All the same, under the skin. Whores." Anguish was a gale that raged through Ellen's being. She tried to stand but could not, as he flung coins at her feet.

"There. All that remains. Have it. I shall see myself out, *Mrs.* de Valentin."

"Raoul. Do not go. Please." She heard him blunder down the stairs. Heard, but did not truly understand. A desperate effort roused her.

"I love you. You are married to me. Not her."

Raoul de Valentin stared up at the white-faced girl standing alone at the top of the stairs. He said, without emotion, "It is no good, my love. It's finished." As if he had made the most unexceptional statement in the world, he pulled the front door open. And closed it behind him with exaggerated care. He was gone.

Ellen stared at the place in the hallway where he had stood.

As if from another place, she watched as Ellen, the girl she knew she was, placed one hand upon her abdomen. And observed as that girl began to cry.

"I tell you, Carolina, I did not look for this. Not brats. Not so soon."

Raoul was slumped before the kitchen fire in Minories Court.

"Did you not, my brave?" The sarcasm registered and he flushed. Mrs. Wilkes continued, dispassionately, "But you thought you could crawl back to this nice warm crib when it all went wrong."

Carolina picked up a poker and punished the coals in the fireplace. "You brought the creature here. And I *knew*, I knew she would entangle you." An angry sigh. "Men. A girl like that." She shook her head, held up a little finger. "Twisted you, she did. Around this. Old or young, it remains the same." Carolina waggled the digit.

Raoul looked away. It seemed obscene. She was wrong, too.

Part of him was insulted that she thought him so easily gulled or Ellen so calculating. At the beginning there'd been real feeling there, on both parts.

"And so?"

Raoul shrugged, sullen. Walking through the door two days earlier and making his peace with Carolina had been easier than he had expected, but that did not mean he desired to be at Minories Court again.

The woman rolled her eyes. "Our investment in the girl and her mother? Docile, you said she was. Split the costs *and* the profit. Dressmaking. Pah. And I believed you, fool that I was. Whoring is always more certain but oh, no, you would not listen, would you?" She folded her arms as she stood. A bad sign.

Raoul would not meet her eye and he hunched a shoulder. "The girl was wrong for that work. I said that to you."

She snorted. "Went soft, is what you did. Remembered you was a *gentleman*. But marriage? What were you thinking?" She hardened. "I want my money, Raoul. Shove over."

Irritated, Raoul made room on the settee. "No good looking to me, *ma belle*. Not a penny piece remains from this little adventure." He shifted in his seat. A man could swallow only so much. And he would not crawl back to Angelique, either.

Mrs. Wilkes knew the signs. A moment more and he'd be as likely to walk as to stay. "Do not take on so. We can come to some arrangement. Of course we can." She smiled cautiously at him. The smell of him. That young male smell. How she had missed him in her bed.

In a mollified tone, Raoul said, "I am not proud of what has happened." He patted her hand. "But this is a mark of the generous woman you are known to be." He gathered himself. "It is good to be back." It cost him an effort, but Carolina did not see the disappointment masked behind his glinting smile.

The landlady of Minories Court grinned broadly and hurried to a locked cupboard. In it was a stone jar of whiskey. The good stuff.

Raoul narrowed his eyes. Carolina was not as pretty as Ellen and never would be, considering the life she lived, but her body was better than her face and she would do.

The young woman pulled out two tankards. Raoul suppressed a grimace. Another long night. "Come then, let us toast the future. To a new partnership. Old friends and good business."

"Our new partnership," Raoul echoed as he touched her pot with his own.

Mrs. Wilkes said with a wink, "Good money to be had in babes, my brave. Very good money if the matter is handled just right."

Raoul glared at her. "There are some things, Madame, that—"

She spoke over him hastily. "Just a little joke, my love. Only my way. Drink up."

CHAPTER 29

"YOU HAVE references?"

Ellen blushed but shook her head. She was the first in a queue of girls, all of whom seemed better dressed and more confident than her. She had waited two hours already.

Mrs. Ikin was hard, but she was not unkind. Sometimes. She peered over the steel rims of her pince-nez and, observing the wedding band, said, "Well then, Mrs.?" She could not be expected to remember every name when so many came to her for work.

"De Valentin. Ellen de Valentin. I have no references because I ran my own business." Ellen was desperate. There was so little food left in the house, but she had to feed her growing baby. And herself.

Saying nothing, the woman stared at Ellen. She was shrewd, Mary Ikin, and acknowledged as such by Mr. Manicore, the owner of this large business. No one had a better nose for workers, he said. Little Mrs. de Valentin, for all her refined accent, had the hands of a working woman. And she wanted this job. But then they all did. It was a buyer's market for labor.

Behind Ellen the line of seamstresses grew restive. This girl had had an unfair amount of time.

"Ran your own business, did you? Now that is very fine. Why do you need work for Manicore and Son, then?"

Ellen dared to hope. She said, humbly, "It failed, Mrs. Ikin, though we worked very hard, my husband and I. We could not find enough customers. And the money ran out."

Remembers names. Very good sign, thought the lady. But she sensed the genuine devastation, and asked, "Why did you not find clients?"

Ellen lifted her eyes, clear as water. "I do not know. I can show you my work." From a large cloth bag she extracted a sheaf of designs. Clothes for the morning. Clothes for the afternoon. Tea gowns. Riding costumes. Even a ball dress. Clever interpretations of gowns that Mrs. Ikin recognized. She sighed. Paris. Why did every little home worker try to compete with Paris? All these fol-derols were far too grand for Hackney. That's where the problem lay. But she said nothing as, quite carefully, she inspected each page before giving it back.

"These are truly your work?"

Ellen nodded. She saw something in the other woman's eyes. Could it be respect?

"Do you have samples?"

Ellen began to sweat. She could feel the beads gather on her upper lip and beneath her arms. But she opened the bag again and found the folded calico. "These are some of my toiles." She shook them out, one by one. "And, also . . ." She took out a blouse of white voile. Tucked and embroidered, adorned with pearl beads and black ribbon, it was a pretty thing. "I did this in half a day."

"I see." Mrs. Ikin tried not to show she was excited. But she was. This pale, gaunt girl had real talent. Talent was rare.

"Very well. You will start with us on Monday, Mrs. de Valentin. Six days. Three shillings and sixpence a day. Seven thirty until six thirty are the hours, and you eat where you work. We shall try you in the cutting room."

"Mrs. Ikin, I am so grateful. I will not let you down." Ellen's eyes glowed with unshed tears. The effect was disconcerting, as if a lens had magnified their size. The older woman frowned. Had she made a mistake? Would this intense young woman serve her purpose?

"See that you do not. There's many that would be glad of the place." She did not need to say more as she stood. "Thank you,

Ladies. We shall post further vacancies as they arise on the side gates."

The disappointed murmurs grew in volume as Mary Ikin left the room. And many pairs of hostile eyes swiveled toward Ellen. But she did not care. She could not afford to care what they thought of her.

The business of Manicore and Son was conducted on three nearly windowless floors of a converted flour mill. Mr. Manicore's father had been a jobbing tailor and his mother an outworker in the garment trade, but Thomas, their child, was cut from different cloth. He had ambition. Brought up from the age of seven to help his family by sweeping workshop floors, pressing seams open, and delivering finished garments to the factory owners, he very soon saw that there was money to be made from clothing, but not as a worker. As England's empire grew, bales of cheap textiles from India and China crammed London's wharves. And as the city, that center of commerce, swelled up and out, demand for finished goods increased, and Thomas set up business on his own account. And from a stake of five painfully saved pounds, he managed to do what Raoul had not.

Now, Ellen joined the forty or more women who worked for Thomas at the mill. Some cut patterns and cloth, and others finished the garments, while an external army of men, women, and children in kitchens and parlors all around Hackney assembled the clothes and returned them within a day.

And the key to Manicore's success was this: Thomas never aimed too high. He did not seek custom from among the affluent (bad payers and fickle clients) but addressed his handbills and advertisements to the increasingly prosperous middle and lower classes.

In spacious rooms looking out on Hackney high street, the wives of local families were enticed through Manicore's doors with one simple promise: A dress or coat or mantle selected from already-made garments, and commissioned and paid for on, say, a Monday, would be received at home by Wednesday evening. A three-day service.

Money up front, high turnover, fair quality, and a middling margin, plus a guarantee to deliver to any address within the greater London area, were the foundations of Thomas Manicore's business. And, as England became rich, so did he.

But the ever-flowing river of orders had to be serviced.

"You will work here, Mrs. de Valentin." Mrs. Ikin pointed to a high desk with a sloping front. There was no chair. It stood beside one of only two windows on the cutting floor, which was otherwise laid out in rows of long tables. This was where the pattern cutters and the cloth cutters worked, one woman per table.

The manageress was a busy woman and had many things to think of. Her chief task each day was to see that work flowed smoothly, since orders from the showroom arrived promptly on the hour, every hour.

"We have our standard lines, of course." The supervisor plumped down a large clothbound folio on the work surface. "I expect you to familiarize yourself with them this morning. Then you will begin. Bess!" Her attention was caught by a cutter staring into space three tables away. "We are waiting on that mantle!"

Ellen was confused. "Mrs. Ikin?"

The supervisor said, impatiently, "Yes?"

"Am I not to cut?"

Mrs. Ikin shook her head. She said, briskly, "I have suggested to Mr. Thomas that you be permitted to look over our designs. This spring we expect to augment the range. By six thirty sharp this evening, I will expect sketches from you. Front, back, side, detail, *and* making instructions for two new skirts, two matching blouses, and two light coats. Economical and simple. But pretty."

Mrs. Ikin softened. Ellen's expression had changed from shock to astonishment. Mrs. Ikin approved of modesty. She approved, too, of Ellen's appearance. Though she wore black, the girl's peplumed jacket of cheap broadcloth was well cut, and distinguished by a long row of tiny jet buttons from collar to waist. The small hat, too, with its spotted veil, was elegant and understated. "Who made your clothes?"

Ellen had worried very much that morning about what she should wear to her new position. In the end, the sample garments that she had made for the business (she had only herself to practice on) were in the best condition, and she chose the least elaborate. She managed to say, "I did, Ma'am. And I am very grateful for the opportunity, Mrs. Ikin."

The older woman nodded. "See that you are. But if your work does not satisfy Mr. Thomas, it will be the cutting table for you. If he approves, you will make toiles. And *then,* we shall see. In that cupboard are the things you need." She rustled away, marching toward the hapless Bess as if she were the hordes of Assyria descending upon the plain.

Ellen unpinned her hat and looked around for a peg. The girl on the nearest table whispered, "Over there. Behind the screen."

In theory, talking was forbidden during working hours. In practice, it was Mrs. Ikin's presence that stilled tongues. The cutter, with red hair and freckles, and only a little older than Ellen, was Irish. Her accent was thick, and Ellen did not understand. Blushing, she said, "I am so sorry. What did you say?"

The other laughed loudly, to attract attention. "Ho! So it *is* a lady. Too good for us, girls!"

Mrs. Ikin having left the floor, a titter spread around the tables and heads craned to see better. More than one of the cutters had wondered what the well-dressed stranger was doing there, and a girl called out, "What's your name, Lady Jane?"

"Ellen de Valentin. And you are?"

"Annie." The girl scurried closer. She snatched Ellen's left hand and held it up. "Look, girls, Lady *Ellen* is married!" The laughter was not unkind, but Ellen's eyes filled with tears.

"Let alone, Annie. See what you've done? You were new, too,

once." Ellen was staring at the floor, willing herself not to cry, but her head snapped up. That voice!

"Polly?"

The maid from Wintermast had grown up. Larger breasts, wider hips, and a tiny waist, she was shorter than Ellen. And sturdier. "Is it really you?"

"True enough." Polly grabbed Ellen's hands. "*You* haven't changed, Miss Ellen. Not really." Privately, she thought Ellen's early prettiness extinguished. The girl she saw now was spare to the point of starvation.

"But, what are you doing here?"

"Same as you, I should think, Miss Ellen." She held Ellen at arm's length, curious.

"And are you really married?" Ellen nodded. "And your mam? Will you remember me to her?"

The younger girl's face worked. "My mother died, Polly. Last summer."

A low whistle signaled that the supervisor was back at the workroom door. Polly hurried to her table, and Ellen, in turmoil, wiped her face, trying not to sob. Ducking her head, she went to the cupboard she'd been shown. Inside it were paper, colored inks, and charcoal.

That first day at the mill passed in an anxious blur, and though Ellen yearned to talk with Polly, the need to prove herself, to secure her place, forced all distraction away. But standing tired her very much and by the time Mrs. Ikin returned to see her sketches, as evening drew on, Ellen was ghost pale.

"Are you ill, Mrs. de Valentin?" The sharp glance frightened Ellen. She stood straighter.

"No, Mrs. Ikin. Not ill. When I draw, time flees. It's as if I go somewhere else."

The response was dry. "Not too far away, I hope. Let me see your work."

Ellen's mouth dried. She swallowed painfully. All she could see were mistakes and clumsy forms, but the sketches contained all the elements she had been instructed to create. And one of the skirts, at least, had a pleasing drape, since she had dared to suggest cutting on the bias. More material would be used but the effect was appealing. "I do not know if they will be satisfactory."

"There is only one way to find that out, Mrs. de Valentin." The supervisor was not unsympathetic, but she was a practical woman.

The silence was suddenly profound in the cutting room as the little drama played out. The cutters watched the white-faced girl with interest. Watched, too, for signs that Mrs. Ikin liked (or did not) the offered drawings. Only Polly dared to wave support. Mrs. Ikin said nothing as she gathered up the sketches. She hurried to the door, calling out as she went, "Work is finished for today."

Is that it? thought Ellen. She stared at her fingers. She had kept them scrupulously clean so the drawings would not be marked or made grubby by charcoal or ink, but she wondered why she'd done it, now. Did such care even matter?

Polly hurried over, pulling on her woolen mittens against the cold. "You did well, Miss Ellen. Ikin would have said straight out if she did not like your work. The last three drafters lasted a day apiece. But you'll be back tomorrow."

Ellen sobbed a breath. The room swam, and Polly jumped to catch her. A moment later and Ellen's head would have hit the edge of the drawing desk.

Ellen and Polly sat wrapped in blankets, two huddled shapes in a room bereft of light, except for a few candle stubs. They had been talking for hours in Ellen's cold house after Polly bought pies from a stall set up near the factory gates (sited to catch the girls as they made their weary way home).

"*No* money, Miss Ellen?"

Ellen shook her head. "Not after I used up the last of the coins he left me. I am desperate. I must work or starve."

Polly took her hand. "I should think you were. Desperate, that is." She shook her head in disbelief. "I have never heard another story to compare to yours." But then she brightened. "Still, you have a place at Manicore's now. The pay is little but at least the hours are regular. 'Course, with you a drafter, your wages will be greater and—"

"But I am not trained. I shall be found out! All I have is the legacy of Mama's instruction and watching Madame Angelique."

"Poor Mrs. Gowan. May she rest in peace." Polly sighed and licked crumbs from her fingers. She eyed her companion. Ellen had always been thin, but her face now was all angles and sinew. She'd been right. This was starvation. "Here. Have it." Polly extended the plate. A single pie remained.

Ellen's huge eyes were eloquent, but she said, "I have had more than enough. You are far too generous, Polly. You always were."

"Old friends are the best friends, my ma always says." But Polly was warmed by the compliment. "Go on. Eat."

Trying not to shake, not to tear at the food like a dog, Ellen said, "I have spoken so much about my own case, I am ashamed. Did you become a milliner after all?"

"You have a very long memory, Miss Ellen." Polly pulled her blanket tighter as the windows knocked in their frames. It was a windy night. She shook her head. "No. I was fool enough to listen to my brother. I tried though, very hard. Tramped the streets until my shoes holed. I could not stay with Allan. He sleeps in the hayloft with the other ostlers. He let me creep in beside him the first two nights, but I was found out. And so I was without a roof *or* a job. And too shamed to go home. Besides, Ma has it hard in the village. It is worse since you left, much worse. Landlords did not repair many of the houses nor the church. Wintermast is well-nigh empty now." She shivered.

Ellen could not bear more sadness, not that night, and said, "But here you are!"

The other girl's eyes were far away. "At first I slept under bridges, or in doorways. Being summer, the nights were warm. Well, if you do not count the rain. But dangerous a' course. All sorts sleep rough in London now."

Ellen laced her fingers with Polly's. "That must have been very hard."

"It was. Some of it. But you meet with kindness, too." Polly's expression was stoic, but the hand gripping Ellen's told another story. "Then my luck turned. I saw a notice on the gates of the mill: 'Cutters Required.' I had no training, either, didn't know what a pattern was. I lied. They say Mrs. Ikin is a hard woman, but something made her take me on. Your ma's character must have helped. I like to think that, anyway. I have been at Manicore's two years nearly, though putting money aside is difficult. But I will not readily leave. It is a cruel world, and desperate times breed desperate acts, so they say." She shuddered.

"Where do you live?"

Polly shrugged. "I doss in a room with three other girls over a tobacconist shop. We share a bed. It is not so very big—neither the room nor the bed—but we are warm, in this weather." She stared admiringly at the parlor fittings. "You've done well for yourself here even if he, your husband, has scarpered." She stopped. "Miss Ellen, forgive my rattle tongue!"

"Gone. Yes. Polly, you spoke the truth. And it *is* pretty. I do not know what I shall do, if I lose my house." Unconsciously, both hands strayed to her belly.

So that is how it is, Polly thought, but instead asked, "Have you nothing to sell? The furniture?"

"Only my clothes. The fittings came with the house when we took it. Unless . . ." Ellen fingered Connie's locket on its chain around her neck. She would not do it! Could not. The tiny portraits of her parents were the last comfort she had left.

"Miss Ellen, something is worrying at you. Something else?" Polly did not ordinarily pry, but her friend was wound tighter than steel ribbon. At any moment, she might spring apart.

Ellen's hands covered her face. She said, very low, "I am enceinte."

Polly rallied. "Well then, we must see that your well-being is safeguarded. And the child's also."

Impulsively, Ellen turned to her friend. "Will you live here with me, Polly? There is a bed. We should have to share it, but I think there would be more space than you have at present. We could help each other. The costs of two are less than one alone." She faltered. She had thought that to be the case with Raoul.

Polly jumped up with excitement. "Miss Ellen, are you sure? Really, truly sure?"

That drew a smile. "Yes, I am sure. I have been so lonely, and so frightened."

"Not anymore," said Polly. "I am here now." But then her bright spirits dimmed. "But if your husband should come back, you'd not throw me out?"

Ellen stared into the candle flame. Her heart twisted in her chest. She had longed, for days, to hear his footstep, longed to hear him call out her name. But he had not come. *Would* she have him back now?

Taking Ellen's silence for agreement, Polly spat in her palm and thrust it forward. "Done!"

For the first time in a very long time, Ellen smiled. She spat in her own palm and grasped Polly's hand. "Done indeed."

And that night, as Polly snored lightly beside her, Ellen drifted into sleep and dreamed happy dreams of a laughing child holding out her arms.

CHAPTER 30

"M RS. IKIN wants you."

Ellen jumped. She had been drawing a set of ruffles and calculating the yardage that had to be allowed. "Annie! You startled me. Did she say why?"

The girl shrugged, but her eyes slid down to Ellen's belly. For more than five months Ellen had let out the seams of her few dresses at night and tried to disguise the bulge of her pregnancy with shawls. But it was hot on the cutting floor as summer arrived, and the extra drapery was stared at. "Very well."

Ellen stood and ignored the urge to stretch her back. She had begged for a stool from Mrs. Ikin, a privilege grudgingly conceded (a mark of respect, Polly said, for Ellen's work) but one that made the long days tolerable. To an extent. Her hands were shaking as she gathered up the day's work—a walking-out dress with frogged button-keepers and a matching bonnet. She ignored Polly's whispered "Good luck." If she acknowledged the sympathy, she might yet need it.

The women on the cutting floor were her friends now, even Annie. And if none of them had openly commented on the pregnancy that she did not wish to declare, Ellen took that as a kindness. But everyone knew what the outcome of this conversation would be. She would be asked to leave.

"Sit down, Mrs. de Valentin," Mrs. Ikin said as Ellen entered her office.

To describe Mrs. Ikin's domain as an *office* was to flatter the space. An entire wall in that windowless cupboard was occupied by shelves, each divided into numbered compartments; one for each day of the working week. In each compartment there were customers' order sheets to which were clipped swatches of cloth, the design of the commissioned garment, and, circled in red, the date upon which it must be delivered.

The only other furnishing, besides a table that functioned as a desk, were two chairs. Mrs. Ikin occupied one, and Ellen took the other. It was frail and it creaked when she sat.

Neither woman knew how to begin the conversation, until Ellen offered her sketches. "This new skirt will work well in the wool jersey, Mrs. Ikin. It is an inexpensive fabric and the drape will be excellent. As you see, I have suggested the rose, but it would do just as well in blue, or black."

Mrs. Ikin steepled her fingertips, apparently listening. Courteously, she allowed Ellen to finish the description of the matching bonnet. Padded velveteen on a wire frame, with satin ribbons of a complementary color and a trimming of small rosebuds, made from scraps of silk. "Very easy to make, and quick. Not expensive at all, since we will employ offcuts that would otherwise be sold to the rag men. The effect is pleasing, and it will seem more luxurious than it is."

"Thank you, Mrs. de Valentin. As usual, your work is ingenious. Mr. Manicore continues to be pleased in this regard." She hesitated. Ellen's heart beat faster. "However, there is another reason that I have called you here."

"Another reason?" Ellen mastered the puzzled tone well.

"Yes." Mrs. Ikin leaned forward. "Mrs. de Valentin, did you not think to tell us that you were with child?"

Ellen thought about lying, thought about denying the obvious. Her face drained of color, and then flushed. *Do not cry. I forbid you to cry!* "A child?"

"Come, girl. I am not a fool. You cannot deny the truth." Mrs.

Ikin was severe. This was always a disappointing situation, especially since the girl had such promise, and time had been expended in her training.

Ellen nodded, and then, alarmed, shook her head. "Not a fool. Not at all." She stared down at the hands joined in her lap. What remained of it. "I needed the work, you see. I hoped that if I could prove myself, you would understand."

Ellen's imploring eyes made Mrs. Ikin shift in her seat, but she had her duty. "*You* must understand, Mrs. de Valentin, that Manicore and Son cannot be seen to employ—"

"You expect me to leave?" Ellen spoke over her.

Mrs. Ikin nodded.

Ellen threw the dice of her life upon the table. "Is Manicore and Son satisfied with my work?"

The other woman cautiously nodded again. "Mr. Thomas himself has said that our new spring and summer lines are superior to those of last year."

Ellen pressed her advantage. "And, the designs are well received, are they not? The figures show that?" When Mrs. Ikin did not respond, Ellen leaned forward. "Does Mr. Manicore know of my condition?"

Mrs. Ikin coughed. Those eyes, too intense to be avoided. She said, crisply, "He does not. But I shall shortly tell him."

Ellen forced her voice to steady. She tried not to implore, tried to be businesslike. "Allow me to continue to work for you, Mrs. Ikin. From my house. I live close by. Manicore and Son need not be embarrassed or reproached by my situation. It would be another form of piecework, in its way."

Mrs. Ikin stared at Ellen. For a moment she said nothing. "But as"—she gestured at the bulge; Ellen had ceased to drape the shawl across it—"as your baby nears term, you will be tired."

"You mean I will be less efficient?" Ellen laughed. The sound was grating. "I do assure you I shall provide all that you require. If I do not, my baby and I do not eat." *Would you see us starve?*

"But afterward? With a child to look after, what will your husband say to your continuing to work?"

My husband. Ellen stood. "My husband, Mrs. Ikin, will be of no concern to either of us. I assure you of this."

The other woman said nothing, but her eyes searched Ellen's face. At last she said, "I shall speak with Mr. Manicore, though I guarantee nothing."

Ellen's hard-won strength lasted only so far as the door. Grasping the knob to steady herself, she could not control her voice any longer. "Bless you."

It was August and Ellen's sixteenth birthday had come and gone. She was in the scullery, staring out of the window as she washed the few breakfast dishes. The apples were nearly ripe again.

Abstracted from the present, she saw another green garden. And children—boys and one small girl—climbing among the trees there. She smiled. If she closed her eyes, she could almost hear them. But a kick in her diaphragm plucked her from the past. She patted her belly. It was tighter than a drum skin.

Ellen talked happily to her child. "I thought you were asleep. But you and I must work soon, or Mrs. Ikin will not be pleased."

Behind her on the kitchen table was a pile of sketches. An odd effect of pregnancy was that ideas seemed to flow faster from her fingers' ends to the page. Or perhaps that was just the practice, after all these months. She knew so much more now.

"Ellen? Do you need anything?" Polly, getting ready for work, was pinning on a straw bonnet in the doorway.

Ellen picked up the last plate. "You are kind, Polly, but you'll be late if you do not go. We have much to keep us busy here." She smiled dreamily and cradled her belly.

Polly did not like to leave. Ellen did not know when her baby was due but, in profile, it was clear that the child had dropped down. And yesterday, as if impelled by a force outside herself, Ellen had scoured the little house, even cleaning the windows and washing the kitchen floor with hot lye.

Not long now, thought Polly. *At least she has flesh on her bones to see her through.* It was true. Polly's care and two wages had brought food to the house again. Ellen was not the gaunt creature of all those months ago. And today she was happy.

"Well, if you are quite sure?"

Ellen made a shooing motion. "Go!" She smiled as the front door closed. *Dearest Polly. How lucky I am, Mama, that we have found each other again.* She had not visited Connie's grave this week but perhaps she could be forgiven, just this once.

Humming, Ellen walked out into the garden with a basket on her arm. It was warm today, and the drowsy fizz of bees drew her to the lavender she had planted last autumn. Bending, she closed her eyes and drank the scent. Her back was sore this morning. Perhaps that was the cheap mattress? She wandered farther.

"You are very fine, are you not?" Ellen asked, looking up at the apple tree.

Standing beneath its laden bows, Ellen was pleased with her work. Last autumn she had hard-pruned the neglected limbs, as she had seen her father do with the oldest trees in their garden. She had been concerned that she might have killed it, but this season the ripening crop was greater yet. "I hope you do not mind, friend, if I pick just a few?" It was a strange fancy addressing a tree as if it were a person. Ellen reached up to test an apple, smiling. It came away easily from the stalk, there was no need for her little knife. The harvest would soon be ready to take.

What was the old saying? *Hide knives from the wife as she bears.* Ellen remembered it too late, as pain sliced her side.

The apple, the basket, and the knife fell to the grass unheeded, and Ellen, gasping, collapsed to her knees. She grabbed the trunk of the old tree and clung to it. As the pain came again, she cried out and the canopy trembled above her head.

CHAPTER 31

"E LLEN?" POLLY had begged off work early. All day she had been uneasy, the picture of Ellen's swollen belly too vivid to banish. She called out again as her key turned in the lock. "I'm home."

Polly climbed quickly to the bedroom. It was tidy, the bed made. *Where are you?* The curtains had not been drawn back. She went to the window.

Ellen lay beneath the apple tree. Polly gasped and ran.

A warm and beautiful evening had succeeded the radiant day, but Ellen saw nothing of the flaming sky. She did not know how long she had lain there, for time had departed. There had been nothing else but pain, her dark companion, as the shadows slowly stretched out toward her. Twice she had tried to crawl to the house but he would not permit that. He had her, gripped her and would not let her go. So she stayed with the apple tree. Her friend, too, was strong, and if she held on, with hands made raw from his rough bark, *his* strength would help her endure the power of the other.

"Oh, Ellen." Polly arrived at a run.

But Ellen did not know. She was caught in a toil of bloody skirts. She screamed out, but Polly did not understand since the word was a howl, not a name. "Raaaaaaouuuuuuul. Ah, Raaaaaaaaouul."

Ellen began to pant. Quick, short, shallow. Polly, who had helped birth brothers and sisters since she was old enough to hold a basin, tried to prise Ellen's hands from the tree trunk. "You must kneel."

"No!" Ellen bared her teeth. But she was weak. Polly understood the fury of a woman close to bearing. Ellen would remember little of this agony. Soothing the wild hair from her friend's eyes, Polly caught hold of one hand and then the next, crooning, "Hush now, little one. Do not fight me."

Putting her arms around Ellen, Polly hauled her partially upright. And instinct took over as Ellen knelt on all fours, her head down.

"That's right, my beauty, breathe deep now. Store breath for the pain."

Polly pulled Ellen's skirts away from her body. They were heavy and wet and would impede what must be done. The small knife lay in the grass. The dress had to be sacrificed. "Stay still now."

Ellen groaned from the pit of her being and arched her back to a hump, but Polly managed the task. Ripping the skirt from hem to waist, she pulled the bloodied cloth aside. Ellen panted faster. The washhouse was close by. "I must get linen and water."

"Do not go. Do not leave me." There was no time for linen. A wrenching groan turned to a howl, and the child slid from Ellen's body and into Polly's hands in a gout of blood and water. Ellen's daughter began to scream, turning from purple to scarlet in an instant.

Ellen raised her head, her face a white mask, even her lips were bloodless. "My baby." It was barely a whisper. Polly cut the child's cord with the paring knife, and helped her friend sit up. She braced Ellen's back against the tree. The infant struggled as Polly wrapped her in a piece of the bloody skirt. For the moment, there was nothing else.

"Here is your little girl. Healthy and fine."

Ellen's arms enfolded the infant, and the child ceased to cry. Mother and baby gazed at each other, a universe of two beneath the apple tree.

Raoul de Valentin had been drinking with Carolina Wilkes in a Spitalfields crib for two days, and it was there that Polly found him after hours of searching. Unshaven, his fine clothes were discolored by sweat and worse. The velvet cuffs of his frock coat were particularly filthy, long past the ministrations of a laundress or his careful wife.

Ellen had said Raoul was handsome, so when the barman pointed to the red-faced lout in one corner, Polly was uncertain. But just then the woman with him wheedled, "Just one more gin. Only a little one, Raoul," and his identity was confirmed.

Ellen's husband was younger than Polly had thought he would be, more youth than man. She stepped into his path as he made his uncertain way across the taproom. "You have a child, Mr. de Valentin. A daughter."

"A daughter?" Raoul's eyes misted. Spirits made him sentimental. "Carolina, do you hear? My baby is born." Polly stared from one to the other with disdain.

Mrs. Wilkes narrowed her eyes. "And who are you?"

"A friend." Polly turned to go but Raoul stopped her, slopping grog on her dress. "Wait, girl. Is the child well?"

"Tolerably, but not her mother." Polly mopped her gown with a handkerchief. It was hard to be civil.

"Not well?" Carolina asked hopefully.

Polly ignored her, glaring at Raoul. "That is why I have come."

As plainly as if she had spoken, he heard *More's the pity.* "I must go to my wife." Raoul waved grandly, as if to part a crowd, and tried to turn toward the door. But his legs let him down and he fell like a tree to the sanded floor, to the shrill consternation of his companion.

Polly did not stay for more. She had done as she had promised.

"Did you find him?" The call came from the bedroom.

Polly grimaced. Ellen must have heard the key in the lock. She had hoped her friend would be sleeping. The baby began to cry fretfully. Polly called back, "Yes. Would you like some more of the broth? It will take but a moment to heat."

The crying ceased. There was silence at the top of the stairs. Polly tried again. "For the baby? Just to help the milk. There's plenty left in the pot."

"I am not hungry." Ellen's voice was weak.

Light shone from the bedroom at the top of the stairs. Polly sighed. Best to get it over.

Lamplight is kind. The baby, rose and white with a quiff of dark hair, seemed content as she suckled, and Ellen's bright cheeks, clean nightdress, and freshly washed hair—Polly's ministrations that morning—were all they should be in a new mother. But it was fever that brought color to Ellen's face and Polly knew it.

She sat on the bed. "You must eat, Ellen. For her sake." She touched the baby's cheek, and was dismayed to see that the tray she had left with a covered bowl of broth, a large piece of cheese, and buttered bread lay untouched beside the bed. "We shall call a doctor for you."

Ellen shook her head. "Doctors are expensive." Her breath was short, and that worried Polly also. Any village girl knows the symptoms of childbed fever. Ellen was hot to the touch and her pulse was far too fast. "Listen to me, Ellen. Many women die needlessly after their baby is born. You daughter needs you. Let me get the doctor. Please."

But Ellen was stubborn. "I am young. And strong."

Too young, thought Polly. *And as to "strong,"* "Strong makes no difference. The fever takes whom it chooses. That is why—"

Ellen spoke over her friend. "Tell me about him, Polly. Please. What did he say?"

Polly stood. "You will feel better when the bed is tidy." She busied herself shaking the pillows and smoothing the bed covers as the yawning baby detached from Ellen's nipple. Polly held out her arms. "Give her to me. She will need her napkin changed, the dear thing. Have you thought of her name?"

Ellen allowed Polly to take her sleeping daughter. She slumped against the bolster and closed her eyes. She'd been oppressed by a headache these last hours. "I shall call her Constance. For my mother. But you saw him? Tell me. I do not mind what he said."

Polly made a business of changing the napkin. She'd hemmed them herself from linen offcuts begged at Manicore's. "He seemed happy when I told him." The baby woke and squirmed. She was not pleased to be uncovered. "There, little one. Only a moment." But Constance began to whimper.

Ellen sat up. It upset her when the baby cried. "Give her to me, Polly." She winced. Her throat was sore and it was hard to speak.

Polly put Constance in Ellen's careful arms and the screaming ceased. The instant contentment of mother and child in each other's presence touched Polly greatly, and she blinked away tears. After a moment, Ellen asked, "But does he want to see her?" She meant, Does he want to see *me*?

Polly dropped the napkin in a bucket. She would wash the soiled ones before she went to bed. "He has said as much." She knew that Ellen yearned for Raoul to come back, but how could that be a good thing? "I shall make something to eat. We can have supper together. Shall I put Constance in the cradle?" Ellen had bought a rocking cradle in the market for pennies and sewn the bedding herself. It stood beside the bed.

"Not yet. I like to hold her as she goes to sleep."

Polly silently cursed Raoul de Valentin as she left the bedroom. The vulnerability of the frail young mother and her tiny child was painful. How could he have done what he did?

"You have decisions to make, my brave. You know it would be a kindness to them both." Carolina stared at Raoul. It was early, or, rather, late, and they were the last patrons in the taproom. When Raoul began to cry some hours earlier, Carolina had drunk herself sober, but her lover was still a befuddled mess.

"Raoul? Do you hear me?" He raised his head from the bar

counter but could not focus. "My little baby. Ellen, dearest Ellen. How could I have done this to you? I am a father." Each word caused the room to spin faster. His head hit the counter with a *thud* he did not feel, his cheek resting in a puddle of beer.

Carolina was annoyed. She grabbed Raoul by the hair. "You *know* there is the better choice. How can she give that scrap the life she deserves? Your wife has nothing. And you owe me much. All your fine clothes and fancy ways do not come cheap."

Carolina Wilkes had partnered with weak men all her life. They were easier to manage than the strong ones. But when shown unpleasantness, especially of their own making, they wavered. They were all the same: talked much, did little. Her first husband had been like that until the day he died, drunk, when he fell under the wheels of a dray. She sighed. She wished she was not drawn to Raoul de Valentin but she was, and while she was, she would arrange matters as seemed sensible. He would thank her one day.

She shook the boy, and he flopped like a rag doll. "I know people of influence who would be glad to adopt your daughter. She will have a loving and wealthy home. This is to her advantage. Do your duty by the child." She did not mention Ellen's name. If she did, he would blubber more.

Raoul found his voice, and a little of his strength. He took hold of her wrists, and for a moment saw Carolina Wilkes with terrible clarity. "This I shall not do. Sell my daughter?" He stumbled upright, beyond the reach of her hands. "This is not worthy. Not the action of a de Valentin." Pride was discounted by his appearance.

Carolina considered the outburst. And smiled.

"Come here, sweet boy. It will not be so very bad." She was crooning, almost. As he stared at her, Raoul's vision blurred. He slumped onto a stool and felt Carolina's arms encircle his chest. He leaned against her shoulder. If he could just rest, all would become clear.

CHAPTER 32

WHEN RAOUL de Valentin returned to Carnarvon Avenue the next afternoon, he was no longer drunk and was cleaner than he had been. But if haunted eyes and a pale face declared remorse, Polly was not inclined to believe it when she found him in the hall. "What are you doing here? How did you get in?"

Raoul, drunk though he may have been, remembered Polly's face from the pub. He glared. "This is my house." He thrust his keys in her face.

Polly did not flinch. She glared back. "I live here now. *Someone* had to look after Miss Ellen."

"*Miss* Ellen?" He laughed, an uncharitable bark. "Mrs. de Valentin, you mean. Leave. Now."

Pushing the girl aside, Raoul took the stairs two at a time. She called after him. "She needs me. I will not go."

"Yes you will, deary." Carolina dipped her head as she entered. The feathers on her bonnet were taller than the door frame. "Jikes, remove this woman." Behind her, a very large man bulked through the open door. Removing her gloves finger by finger, Mrs. Wilkes stood aside.

As the man grasped her shoulders, Polly shouted, "The doctor says she is ill, very ill!" A slam cut off her words, but Polly yelled even louder on the other side of the door, "The child must be reliably suckled, or she will starve!"

"Ellen?" Raoul could hear the scuffle below, but ignored it as he

265

opened the bedroom door. "I am here now," he said. But Ellen was deeply asleep. Her color was hectic and her breathing rapid. The baby mewled fretfully in her crib, but when Raoul picked her up, she cried and squirmed in his arms.

"Her below's right. That child is hungry."

Raoul scowled at Mrs. Wilkes as she entered. "I can see that." He tried to wrap his daughter with little success. Carolina sighed. "Give her to me." But Raoul, agitated, stepped back on her toe by mistake.

"Oaf!" The agonized exclamation frightened Constance. Her clamor grew louder, and Ellen stirred. Unnerved, Raoul passed the baby to Carolina.

From outside the house, they heard pounding. "I shall return. Do you hear me?"

As she tried to soothe the increasingly angry child, Carolina stared down at Polly through the window. "Persistent, ain't she?"

They both jumped when Polly used the knocker to brutal effect, yelling out, "I said, do you hear me?"

Through the door, Jikes bellowed, "Clear off. Go on!"

But Polly would not be deterred. "I mean it."

Ellen woke and saw Mrs. Wilkes. "Give me my baby!"

Raoul, standing between the women, paled as Constance arched her back. Her screaming hurt his ears. Ellen was distraught. "Raoul, she will drop our child!"

Between the outrage of Raoul's daughter and the terror of her mother, Mrs. Wilkes had some trouble transferring the infant to Ellen's outstretched arms. At last this was accomplished, and the girl opened her nightdress with a shaking hand. Earnest snuffling replaced cacophony as Ellen cupped her baby's head against her chest. "How could you?" She ignored Mrs. Wilkes, but Raoul felt Ellen's glance like a brand.

He coughed nervously. "We wish to help, Ellen."

She shook her head. "Too late." Tears dripped on the baby's

head. Constance frowned but did not stir as she sucked. And Raoul's expression changed. He was enraptured.

Why, thought Carolina, had Raoul never looked at *her* in that way? The rings rattled as she twitched the curtains closed. "Yes, a *very* touching sight. Proud father that you are." Her eyes were gimlets.

Raoul flinched at the sneer, but Constance had hold of his forefinger. Gradually, her eyes closed as she suckled. He spoke very softly. "Do not send me away. Our daughter is beautiful and so are you. I am so sorry for all that has happened."

Over her daughter's head, Ellen gazed up at her husband. He meant what he said. In that moment.

Carolina raised her voice. "Come, Mrs. de Valentin, you are not well. As Mr. de Valentin says, we have come to render assistance. In the best interests of your baby and you."

"Tell Mrs. Wilkes that she is not welcome in my house." Ellen spoke only to Raoul.

"Our house, *chérie.*" Raoul sat on the bed. Tenderly, he smoothed a curl from Ellen's eyes.

This was the action that, above all else, provoked Carolina Wilkes. "Your wife may not know we are here on a matter of business, Raoul." Her voice had an edge to cut glass.

"Business?" Ellen's grip on Constance tightened.

"Tell her. Go on."

De Valentin swallowed. "I have changed my mind. My daughter is far too young."

"To leave her mother? But this is the perfect time. The child will remember nothing."

"Leave? What do you mean." As Carolina advanced toward the bed, Ellen reared up and the baby woke, confused. She was being held extremely tight. She whimpered. And then screamed. Mrs. Wilkes stopped. Dead eyed, she stared at Raoul de Valentin. "You will remember to what we have agreed. Debtors' prison is a most unpleasant place."

Raoul attempted to stare the woman down, interposing his body between Carolina and Ellen as the child screamed ever louder. But he swallowed.

"Ellen, Mrs. Wilkes believes that . . ."

"It is not what I believe, it is what I know. Your child, Mrs. de Valentin, will have a better life in other circumstances."

"Other circumstances? I do not understand." But she did. Ellen stared at Raoul with disbelief. He would not look at her.

From below came a shattering thump. "Open the door!" A man was shouting from outside the house. Jikes raised his voice. "I will not!"

The rending crash as the door was broken in was succeeded by confused yelling and then a fight.

"Ellen?" A woman's voice rose above the howls and grunts of the men. Polly had returned. And she was not alone.

Mrs. Wilkes lunged toward the baby, but Ellen had the strength of the desperate. Hitting Carolina with a bolster, she wrapped the bedclothes around the woman's head and hobbled to the door with Constance just as Polly burst in.

"That's him!" Polly yelled, and a very large man, larger than Jikes, pushed into the room behind her. Behind him was another. Both were bloodied. If Carolina had the nerve to face them down, Raoul did not. He had always abhorred physical violence. But that did not save him, nor his pretty face.

It was some weeks after the attempted kidnapping that Ellen finally recovered. Often during that time, Polly despaired of her friend's survival, and that of Constance, as childbed fever tightened its grip. But the girls from Manicore saved Ellen's life, especially when Mrs. Ikin heard what had happened.

If the manageress was thought to be a hard woman, her actions toward Ellen displayed another side of her nature. It was she who paid for the doctor until Ellen was out of danger. And it was she who permitted the girls of the cutting floor, in arranging a roster with Polly to help Ellen morning and evening, to arrive late and leave early.

Mrs. Ikin even sponsored the finding of a wet nurse for the baby when, because of weakness and delirium, Ellen could not suckle little Connie for some days. All this the manageress did without informing Mr. Manicore. And somehow, Ellen's work got done. Polly began by tracing her friend's existing designs, and with Mrs. Ikin's active guidance, managed to alter enough so that new sketches were created from the old.

From Raoul and Carolina, not a further word was heard. Perhaps they had disappeared back into Spitalfields, and if so, thought Polly, there they deserved to stay until Hell took back its own.

One warm September evening, Ellen and Polly were shelling peas. They were sitting on the kitchen steps at Carnarvon Avenue as Constance, fat and entirely content, lay on a blanket staring at the leaves of the apple tree.

"She has been so good to me. They all have." Still very weak, Ellen fumbled the pods open. The *she* was Mrs. Ikin.

"I would never have believed it. Not if someone had told me before." Polly was shelling peas at twice the rate.

"But I still do not understand how you persuaded those boys to help you."

Polly grinned, remembering. She had run into a nearby pub and accosted the biggest of the young men in the taproom. Desperation must have worked. Two of them, a farrier and a cabinetmaker, believed her improbable story and hurried back to the house beside her. Both of them proved useful with their fists.

"What are we to do, Polly? We need the second wage, but I will not send my daughter to a baby farm while I work," Ellen said, turning the discussion to their present woes, as her rosy infant smiled and waved her arms.

Polly laid a hand over Ellen's. "Do not distress yourself. I have been thinking. I shall go to Shene this Sunday. Your aunt and your cousin must be told. And letters, plainly, will not serve. Perhaps they can help."

Ellen's head drooped. "I am so ashamed." She stared unhappily at little Constance. "How can I tell them? Not just about Constance, but about her father, also. All that he did. And tried to do." Her tone was hopeless.

"When I see them, I shall say that your husband died. They need not know more." Polly's tone was brisk. Ellen blanched.

"Bury the past, Ellen. For the sake of your daughter." Polly removed the bowl from Ellen's hands. "Here, let me do the rest."

Ellen blinked. "You always have. You always do. You saved us, Polly. I shall never forget that." The baby kicked her naked legs in the late sun and blew milk bubbles.

Polly said, warmly, "You'd have done it for me." The pair sat in companionable silence. Ellen knew Polly was right. Better that Constance grew up thinking her father dead than that he had tried to sell her.

"He *is* gone from my life. For good. I shall be a widow."

"Amen. And the Lord defend us from his ghost."

Alarmed, Ellen stared at Polly. "You think he will come back?" She scooped up her daughter.

"Not soon. Not after that beating. His nose will heal crooked. Shame. But you should move. *He* might be weak, but she, that Wilkes creature, is not. Vengeful, she'll be."

Ellen rocked Constance. Carnarvon Avenue had been a refuge. She and Polly had even been happy there. To leave was to chance the unknown once more—that hollow, hard-surfaced place that did not want her, or her child. But did she have a choice?

"I am so grateful to you, Polly. More than I can say. Go to Shene. I shall consider, then, what is best to do."

Her friend shook out her apron. "No need for that." Polly tickled Constance beneath her soft chin and the baby gurgled.

Ellen said, "If he comes back, I will not have him. Not ever again."

Polly nodded. "He's dead, Ellen. Gone. Good riddance."

CHAPTER 33

29th of September, AD 1846
16 Carnarvon Avenue
Hackney

My dearest Oriana,

Perhaps my words will never reach you, but if you have
read any part of my previous correspondence—or if you
have not and read only what is written here—please let me
hear from you.

It was a late Sunday evening and Ellen put down her pen to
trim the wick of the lamp, which was unnecessary since it had
not smoked. She knew she was procrastinating. After Polly had
brought the news from Shene, it had taken this long just to begin
the letter. Oriana was her final hope. If, once more, there was no
response from her cousin, that hope would wither and die.

Oriana, it seemed, had married Connor Moncrieff. Their run-
away match had caused great scandal and Oriana was estranged
from her father. As Mrs. Connor Moncrieff, she was living now
at Clairmallon, mistress of the estate since the recent death of
Connor's father. Daisy had not been so lucky. She was trapped at
Shene, still, and rarely seen outside its walls.

Above, in the quiet house, Constance stirred. Polly had
woken, too. Ellen heard her friend singing as she rocked the
cradle, and soon all was still once more. Ellen sighed, and picked
up her pen.

If you have not had my letters, you will not know
that Mama and I stayed almost a year at Richmond with
Madame Angelique. After that, we went to London.
There, my dearest mother most tragically died. I miss her
each day of my life.

Thirteen months in which she had married and been deserted,
and borne a child. And nearly died.

I should explain that I have been very ill. I was married
on the day of my fifteenth birthday, and after my daughter
Constance was born last August, I suffered childbed
fever and lost my husband also. Little Connie is my sole
consolation.

It was true. Raoul *was* lost to her, and her daughter was all, now,
that anchored her to life.

There is so much to tell you—too much to write here.
I think of you so often and am glad indeed to have news of
your happiness. Remember me to your husband? I hope
he knows how lucky he is.

Ellen closed her eyes. Connor Moncrieff. Had she really thought
herself in love with him, a hundred years ago? Love between a man
and a woman. What was it? Was it even possible?

I long to hear more of your life together, dearest
cousin.
Write to me when you can?

All my deepest love.
Ellen d

Ellen began to write her name but paused. Carefully transforming the *d* of *de Valentin* into a *G,* she wrote *Gowan* instead and then blotted what she had written. She stared at her old name and smiled. Tomorrow she would post the letter.

Three days after she wrote to Oriana, Ellen began working on new sketches for Manicore, with Constance asleep beside her. The baby lay in a washing basket lined with calico, her portable day crib. Polly had arrived home the previous evening with an urgent request. The Christmas season loomed and there was a rush on at the mill. Advance orders had to be cut, and designs from last year reworked for the coming spring season. Was Ellen well enough to take back some of the work?

Ellen instantly agreed, though she was frightened. What if the flair was gone? And would Mrs. Ikin permit her to work again from home? As luck would have it, Mrs. Ikin was in fact desperate. She would have been happy to agree that Ellen work in the fork of a tree—if that was what she wanted—so long as the work got done.

In the parlor, Ellen was now carefully rubbing crumbs of new bread across a charcoal smudge to clean the mark from the page. She had always been proud of working cleanly, but her hands would not always obey her mind or her eye for she was unpracticed and weak, still, from illness. That was upsetting enough, but it was galling to be clumsy also. For when Ellen brushed the dirty morsels of bread off the desk, they fell on the face of her sleeping child.

But Constance did not stir. She merely sighed and half-smiled. Ellen was overwhelmed. How beautiful her daughter was, how perfect. And yet she was *his* child also. Did that make a difference?

Ellen softly blew the specks away, and Constance giggled in her sleep. Little, happy Connie was her own person. A flower that had bloomed out of mud. No. It made no difference at all. Ellen Gowan loved her daughter with a piercing, tender ache and always would.

Her mother would have adored her tiny namesake; Edwin, too. That certainty made their daughter happy today.

Humming softly, Ellen returned to her work. She began to enjoy herself at last, and saw the drawing she had made with new eyes. A gown for an evening family party, readily adaptable for grander gatherings if required. Perhaps it was not so bad. Perhaps with a little more work . . .

The knocker crashed against the gorgon's head. Ellen jumped. She was wary of visitors, though the anxious dread of the last weeks was fading.

"Yes?"

"I have a letter for Mrs. Gowan. Special delivery." Ellen opened the door. The postboy looked her up and down, noting that she was pretty, and about his own age. Perhaps she was the maid? He puffed out his thin chest.

Ellen held out her hand. "I am she." The postboy saw the ring. His smile withered. "Beg pardon, Ma'am." Confused, he tipped his hat, and Ellen, with a tiny smile, watched as he hurried away. Maybe it would be nice to be admired again.

But then Ellen Gowan forgot the postboy.

> Clairmallon
> Norfolk
> 1st of October, AD 1846
>
> My dearest Cousin,
>
> I sat down to write to you immediately upon receiving your letter today. In so doing I began—and destroyed— many sheets of paper, since the words on the page seemed poor shadows of what I wished to say. Please, I beg therefore, accept these sentiments as true even if their expression is imperfect.
>
> My poor aunt and your own situation: both are inexpressibly sad. Dearest, dearest cousin, I long to

offer comfort. However, I am distraught that no other letters from you have reached me, and for that I have no explanation. Know that I am thinking of you as I write these words, that I see your face, that I care for you very much.

Soon, I hope, we shall have all the time in the world together. I miss the sister I never had until you came into my life, and I have grieved your absence each day since you fled from Shene. How much we have to say to each other!

But before all, Connor and I hope, so much, that you will consent to come to us here. Ellen, make Clairmallon your home. Allow me, personally, to amend the unhappiness you have suffered. Constance shall grow up here, happy and safe, with the babies we hope to bring into this world. The children who will become her loving friends and companions. Clairmallon is very beautiful and this old house is more than big enough for us all.

Please, dearest cousin, permit us this happy anticipation? Write to me. I shall find it hard to sleep without your reply. Until then, and until we meet again, my dearest love to you and to little Constance.

Your cousin,
Oriana

Ellen sank down beside her sleeping child and stroked her brow. It was too much to take in. She was holding, actually holding, a letter from Oriana. And with it came the offer of a home.

"This is tasty, Ellen. The room looks nice, too."

It was the first really cold night since summer's end, and Ellen had taken particular trouble with the evening meal. Two shillings had been consumed for the baked leg of mutton and a pound of Cream Turtons (densely fleshed potatoes, just then at their best). Along with their own peas and an apple pie, there was even a bottle of burgundy to accompany the feast. Ellen gazed around the drawing room. She would leave so much behind.

Polly asked, brightly, "And so. What is the celebration?" She knew there were things to be said.

Ellen offered Oriana's letter.

"Is this what I think it is?"

Ellen swallowed. "Yes. Oriana replied."

Polly handed it back. "Read it to me."

The paper was stiff and thick but it shook in Ellen's hand as she began to read.

> My dearest Cousin,
>
> I sat down to write to you immediately upon receiving your letter today. . . .

She stopped. Polly gestured. "Read on." Her eyes were suspiciously bright. But Ellen could not continue.

Polly asked, "They want you to go to Clairmallon?"

Ellen nodded.

"Then, you should go. Truly." Her mouth twitched into a smile. "You'll have to say good-bye to the girls, though. And Mrs. Ikin."

"But what about you, Polly? All your kindness to me and—"

"Go and do not look back. These are your people. I know what I am."

"No!" Ellen grabbed Polly's hands. "Come with me."

"Me at a grand house? And it *will* be grand, with a name like that." Polly shook her head. "Can't see me in the drawing room, can you?"

Ellen began to protest, but Polly laid a finger across her friend's lips. "You belong there. I do not. Besides, I've had a taste of making my own way now." Polly held the burgundy up to the light of the fire. The dense scarlet pleased her. "Mrs. Ikin talked to me today. She thinks, well, she as good as said that—"

"You'll be a drafter?" Ellen finished the sentence, joyfully. "Of course! You have been too modest to believe in your own talent."

"You taught me well."

"I?" Ellen was astonished.

Polly nodded. "I watched you. At the mill and here. I shall never have your ability, not for one moment of my life, but Ma taught me persistence. That will do, for now." She kissed Ellen on the cheek. "Go with my blessing." She sniffed and wiped her nose on her apron from habit. They both laughed. "And *that* proves it. No drawing room for me. I should spend my life in mortal fear among all the grand people." But she rubbed her eyes vigorously.

Ellen smiled mistily, and said, "But if," then corrected herself, "*when* I leave, what about this house?"

Polly hesitated. "I shall live here. With Annie, maybe. Or one of the other girls. We could get a small bed in the box room I reckon? Three of us to split the rent. And drafters' wages is better than cutters'. I like this house."

Nodding, Ellen said, "So do I. Very much." They both knew what she meant.

Polly gathered their plates and knives and forks with a rattle. "The little one will like it in the country. More room to run. And a pony, I should not wonder."

"Polly?" Ellen's friend turned in the doorway. "Thank you. For everything. Do not think I shall ever forget."

Polly gazed at Ellen for one long moment. She nodded. "I'll bring the pie." She left Ellen gazing into the fire. The embers crumbled and sparked, and the glow picked up the glint of tears.

Carnarvon Avenue was narrow, and the arrival of the grand landau at number 17 on that sunny October morning caused considerable comment. And that was because the carriage was wider than half the roadway. The neighbors awaited catastrophe with happy anticipation, as wheeled traffic began to bank up before and behind the opulent carriage and voices were raised.

Peering through the window beside the front door, Polly called out, "He is here! No, Constance! Take the key out of your mouth."

Ellen had known before Polly had. She was pinning up her hair when she heard the carriage arrive, and now the day was upon her.

Gazing around the tiny bedroom one last time, Ellen took mental leave of the bed, the press, and even the small mirror reflecting her face beneath the bonnet. To leave this house was to leave Raoul de Valentin, truly, behind. And begin again.

Below, the knocker sounded. "Ellen!" Polly was panicked. And Constance, no doubt because she sensed it, began to cry as the door creaked open. That creak. It had been there from the day he carried her over the threshold.

"Is this the residence of Mrs. Gowan?" a man's voice said, addressing Polly.

Ellen stood at the top of the stairs. She answered the man before Polly could. "I am she. Madame Ellen Gowan." Ellen ignored Polly's raised brows though she flushed a little. She had not told her friend of the change. As to *Madame,* Ellen had no idea why, suddenly, she called herself thus.

The footman stood to one side as his master entered the crowded hall. Ellen's heartbeat accelerated. Since the time and place of this meeting had been confirmed, she had tried to imagine the moment, tried to imagine what Connor Moncrieff would look like now and what *he* would see when he saw her. Yet, sight was one thing and feeling another, for something, unasked for, flared in her chest. An ache. Ellen ignored it. Connor Moncrieff was Oriana's husband. She hoped they would be friends. Friends were more important than lovers.

"Madame Gowan." He had heard her. "I trust you are fully recovered? Mrs. Moncrieff has been most concerned." Connor bowed. Why was he so little changed from the handsome boy at the children's ball? And yet, as he raised his head, she saw that he had the purpose of a man in his eyes, and a man's shoulders and chest. Ellen paused. She raised her skirt a little as she descended the stairs neither fast nor slow. He remembered a child, but she would show him the dignified woman.

"Thank you. I am quite well."

Connor, perhaps because of the *Madame,* picked up one gloved hand and kissed it. He had almost forgotten what Ellen looked like. How old was she? Sixteen or seventeen? This slender, serious-eyed girl might have been twenty-five. Time did strange things to human faces.

"We shall drive by easy stages to Clairmallon, Madame. My wife has instructed me—exhaustively—that I am not to tire you. Or this charming young person." His smile was warm as he waggled his fingers at the baby in Polly's arms. That solemn little face—all eyes—split into a wide, engaging grin, and laughter from all three (even the manservant, who tried not to smile) lifted the tension from Ellen's heart like a troublesome curtain. *All will yet be well.*

"I wish you a pleasant journey." Polly clipped her good-bye to a spare few words. The street was now convincingly blocked and more loud voices could be heard. "You shall find me here when next you come to London, Madame Gowan." Formality was a balm, sometimes.

But Ellen would have none of it. On the step, she folded Polly tightly in her arms. "Soon. Constance and I will visit soon." Connor was surprised by the informality. Embracing the maid?

In the street, a man cursed as he tried to inch past the barouche. Unsuccessfully. "Oy! Shift this thing!"

Polly was scandalized. No manners, these days. "Hold your noise," she shot back. "The lady has a child to think of!"

"Lawrence, the trunk, if you please." Connor spoke quickly. "And the cradle."

Ellen's wooden box was heavier now. Not with her clothes but with toys and her daughter's layette, much of it presents from the girls at Manicore. Even Mrs. Ikin had tatted a shawl, which Ellen received with tears when she'd visited the mill for the last time with Constance in her arms. Polly, with a last kiss, surrendered the baby to her mother. The house would be empty tonight.

As Ellen was escorted to the carriage, she held up Connie's arm so that she, too, could wave to Polly. And then, they were away. Bowling at a good pace from the tangle of carriages they left in their wake, the matched bay geldings pulled away strongly. Wrapped in a fur rug, Ellen breathed deep behind her veil. She would not upset the baby with tears.

And if Ellen had been apprehensive about what she and Connor Moncrieff might talk about, alone on the daylong journey to Norfolk, she was soon at ease. He, tactful and sympathetic, did not press his guest for the details of the last disastrous years. And, noting the wedding band, did not ask why Ellen chose to be called by her maiden name. He found he enjoyed her company, remembering how clever he had thought her from their brief encounters. It was a serious thing to take in two poor relations, but perhaps, with Ellen's arrival, the wounds of the past might begin to heal for Oriana.

Connor waved at the baby and Constance gurgled. An engaging child. He liked children.

It was evening before they arrived at Clairmallon. Seen from a distance, the house did not seem so very big set against an immensity of sky. But that was an illusion.

As the carriage drew closer, sweeping around in a long curve through the home park, the house unfolded like a flower viewed from all sides. Only then could its true extent be understood. A Tudor mansion of warm brick and mullioned windows, cupola-surmounted turrets were set at every turn on the building's perimeter, each one more fanciful than the last, as if the builder's only intention had been to surprise and delight the visitor.

As the horses' heads turned finally for home, and the carriage passed beneath a tower to a central court from which ranges of rooms climbed toward the early stars, Ellen cried out, "How wondrous!"

Every window of the old building had candles lit behind the glass. Connor nodded. "A family tradition. Homecoming for me. Welcome for you."

"Cousin!" Pink silk and attar of roses enveloped Ellen as she stepped down into her cousin's arms. "Let me look at you. And Constance." The baby was asleep, cradled against Ellen's chest.

Entranced, Oriana whispered, "How lovely she is. A rosebud. And so like dearest Aunt Connie." Oriana was right. Ellen's daughter did look like Connie, though she had never seen it so clearly before. There was little of Raoul in her face. Emotion made it hard to speak.

Connor cleared his throat. "Perhaps, wife, we should go in? Your cousin is tired."

"Connor!" Oriana hurried to her husband. Kissing him lovingly, she said, "I am glad indeed that you are home."

But Connor's glance was drawn to Ellen. How wistful and alone she seemed with the child in her arms. He held out his hand to his wife's cousin. "Food and rest are required, Madame. Tomorrow is another day."

Oriana was proud of her compassionate husband. She linked her arm through Ellen's. "Come. There is so much to say. Where shall we begin?"

On the second floor of the old house, three interlinked rooms had been prepared. One held a four-poster bed of carved black oak. For a moment Ellen balked when she saw it, but this, of course, was not the Genesis—the carvings here were only of fruit and flowers. Through a door was a white-painted nursery with a pretty crib and a smiling nursemaid. A small fire crackled in the grate to warm the air for Constance. "Lily, this is Madame Gowan, my dear cousin. And Miss Constance, her daughter."

"Shall you like me to undress Miss Constance, Madame? The

crib is prepared." The girl had a soft voice and a calm presence. Ellen said, gratefully, "Thank you. But can the cradle be moved beside my bed? We like to see each other when we wake."

"Of course, Madame." Lily took Constance from her mother's arms. The baby did not stir. Relieved of the weight of her child, Ellen swayed where she stood.

Through yet another door there was a low-ceilinged room with a window seat looking out over the home park.

"Do you remember how we used to sit in our aerie and watch as the world arrived?" Oriana asked, and Ellen was touched. But the contrast between this pretty room and the spartan nursery at Shene was noticeable. Here, at Clairmallon, soft carpets caressed the feet—no oilcloth—and candles were set in profusion before gilded mirrors on every wall. Beeswax, not tallow, so that the air smelled of honey. Damask curtains of rich dark blue, the same color as the highest parts of the evening sky, were held back by silk cords, and silver bowls had been filled with white and pink roses. Their scent summoned memory.

"There is just enough light to see your new home."

Shadows lay deep across the grass below, but in the distance there was a shining lake, and the sky behind it was caught in fretwork, the branches of great trees. The beauty and the peace caused Ellen's heart to lift. Oriana drew her cousin toward the fire where two chairs, stuffed with feather down, had been arranged. On a side table there was food in profusion.

"Let me serve you while we talk. Then you must sleep. And happily dream."

Happiness. Perhaps it was possible here. Ellen gestured around the pretty room. "You escaped to the haven you deserved." She received the plate of food gratefully from her cousin.

Oriana sat in the other chair with another plate but did not eat. "Mama did not. She is a prisoner still." Staring into the heart of the fire, Oriana said, "Papa was so angry when I told him about Connor, and about our marriage. He blamed Mama."

"*You* told Uncle Isidore?"

Oriana nodded. Her face pinched at the memory. Unconsciously, a hand strayed to her jaw.

Ellen frowned. "He hit you." It was not a question.

Oriana crumbled an uneaten roll with her fingers. "Do you know, I was almost glad? Perhaps that sounds perverse. For such a long time Papa used Mama in this same disgraceful way. And Aunt Connie also." Her gaze was haunted. "Can you forgive me?"

"I forgive *you*? It was not your fault."

"Sometimes, I feel cursed." There was shame in Oriana's voice. "What if, somewhere deep in my heart, I am like him?" Her look was painfully frank. Ellen went to speak but Oriana quickly continued, "Do you know why I did not challenge him in all those years?"

Ellen said, "You were a child, cousin."

Oriana shook her head. "If I was defiant, he punished my mother. But *I* was never abused. Not in that sense."

Ellen nodded. Abuse had many forms. "And yet here you are, married and happy. As you deserve to be."

"I do not know what I deserve." Oriana held out her hand. "But I am grateful to call Clairmallon my home. Connor loves this place. So do I. There is joy here. His ancestors created beauty with each tree they planted, each wall they built. Clairmallon welcomes the terrified stranger. That is what I was when I came here first. I thought my father would drag me back to Shene. Drown me in the shadows once more. And I had dreams, terrible dreams, for months, long after Connor and I were married by special license. Mama knew, of course. She was our only witness. Without her help it could not have happened."

And mine was the sexton in that dusty old church . . .

"Connor had wanted to tell Papa, but I would not let him. I wished to face him, at last. But Papa hit me and then Connor knocked him down. I have not seen my father since that day."

So many echoes between our lives, thought Ellen. "And Aunt Daisy?"

Oriana stared at her hands. "I write to her, but my letters are not answered. I do not know if she is alive or . . ."

Ellen leaned forward and said, urgently, "You would know, Oriana. You would feel it."

"Do you think so? Through his solicitor, Connor wrote to my father inviting Mama to come to us. Just for a visit. That letter was returned, the seal unbroken."

Ellen mused, "My letters and Mama's . . . We wrote often."

Oriana broke in earnestly, "I swear to you on the heads of my unborn children that I never received even one."

Ellen said, gently, "I should so like to forget the past. Or, at least, think of other things. Happier things."

Oriana said, shakily, "I, too. But now we have the present. And each other."

Part Three

CHAPTER 34

A SIXTH BIRTHDAY is suffocatingly important. And for Constance Gowan, waking in the half dark, it was impossible that this day of the year, most of all, could ever begin too early. A cock crowed and on that signal birds of all kinds stirred in the trees Connie could not see. Blackbirds, starlings, rooks, and somewhere, quite close, a peacock. Shivering, she ran from her bed to pull the heavy curtains back. The rings on the curtain rods chattered together but she was strong enough. Just.

Before her, the low hills were turned pink where sky met land, and the emerging sun flashed black trees and gray hedges from gold to green. As she watched, the dark lake at the end of the garden became a sheet of silver. The fairy tales that her mother read aloud spoke of magical lands, but for Connie none would ever possess the enchantment of Clairmallon's garden in the rising light.

The little girl unlatched a window and leaned out beyond the sill. She knew it was forbidden, but the air smelled of cut grass and earth, and below, parading the length of the stone-flagged terrace, was a peacock. As if just for her, he spread his shimmering tail in a wheel of turquoise and green and black-blue.

Little Connie rested her chin on her hands. The house was asleep but she was awake. This was her birthday morning and all the world was hers. She sighed. Today was good.

The child turned back, her eyes adjusting as dim shapes resolved to familiar objects. The dark mass in the corner became her dollhouse. It had eight rooms and a servants' hall. Uncle Connor had made all the furniture, and Aunt Oriana, the curtains and the rugs. Her own mama had made the tiny paintings on the walls and dressed the family of dolls who lived there. Connie frowned as she inspected each little room. She'd put everyone to bed the night before but, somewhere, someone was sobbing. The soft hairs on her forearms stood up. Had the dolls come alive? But they were not the source of the sound. It came from outside her room.

A moment later, Connie turned the handle on her door with both hands. She could hear the noise more clearly now.

A house as old as Clairmallon moves in the night, and some of the sounds were comforting, for she had heard them all her life. But human distress Connie had rarely heard. Like a pin to a magnet she was drawn onward. *Hot. Getting hotter.* She had played the game often enough in daylight. It was no more frightening in the half dark. Was it?

The sound was clear though not constant. It came from beyond the door that she faced now. Her hand was pale enough to see in the dark as she reached up.

"Mummy?" She turned the handle. "Are you crying?" The curtains over Ellen's casements were drawn back. They fluttered in the first breeze of the morning.

Ellen sat up in her bed. "Crying? No."

"Are you sure?"

Her mother said, smiling, "Of course. But here *you* are. Happy birthday, my darling girl." Connie skipped to the bed and clambered up, relieved of confusion. Ellen made a nest among the sheets and blankets. This was a familiar ritual.

Ellen whispered, confidentially, "Six. This is a very great age."

"Yes. And after, I shall be seven. And then eight." Connie sighed happily. Ellen said, solemnly, "With even more to come. Soon you will be an old lady indeed."

"But not as old as you, Mama!" They giggled as Ellen hugged her cheeky daughter.

The morning grew lighter, and piece by piece the furniture took back its substance from the night. The edges of a chair and then the line of an armoire's pediment emerged from shadow. Star-like, a crystal jar briefly glittered, and at last, the great black bed appeared in the mirror. Ellen and Connie waved to the girls in the pier glass, and the girls waved back.

"Your eyes are rather red, Mama." Connie touched Ellen's face gently. "Did you have a bad dream?"

"Yes, my darling. Very bad. That happens sometimes."

"You will be happy at my party, though?"

"Certainly! How could I not be?"

Connie hugged Ellen. "Is it time now?"

"Soon."

Connie slid down from the high mattress. It was a long way to the floor. As she ran to the door, Ellen called out, "But first, look in the armoire!"

The little girl turned. "A surprise?"

Ellen nodded solemnly.

Squeaking with anticipation, Connie ran to the mirrored cupboard.

"Shall I help you?" Ellen had draped the dressing gown around her shoulders.

Connie could just reach the handle on the door. "No. I can. Oh! Mama, is this for me?"

Ellen was standing at Connie's shoulder as the little girl brought out the dress—pale pink and sage green silk. Ellen had sewn it herself. "Yes, my darling. Here is your party dress." She held it up against her daughter. "I had a dress for my birthday once, just like this one. Your granny sewed it for me. And slippers, too. Your grandfather made them." From behind her back she held out a pair of slippers fashioned from the offcuts of the dress, just as her own had been.

"Granny made your birthday dress?" Connie loved to hear stories of Ellen's childhood. The mother met her daughter's bright eyes in the mirror. "Yes, my darling. And I wanted your dress to look as much like mine as I could make it." She touched the silk gently. "Granny liked pretty things. We can show Aunt Oriana and Uncle Connor as soon as you are dressed."

"Will they think me pretty?"

Ellen laughed. "Very pretty. You will be the prettiest girl at your party, of that I am certain."

"Did you have a party, Mama?"

"For my thirteenth birthday? Yes." Ellen busied herself closing the door of the armoire. "Come along, we must be quick or we shall miss breakfast. And presents."

"Presents?" No further encouragement was necessary. As Ellen washed and dressed her impatient daughter, she thought of what she had to say, today, to Connor and Oriana.

Oriana touched Ellen's arm as she poured lemon squash for a line of thirsty children. Both cousins were flushed from blindman's bluff, still being played on the lawn in front of the house. "Connor has told me. You wish to leave Clairmallon?"

"It is not my *wish* to leave you. I love this family, and this place."

"Why then? Connor said you spoke of becoming a governess?"

"Perhaps." Children shrieked and fled as Connie, blindfolded, stumbled on, arms outstretched.

"But you would be so unhappy." Oriana was horrified.

On the other side of the lawn, maids were laying out the birthday feast on long trestles in the shade of the lime trees.

Connor, conferring with the harassed butler as children surged toward the tables, waved—the sign for *We need your help!*

Oriana waved back. Ellen's glance followed Connie as the little girl fell into a rowdy, happy heap with her friends.

Oriana spoke softly. "You must wish for your own home. I do understand. We could give a ball. There are so many eligible young men."

"I do not wish to marry again." Ellen spoke quickly. "Oriana, I

am more than grateful to you both, but I must support my daughter. For that I need independence."

Oriana found confrontation difficult, but she was courageous.
"I know you are proud, Ellen. However, I suspect you judge your
situation here too harshly."

Ellen stopped her cousin. "It has been delightful being your
companion. Please believe me."

Oriana was hurt. "You are not my *companion* in that sense. You
are my dearest friend and cousin. And luckier than you know."

Ellen followed her cousin's glance. Connie. Eight years of marriage to Connor had brought Oriana two miscarriages and a still-
born son, an enduring sadness to everyone at Clairmallon. Oriana
murmured softly, almost to herself, "What should we do if Connie
went away?"

Ellen had no answer. She pointed to a carriage just then rounding a corner of the house. "A late arrival?"

"Very late." Oriana shaded her eyes.

"Cousin?" Ellen was puzzled. Oriana's grip had tightened on
her arm. Blanched white, she whispered, "Look at the crest on
the door." The closed carriage bowled closer, and Ellen saw the
escutcheon clearly.

As the brougham drew up, Oriana backed away, a hand to her
mouth. "Shene."

Ellen clutched her cousin's hand. "Your father cannot harm
you. If it is he, he has no power at Clairmallon." But Ellen moved
in front of her cousin. Could it really be Isidore?

Connor hurried to the unexpected visitor.

Oriana was breathless. "Call him back!"

Too late. Ellen said, softly, "Do not be afraid, Oriana. Look."
In the distance, Connor bowed over a gloved hand emerging from
the carriage. Suddenly her cousin was running as a black-gowned
woman emerged. "Mama!"

Ellen hung back. She watched as her aunt, gaunt and a little
stooped, opened her arms. Watched as Oriana ran to her, crying.

Watched, too, as Connor embraced his wife and her mother together. Ellen turned away.

Clasped in Daisy's arms, Oriana raised her head. "Where is Ellen?"

But Ellen had retraced her steps toward the picnic tables where the children, oblivious, were eating and shrieking in equal measure. She was not jealous, or envious. She was alone, that was all. But Constance ran to her and tugged her hand.

"Mama! Come and see the presents. Look! So many!"

Ellen stroked her daughter's curls. "So there are."

Constance was suspicious. She touched Ellen's face. "This time you *are* crying."

"Me? No. Or if I am . . ."

"Your mama cries for joy, Constance." Oriana was suddenly there, with Daisy at her side, and Connor just behind.

"Child. Dearest, dearest niece." Daisy hurried to Ellen and cupped her face in her hands. "How I have yearned, all these years, to know that you were safe. And now I find you at Clairmallon with your little daughter." She turned her soft, tired eyes toward Connie.

Ellen held out her hand. "Constance, this is your great-aunt. Aunt Oriana's mama."

But Constance Gowan, though she curtsied, was exasperated. "Great Aunt Daisy, would *you* like to see my presents? I can interest no one else."

"He is dead. Truly?"

It was evening, and in the last of the long twilight, Ellen, Daisy, and Oriana slowly paced the terrace.

"Yes. An apoplexy." Daisy gave no further explanation. In the silence that followed, the night garden seemed noisy from an orchestra of frogs. The trio reached a stone seat, and with unspoken agreement, sat.

"Did he suffer?" Oriana asked.

A further pause. Daisy answered, "I do not know. I was not there. He died in the library. Warwick found him."

Oriana said, without emotion, "I cannot mourn him. Or forgive him."

Ellen spoke half out loud. "Perhaps it is better to forget."

Daisy shook her head. "He did much damage to us all. If my sister died because she was cast out, then . . ."

Ellen said nothing. How hard platitudes were. She would not speak them.

Oriana said, "Will you live with us here, Mama? Ellen and Connie and Connor and I? You have been so long without your family." She did not look at her cousin.

Daisy pressed her daughter's hand. "Bless you. I shall stay a little while, but there is much to resolve. Shene, for instance. Perhaps, at last, conscience moved your father. It seems Isidore broke the entail. He made you the heir."

Oriana stared at her mother. "How?"

Daisy shrugged. "He was a lawyer, child. And Isidore was nothing if not well connected."

Oriana's face darkened. "But you were left nothing in his will? Not even a lifetime interest?"

Daisy did not answer.

Oriana stood, her face full of emotion. "We shall sell that house, Mama, and everything of his. *Then* you will have the means to live as you choose." Despair broke through. "Why was my father so cruel?"

Ellen glanced at her aunt. Cruelty. Weakness. Perhaps they were the same. In effect.

Daisy replied, "I do not know. But he shut himself away among his books after you left Shene. We hardly saw each other. That, I think, speaks of loss and of love."

Oriana grimaced as her mother continued, wearily, "In some sense, you were the rope that moored him to life. What he felt for you gave him hope, I think, that more was possible. You were not, in the end, just a thing. I think he discovered his heart was broken, when you left." Her voice was terribly sad.

Oriana broke in. "Heart? He had no heart. But am I like him? Does God wish me to be barren because I am evil, as he was?"

Daisy, appalled, glanced at Ellen. "No!" She took Oriana's hands in hers. "There are always reasons. Your father was strange, but his childhood was very violent and sad. Something was twisted in him, the result of that early, brutal existence." Daisy's voice broke as she struggled on. "And yet, I never stopped believing in all the years of our marriage that I could help him to love. If only he had permitted me to do that."

Ellen murmured, "I pity my uncle. I really do."

Daisy nodded. For a moment she said nothing. And then, "But we three remain. We have one another."

Ellen's eyes filled with tears. That unconscious echo of her father's words on the day he died cut deep.

Offering comfort, Daisy touched Ellen's hand. "The future is a different place, niece, a happier place. And we can dwell there, if we choose to, rather than in the past."

CHAPTER 35

THE LAKE at Clairmallon had been made, not created. At the very end of the garden, past the terrace and the yew hedges, beyond the walled orchard and the herbaceous borders, it lay cupped in a bowl of grassy slopes.

The day following the party, the wind accompanied Ellen as she walked beside the water. It billowed her skirts and, tugging at her bonnet, seemed to demand attention. Ellen stared at the agitated surface of the lake. "What would you say to me, if you could speak?" The water fled from the wind, escaping among the reed beds and setting them to rock and bend and whisper.

Ellen faced the sky and turned in a circle, her arms spread wide. "What is my future? Should I leave this place?" She was tortured by indecision. She did not blame her mother for what had happened at Shene, or her aunt, but dependency and lack of choice had created the cascading disasters that had shaped her life and filled it with secrets that even her cousin did not know.

Ellen loved Oriana dearly, and Connor had become her friend. It seemed odd, now, that she had once been so jealous of her cousin. But life at Clairmallon could not drift on forever. If her daughter was to be an independent woman, she must be properly educated. For that, more than the wages of a governess were required. But what should she do? What *could* she do?

"Set up in a business?" Ellen was taken aback.

"Yes. It was Oriana's idea." Connor patted his wife's hand. On a warm evening some days later the three were strolling beside the now-tranquil lake. "You need a proper occupation, cousin. Or that is what my wife believes." His eyebrows rose humorously.

Oriana interrupted her husband. "What have you been about all of this last year, Ellen? And the years before, since you came here?"

Ellen gazed toward the distant hills. "Drawing. And painting, I suppose. Teaching Connie."

"No. You have been making clothes." Oriana displayed the skirts of her gown, holding them wide to prove her point. Blue-and-white-striped paper-silk rustled. The gown, modeled on a French Bergère dress of the previous century, was charmingly fresh with its muslin shawl and ribboned half sleeves. Oriana had worn it at the party. She continued, "*And* designing all that you make. Besides cutting the patterns, choosing the stuffs and the buttons and the trimmings, and I do not know what else. Well, there you have it. Such artistry is rare and deserves support."

Connor nodded, tolerantly. "Even I, mere mortal male, must agree." He was sincere. Oriana's cousin was never less than elegantly dressed, even if she wore only black or white or gray.

Oriana continued, enthusiastically, "At the party all the little girls were *so* envious of Connie's dress, and their mothers of mine. And it would not quite be trade. As I said, you are an artist." The three had reached the margins of the water. The breeze was stilled on that breathless evening.

Ellen stared out across the lake, considering. "A happy thought. But what you suggest is impossible. It would not work here."

Oriana was dismayed. She turned to Connor. "Will you speak sense to her, husband?"

Connor cleared his throat. "Why not at Clairmallon, cousin?"

Ellen picked up a black pebble, smooth and round. Bending, she cast it skipping across the unmoving surface. The ripples left behind widened out in ever larger circles.

"What you suggest would amuse me, certainly, and entertain

the gentry hereabouts. For a time." She picked up another stone. It skipped farther before it sank. "But a business, a real business of fashion? London is the place for such an enterprise. Perhaps, in time, I might rival Paris and Mr. Worth." The tone was ironic.

Oriana said, troubled, "But that would be a very hard road. And what would happen to Connie in London? The city is filthy and crowded and she so loves Clairmallon. This is her home."

Ellen smiled, a little crookedly. "Children adapt, cousin. I could hire a nursemaid and live above the shop, as many families do. We would manage." Ellen gazed into the soft distance, seized with a vision of a future that she had not considered until now. "But this is fantasy. I do not have the capital."

Oriana stared at Connor. Neither of them had expected this response. He cleared his throat. "If this is your true desire, Ellen, I could back you."

Oriana began to speak but could not continue. Her heart wailed, *Constance.*

Ellen, for once oblivious of Oriana's distress, said, quickly, "But I could only consider such a thing if we were partners. An investment. A real one. Not a charity scheme." She winced. Why be so blunt?

Connor Moncrieff picked up a pebble himself. Pitched across the lake, it sank short of the others. "You are certain you want this?" He turned to meet Ellen's gaze.

"Yes." And suddenly it was true. This *was* what she wanted. It had been her dream.

A long moment, and Connor Moncrieff nodded. "Very well."

"No!"

Ellen and Connor stared at Oriana.

"My dear, do not upset yourself."

Oriana pushed Connor's hand away. "Ellen, you cannot do this to your daughter. How can you be so cruel? To take her away from all she has known and loved? To grow up in some dark slum without sunshine, without her pets? Without this garden?" The impetuous words sank into silence. Oriana whispered, "I shall miss her so."

Ellen said, gently, "I must decide what is best for Connie, cousin."

Oriana twisted her hands together, almost too distressed to speak. "Of course. She is your daughter." She sobbed a breath. "But if you go, leave her here with us. I beg you, Ellen. For Connie's sake. You will work so hard to become established, and I could not bear to think she might cry herself to sleep, homesick and lonely and in the care of strangers."

Bald words, which came with the shock of cold water.

How ironic that Ellen wanted, no, *needed,* to work to secure the future for Connie and yet might break her daughter's heart.

"Will you think on what I have said, cousin? Please?"

Oriana was rarely so persistent or so brave, but Connor spoke over her. "We will not mention this again, Oriana. Come." He took his wife's hand and led her toward the house.

But Ellen called after them, "Wait!" Catching up to Connor, she said, "Is this offer of investment a real one?"

Connor nodded. "It is."

Ellen swallowed. "Very well. Oriana, I shall think of what you have said. You shall have my answer in the morning."

"Have you said your prayers?" Connie was in her nightdress, putting her dolls to bed. She bent her head to the smallest doll and smiled approvingly. "You are a very good girl. But if you should wake in the night, do not worry. Mama and I are here." She glanced at Ellen, waiting to read her a story.

"Are you ready, Connie?" Ellen turned back the counterpane and patted her daughter's pillow.

Connie sighed. "I do hate trying to sleep while it is still light, Mama. Besides, I am not at all tired." Yawning, she scrambled under the covers.

Ellen laughed. "Of course not." She settled herself beside her daughter. She had a copy of the Mabinogion on her lap, and she smoothed open its thick pages.

"Fairy tales." Connie pouted.

Ellen was a little hurt. "I thought you liked them?"

Connie snuggled against her mother's side. "I do, but Aunt Oriana reads me all sorts of things. Not just legends and magic."

Ellen gently closed the book. "Shall we talk, instead?"

The little girl nodded. "What shall we talk about, Mama?"

Ellen's heart jumped. "I do not know. You choose."

Connie shrugged. "Why are you unhappy, Mama?"

Ellen stifled a gasp.

Her daughter continued, "It is different for Aunt Oriana. She's sad because of the babies. But"—Connie groped for Ellen's hand—"I do not know why you cry."

At a loss, Ellen finally said, "Mummy has a lot to think about. That is all."

Connie nodded. "It is because you are an adult. Uncle Connor said it is easier being a child. But I do not agree with him sometimes."

Ellen blinked. "No?"

"Yes. I mean no." Connie tried not to giggle. This was a serious conversation. "*He* said not to worry about it. That everyone is sad sometimes. But I do worry. I want you to be happy, Mama. We all do."

Out of the mouths of babes. Ellen drew her daughter close. "And I want *you* to be happy, too, Constance. Really happy. That is why I must make difficult decisions."

Connie yawned and closed her eyes. "Well then, I think you should go to London. I can stay here with Aunt Oriana and Uncle Connor." Ellen gasped, and one blue eye reopened. "You will come back, though?"

"Of course, my darling. If I go." *How did you know?*

Connie said, matter-of-factly, "I was playing by the lake. You did not see me when you were there with my aunt and uncle. Yes, I know I am not supposed to be there by myself but it was hot."

On any other night, Ellen would have questioned her daughter. Why was she so far from the house and alone near the water? Why had she not told them of her presence? But she did not. Instead she said, "But you might not like it if I go."

Connie said consideringly, "You will be more unhappy if you do not. I like it best when you smile. Besides, Clairmallon is our home. You have said you will come back." Breathing softly, she slid into sleep.

"And so, your trip was successful?" To stay out of the way, Oriana was sitting on Ellen's bed, as her own maid, Frances, and Lily— Connie's nursemaid—methodically stripped the armoire and the clothes presses of Ellen's gowns and hats, her mantles and shawls, gloves, boots, and shoes. All the things she had accumulated in her years at Clairmallon.

"The day gowns can go in my old box, Frances."

The maid eyed the battered wooden trunk dubiously. "I might use extra tissue if you are certain, Madame?"

Ellen, distracted, nodded. "Yes. But the heavier garments should be placed in the traveling trunk, along with my spare winter boots." She frowned. "I am sorry, cousin. What did you say?"

Oriana said, patiently, "The London visit? Connor tells me you found premises?"

"Yes. It took a little time. Careful, Lily! The feathers will break." Ellen rescued a bonnet just in time, removing the plumes so that they would not be crushed when the bandbox lid was closed. She stared around her bedroom. "This is all I shall take. If you will call the men, the boxes may be carried down to the wagon."

She joined Oriana on the bed as the maids hurried from the room. "You have been so generous, Oriana. All these clothes!"

Her cousin chuckled. "You made most of them, I merely purchased the material."

"But still."

"Now, Ellen, we have been over this. You owe us nothing. It is my family that owes *you* thanks." Constance. The child's name hovered unspoken. "But tell me more. Describe the house. Connor was scant with detail."

Ellen laughed. "A house? It is not as we understand a house to be. But Connor was so helpful. It would not have been possible in so short a time without all that he did. He interviewed commercial agents each day we were at the hotel, but the key was placing the advertisement in the *Times*. And that was his idea." She retrieved her reticule from the mantelpiece. "Here it is."

Oriana took the proffered clipping and read, "A lady wishes to establish a business as a dressmaker of the highest order. Practical premises with living quarters, a showroom and a workroom are required in the vicinity of Piccadilly, The Strand, or similar. An excellent rental will be paid for a long lease. All correspondence to be addressed immediately to Mr. Connor Moncrieff, care of the Grosvenor Hotel, etc., etc."

Oriana folded up the slip of paper. Handing it back, she asked, "And were there many replies?"

Ellen nodded. "Enough. And the third we inspected was entirely suitable. Number 8a, Vine Street, Piccadilly. The family accommodation is spacious, for a back-lane building, with three bedrooms and a sitting room on the second floor. There are several rooms, too, in the attic. Excellent storage for the business and a playroom also. On the ground floor is a wide hallway for the clients to wait in, a large fitting room, and behind, kitchens, and a room that can be adapted for cutting. There is also a dayroom for the girls who will work with me. And even a tiny garden with a stable near the washhouse. All that could be required."

"A back lane?" Oriana was dubious.

Ellen shrugged. "But a back lane in a very good part of town for this business, I do assure you. It will provide all we need as Polly and I establish the enterprise."

"Polly?" Oriana was puzzled. Then she remembered. "Was this the girl who—?"

Ellen finished the sentence. "Worked at Manicore's? Yes. She was our maid at Wintermast, and then we shared Carnarvon Avenue." She paused. Polly had agreed, immediately, to join this new venture when Ellen had written to her, which cheered Ellen greatly. "Polly saved my life and Connie's, too, after she was born. I would not think of starting this without her. She will live in with me."

Oriana digested that slightly defiant statement. "As your maid?"

"As my friend."

Oriana's eyebrows ascended, which Ellen chose not to see. "Polly is a fully trained cutter and drafter now. An asset to our business." She colored slightly at Oriana's level glance. "She is a very nice person. And clever."

Oriana murmured, "I am certain she is all you say she is." She stood. "We must dress for dinner. That is, if you have not packed quite everything for London?" She smiled warmly.

Ellen also stood. And swallowed. "I want to thank you, Oriana. You were right about Clairmallon. This house does work its magic on terrified strangers, of which I was one. I am very grateful."

At the door, Oriana turned. "You were never a stranger to me, Ellen. Clairmallon will always be your home." She held Ellen's gaze for a moment. "Do not forget that. Go away slowly, hurry back."

"What is my new room like in London, Mama?"

It was the night of Ellen's farewell dinner and candles had been lit in every window of Clairmallon, just as they were when she and Connie had first arrived. Daisy had returned for the occasion, and the child had been permitted to stay up and eat with the adults. "You will have to wait and see."

But this was not a satisfactory answer. Connie was suddenly alarmed. "But it is nice, is it not?"

Ellen hugged her daughter. "Of course! I shall count the days to your visit. I have already made pink curtains for you, and there is a nice new bed as well."

Connie sighed, relieved. "And *that* is just as it should be." Unconsciously droll, she made the adults laugh. And the tension of things unsaid dispersed like smoke.

"The business, Ellen."

Oriana laid a hand on Connor's arm. "Ellen's *salon,* husband. *Business* sounds so mercantile."

Ellen spluttered into her wine. What was this venture but mercantile?

Connor continued, "Very well. What is your salon to be called, cousin?"

Ellen smiled at her bright-eyed daughter. "Chez Miss Constance. That has a nice ring."

Connie beamed. "For me?" Ellen nodded. "Certainly. You will be famous."

Saucer eyed, the child squeaked, "Famous? Did you hear that, Aunt Oriana?" She danced from her chair and skipped around the table, chanting, "Famous! Famous! Famous!"

Beneath the laughter, Oriana touched Ellen's hand and murmured, "We will make this work between us, cousin. Connie is our greatest concern, yours and mine. I will never be her mother, but I am her loving friend. And nothing is forever."

Connie stopped by Ellen's chair and plumped herself on her mother's knee. She looked from face to face. "You were talking about me." She patted Ellen's cheek. "It is an adventure going to London, Mama. You will have lots of stories to tell. And you can bring me surprises, when you come home." Healthy self-interest saved the moment.

Ellen said, brightly, "Certainly! No more fairy stories for you, Miss Constance. In my letters you shall hear all about the people I meet and what I do in London. And Aunt Oriana shall read them to you." She swallowed. This was hard, now the moment was close.

Connor cleared his throat. "Mother-in-Law, you wished to give us a toast?"

Daisy nodded. She raised her glass. "To dearest Ellen. And to Constance." She bowed to her great-niece, who blushed at being singled out by the nice old lady she hardly knew. "The future begins tonight. We will remember this moment all our lives—even you, Constance—and the happiness it portends. It is my heartfelt wish that Chez Miss Constance is the success it deserves to be, and that, indeed, you *both* become famous. To Madame Ellen Gowan and Miss Constance Gowan." Connor and Oriana echoed Daisy's words.

As the toast was drunk, Ellen put her arms around Constance. Could she really do it? Could she face that pitiless, teeming place and not just survive, but prosper? And Raoul. Perhaps he lived there still. In all these years he had never attempted to find her. Perhaps he really was dead. Sometimes she looked back on Richmond and London as if viewing someone else's life. Angelique had been such a good and kind person, but her son bewildered her still. She had thought she loved him, that fate had given her a man to trust and cherish, but she had been wrong and her mother right.

"Are you happy now, Mama?" Connie snuggled against her mother. Ellen kissed her daughter and they shared a long look.

"Sometimes joy and sadness feel like the same thing." She pushed back an errant curl from Connie's eyes. "But yes, I am happy now." She smiled at her daughter. There were times when Connie looked like her other grandmother, Angelique.

One of Ellen's lasting regrets was that she never made contact with Raoul's mother after he left her. She had not had the strength, then, to say what had to be said. And Connie knew so little of the true circumstances of her birth. How could Ellen lay to rest those ghosts of loss and longing, and not tell her daughter the truth?

CHAPTER 36

"I DO NOT think we can afford another cutter, Polly. Besides, Dorcas is quick and good at her work."

Polly said, a touch stubborn, "Another cutter will double our capability. I know just the girl. I have my eye on her at Manicore."

"Mrs. Ikin has been very good to me. I will not take her staff."

Ellen and Polly were in the workshop dayroom at the back of the house in Vine Street. It was a cold mid-February day, and at seven the morning was still dark. In half an hour Dorcas would arrive to begin the working day, but meantime Polly and Ellen warmed their hands holding thick china cups of tea.

"No. We need more commissions first." Ellen tapped the order book that lay open between them.

Polly inspected the pot. It was nearly empty. She got up to retrieve the kettle from the trivet. "Only five months and we have completed seventy-three orders, have twenty on foot with more expected. *And* you've dressed your first bride. I would say that's achievement enough to give you confidence." She poured boiling water onto the already used tea leaves. They would stretch to another brew. "Word is growing. Soon there will be a flood of orders. We shall need that cutter then, nothing more certain in this world."

"Flood first, cutter later. We can manage at the present." They eyed each other. Polly blinked first.

"Is there more tea?" asked Ellen, bland as you like.

Polly poured and tried again. "I'm only saying, spend money, make money. That is what Manicores always did."

"But they have deeper pockets. *Much* deeper." Ellen rubbed her eyes, tired from late-night sewing.

Polly shot back. "Not at the beginning. Had to take a gamble then. Paid off for the old rascal though, did it not? You have backers. Rich ones. Ask for more." It was still amazing to Polly that Ellen had walked away from her comfortable life in the country to take up the challenge of trade again. Especially since the cost had been so great, in spirit and in flesh, all those years ago.

Ellen said, pleasantly, "No, Polly. They have been more than generous with establishing capital. I shall be happier to increase our trade and I will not borrow more to do it." But she worried at her bottom lip. A large order of materials was expected, and the terms were payment on delivery.

Polly got up. She would say no more. For the present. "If we finish the walking-out dress for Mrs. Mackenzie today, I could ask for payment by the end of the week. Nothing like the wife of a prosperous butcher to spread the word among her friends. I'll go and open the workroom for the girls."

Ellen nodded as her friend left the room. She must write quickly to Constance before the working day began. It had been three days since her last letter. She blew on her fingers. The room was still icy, as the fire had not been long lit. Should she be extravagant and add more coals? Ellen smiled faintly. She was out of practice with frugality.

Clairmallon. It was always with her. There was her small desk. On it was the silver writing stand that Oriana had given her as a going-away gift. "Think of us, dearest cousin. And write often." Ellen touched it with a gentle hand. Oriana's gift had come to signify good luck. She often had ideas sitting there at night when all the world was quiet. Gowns and skirts and bodices, jackets and coats and bonnets arrived in her head and almost drew themselves.

Though she was tired, Ellen smiled as she began to write.

My darling Connie,

Just a little letter this morning to say that we are very busy here, but not too busy to think of you.

Do you know, I miss the silence of Clairmallon? I look forward to being in the garden with you very soon. Here there is always noise. But it is useful noise, too, for if a man walks by and calls out for me to buy his pies—oyster pies are very good in London—another will have milk for sale, or hot chestnuts. Fish, too, comes in a handcart to my door, and skinned rabbits—"Caught in the country, Missus!" Or so they say.

And I had a rat-man come by yesterday. I thought he wished me to buy *his* rats at first. But no. He was offering to catch them for me. I do not think we have rats in Vine Street, but I know there are mice in our kitchen. On your next visit, shall we get a kitten? Would you like that? I should. And when she grows up—or, perhaps, he—the mice will have a worthy opponent.

Polly sends her love to you as well as me. She is very excited to know that you will be coming to visit us again soon.

Ellen smiled. Constance was a lucky child. All the women in her life adored her, including Polly. Only she knew how many evenings Polly had labored over the pretty coverlet that she'd embroidered as a surprise for Connie's bed.

A crash sounded. The knocker. Ellen frowned. It was early still. Who could it be? She hurried to the hall to find Polly staring, transfixed, at the panels of the front door. They visibly shook as the knocker descended again.

"Well? Open it before it breaks."

Mute, Polly shook her head. She was quite white. Alarmed,

Ellen peered from behind the walking costume displayed on a dressmaker's form in their bowed front window to see who their visitor was.

A brougham, a large one drawn by four matched chestnuts, was blocking Vine Street. There was a coachman upon the box and a very large footman on the back plate, and both these brave souls were liveried in excellent black broadcloth. By their expressions, it was obvious that they considered themselves very superior persons.

This was a considerable development. "Open the door, Polly."

"Very well, Madame." But she hesitated. Polly was rarely abashed, but suddenly she was a maid again, a country girl, gauche in the presence of London toffs.

Ellen clasped her hands together. She, too, was intimidated but better at hiding the fact. "Quickly, Polly." In that moment she was very glad to have spent more money than they had on the appointments of the business. The lacquer on the door was lustrous, and the fittings of the lock and knocker impeccably shiny. These at least were brave. Yet this elegance meant nothing to the man who was revealed by the opened door.

From a position above their heads, another footman stared down at Ellen and Polly with a half sneer, one eyebrow raised almost to the brim of his glossy hat.

"Is this the *Hes*tablishment of Madame Ellen Gowan?"

Ellen said, pleasantly, "It is. I am she." She refrained, but only by swallowing the word whole, from adding *Sir*. The footman sniffed. "My mistress kindly offers to speak to you."

The profile of the visitor in the brougham was turned away. Perhaps Ellen was expected to hurry across the laneway to the window of the carriage and transact business in the open air.

Ellen said, politely, "It is warm within. Please convey my compliments and my invitation directly to your mistress. I do not like to see her kept waiting in the open street."

She heard Polly swallow a gasp, but Ellen did not move. A sullen nod was her reward. Turning his back, the footman stalked the bare six feet that separated her door from the carriage.

By now a market dray piled high with baskets had stopped behind the carriage; their lane was a backway to Covent Garden. "Shove on, there!"

Ellen smiled charmingly at the carter as she muttered, "Quickly, Polly. Ask the man to hold his horses. Only for a moment." The carter was big and not best pleased. But Polly hurried to the wheel of the dray. Gazing up winningly, she said, "Good day to you, Sir. . . ."

Ellen tried not to show the strain while she waited, but her heart bumped in her chest as she (discreetly) strained to hear what was said by the lady in the carriage. Eventually, and very slowly, the footman procured a stepping block and reached up to open the door with one gloved hand.

The feathers on the lady's bonnet advanced from the carriage first. The dense black of best jet, they adorned the brim of the highest-crowned bonnet Ellen had yet seen on a human head. Very elegant, very French, was the effect, for the ebony straw had broad ribbons of mint green tied beneath. The face of the bonnet's owner, when revealed, was not quite in its first youth, although it was appealing.

Ellen fervently hoped that she made a stylish impression on her visitor. Her sharply waisted, ivory-colored gown was of wool crepe—a good cloth for draping over skirt hoops. Ellen also wore a Basquine jacket of gray-and-black-striped silk; light, yet warm. These garments had been among the first productions of her new workroom. Her skirt fluttered suddenly and a freezing draft declared that her ankles, and possibly more, must have been visible.

The carter, cajoled to friendliness by Polly, called out, "Very nice, Missus. Werry pretty!" Ellen giggled. And was mortified. Blushing, she smoothed her errant clothing.

At the sight, their visitor paused, then descended to the road. Her expression changed. She smiled at the man. "I do agree. And

I thank you for your patience, Sir." Her voice was high and clear and, as she waved her coachman on, the humor was unmistakable. "Michael, wait at the street's mouth so that we shall not inconvenience this gentleman—and this lady—one moment more. When I am finished here, you will be called."

Graciously inclining her head as she entered Ellen's house, their visitor declared, "And so. You are Madame Ellen? I am Lady Hawksmoor. Your work interests me."

Lady Hawksmoor? All Ellen could find to say was, "You honor my house." Hoping that her bow was sufficiently graceful, she stepped back indicating the salon. *My work. How had she seen it?* "Will you be seated? And perhaps we may offer refreshment?"

Lady Hawksmoor gazed dispassionately around the salon before selecting a Hepplewhite sofa on which to sit. The one good piece in a stylish but inexpensively furnished room. But the space, if interesting, was small, and Ellen instantly saw it as her visitor would. All an effect of color and light and pretty fabrics, with no real substance. No *luxury*. Lady Hawksmoor would be used to luxury.

"Thank you. Tea, if you have it." Polly, falling back into a familiar role, curtsied and sped away. Perhaps there were refreshments suitable to the occasion in the tiny kitchen, perhaps not. Ellen did not want to think about that. She cleared her throat but before she could speak, her visitor said, approvingly, "A charming room, Madame Ellen. Particularly interesting for its use of color. The rose silk on your walls is an inspired thought."

"Charming?" In a dazed way, Ellen could only repeat the compliment. Lady Hawksmoor smiled. "Certainly." She began to unbutton her gloves.

Ellen took a deep breath and collected herself. She was not brave enough to sit but she controlled her voice well, considering.

"And so, Lady Hawksmoor, how may I assist you?"

"By making me a dress, Madame Ellen. A ball dress."

Now Ellen did sit, but only because it became impossible to stand since her knees began, inexorably, to buckle. *A ball dress? I am being commissioned to make a ball dress by the leader of London society?*

Perhaps Ellen's visitor was a mischievous woman. She continued with a hint of amusement, "Something rather grand, I think. A gown that people will talk about."

"And here is the tea. Set it down, Polly. I shall pour." *If I can,* thought Ellen. Between the rattling of the cups and the pouring and the offering of quite appealing little shortbread biscuits—*where had they come from?*—Ellen had time to collect her thoughts.

"Polly, please see that Lady Hawksmoor and I are not disturbed. Not on any account." As if she had a whole *houseful* of clients clamoring at her door.

Ellen cleared her throat and began again. "Rather grand, I think you said? May I ask what the occasion will be?"

"A reception for the Prince of Wales."

Ellen almost dropped her cup. She repeated, thoughtfully, "The Prince of Wales. I see. An important gown, then."

The glint of that smile again. Lady Hawksmoor nodded as, gently, she sipped her tea. "Quite so. This is excellent."

She could not help it. Ellen had to ask. "I am delighted, of course, to accept the commission, but may I ask why you have picked me to create your gown?" The *me* was almost a squeak. She had not meant to be so forward, but astonishment rattled her tongue, as it did her cup.

Head to one side, Lady Hawksmoor examined Ellen quite carefully. At last she nodded, as if to herself. "Madame Ellen, I shall be honest with you. My maid it was who recommended you. She has nothing but praise for your work. I trust her taste, since she has been in my employ many years. Besides, I have not time to go to Paris. The reception is an unexpected one at this time of the year, and I have much to organize."

"Your maid?" *Stop parroting!* Ellen shook her head. This was becoming tiresome.

But the lady herself said, patiently, "You were commissioned recently to make a bridal gown?"

Ellen was perplexed. The only wedding dress she had designed had been for the girl who had recently married a rather pleasant local fishmonger. She nodded cautiously. "Yes. For the lady who became Mrs. George Folder." *Lady* was a euphemism, of course. Fishmongers' wives and *real* ladies were not to be considered on the same plane of existence.

Lady Hawksmoor inclined her head. "Mrs. Folder. Quite so. A charming girl. She is my maid's sister. I sent them a present." She smiled. "The gown was described to me as a triumph and universally admired by those who saw the bride."

How remarkable the world is. Ellen swallowed. "It was rather pretty, but then, so is Mrs. Folder."

Lady Hawksmoor stood. "Perhaps we may begin. How should you like to work? Measurements first, perhaps?"

CHAPTER 37

"POLLY? POLLY, where are you?!"

"What did she say?" As Ellen closed the door behind her visitor, Polly hurried to the hall so fast she caught her foot in her skirts and almost tripped.

Ellen had an uncontrollable urge to laugh. From relief! Quite weak, she leaned against the wall. "She—Lady Hawksmoor, that is—wants us to make her a dress."

Polly hugged herself. "A dress! Her!"

"Yes."

"What kind of dress?"

Ellen's reply came out in a *whoop* as she ran toward the workshop door. "A *ball* dress! We shall need that cutter, and more besides. The tide has hit the shore!"

The next twenty-four hours left Ellen little time for reflection or sleep, as she created sketch after sketch. Wide skirts, narrow skirts, overlay, no overlay, dropped shoulders, high neck, velvet, satin, silk, lace . . .

"This one, Madame Ellen"—Lady Hawksmoor held up the sketch—"is very daring." Ellen held her breath, but her patron smiled. "I like it. This it shall be. And the material?"

Ellen swallowed, relieved. Lady Hawksmoor was a remarkable client, direct and unafraid. "Peau de soie, for the way it moves, even in great volume, which this gown will contain, of course. And of a shade not white, not yet cream or even light gray, but . . ." Ellen cast her eye around the drawing room at the Hawksmoors' town house for inspiration. It was a grand and chilly apartment, since the fire, great as it was, and blazing brightly also, made little impression on the volume of air contained within such vast space. "The paneling here, for instance, has a lustrous quality, and a color not dissimilar to that which I should like to capture. A cool, pearl-like hue."

"The paneling. I see." Lady Hawksmoor frowned.

Ellen shifted uneasily in her chair. Perhaps she had allowed enthusiasm to run thoughts from her mouth too quickly. "That is . . ."

Her client's brow cleared. "I quite understand what you mean, Madame Ellen. How refreshing I find your approach!" Lady Hawksmoor got up from her chair and peered closely at the paneling. She tapped it with one finger. "Lustrous, you said?"

"Lustrous," echoed Ellen. *Stop that!*

"Perhaps you will send me some samples of the stuffs you prefer before you begin to cut, Madame? When I have made my choice, I shall return them to you immediately, so that you will not be delayed in the making. We have so little time."

Ellen stood. Carefully she gathered up her sketches, restoring them to the artist's folder emblazoned with embossed letters proudly proclaiming,

CHEZ MISS CONSTANCE
MADAME ELLEN
MODISTE & MANTUA MAKER
VINE STREET, PICCADILLY

An extravagance, but one that was merited. Small things of this kind assisted the look of her business. Now, however, there was the material of the gown to be purchased, which was a problem, but one she would not share with her client.

"You shall have samples this afternoon, Lady Hawksmoor."

As the bell was rung for the manservant, Ellen tried not to fidget. There was so much to do, so much to think about, that the demeanor of the footman, as cool as the temperature of the drawing room, had no effect at all. After all, she had been patronized by such experts in her time, he hardly counted.

Once the form of the gown had been decided, and the stuff of the dress agreed upon, the lights in Ellen's cutting room began to burn all day and all night. At considerable expense.

First the pattern had to be made, and then the toile cut so that it might be fitted to Lady Hawksmoor. This was two days and nights of work. Two days in which Ellen had to find a way to pay for the material, as the business was already at the limits of her credit.

Every week since early autumn, when she had moved into her house in Piccadilly, Ellen had faithfully cast up the accounts of the business and made full report to Connor and Oriana. As faithfully as if they had been a bank, and might foreclose at any moment.

Those first months had been nip and pinch. She had been determined to exist within the limits of the investment that Connor had provided, and ingenuity, therefore, had to take the place of extra pounds and shillings. Ellen had learned a great deal from the miseries of her previous time in London, and with Madame Angelique in Richmond, and thus by Christmas she had proudly reported that Chez Miss Constance had made its first tiny profit. Yet this amount would soon be swallowed whole in procuring the fine materials and trimmings that she had to provide for Lady Hawksmoor's dress.

Supply was a difficulty, too, so soon after the Christmas season. Many chandlers had yet to replenish their stocks, and what remained commanded a premium price. This was even without the worry that increased wages brought, for Ellen's existing loyal clients could not be slighted or have their orders unreasonably delayed. That, too, she had learned from the past. So the single new cutter became two, and Polly also found two specialist sewers—one for beading, one for embroidery. How would she pay for them all?

"I will not. I will *not* ask him for more money."

Just past three in the morning and Ellen was still in the work-shop, where Polly had joined her. "You must eat at least. We shall all need your strength." She had brought Ellen a seriously large ham sandwich on a plate. "With good, sharp mustard. I know you like mustard. It will keep you awake."

Ellen massaged her tired eyes, to little effect. But then, every bit of her body felt the same. "Thank you, Polly. You are consideration indeed." She eyed the food, and remembered that she had been hungry hours ago before finishing the toile absorbed her. Now, suddenly, eating became the most important thing in the world. She snatched the food with shaking hands.

Polly looked on with approval. "Now, tell me what I must do."

Ellen shook her head. It was impossible to talk. "Nmming." She swallowed, closing her eyes. How good it was to taste once more, to relish food. "Nothing, I meant. Do not concern yourself, Polly. This is mine to deal with."

Polly looked at Ellen, consideringly. For a clever person, Ellen Gowan could be singularly stupid. "I know about the money. The cost of the stuff for Lady H. And our credit. Or lack of it."

Ellen's eyes widened. Polly rolled her own. "Did you think, in this small place, that I would not understand the stretch this has brought us to?"

Polly took the empty plate from Ellen's fingers and said, kindly, as she left the room, "You are best to do the work God made you for. To the suppliers I shall go. This tangle shall be sorted *and* I'll obtain the materials you require. Just see if I do not."

Ellen was so astonished, she could not immediately summon a considered response. But then she ran to the door. "Polly, come back here. Polly!"

Grinning, the other girl peered out from the kitchen door. "Well? Will you say no?"

Nonplussed, Ellen stammered, "N-not precisely *no*, but—"

"Then *yes* is good enough for me, for that is what I hear." Polly put the plate down in the scullery, and staunched the lamp. To let it burn was wasteful. "You get on now, but only for this hour. You must sleep soon, or you'll not be useful in the morning." *And so must I,* yawned Polly, *or neither of us will finish what must be done....*

"Do you like it, Madame Ellen?" Violet, the youngest of the new girls in the workshop, could stand the suspense no longer. The ball gown was finished. It had taken the work of six women working in shifts over five days and nights.

Polly frowned. "Hush, girl."

The dress, a glimmering confection of silk and silk-velvet and pearl-sewn tulle, had been laced around a workshop form for the final time. Everyone in that silent gathering wore white gloves so that the cloth should be perfectly unsullied if they touched it. They watched as Ellen inspected each aspect of their work, from the seams of the under-petticoats to the facings of the bodice.

But even Polly was worried when, after five minutes, Ellen remained silent. To her own eyes, the gown was perfect.

Ellen said, half to herself, "There is something. I cannot quite see what it is."

The girls stared at each other, deflated. "We think it looks very nice." Becky, older and more confident than Violet, spoke for all of them. Disappointment made her truculent. They had all worked without complaint and were proud of the result.

Ellen rubbed her forehead. She must not lose them now. "I thank you all. The skills you have brought to the creation of this gown are formidable. Magnificent. I apologize for not saying so." But the warm smile was not quite enough to disguise her disquiet. Her eyes strayed back to the gown. *What was it?*

Mollified by Ellen's honesty, Becky asked, "Shall I turn the model toward the light? You will see better." The hopeful tone earned another smile.

"Thank you. Polly, is there tea? And we must send Violet to the high street. The pie-cart will still be there. We all deserve supper."

Polly understood the code: *Leave me alone with the dress.* She said, briskly, "Come, girls. Violet, I shall write down what you must buy."

Ellen, left alone in the workroom, pushed rising panic aside. *What shall I do?* The design had shown such promise, and here, exactly as she had drawn it, was the result.

Something was missing. The gown was a failure. Part of her mind barked, *Method. Examine each aspect, each element of the gown. Then look at the whole.* Worn from days and days of close work, Ellen was exhausted. And lost. But then she *saw it.*

The overlay! The intention had been for the veiling of the wide, bell-like skirt to be held in swags by strands of pearls and crystals. The veil was to be as filmy as mist, so that when Lady Hawksmoor danced she would seem to float in a cloud. *This* overskirt, however, was insufficiently gossamer-like to achieve the effect.

There was no avoiding the conclusion: It had to be remade. *At least,* thought Ellen, *the bodice is all it should be.* Lady Hawksmoor had lustrous skin, and the silk-satin of the upper part of the dress would illuminate those cream-smooth arms and shoulders.

"If I could see another way, I would tell you. But we have only tonight. We must remake the overlay. If all of us work together, it can be done." *What if they walk out? What if they will not help me?*

Crammed into the tiny kitchen at the rear of her house, Ellen ate with her workshop girls. They were all ravenous, and it was fortunate that a small store of pennies had remained in the pin tin to buy enough pies for all.

"Where will we get the material?" Becky spoke up. It was a question, not an accusation.

Where indeed? Ellen had no answer. It was late, past nine at night. Violet timorously asked, "What about the bale of silk sarcenet? It's under the cutting table."

Becky chimed in. "Yes. It was bought for the fishmonger's bride."

"Of course!" Ellen's heart ramped up to dizzy speed. Mrs. Folder-to-be had changed her mind at least twice, which had caused some distress at the time, since Ellen could not return the stock they had begun to cut. The fabric lay, now, in a pile with bolts of more common cloth—calico, muslin, and buckram for padding—beneath the cutting table. What irony, if Lady Hawksmoor should benefit from the indecision of her maid's sister.

Polly said, hopefully, "The fabric, at least, is very soft and fine. Do you think the color will serve?" Ellen swallowed the last crumb of her pie. "It will serve. Better than serve!"

She ran from the kitchen. The girls would follow or not. She had no time to agonize further. Nine hours until dawn, and three more after that before she must present their work to Lady Hawksmoor. She would do it alone if she had to.

Ellen scrabbled beneath the worktable. There! She hauled the bolt of material to the cutting surface and out from its calico cover. The color was perfect, a misty pearl cream. Intent on what she was doing and moving quickly, she bumped into Becky. Violet and Maude and Dorcas were standing behind her. And Polly. Tears pricked Ellen's eyes. She was not alone. "Thank you."

"Well then, girls, hop to." Polly hurried to Ellen's side, helping her unfold the bolt. "We have work to do."

"You have restored what was lost." The words were said softly. "I had thought myself grown old, and yet, in this gown, I am a girl again. You have sewn enchantment into its folds, Madame Ellen. You are a sorceress!"

Perhaps it was the lack of sleep and little food, but Ellen swayed as the world seemed, suddenly, to shimmer.

Lady Hawksmoor was alarmed. "Madame Ellen! Please, sit down. You are very pale."

But Ellen grasped the back of a chair. This feeling, so strange, was elation. A pure surge of joy!

"You really like it?" Ellen's voice was vulnerable. Lady Hawksmoor's eyes locked on Ellen's in the pier glass. A slow smile gathered on her face.

"How unusually honest you are, Madame Ellen." Lady Hawksmoor reached out a hand, and Ellen took it. Side by side they gazed into the mirror. "Yes. I like it. And others will as well." Lady Hawksmoor smiled, a beautiful enigma. "Be careful of what you have wished into being, Madame."

CHAPTER 38

"WELL? WHAT was it like?" Polly was sweeping the workroom as Violet and Becky arrived, yawning, followed by Dorcas and Maude.

"You should have seen the show! We stood in the street outside Lady H.'s house last night, watching the guests and waiting to see the prince. Blurry cold it was, but the gowns! A wonder they did not all catch their deaths. Down to *here* some of them necklines." Becky gestured to an improbable point between her breastbone and her navel.

"All silk and jewels and furs. But none as pretty as her. Gobsmacked, they were, Lady H.'s guests, when they saw our gown." Polly's eyebrows ascended. Shy Violet was nearly often silent, but last night's events had unstopped her tongue.

"*And* we saw the prince. Hot-eyed boy, that one. You could see it. The way he kissed her hand and would not let go. Admired Lady H. more than all the others, wouldn't you say, Vi?" Becky elbowed her friend in the ribs.

Violet nodded enthusiastically, as Polly asked, "Did Lady Hawksmoor seem pleased?"

Becky snorted. Even Violet giggled. "Pleased? Well, what would *you* be, if the queen's son liked what he saw so much. And showed it?"

"Who liked what he saw?" Ellen hurried in on the last part of the conversation.

The girls chorused, "The prince," just as a rapping was heard on the front door.

"Are we expecting a delivery?" Ellen was puzzled. It was just after eight on a dark morning, and the world was only reluctantly beginning to wake.

Polly shook her head. She took off her apron, hurrying from the workroom. "I'm coming." The noise grew louder, more impatient.

Ellen leaned companionably against the table. "So, girls, after all the excitement of last week, perhaps we can get back to . . . Polly! Whatever is wrong?"

Polly, ashen, returned through the door as if pursued by hounds. "You'd better come."

Ellen's anxiety flared. *Debt collectors!* The rapping at the door turned thunderous. She gulped and hurried to the hall, Polly at her heels. Clasping her hands in a strained knot, she nodded. "Open the door." And gasped.

Vine Street was blocked, *choked,* by carriages and agitated women, all of them fashionably dressed and each accompanied by at least one servant. As one, a sea of bonnets turned, and twenty, or perhaps thirty, pairs of eyes were accusingly trained upon the doorway.

"There. There she is!" The ladies left off milling, some politely and others less so, and surged forward.

"I have no appointment, however . . ."

"Perhaps you would be so kind as to see me first . . ."

"Lady Hawksmoor, my oldest, *dearest* friend, suggested that . . ."

Ellen and Polly stared at the advancing, fast-packed horde with some alarm.

The Siege of Vine Street had begun.

Just one garment, Lady Hawksmoor's ball dress, had created this frenzy. And during the days that followed the reception for the Prince of Wales, relays of ladies—great, and those who aspired to be—arrived at Ellen's door.

As if they were explorers thrown upon an unfamiliar shore,

they ventured from their common haunts, the better parts of town, into the wilderness behind Piccadilly with only one aim: to search out the girl who had transformed Lady Hawksmoor. If magic had worked once, it could be made to work again.

And tall, pretty, short, plain, haughty, well-mannered or not, each new visitor to Chez Miss Constance shared one ambition: for Madame Ellen to create for *her*, make for *her*, dress *her*, if not exclusively then immediately, or as soon as might be managed.

Dazed by the assault, Ellen applied herself to the improbable task of just *how* she might satisfy all requests.

"Ladies, we do not have room for all inside the salon."

A voiced *Oh!* of disappointment passed through the crowd.

"*But* if you will kindly provide my assistant with your names"— she indicated Polly, who blanched—"we shall serve you all with an appointment as soon as we can."

The frenzy began again as gloved hands waved white cards in the air. "My card!"

"*My* card, if you please!"

"And mine. Take mine!"

Polly backed up to Ellen, muttering, "Thank you very much! Send Becky with the appointment book."

As Ellen whisked through the door, Polly curtsied bravely. No easy task, since the women had advanced to the top step in a phalanx. She selected the closest. "Perhaps, this lady. Yes, you, Madame, and her friend will enter?"

Unbecomingly triumphant, the couple squeezed forward as Polly tried to keep some order among those who remained and were forcibly expressing their disappointment. "Now, Ladies, one at a time, *if* you please."

Ellen did not like to close the door, but the crowd was intimidating. She had not dealt with a mob before. Collecting herself, she invited the two well-dressed women to sit in her salon.

"You *are* Madame Ellen, are you not?" Her visitor peered at Ellen closely. She whispered something to her friend behind a glove.

Ellen caught the words *very young* and colored. "I am. And whom do I have the honor to address?"

The lady, a handsome forty or so, had had her bonnet knocked askew in the melee. Ellen tried not to stare, though one broken plume was especially distracting. It flapped as her visitor spoke.

"I am Eloise, Marchioness of Kendall. And this is my friend, Alicia, the Lady Kilcannon."

"And how may I serve you?"

The marchioness leaned forward. She fixed Ellen with the eyes of a zealot. "We have come for *clothes,* Madame Ellen."

And that was the tenor of that day, and those that followed. With each new client, Ellen's first task was to display sketches—so far as she had them—and swatches of cloth (a difficulty, since few full bolts were kept at the workshop).

But as commissions poured in and the succeeding weeks became busier and busier, it was hard to retain the semblance of serenity.

"A ball gown, Madame Ellen. Not similar to Lady Hawksmoor's, and yet a little alike. With velvet for silk in the skirt perhaps?"; and "Three tea gowns and two walking dresses with manteaux to match"; and "A taffeta redingote with a mantelet embroidered in silk"; *and* "Do you make bonnets? My milliner's work is displeasing of late"—this from a haughty old woman with a hat more suited for her granddaughter and pinned upon unlikely red curls.

Ellen smiled and smiled until her face ached and her mind reeled with calculations of how much cloth was required, and where to obtain what was needed. What trimmings, which lace, and how much time must be set aside for the making of each commission. So *many* calculations and each one important.

And she tried very hard not to promise what could not be delivered, but it was always tempting to say, "Yes, of course. Next Tuesday fortnight?" when her new clients seemed so eager to spend and spend and *spend.*

Ellen could not sleep. Long after that first tumultuous day, she lay on her bed as the night hours idled past, marked by distant bells.

Her mind was a centerless wheel of anxiety and elation. Images occupied the space behind her eyes, glittering pictures that refused to be banished. Vine Street was already too small, so if the madness continued, where should Chez Miss Constance go?

Sumptuous interiors paraded around in Ellen's head. Adam staircases and marble floors, gilded mirrors and curtains of swagged silk beside tall windows. Mayfair, perhaps, or St. James? Discreet, stylish, opulent, her rooms would one day be legendary.

Should she have a double salon? A client might be greeted in one room, and while that lady disrobed, another in *another* room could be fitted in her toile—and more ladies could be accommodated. But then, of course, more cutters would be required—and another drafter, possibly two. Polly had the knack, it seemed, of scheduling, but she had to see the clients herself. Neither she nor Polly would have time to draw up every design. Who would do that, the most important thing of all?

The cost. Think of the cost.

Ellen sat up and hugged her knees in the cold night. No. She would not think just of the cost, for the future was no longer burdened by dread. Her dream was real.

CHAPTER 39

Several months had passed since Lady Hawksmoor's gown had transformed the fortunes of Chez Miss Constance. Summer smothered London now, as a gray, hot day simmered into evening. Away to the west, light split the sky as wind began to rise. Soon there would be rain. *Let it pour!* thought Ellen. The city was suffering because of its ancient drains, and even the river reeked as it tried, in vain, to carry the weight of London's waste. Only rain, great gouts of sweet water, would flush the Thames to the sea and allow Londoners to breathe without choking.

"Ellen?" Polly knocked. Ellen knew that knock. Her usually forthright friend was tentative. Polly had something important to say. "Come in."

"Here you are. For Constance." Polly had one of their new gown boxes in her arms. They were glazed a smart black and embossed in silver, and they'd cost a ruinous two pennies each but were worth the price for the distinction they brought to the business. "I made this for her birthday. A girl cannot have too many party dresses."

"May I see?"

Polly colored slightly. "Of course," she said, putting the box on the bed.

Ellen untied the bow of silver ribbon carefully. Inside, between sheets of tissue paper, was a white dress with an overskirt of soft pink gauze and tiny pink sleeves edged with white lace. "Pink and white! How did you know?"

Polly shrugged. "Little girls. Can't go wrong with pink. Besides, seven is important. I remember being seven. Hard work with four

326

brothers and sisters. I hope she has more fun than I did." But she grinned engagingly.

Ellen nodded. In a different life, she might have had four siblings at her seventh birthday, too. "Connie will bless you. And I thank you, Polly. Very much. What a lucky child she is."

Polly said, impulsively, "She has much of your mother about her." She paused, a little abashed. How sad Ellen must feel that Constance Gowan had never met her namesake grandchild. She hurried on. "And *this* is for you." Another parcel emerged. "Do not look so wide eyed, Madame Gowan. Did you think I could have forgotten your birthday? You'll have it at Clairmallon."

Ellen took the parcel from Polly's hands. She had never welcomed Lammas Day.

"This year, wake up on your birthday morning and smile. Thank God for all you have. For the success here. For those who love you. Love is most important of all." Polly's tone was compassionate, but she stopped. Quite abruptly. And blushed.

Ellen quirked an eyebrow. "Perhaps He answers your prayers more frequently than He does mine."

"Perhaps." Polly colored deeper. Ellen was suddenly alert. She had never seen Polly look quite as she did tonight. Nervous and . . . happy.

Polly swallowed. "When Raoul tried to take Connie, do you remember those two boys?" She paused. Ellen sat on the bed and patted the space beside her. Her smile grew wider. Polly swallowed again, then said, "Well, the really big one has declared his intentions to me."

Ellen jumped up. "But, Polly, this is wonderful." She did not say, *Finally!* Polly fondly imagined that no one in the workshop knew she'd been "walking out" for some time. "Truly! I am so very, very happy for you. If anyone deserves happiness and companionship, it is you."

Polly was relieved. "I do not want to desert you, but perhaps it is time to find an assistant for you. A proper one?"

"What, and you are not that? And as to deserting me? No! You will add another member to my family. That is all. I shall make your wedding dress. That will be my gift to you."

Polly plumped down on the bed in an expiring cloud of skirts. "William will be very happy. Will Redcliffe. He is a cabinetmaker. Did I tell you that, then? The other one was a farrier, if you remember."

Ellen nodded. She said, carefully, "An excellent trade. Does your Will have a view about you working here?"

Polly's face clouded. She nodded reluctantly. "That is why I thought about the assistant—in case I cannot sway him. And why I would not listen to him for so long. I like what I do." She heaved a stalwart sigh. "But the time comes to choose. Shall I look while you are away at Clairmallon?" With the August heat, London would empty of the gentry, and the wildly successful Chez Miss Constance could afford to close for a month.

Neither agreeing nor disagreeing, Ellen said, "Let us talk when I return. Shall you bring Will to dinner here?"

Polly beamed. "Thank you. But be warned. He is quite in awe of you."

Ellen chuckled. "How odd. But I *think* I remember him as handsome."

Now Polly *really* blushed. "I find him so."

Ellen nudged her friend in the ribs. "And he? Does he know how lucky he is?"

"Lucky?" Polly's heart was in her eyes. "I am the lucky one. To be so loved and cherished. I had thought myself too old and past the age when a man would want me."

Loved and cherished. The words sliced Ellen's heart. It was eight years since she had married Raoul de Valentin. Eight years since she had permitted herself to be someone other than Constance's mother. "Twenty-six is hardly old, Polly."

"And neither is twenty-three." Polly had often wondered why Ellen had not accepted other suitors after the contemptible Raoul, but from lack of courage she had never raised the subject. Until tonight.

"Ellen," she asked, gently, "do you never think of love? Of marrying again?"

"How can I? My husband is still alive."

There were so many things that Polly wanted to ask. And so much that Ellen, too, might have said. But the moment passed as Ellen stood. "I must finish packing."

Polly followed Ellen's lead, then embraced her friend tenderly. "Sleep well, dear heart. And I shall pray for you. Tonight and always. May God hold you in the hollow of his hand. You deserve happiness, too."

Four precious weeks of summer at Clairmallon. Four weeks of peace and space and beauty. And her family.

"Stop, Giles. I shall walk from here."

"Very well, Madame." The barouche slowed and stopped, crunching on the gravel. Ellen, not waiting for the steps, climbed down. It was late afternoon and they had made good time from London.

Giles, shading his eyes, watched as the girl set off toward the great house in the distance, her black skirts trailing across the velvet green. In the pretty light, the coachman could understand why Madame Ellen might want to walk the last quarter mile alone. Coming home to Clairmallon must be sweet indeed after the filthy, crowded city. The grass, too, would be soft beneath feet more used to cobbles.

"Come along, my dears." The man tightened the reins and his leader whinnied. "Home for us all." The carriage picked up speed as the willing horses stretched out. Behind them, a plume of white dust rose against the gold and azure sky.

Ellen paused and listened. Already the sound of the wheels, the snap of the whip was receding. Soon, she would hear only birds and the soft breeze as it sighed through the meadow grasses.

Clairmallon's voice was an active silence. Ellen relished even these few minutes by herself. So little of her life in London was solitary, and she had always liked her own company. There was always too much to do now, and so little time for contemplation.

Her skirts hushed to a rhythm as she walked across the grass. If she thought about the sound a different way, it might have been the sea, calling from a distance. That endless wash of water, the reach of childhood into the present.

"Wait for me!"

Ellen stopped. That voice . . . She shivered. It could have been her mother calling.

"Where are you?" She gazed around the meadow.

Someone laughed. "I can see you, but you cannot see me." Up. The sound came from on high.

A lone oak stood sentinel about ten feet away. Its canopy was richly dense, but when Ellen looked carefully, she saw a pale, small, bright-eyed face among the leaves. Connie.

"You look like the Green Man. Or Green Girl, rather."

With a giggle, her wood-sprite daughter disappeared, and then, with a certain amount of sliding and shouting, descended from branch to branch. "Catch me, Mama."

Ellen held out her arms and Connie jumped fearlessly. But the distance was a little too great, and mother and child collapsed to the turf in a tangle of skirts.

"Mama!" Connie was panicked. "Speak to me!"

Ellen struggled to a sitting position. "Certainly. When. I. Have. My. Breath." But she was grinning as broadly as her daughter. Connie dropped backward into the grass, arms spread wide. "What a relief! I could not have borne killing you. Not when you've just got home."

Ellen propped herself on one elbow, gazing down at Connie's face. Her heart caught on a snag of love. Polly was right. How like her grandmother the child was becoming. And Edwin was there, too, in the wide, gray eyes. But she did not see Raoul. She never saw Raoul.

"Do you mind very much, Connie, that I am away in London?"

Constance Gowan rolled over onto her stomach. She considered the question carefully. "Yes. I miss you. I get into Aunt Oriana's bed in the morning, but it is not the same."

Ellen sat straighter. In Oriana's bed? It was mean-spirited to be jealous.

Connie looked at her mother. Her gaze was very direct. "But I understand. You are doing it for me."

Ellen spoke cautiously. "Did Aunt Oriana tell you that?"

The little girl plucked a blade of grass and sucked it. "No. I worked it out by myself." She patted her mother's face. "You are very clever, Mama. Everyone says so."

Connie stood and reached down her hand. "Come home."

Home. Mother and child ambled together toward the old house, singing, *London Bridge is falling down, falling down, falling down. . . .*

What was it that Oriana had first told Ellen? *Clairmallon welcomes the terrified stranger.*

Well, Ellen Gowan was no longer terrified. And she had taken hold of the direction of her life. For Connie's sake, and her own.

"Uncle Connor says that Aunt Oriana is resting. She has been sick for a little while."

Connie was watching Ellen as she washed. Soon her mother would dress for dinner, and Connie would be taken to a nursery supper with Miss Egglestone, her new governess.

Wiping her face with a piece of wrung-out linen, Ellen met Connie's eyes in the looking glass. The child was anxious. Ellen said, soothingly, "Then rest is the very best thing. I expect it is just a summer cold."

"No. Aunt Oriana cannot eat very much and says she feels ill. She is tired all the time, too."

Ellen frowned. It was odd that Oriana had mentioned nothing

in her last letter. And then she reproached herself. Perhaps she'd been so busy, she'd not picked up a hint of how things stood.

Connie scrambled down from her chair and wandered to the bed. An evening gown was laid out on the coverlet. "This is very pretty, Mama. Did you make it?"

"I did. Or, rather, the girls in the workshop made it for me. A new design."

Ellen rang the silver bell on the dressing table. She did not like heavy fabrics, least of all in summer, but on any scale this gown was daringly light. Pale Indian muslin was printed with a repeating pattern of black roses and soft gray leaves. It caught up in billows over an underskirt of chalk white silk, and the black velvet bodice was quite severe, though it dropped prettily off her shoulders. Tonight she would wear short black gloves, and her only jewelry would be the cameo that Oriana had given her.

A knock at the door announced the maid. "Mrs. Moncrieff has sent me, Madame. I am to help you dress." The pretty girl had eyes as black as currants and a melodious Irish burr. Ellen nodded pleasantly. "And, your name is?"

"Maggie."

"Very well, Maggie. Would you lace my stays?"

Ellen disliked the fact of stays but enjoyed their effect. Connie observed the operation carefully. First her mother stood, then, when the hooped petticoat stopped swaying, she held tight to a bedpost as the maid pulled the corset laces through eyeholes in the reinforced back.

"Shall I have stays, too, Mama, when I am grown up?"

Ellen put a hand to her abdomen. When first laced, it took time to remember how to breathe. "I do not know, child. That will depend."

Connie eyed her mother critically as the gown was dropped over Ellen's head and Maggie did up the hooks at the back. "On what, Mama?"

Ellen winced. The dress sat snug around the corset, but the compression of her ribs was no easy thing to bear.

"Connie, your grandmother once said that *pride knows no pain.* I think she meant that we would suffer whatever might be required to obtain a pleasing effect. But sometimes, even as a modiste, I wonder. There has to be a better way!"

Maggie stepped back and observed Madame Gowan with a professional eye. "But, Madame, there is no substitute for stays. As I am sure you know. And, if I may say so, you appear to magnificent advantage. The waist. It is tiny!"

Ellen bowed to the inevitable. She could not ask her clients to suffer what she did not.

"Will your mistress be down to dinner, do you suppose?" Ellen's tone was even. She would not make Connie more anxious than she was.

Maggie's expression did not change. "I believe Mrs. Moncrieff hopes to be. The doctor has been in a little earlier."

Doctor? Now Ellen was seriously worried. But she smiled at her daughter.

"Very well, Connie. Should you like me to take you to the nursery, before I go down to dinner? We must not keep Miss Egglestone waiting."

Connor blinked as Ellen entered the dining room. If he had not noticed it before, he did now. His wife's quiet cousin had acquired real polish in London. It was there in the carriage of Ellen's head, in the graceful swirl of her skirts as she turned to acknowledge him. This truly was *Madame* Gowan, and not a girl masquerading as a grown-up in her mother's clothes.

It occurred to him, with a little surprise, that here was a most handsome woman. The early promise was, at last, fulfilled.

"Cousin." He bowed over Ellen's hand punctiliously, and kissed it.

Her chuckle was unforced. "Dear Connor, so gallant. Have you been reading your wife's French novels?"

"Not at all. But we have champagne." He conducted her to an armchair drawn up beside open casements. Scent poured in from the garden outside. Night-opening lilies and late jasmine, blooming by the moon's light.

Flicking out the tails of his coat, Connor offered Ellen the flute and sat opposite her, with a glass in his own hand. "We have all been looking forward to your return. Especially Constance."

Ellen stared into the depths of the bright wine. "And I am glad to *be* home." She was unaccountably nervous. Tipping the glass too quickly, the bubbles fizzed and she sneezed.

Without comment, Connor extended his handkerchief. Ellen said, ruefully, "I try, I really do. But something always spoils the effect. I shall always be the girl from Wintermast. And happiest in my workshop."

"And is that so very bad? Wintermast is beautiful. As you are, cousin."

Oriana appeared. Dressed in night blue satin, with a collar of sapphires and diamonds at the base of her throat, she carried her head like a queen.

Connor hurried to his wife, and with an arm beneath her elbow, escorted her solicitously to a chair. Oriana sat in a sighing rustle of fabric.

Ellen kissed her cousin. "I did not know you had been to Wintermast." To say that name had a strange effect. It was as if she had talked of someone long dead. Joy and sadness welled up together with a force that she could not have imagined.

Oriana nodded. "I traveled there on a whim one day. It is not so very far, after all. Just to see what you had talked about so often. The church has been repaired and some few of the houses. The churchyard, too, is well tended."

Ellen remembered her last day in the village. Her mother lying on her father's grave. She swallowed, and changed the subject.

"Connie tells me you have not been well, dearest cousin? I hope you are feeling better tonight."

Connor took up Oriana's hand. "My thoughts exactly, wife."

"I am indeed, Ellen. No more nausea at the present, though Doctor Abel has recommended I keep to my bed as much as is reasonable. But I am becoming impatient. I dislike bed rest very much, and Connor will treat me as if I am made of glass!" Oriana smiled broadly at her husband.

Ellen leaned forward. "Do you mean, cousin . . ."

"Yes." Oriana's hand strayed to the waist of her gown. Only now did Ellen see that it had been raised, and below it was a discreet bowing out of the fabric. "I carry a living child. The baby quickened yesterday. We did not want to speak of my condition until we were certain all was well." *This time.*

"How delighted I am for your joy." Ellen raised her glass and Connor touched her flute with his own.

He did not mean to be tactless when he said, "Constance will have someone to play with at last."

Ellen's smile did not falter. "And she will relish the role of older sister, just as you did all those years ago, cousin."

"Perhaps, in the morning, we might let Connie know together?" Oriana had seen the flicker of distress in her cousin's eyes. "This new life will mean so much to us all." She extended her hands and Ellen took them. "Family, in the end, is all we have."

Why had she allowed herself to be persuaded? Ellen asked herself the question again as the barouche slowed a little. It was a perfect summer's day, but now, with dread, she began to see familiar landmarks among the hedgerows and the fields.

Soon, just around the bend that was now rapidly approaching, she would see the long, straight village street. And, at the end of the road, the church.

Constance pulled at her mother's sleeve. "It is so exciting, Mama. To think we shall see your house, and the garden, and the apple trees you used to climb."

"Hush, child." Oriana was increasingly worried. It had been her suggestion that they drive to Wintermast on Ellen's birthday morning. And though her cousin had readily agreed, she had become increasingly silent during the drive from Clairmallon. Oriana noticed that now Ellen's eyes were unhappy.

"There it is, Mama! Look, someone put the tower back."

"Shall I ask Giles to stop the carriage, cousin? We could walk from here."

Ellen nodded. She had seen their house. It was empty, the windows on the lower floor boarded up and blinded to the world, and it seemed so small.

After a pause, Connie said, "Your house looks lonely, Mama."

Ellen cuddled her daughter. "Shall we find the orchard, Connie?"

The little girl brightened. "Yes, please." She scrambled down from the carriage and ran across the dusty track to the gate.

As they got closer, the cottage didn't appear as decayed as it had at first. Well built of brick and stone, it still stood solid, though the thatch needed replacing. The roses and woodbine planted around the door by her mother had formed a riotous, twining mat. If not cut back soon, the creepers would find their way inside, and that would begin the true ruin of the house.

"It is all so pretty, Ellen. I can see why you loved your home." Oriana spoke tentatively.

Ellen nodded as her senses took in all that they could. The smell of high summer, dust and grass and recent rain, brought back so much. It was almost as if, in a moment, she might hear her mother calling, *Ellen, have you fed Sally?*

Or, rounding the corner to the back of the house, find her father harvesting potatoes. *Very fine this year,* she heard him say, and she smiled faintly. *As they always are, Papa.*

"Mama, come and look!"

Ellen's reverie broke. She smiled at Oriana. "She has found my favorite climbing tree."

Oriana breathed more easily. "Perhaps she has."

The path to the back of the cottage remained, and there was Connie grinning from a fork in an ancient apple tree. It was still alive. And not *just* alive. There would be a crop of fruit to be picked soon.

Connie patted the branch she was sitting on. She had skinned a knee and snagged both stockings but her smile was seraphic. "It's very big, Mama. Bigger than you said."

Ellen, too, patted the trunk. *Hello, old friend.* Gazing around the garden, she saw that someone had been tending what remained.

"Which one was your bedroom, Mama?"

Ellen turned to look at the back of the house. The sun warmed the old brick, and the windows shone. Odd in a deserted building. "That one. There, beneath the eaves. The little casement." Something white stirred behind the glass. Were those her curtains still?

Connie said, regretfully, "I tried the back door. I am afraid the house is locked. Can we see the church, Mama? Perhaps we can go inside there."

Oriana tensed. "Now, Connie."

"If you would like to, my darling." Ellen had no desire to try the door of the house. Let the pictures of her home remain as they were in her head, when it was clean and bright and cared for. The church was different. If the tower had been restored, someone must have repaired the fabric of the building. Certainly some of the cottages, too, had been rebuilt—though more had fallen to ruin.

It was late in the warm morning as the trio wandered the road toward St. Michael's, eating fresh-picked apricots.

The Wintermast green was the same as it had been. Would she hear her friends shouting if she listened hard enough?

Ellen stopped. She reached for Connie's hand. "I have something to show you."

It was true. Someone had been tending the graves. There were no weeds around the Gowan headstones, and posies of daisies had been neatly placed on each.

"These are your family, Constance. Your aunts. My sisters. Eliza and Mary. And, Thomas and Edward. They are your uncles. And here is your grandfather's resting place." Ellen knelt in the bleached grass beside Edwin Gowan's headstone.

"Mama. Where is my papa buried?" Constance stared at her mother with troubled eyes. "You have never told me."

Oriana broke in quickly, thinking to spare Ellen. "To remember the past is good, but I declare I am hungry! Shall we drive somewhere pretty and have our birthday picnic?"

Connie's breath caught in a sob. "But you never talk about him, Mama, though you speak about your family often. Did you not love Papa?"

Ellen's heart wrenched. She put her arms around her daughter. "Your father was my beloved." *Until he betrayed us both.*

Oriana leaned against a gravestone. The happy day had turned miserable. And it was her fault. The color of the world leached to a gray fog.

"Oriana!" Ellen hurried toward her cousin, but it was too late. Fortunately, Nod was not.

Nod's strength was not what it used to be, but he reached Oriana quickly, and the lady fell into his hands like a piece of fruit.

"Nod!"

"Hello, Miss Ellen." He grinned. "Lucky that I was just scything the grass. Shall I carry the lady to the church? It is cool inside."

"Can you?" Connie asked, innocently. The old man did not look very strong. She wiped her eyes on her sleeve. She was feeling better.

"Hush, Constance! Mr. Noddington is my friend. That was discourteous."

Nod smiled broadly. "Fair question, though. This would be your daughter then, Miss Ellen?" He winked at Connie, who colored a little but said, politely, "How do you do, Mr. Noddington. I am Constance Gowan."

Oriana's eyes opened and focused. She frowned. A man was holding her up. Someone she had never met.

"Just lean on me, Missus." Nod offered to help her stand.

Oriana was bewildered. "Who are you?"

As they walked together slowly through the graveyard, Nod and Constance trailed a pace or two behind the cousins. It *was* cooler in the church, but there was less light than Ellen remembered. "Are there fewer windows, Nod?"

"Yes, Miss Ellen. When the new bishop in Norwich said the tower must be rebuilt—only last year, mind you—they saved money with the glass. Mean of spirit, that man, just like the last. And now they need more candles."

Ellen's gaze roamed the interior. That scene, the chaos of stone, her father's broken body, the hole in the sky, was carved deep in memory. Now it was as if that disaster had never happened. All was neat, the altar restored to its place and the brass polished. Only the bell tower had been closed off from beneath. The tragedy would never be repeated. It should not have happened then.

"Is this where my grandfather preached, Mama?" Connie pointed to a gilded pulpit. Ellen shook her head.

Edwin's old pulpit had been modest, with railings of black oak and steps worn into hollows. Priests had trodden those stairs for a thousand years. Now it had been replaced by this florid object.

Nod shrugged. "The Greatorexes did that. William had it made. Conscience money after how they treated this village—owned half of it and never rebuilt the houses. But there was a special service of dedication, of course. Bishop and all. Bah!"

Ellen was not angry, but she was not resigned either. If the church building had no memory, she did. She smiled at Nod. "It is you who tends the graves, is it not? And puts the daisies there?"

Nod shifted uneasily. "A shame to waste them, this time of year."

He took Ellen's hands in both of his own. "You take care, Miss

Ellen. And Miss Constance also. Do not worry about your family. I shall be here."

Tipping his hat to Oriana, he turned to go, but hesitated. Drawing Ellen to one side, he asked, "Mrs. Gowan, Miss Ellen? Is she well? I did not ask before."

Ellen swallowed. "She died, Nod. In London."

The old man absorbed that. "I wondered. Since you came without her."

Ellen watched the old man walk away. His shoulders had slumped and his gait was slower than before. She hurried after him.

"Nod?"

He stopped.

"I hope the potatoes are good this year." She kissed one whiskery cheek.

Unconditional kindness was real. Perhaps she had forgotten that, to her detriment.

CHAPTER 40

22nd of December, AD 1853
Vine Street
Piccadilly

Dearest Oriana,

Time has fled, chased away in an ever-greater whirl of business as we come closer to the end of the year. But I have been thinking about you and how much I am looking forward to being at Clairmallon for Christmas.

In London, we have had our first snow. For a day the city shone like a bride, but then, so quickly, she was sullied by soot as London tried to warm herself in this bitter winter.

When I picture you and Connor, and think about what you are doing now, I see you as well and happy and cozy. As I write, I am certain you are tucked up before the fire—wood, not coal!—as you happily await the appearance of your little one. Constance cannot be more excited than I am. Kiss her for me and let her know that Polly sends her love, as she does to you, also.

Since your days will be leisurely at present, as an entertainment I have included a little sketch with this letter. It is a drawing of our new premises.

After two months of searching, I have at last secured the perfect home for our growing business, and we shall move there in the new year. Now there is just (just! Such

a little word) the task of packing up Vine Street. And
working each day, as usual, as we do that.

We may have more girls in the workshop, we may be
better organized than we used to be, but still new clients
arrive at our doors in an unabated flow and I do not like
to turn them away. Every lady in London desires, it seems,
gowns and mantles and hats and I do not know what
else, in this Christmas season. Success is a blessing and a
curse, as I am beginning to understand.

But, to return to our new establishment.

As with Vine Street, 38 Berkeley Square will be salon
and workshop combined. I shall live above the shop again
but with a great deal more space. And, our new building is
very elegant. If you were here, I know what you would ask
me. First, how did you settle on the area, Ellen? London
is so very large!

Exactly so, dear cousin, but I did not wish our
business to be located on a shopping street. A discreet
address among fine houses was my aim, as if my ladies
were paying me a private visit (shades of your plan for
my work at Clairmallon!). It is a novel way to pursue
my trade, and I am not ashamed of that word. That very
difference will distinguish Chez Miss Constance from
other dressmakers. For in fashion, newness is all.

And so, as you may see, we have a stuccoed facade
and a pillared portico with a pediment above. These
are very grand! We also have a front door of great height
and width. Do you see the little figure of the lady I have
drawn beside it, to illustrate the fact? I will take down the
knocker from Vine Street to place on that fine new door.
Just for luck, and to remind me always from where we
have come. I did not like the Medusa at first, but now I am
quite attached to her.

Ah, if my dearest mother could have seen where I shall

shortly dwell. Instead of a room or two, there is a whole apartment on the third floor of the building just for me. There will be a study in which to draw up my designs, as well as an office for business, a spacious bedroom for me and one for Connie also, and a dining room and a drawing room besides. In time I shall have my own kitchen and domestic offices, but for now a common kitchen will serve us all at Berkeley Square, including the workroom and cutting floor.

There is also a long garden with an arbor and a rose walk. Sadly neglected. That will change! And even a small lawn. There is much to do, but the garden will be a retreat on warm evenings next summer, and I shall look forward to your first visit with young Master (or Miss—forgive me!) Moncrieff. Mama would have been so happy there, showing the flowers to your baby. As I write these words, her face is before me, and she smiles.

I shall think of you tonight when I go to bed. Please know that my loving thoughts are always with you. And kiss Constance (again!) for me. I shall count the few days that remain until Christmas!

> Your loving friend and cousin,
> Ellen

Ellen yawned as she blotted the letter. It was barely light outside, but the clock in her bedroom insisted that it was past seven in the morning. There was much to be accomplished if they were to close up the business for Christmas, especially since a lunch had been organized for the workshop girls. There were eight of them now. On the bed behind Ellen were gifts for each one. A testament to the success of Chez Miss Constance. A year ago, this would have been too great an expense.

"Yes?"

Polly was at the door. "May I come in?"

Ellen panicked. Polly's present was wrapped in tissue paper only. She still had to place it in a box and tie the ribbon. "A moment, if you please."

The dressing shawl! Ellen flung the pretty thing over the gifts, resulting in an interesting landscape of mounds and bumps.

"What are you doing?" Polly looked at her friend narrowly when she entered. Ellen had the air of a naughty child.

"Oh, nothing. Just getting ready." Ellen took an innocent step back, planting herself in front of the bed.

Worry distracted Polly. "You are certain we shall close the order book this morning? Because, if you do not, the girls must work to Christmas Day and even beyond."

Ellen said, fervently, "Please no! I have told everyone that, delighted though we are to accept their commissions, delivery will be after the New Year. . . ."

"Well after," Polly muttered.

Ellen nodded. "At a date to be confirmed. There. Does that satisfy you?"

Mollified, Polly nodded. "I shall give the girls the news."

"Polly. Before you go?"

At the door, Ellen's friend turned. She was as tired as Ellen. "Yes?"

"Close your eyes."

"My eyes?"

"Of course! And hold out your arms. This is Christmas!" It took but a moment for the tissue-wrapped present to be placed in a box and a silver ribbon tied around it. "There." Ellen placed the box across Polly's arms. It was large, but light. "Happy Christmas."

Polly opened her eyes.

Ellen said, "This comes with my gratitude for your unfailing kindness."

Polly was touched, and abashed. She coughed. "Can I open it?"

"If you like."

Polly carried the present to Ellen's desk and untied the ribbon carefully. She eased the lid off. Her eyes widened.

"Do you like it?" Ellen asked anxiously.

Polly wiped first one hand and then the other on her work apron. "I . . . don't know what to say." A length of Honiton lace emerged from the box, many yards long. Very old and very rare.

"If you like it, this might be your wedding veil?"

"This is what a lady would wear." Polly could hardly speak.

Ellen cleared her throat. "I shall enjoy watching Will's face when you walk down the aisle toward him next summer. But we shall miss you, when you become Mrs. William Redcliffe."

What she meant was, *I shall miss you, and this house will seem empty.*

Polly put the veiling back between the tissue. "He might not want me to work, but at least he understands now. About the advantages." Polly would not use the word *money,* but she was well rewarded and proud of that fact. "He knows I like the business." A quick grin. "It is just, his pride and his mother's need smoothing."

They both grimaced. Will was an only child, and Mrs. Redcliffe, a force to be reckoned with. She did not hold that married women should work, and her son echoed his mother's forceful views.

And then Polly did something she had never done before. She kissed Ellen on the cheek. "Good team, you and me. Happy Christmas, dear friend. But if I do not get down to that workshop soon, the day will be behind before it begins, and we'll have no time for our Christmas lunch."

She winked as she closed the bedroom door, and Ellen smiled. Mrs. Redcliffe versus Polly? She knew whom she would back.

The world must have a skin of ice. Ellen could feel the frost when she put her nose outside the bedclothes into the frigid air. She had been trying to stay asleep for just a little longer, to avoid the fact that she absolutely had to get up.

The previous night she had fallen asleep at her desk, and now there was too much to do before the carriage, sent from Clairmallon, would arrive.

"Oh, very well." She took a deep breath and skipped from the warm coverings, whimpering. Once her bedroom fire was lit, the cold could gradually be forgotten as she packed.

Polly, too, had risen early, though a headache, a relic of yesterday's rum punch, made her more taciturn than usual (Polly was never good in the mornings).

Having banked the ashes in the kitchen stove last evening, she was trying to heat a pot of water. But whichever way the damper was turned, acrid smoke filled the room when she added coals to the sulking fire, sorely trying her temper and causing her temples to pound.

"Polly, I *must* get dressed," Ellen called down over the banisters.

"You can have it hot, or you can have it now." Polly winced. Shouting was painful.

"Now! I shall be late."

Polly shrugged. *Do not blame me.*

Ellen went back to her bedroom. The dress she had chosen for the journey was modestly hooped beneath charcoal velvet, the bodice laced with white frogging in the military manner. From the armoire she pulled out a caped mantle of black cashmere and a bonnet of stiffened, white velvet ornamented with silver rosebuds and black ribbons. Darker gray half-boots of Russian kid with black silk tassels, and a black-and-white-striped winter parasol completed the ensemble. But she could not put the dress on without help. And she must wash! Perhaps Polly was right. At Berkeley Square she would need not only an assistant but a proper maid!

"Here I am. I shall not be sorry to leave that stove behind."

Polly was making an effort at civility. For all her queasy stomach and unreliable head, she would miss Ellen. And she was nervous. Mrs. Redcliffe had invited her to share their Christmas table. The woman was a snob, and Polly was terrified of transgressing Will's mother's rigid code of behavior.

"While I wash"—Ellen grimaced, the contents of the copper cans was barely tepid—"there are a few last things to be folded."

"Very well." From the corner of an eye, Polly caught a glimpse of Ellen half-turned away for modesty's sake as she washed her breasts and arms. Waste annoyed Polly. Her friend seemed oblivious of the impact she made, and not just on ladies of fashion. Men stared at Ellen in the street, and it was certain they were less interested in fashionable attire than they were in the person who wore such pretty things. But Ellen, somehow, considered herself invisible and did nothing conscious to encourage male interest.

Polly sighed as she added the last of Ellen's linen to the new traveling trunk. If she could give her friend a real Christmas wish, it would be for Ellen to fall in love with a decent man. And for that love to be faithfully reciprocated.

Yes, Ellen was married, but Raoul had disappeared into the London stews when Ellen left to live at Clairmallon all those years ago. With the kind of habits he'd had, it was likely that he *was* dead by now anyway, and Ellen a widow in truth.

Madame Gowan was a success, and pleasingly notorious since she was so young. Soon, if things continued in the same way, Ellen would be worth something. And a wealthy widow, a *pretty* wealthy widow, could have her pick in London town. If Ellen would only allow herself to see that . . .

"Are you ready for lacing?"

"I am." Ellen was clad in a hooped petticoat and underlinen. In haste, she had dried herself less than thoroughly, and now stood shivering before the guttering fire.

"Very well then. Here's to a warm Christmas for us all!"

Ellen had a final errand before her journey to Clairmallon. "Stop at Fortnum's, Giles, if you please? I shall be but a moment." The hard frost had cleared to a brilliant, sharp blue day. Even the air, so cold it stung the nose to breathe it, was as giddy making as wine.

"Fortnum's it is, Madame Gowan. I shall wheel around the block and return. Take what time you need."

181 Piccadilly was thronged with Christmas crowds as the well-dressed and well-satisfied classes of London converged on the doors of the most famous grocer in the world. But Ellen's errand was quickly accomplished. A pound of the best sugared almonds for Constance, a Christmas treat, and a tin of rose water Turkish delight for Oriana. Connor had sent Ellen a note, begging the favor since Oriana craved sweet things in this last month of her pregnancy.

Outside the shop, Ellen looked in vain for Giles and the Clairmallon landau, while discreetly stamping her boots in the cold. But she was noticed as she stood among the cheerful press of people and carriages, and by more than one gentleman.

"Do stop staring, my dear. It is a little vulgar." The pretty lady of forty or so tapped the rather younger gentleman on the arm. Her tone was humorous. To a point.

"What?" They made a striking couple. The young man was exquisitely dressed in well-cut broadcloth, set off by perfectly laundered linen, a very tall (and very glossy) hat of brushed beaver skin, and a black cashmere coat lined with scarlet silk. The lady was in half mourning, her velvet gown like burnished steel to his charcoal. And though her bonnet was impeccably black, it was set off by a scandalously scarlet feather.

"You know very well what I mean. That lady there. You have watched her for five minutes now."

"You do not understand, *ma chère*." The French accent was pleasant. As if it tickled, his companion smiled when he spoke in her ear. "No. It is just that I think, in fact I am certain, that I know this lady a little. And yet . . ." The gentleman frowned. He was surprised by what he saw. The magnificent clothes were evidence of wealth.

Many a worldly woman would not have believed anything that a young buck said when he stared at a pretty girl, but the widow Ondle flattered herself that she knew her companion tolerably well by now.

"As it happens, I am acquainted with the lady also. Or rather, I know who she is, and would like to know her better." It pleased Mrs. Letitia Ondle to be enigmatic.

The young man stared at his companion. "How so?"

As they watched, Giles returned. The Clairmallon carriage with its escutcheoned doors and the matched pairs of horses commanded respect from Fortnum's doorman. Parting the crowd, the man managed a path to the curb for the barouche, and assisted Ellen to climb the carriage steps.

"*That* is the increasingly famous Madame Ellen Gowan. She dresses Lady Hawksmoor. I saw the gown that made her name, for I was at the ball that the countess gave for the prince. Lady Hawksmoor was a sensation that night. It is impossible to obtain an appointment with Madame Ellen in under six months, since she has become the rage."

"A dressmaker, you say?" The young man stared with great interest at the Clairmallon carriage as it rolled away.

Mrs. Ondle tweaked his arm. "Should you like to renew your acquaintance with the lady?" She raised an eyebrow in what she hoped was a roguish manner.

Raoul de Valentin shrugged. "*Chérie,* I have so much more interest in knowing a certain lady better. She who commissions the clothes for her back, rather than makes them." He grinned. "Then again, clothes, I find, are an impediment. A person in a state of nature is so much more free to . . ." He whispered in the widow's ear. And whatever he said caused the lady to giggle like a girl.

Raoul de Valentin dressed well. For that skill he was grateful to his mother. Today, as he strolled beside the frozen Serpentine in Kensington Gardens, he knew he presented the very picture of gentility. A long jacket of checkered tweed with silver buttons, a waistcoat with narrow black and gray stripes, linen of the most superior quality, and straight-cut trousers of fine wool. Around his shoulders he had thrown the black cashmere overcoat, and his laced shoes—a fashionable innovation—were brilliantly polished.

Remarkably, the entire ensemble had been cared for without a manservant. This was a closely guarded secret, one that may have surprised those fashionable blades who passed for his friends. Something else for which Madame de Valentin could take credit. If Raoul had learned her lessons reluctantly, he had at least learned them well.

Raoul was a little early to call on Mrs. Ondle for the Christmas drink he had been promised, hence the pleasant amble through the gardens. Even on a cold day, he enjoyed the busy scene. But although he had every reason for optimism, this Christmas season made him melancholy. Raoul embraced some aspects of reality and rejected others at will, yet very deep in that part that others might call a soul, he knew the source of this present unease. It was the fleeting sight of Ellen outside Fortnum's the other day, so prettily dressed and prosperous looking, that had unsettled him.

Because of fear he had abandoned her all those years ago, when she had been close to death. As Letitia said, a broken nose conveyed a piratical air, but he did not like to think of how he got it. From time to time, he felt remorse over that desperate episode. Even *he* acknowledged that almost selling his daughter had been the lowest point among many after that disastrous year with Ellen.

Raoul paused for a moment. He stared sightlessly at the sauntering crowd. Would he permit himself a cigarillo as he strolled? Tobacco, he found, calmed the nerves, though it was thought raffish to smoke in a public place. With regret, he decided against it. Letitia had complained she disliked the smell. He sighed. Women. So unreasonable sometimes. *But Ellen was not unreasonable, was she?*

Raoul de Valentin shook the unease of that thought away. What they had tried to create together in Hackney had been a mistake from the beginning, why had he not seen that? His lonely childhood with Angelique—as she tried to keep food in both their mouths after his father died—should have provided ample evidence that hard work in an unjust world offered only more toil, with little real reward.

And though, through charm and drive, his mother's business had eventually succeeded, Angelique had never allowed herself to enjoy a sense of achievement. Her clients admired the *French dressmaker* for what they saw as a glimmering joie de vivre, but Raoul knew what lay behind Angelique's wit and breathy giggle. The penury of her early married life had profoundly frightened his mother, and from the time he was old enough to hold a broom, she had driven him as she drove herself. There was always so much to be done. Spring gowns were designed in autumn and sewn in winter; summer's range were designed in winter and sewn in spring, which gave way to clothes for autumn. The pace was unrelenting, and as he grew older, Raoul resisted his mother as she tried to force ever-greater responsibilities on him. Of course, he had made an effort with Ellen, a sincere effort, to set up an enterprise for himself, but he knew now, as his ancestors had also found, that he was entirely unsuited to a life of business.

For, what was the point of *working* when so many well-off widows crowded London during the season? With much less effort than it took to sweep a workshop floor, he could have his pick of that eager little pack, since each was anxious to be seen on the arm of a handsome young man, and happy to pay for the privilege.

Perhaps his first widow, the formidable Carolina Wilkes, had taught him the most. Not least how to take what was offered without scruple, and ignore the consequences. An excellent training as it turned out, more practical than anything his mother had tried to teach him.

And if Carolina had not received his services for some time,

Raoul still smiled when he thought of her. His childhood friend might have humiliated him, might have, on occasions, unmanned him, but in the end Mrs. Wilkes had paid dearly for those little games, for he had deprived the lady of that thing she loved most: money.

One night, not long after abandoning Ellen, he had found Carolina's hoard. It was hidden behind the false back of a cupboard in the Minories parlor. The work of a minute, and nimble fingers managed to remove that weighty leather bag. At dawn he had left with relief, and without farewell. The drab had not deserved those pretty gold coins, the rings and notes and bits of jewelry fleeced from her lodgers and their clients. She had not deserved *him.* Raoul flattered himself that by this second desertion he had broken Carolina's heart (if she had one), a fair part-payment for the suffering she had heaped on him. No doubt he had taken a risk in removing her property, for the lady was vengeful. But life *was* risk, and after decamping to Paris for some months—to reinvent himself as the Marquis de Valentin, wealthy young man about town—he discreetly returned to London, and an altogether better milieu. In time, too, he ceased looking over his shoulder, for he had not seen the woman since, nor any of his old cronies from Spitalfields.

Yes, his first widow had done him two services. Mrs. Wilkes had unknowingly helped him claim a place in the world that should always have been his, and she had shown him that there was such a thing as justice to be had—if one would only take it.

Buoyed by this cheerful thought, Raoul paused to allow a small child to bowl its hoop across the path. He raised his hat and winked at the boy's pretty mother. Her blush was his reward. Much encouraged, he strolled on.

Yes, the years since Hackney had served him tolerably well, even if he was low on the readies at present. But better times were again in prospect, if he could just entice Letitia Ondle over the line. Perhaps a kiss beneath the mistletoe and the gift of the pearl-embroidered garter that he had in his pocket would do the trick.

Twirling his stick, Raoul gazed at a duck. She had dragged a little waterweed from under the ice and was now being deprived of it by her drake.

Marriage. Could he do it? Did he really *want* to do it? Letitia was pretty enough, if a little old for a man of his age. How old, he was not sure, but her skin showed that she was somewhere in her forties. He did not especially care. This transaction was not about appearance, not on her side. It was about wealth. Hers.

But the rub was this. In an unusual fashion, a good deal of his own smallish capital had gone to entertain the lady over the last months and to dress the part. Letitia's circumstances demanded that effort—she must be proud to be seen on his arm.

At first, he had thought that the title, his personal appearance, and undeniable charm might be enough, especially since Letitia seemed to find the French accent he affected (thank you, Angelique!) irresistible. Of course, to become a marchioness was a substantial lure as well, especially when Raoul talked of the family estates in the Loire. His inamorata was not to know that others now lived in the fine chateau and farmed the ancestral de Valentin lands. Raoul dreamed of buying it back, every chain, every perch and rod, but Mrs. Ondle would have to accept his proposal for that vision to be made manifest.

She needed him, too, of course. A title launders the stain of trade with remarkable ease, and her lamented husband's fortune had been made from fish. A fair exchange, as these things go. Raoul would be inept indeed if he could not persuade Letitia to the altar, after so carefully laying the groundwork to his siege. His prior entanglement with Ellen would need attention, of course, but he did not see that situation as an obstacle to his happiness. In fact, a plan was beginning to form in that regard.

Pulling out his watch, Raoul glanced at the time. Another five minutes and he would turn back toward the Ondle town house. It was situated on an appealing street not far from Kensington Palace. Its refurbishment was a tribute to the depth of the late fishmonger's pockets and his wife's unexpected good taste. Well-chosen furniture, excellent pictures, brocaded silk on the walls, and silver and crystal of the very best quality. Now *that* had impressed him. What a very good catch the widow was, if emotion could be put to one side.

Idly he watched a couple stroll past. The lady twirled her parasol as her companion, laughing boldly, attempted to kiss her hand. She slapped his fingers away and giggled. Raoul frowned. A game was being played here. The lady was eager one moment, dismissive the next.

Was Letitia playing that game with him? Was he, perhaps, a useful adornment at the opera and nothing more? After all these months, perhaps he might have expected *some* generosity from such a wealthy woman—apart from her bed, naturally, which he did not especially enjoy. He was practiced in the art of dissembling in that area but still, it had become more tiresome lately.

As if the point of something cold had touched him at the hairline, Raoul flexed his shoulders. He swung his cane and picked up the pace. When he thought of it, Letitia had recently not seemed so ready to respond when he had dropped hints of his intentions. Yes, the time had come. He must shortly present a ring and declare himself.

The stone must be of the first quality, of course, and he would require new clothes as well. Letitia had made some passing comment about the fact that he seemed to have only three suits. He had laughed it off, declaring that he was indifferent to clothing, that all he needed was the care of a good woman to remind him that it was time to visit his tailor again.

Should he pay a call on his wife, perhaps? His *very successful* wife. He had taught her well in Hackney. She had much to be grateful for, in retrospect. Perhaps that gratitude might take tangible form.

And then there was his daughter. What had happened to her? Undoubtedly, it was time to find out a little more about the very enterprising Madame Ellen Gowan. He wondered, though, why she had not kept his name? If that disrespect offended him in one sense, in another he was not unhappy. Letitia might have asked awkward questions if a Madame de Valentin had made the splash that Ellen had achieved in London.

CHAPTER 41

"E LLEN." THE knock was urgent. It came again. "Ellen. Can you hear me?"

Ellen sat up in bed half-aware, half-awake. Connor. She fumbled for her dressing wrap. "I am coming."

It was dark in her room on this moonless Christmas Eve, but he was carrying a lamp. And plainly agitated, for the line of light beneath the door moved back and forth. She could hear him breathing, too, short and shallow.

"Yes?"

She pulled open the door, conscious that her hair was loose. One look at his face and she knew. "The baby."

"I have sent for the doctor. Oriana is joyful but frightened. She remembers the others." His eyes were dark. He, too, suffered from those memories.

"Of course." No time to dress, Ellen tied the belt on her gown tighter and hurried after her cousin's husband. As they came closer to the bedroom, they heard a keening sob. And then another. Oriana was trying to swallow her pain.

"Here we are, sweetheart."

Oriana was lying in a vast half-tester bed clutching Maggie's hand. "It hurts, Connor. It tears at me. I am so afraid our child will not be safely born." Her body flexed as she bit back the agony. The pair hurried to the bed. Maggie quickly gave her place to Connor. He grasped Oriana's hand strongly in his own.

"My brave girl. I am here now." His voice was calm, but his face worked. To see Oriana suffering upset him very much. "My brave, brave wife."

Ellen took over. "Maggie, do we have linen prepared? Dr. Abel will need it. And wake cook. We shall require hot water, and Mrs. Moncrieff must have sustenance through the night."

The girl scurried from the room almost too quickly to nod. Ellen looked uncertainly at Connor. His fear might compound Oriana's own. *Give him something to do.* "Connor, shall we make the bed more comfortable? Could you lift Oriana, please."

"Of course! Rest, my darling. Lean on me." Oriana's contractions were still some minutes apart, and in the quiet space between the pains, she slumped in her husband's arms.

Ellen created a nest from bolsters and pillows in which her cousin could half-sit up. "This will feel more agreeable, cousin."

Oriana opened her eyes, already shadowed. "I thank you, Ellen. You are very good to me. You always have been." So early in the labor, and Oriana was already exhausted. *Not a good sign,* thought Ellen as her cousin's eyelids drooped closed.

Connor stared in anguish at Oriana. He spoke quietly. "What can I do, Ellen? I feel so helpless."

"You could ask cook for some broth. It will do her good. This night may be long."

Connor stood reluctantly, ceding the place beside his wife. Ellen was right. This, at least, was something practical to do.

In the distance, horses whinnied as a light carriage clattered across the Clairmallon forecourt. "Doctor Abel. It must be. I shall bring him immediately." Connor strode from the room. Ellen called after him. "The broth, Connor?"

Oriana startled awake as the door closed. "Connor? Where did he go?" She tried to sit straighter but as another contraction began, she folded around herself, rocking. Ellen massaged her cousin's back with both hands. "To groan brings relief. Do not be stoic, cousin." The pain beneath her fingers, under Oriana's skin, had a tangible force. She would sweep it away if she could. "Breathe with me, breathe deeply. Breathe the pain from your body."

Doctor Abel arrived. He hurried into the bedroom removing his coat, followed by Maggie, bearing water, soap, and towels.

"Well done, Madame Gowan. And again, if you please while I wash." Ellen was pleased to see how scrupulously he cleaned his hands. So many doctors thought it of no account. "And now, Mrs. Moncrieff."

Ellen stood back and watched as the doctor drew the sheet away from his patient and gently assessed the position of the baby. He smiled at her frightened cousin. "All is satisfactory. Soon your baby will be born, Mrs. Moncrieff, and here we are, your friends and family, to share in your joy."

Connor was staring into the room from the doorway. It was as if he did not trust himself to come closer. "Mr. Moncrieff, if you will make sure that the house is quiet and warm and all is in order to receive your child, I am sure that will comfort Mrs. Moncrieff."

Ellen had been lonely for so much of her life, she understood Connor's desolate expression. Here was displayed the harsh reality and peril of birth. If he lost Oriana, as so many women died in childbed (she, herself, almost included), what would he do?

Connor felt Ellen's glance. His own was fathoms deep. Oriana was taken by another contraction and as she wailed, his shoulders slumped. He left and Ellen ran after him. "I shall come and find you. You must not be fearful. She needs us to be strong."

He stared at Ellen, uncomprehending. "Strong? What use is it that I am strong? She is not."

Ellen said, simply, "But she needs *you*. Remember that." Connor Moncrieff was a good man.

Oriana's labor was not long, seven hours, but it was nearly too much for her frail body. There were some periods of the night when Doctor Abel and Ellen thought Oriana would not survive.

And yet, at last, death lost the struggle, for the birth of Oriana's son came with the first rays of the sun on Christmas Day. The child was not large but he was healthy, and he screamed with indignation at all that he had had to endure. His mother held out her arms. "Give me my boy."

Ellen, tears in her eyes, gave Oriana her son. And all grew quiet as they gazed at each other for the first time.

Ellen found Connor Moncrieff in the stables. Anything, even cleaning tack, had kept him awake through the night. And out here he could not hear the screams. But he saw Ellen coming and turned away. He could not look at her face.

"A son, Connor. Your son. All is well with them both."

The sinews of Connor Moncrieff's knees gave way. Slowly, and then faster—as if he were a building coming down—he crumpled to the brick floor. Ellen knelt beside him, still in her dressing wrap and nightgown.

"She is not dead?" Suffering had cut Connor Moncrieff open like a surgeon's knife. His heart was undefended.

Ellen reached out to the man, arms open and imploring. "Your beloved wife lives. And so does your son."

Connor stared into Ellen Gowan's eyes. Joy flared like a storm or a fire. "She is alive!"

He sprang to his feet and ran from the stables. "Happy, happy Christmas, beloved cousin."

Ellen stood more slowly as feeling drained away. Joy, fear, confusion, love. From the rigors of the night she felt hollow as a vase. But there was something more. And she would not admit it, even to herself.

Loss.

CHAPTER 42

"D o you like it?"

Connie's new room at Berkeley Square had been a secret. She had been told only that she would have an annex off her mother's.

Ellen's daughter stared, big-eyed, around the bedroom. New rose velvet curtains hung from brass rods; there was a delicate, white-painted bed; and she had her own fireplace, just now filled with a cheerful blaze. The little girl hugged herself. "Very much!" She ran to the bed and, climbing up, bounced happily on the coverlet. "It is much bigger than the one I had at Vine Street. And so cozy!"

"Since this is your first visit to our new home in London, Polly has very kindly agreed that I may run away for all of today. Where would you like to go?"

Connie hugged her knees. She adored visiting Chez Miss Constance because the bustle and noise of London was so different from her home in the country. And her mother was always so much fun. That was different from Clairmallon, too, at the moment.

"The museum? Could we go there? I should like to see the mummies and all the statues."

"Very well. The museum it shall be. That will keep us busy. And morning tea, too, I should think." It delighted Ellen that Connie had a natural interest in the past. Part of Edwin Gowan would always live in this child.

But spring is an uncertain season, and it proved a wild morning as Ellen hailed a hansom. She had difficulty securing her bonnet *and* holding her skirts down as she held Connie's hand at the curb.

"Great Russell Street, if you please."

Connie giggled as Ellen climbed into the carriage, her dignity barely intact. "Mama, if you are not careful you will float away!"

"Then you must hold on tight, and we shall fly over the rooftops together."

But worse was to come. Even the weight of the skirt hoops made little difference as Ellen and Connie began the long walk across the museum's new forecourt. Ellen's skirts very soon threatened to become uncontrollable in the fierce gusts, and since more than one gentleman took interested note of her predicament, her embarrassment was acute.

Blown across the forecourt as if ships of the line, the pair at last made safe harbor inside the echoing entrance hall. Connie was secretly delighted by the drama caused by the savage weather. "You still look very pretty, Mama, even all ruffled about. I saw the gentlemen look at you."

Ellen was startled. She had not thought her daughter aware of such things. "What an imagination you have, Connie."

The child shrugged. "Just as you please, Mama. But I know what I saw."

Ellen quickly changed the subject. "And so, where shall we begin?"

"The Greeks first, and then the Egyptians. And then tea." Connie looked critically at Ellen. "But we should brush our hair first. Or rather, you should."

Ellen's hands flew to her bonnet. Tendrils of hair had dislodged in the wind and fallen to her shoulders. She said humbly, "Thank you, Constance."

"Do not mention it, Mama."

A restorative visit to the ladies' cloakroom took only a few minutes, and then, as the pair sauntered toward the hall of the great Athenian friezes, Ellen asked, "And how is little Kit? Your aunt, in her recent letters, says he continues to thrive."

Connie said happily, "My cousin is very well. I *think* he smiled at me last week, though Uncle Connor says he is too young. Aunt Oriana is still in bed though."

The news worried Ellen. It was more than three months since Kit's birth. But she said, "It is best to recover slowly, of course. Here they are, Connie."

Holding hands, Ellen and her daughter gazed at the Parthenon friezes in silence. Time had been caught among those marble draperies. The horses, the young men, the girls on their eternal processional journey toward the temple would never change.

Ellen could have been one of those girls, or Connie one of the children.

Connie whispered, "I feel as though I am in church." Ellen squeezed her daughter's hand. Constance was an unusual little girl, sensitive and thoughtful. But having stood still for a long while, she began to fidget.

"Yes, Connie?"

"Could we see the mummies now? And then have tea a little later?"

"A little later. Now that is an excellent span of time. Much more useful than mere minutes."

Mother and daughter giggled as they wandered on through a growing crowd. The audience from a lecture on Mr. Charles Fellows's expedition to Xanthus in Asia Minor was just then departing from the rooms of the museum members. Neither Ellen nor Constance noticed the interested observer among the throng.

"Raoul, you are staring."

"Only because the lady is so elegantly dressed."

"Which lady?" Letitia Ondle was curt. It was hard not to be proprietary sometimes. But then she saw at whom her companion discreetly pointed. Madame Ellen Gowan was indeed dressed delightfully today in dove gray jersey wool, with a mantlet of rich black velvet lined with white fur.

Mrs. Ondle had an inspiration. "Raoul, you might introduce

me? I am in desperate need of at least two new ball gowns for the season. It is such a bother going to Paris."

Raoul appeared not to have heard. "Who do you suppose that child is?"

Mrs. Ondle was annoyed. Soon Madame Ellen would have walked on too far. "How should I know? It is said she has a daughter. Well?"

Raoul stared after the little girl with great intensity. "A daughter."

Letitia Ondle tapped an impatient foot. "You *said* she was a friend of yours."

"A friend?" Raoul shook his head. "That is to overstate the case. Madame would not remember me." Letitia Ondle's lips tightened. Sometimes Raoul de Valentin, for all his pretty manners, was annoyingly elusive.

Raoul sensed the chagrin and smiled brilliantly, his full attention focused on his companion. "But why should we care about mere dressmakers? We have the day before us, Mrs. Ondle. And I can think of at least three things that I should like to do."

"Indeed, Sir." The widow was not inclined to be immediately mollified.

Tenderly, Raoul folded the lady's arm through his. "Certainly. And two of them, I should think, will please you enormously also. The third will please *me*."

Her eyes brightened. "And where shall we discuss these proposed activities, Monsieur?"

"Why, in your drawing room, of course. Unless you can think of another, more suitable place?"

CHAPTER 43

ELLEN STEPPED back so that the full effect of the gown could be seen. "There. Just as we imagined."

Polly stared at herself in the long glass and could not immediately speak. A stranger, a startled girl she had never seen, gazed back wearing a gauze and satin gown.

"I look like the fairy on the Christmas tree!"

"Well, *I* think you look lovely. And Will, will, too. You wait!"

Constance was hopping from foot to foot. She had been told that she must not sit down, for fear of crushing her dress.

Polly's voice wobbled. "This is even *better* than the dress." The *dress* was that fabled first ball gown created for Lady Hawksmoor. Polly touched the veil, secured to her head with a neat coronet of pearls, a gift from Oriana and Connor. "Pearls. And real lace. It's a brave show, all right. Not bad for a village girl." Polly turned carefully, to inspect the back. She was still uncertain about managing a train, though Ellen had made her practice with a length of curtain attached to her waist for the last week.

Ellen said, "I'm sure Mrs. Redcliffe will be delighted by your appearance."

Polly sniffed. "She will not. She does not like me. Or, I should rather say, she would not like *anyone* who took her precious boy away. She wanted us to live with her, did you know that?"

"You have told me. Several times." Ellen handed the bride her gloves.

Polly indelicately snorted. "As if I should have agreed to that. I can tell you, I put my foot down." She waggled a satin slipper from under the hem of the gown. "Besides, Will has found a very nice little house for us on a long lease. It puts me in mind of Carnarvon Avenue. Dinner with us once a week you said, and I shall keep you to that arrangement, Madame Ellen."

Head to one side, Polly stared at her friend. Her eyes misted. "Your ma would be proud. *You* look very nice, too."

As chief supporter of the bride, Ellen was dressed in silver lace over silk velvet of a darker hue. She shook her head. "Today is about you and your groom, Polly. No one else matters."

Violet hurried into Polly's bedroom. In an anxious flurry she said, "I am so sorry, Madame Ellen, but the bouquets were late being delivered."

Ellen said, patiently, "We know. The bride's first, if you please." Violet carefully handed Polly a trailing posy of spring flowers. The beguiling scent of lily of the valley and jasmine wove through the air like a first benediction of the marriage.

"This is for you, Madame." Violet gave Ellen a smaller version of the same. "And, Miss Constance, here is your basket." Loose white rose petals filled a ribbon-twined basket for Polly's excited little flower girl. "Just be careful as you walk out into the street, or they will blow away."

Not bad for a village girl. Ellen smiled as she hurried down the stairs. She had been determined that Polly should have the finest wedding she could arrange in the grandest church that could be found.

As Connie and Violet helped Polly from the bedroom, which included navigating a doorway too narrow for the hoops of the dress, Connie said, confidentially, "I know Uncle Connor is sorry he cannot be here today. And Aunt Oriana, too. They were both looking forward to seeing you married, Polly. They like you."

Polly said cheerfully, "Much better they stay where they are since Mrs. Moncrieff is not well." Polly touched the pearls for luck. The trio had arrived at the bottom of the stairs. No turning back now. She took a deep breath.

Ellen stood smiling at the open door. "Ready?" Beyond, the Clairmallon carriage was decked out with broad white ribbons, and each of the horses wore a plume of ostrich feathers, precisely the same color as the froth of blossoms in the gardens of Berkeley Square. Giles stood beside the carriage steps, beaming, with a white cockade in his hat.

Polly blinked back tears. "I am." They had come a long way from Wintermast, together.

Clairmallon lay in the last light of a gentle dusk as if waiting for her. Homecoming, after so long away, was precious.

"Driver." Ellen rapped on the ceiling of the hansom cab. "Will you stop, please?"

The cabbie almost swore. He had to hurry if he was to take this lady up to the house and still pick up custom from the last London train of the day.

"It will be worth it to you, Sir." His passenger was polite. That was something in these fast times. The man hauled on the brake, locking the rear wheels.

The lady unlatched the door herself and dropped the step down. "Take this for your fare." The half sovereign cheered the coachman. He called out as she walked toward a lake between the drive and the house. "Where shall I take the trunk, Ma'am?"

"To the stable yard. Knock on the kitchen door. Say I shall be along directly."

Ellen did not wait to see if the driver had done as she asked. She was too occupied breathing in the scent of the evening and watching the dragonflies hover above the silver waters of the lake.

A dark figure waved from the terrace. "Ellen!"

She could not hear her name distinctly but imagination supplied the sound. Connor. Behind him a smaller person jumped up and down.

Ellen gathered her skirts in both hands and ran toward the pair as they hurried down the steps. In the very middle of the lawn, she opened her arms and Connie flew to her. She was tall, almost up to her mother's shoulder.

"Connie! And who is this splendid young gentleman?"

Connor had joined them. He had the baby in his arms. Nine months was very different from newborn. The child stared solemnly at the stranger.

Connor said, encouragingly, "Kit, here is your dear aunt. She has come a very long way to see us all."

Ellen knelt. But the little boy, suddenly shy, turned his face away. Ellen said, "What shall we do, Connie? Shall we kiss him?"

The baby gurgled and giggled and squirmed in his father's arms until, at last, his blue eyes met Ellen's lively green ones, and the little boy beamed. Ellen had truly come home.

Oriana struggled to sit up. "You really are here!"

She had been dozing on a daybed in the summer drawing room. It had been pulled up to the windows so she could see the garden.

Connor caught Ellen's glance. She swallowed. *Why did he not tell me?* But she hurried forward, smiling. She sat on the end of a chaise longue and reached for her cousin's hand. "What's this? Asleep before sunset?" The change was deeply affecting. The pretty young mother had vanished.

Oriana stared at her cousin with painful intensity. "I shall sleep better now that you are here." Her eyes were embers, deep in shadow.

"And I, too. Clairmallon has been calling me, you know. In the end, I could not resist that siren song. Autumn is so pretty here." Ellen tried to smile. Connor stood behind her shoulder, and Connie, unusually quiet, sat on the floor with Kit in her arms.

Oriana reached up to Connor. "Do you know, I should like to walk. Just before the sun is completely gone from the garden?"

"Well then, so you shall." Connor leaned forward, as if to lift his wife from the daybed, but she stopped him. "With Ellen. We have so much to talk about." Connor swallowed. He cast Ellen a despairing look.

Taking a breath between each word, Oriana said, "There. You see? Quite steady." Standing, it was apparent how thin she had become. Ellen had to look away. She cleared her throat and asked, brightly, "Where should you like to walk, Oriana?"

"To the lake. Where else? Just as we used to do." Oriana sighed happily. "This is my favorite time of day. Do you remember?"

Ellen nodded. "Of course." They had always loved evening as the blue shadows gathered.

Connor showed Ellen how to support Oriana, but in spite of Ellen's arm around her waist, his wife wavered where she stood. "You would not prefer to be wheeled, Oriana?" A wickerwork cart stood on the terrace.

"I feel stronger tonight. Doctor Abel told me the liver would be effective. He was correct."

Connie said judiciously, "Aunt Oriana does not especially like liver, Mama. Nor do I."

"But we all eat it together, do we not? Delicious. Especially with bacon." Connor was determined to seem lighthearted. Oriana laughed, a faint silver thread of sound. Ellen's heart contracted. She took Ellen's arm and the pair moved slowly across the terrace.

Oriana joked, "Send men with torches if we do not come back."

Connor said softly, "Do not be long, my dearest wife, or I shall . . ."

Ellen could not bear to see the pain in his eyes. "Here are the steps down to the lawn, cousin. Can you see them?"

Oriana replied, "I can see perfectly well, cousin. Only my body lets me down. Not my eyes."

Ellen was stricken. "I am so sorry, Oriana. I did not mean—"

"You meant only to be kind. Let us enjoy the evening. It has been a long time."

Ellen said nothing, but she thought, *How can I not have known? Why did I not feel the change?*

"You have done so well with the business. I do not wonder you had no time to come to us in these last months. But we have missed you." Oriana's breath came in short gasps.

"It is easy to be busy. There are more important things."

The lake was in sight. "Do not be sad, cousin. We understood why you left Clairmallon. And only think, you did not need to become a governess." They both laughed.

Ellen said, "An escape to be celebrated."

Oriana happily sighed. "It is so peaceful here."

"Shall we pause for a while?" Ellen had brought her cousin to the bench by the lake.

"Yes. But tell me about . . ." Oriana had no breath to finish the sentence as Ellen helped her to sit.

"About London?" Ellen completed the thought, and Oriana nodded. Ellen gazed at the line of fading hills. "I expected, after the first frenzy, that interest would subside. But the opposite is true. And if I continue . . ."

Oriana looked at her cousin, puzzled. "If?"

"*If* I continue, it will be for a very good reason. Though one that eludes me at this moment." She pressed Oriana's hand to emphasize the irony.

Oriana found it easier to whisper than to speak. "It was all for Constance, Ellen. And I have been a very lucky woman. I, too, have had a daughter." *Have been. Have had.* The words struck like a tolling bell. "So much happiness. My husband. Constance and little Kit. And you." The pupils of Oriana's eyes were huge in the dusk. "More than a sister." Tears slipped down her face, but she was smiling. "One day, you will be as happy as I have been. With a family of your own. Yet promise me . . ." She paused.

How could Ellen breathe? It was too painful. "Of course. Anything."

"Think lovingly of Connor. And the children. They will need you."

Ellen could not listen further. She said quickly, "But you will be better very soon, Oriana. The weather is warm, your family is all around you." She would not let herself cry, *she would not.* "I must take you back to the house before you get cold."

Oriana's tears were gone, but the smile remained. "Let us stay a little longer. It is so beautiful by the lake." She took both of Ellen's hands in her own. Her voice was almost spent. "Do not be frightened of death, Ellen. I am not. Something of me will always remain in this place."

Ellen sat beside her cousin, numb, as they gazed across the silver water. Slowly, the last glow of evening was extinguished, and the garden, by degrees, slipped into the dark.

"Why did you not tell me, Connor?"

It was late, and Connie was, finally, in bed after Ellen had read "just one more story" three times.

"You said I was not to worry. That the illness was minor." Ellen could not keep reproach from her voice. She and Connor and Daisy were seated at the dinner table. None had done anything but pick at what they had been offered. Oriana, they hoped, was sleeping after the walk.

"Do not blame Connor. Oriana would not let him tell you how serious things had become. She did not want to worry you." Daisy had bruise-dark circles beneath her eyes.

"But . . ." Ellen shook her head.

"She said you had had enough unhappiness." Connor drained a glass of wine and poured another.

"I could have nursed her!" Ellen's anguish was insupportably raw.

Daisy winced, and said, gently, "Perhaps I am selfish. This was something I wished to do."

Ellen closed her eyes. She whispered, "I am sorry. So sorry. Forgive me."

Connor muttered. "We are all sorry. The truth is, Oriana has never recovered from Kit's birth. Doctor Abel has done all he can, but he is mystified by the wasting. I have had London medical men here, too, in relays, but though they prescribe this or that regime, nothing changes."

Daisy said piteously, "And she has dwindled to bones and skin before our eyes. It is hard for her to swallow even milk." She shook her head in despair.

Connor continued, "But Oriana, and we, have never given up the hope that all may yet improve." He smiled, the pain showing in his eyes. "And now you are here. All week she has waited to hear your voice. As have we all."

That haunted gaze gripped her. "Tell me what I can do."

It seemed cruel that each autumn day was more beautiful than the last as Oriana faded—the skies limpid blue, the sun glorious and warm, the air light.

Daisy and Ellen took turns nursing Oriana; each dawn, each evening a loss, never to be restored, but at least one more day during which she still lived. And when not beside Oriana, they were with the children, reading, kissing, and playing in the garden—providing the comfort that they could not find for themselves. Connor, too, sat with his wife all the hours he was awake. If he had to sleep, he did so on a trundle bed beside her own.

Clairmallon grew quiet. Much life had passed through this old house, many beginnings and many endings. Perhaps it understood how to wait, as if it wrapped those who mourned in a compassionate embrace, a presence hundreds of years older than theirs would ever be. A spirit that surrendered to joy and sorrow on the same terms. Acceptance.

One perfect evening, Connor stood at the foot of his wife's bed. Oriana seemed to be sleeping. Each wheezing breath long and the time in between growing longer.

Ellen asked, "Shall I send for Doctor Abel?" The doctor had

been tireless in these last weeks, never grudging what time he was called to Oriana's bed.

"No. He left a quantity of the laudanum syrup. There is nothing further he can offer my wife." Connor spoke quietly, just in case Oriana could hear him. Hearing, he had been told, was the last sense to depart.

"It will be at the turning of the tide." Daisy was sewing in the window seat. There was always mending to be done for the children, or the household. Her busy hands were the habit of a lifetime.

Ellen sat beside her aunt. "They used to say that in Wintermast."

"The soul leaves with the tide, borne away from mortal sight." Daisy was beyond tears. They all were. The bedroom door opened.

Connie entered the room and ran the few steps to Ellen's arms. Daisy asked anxiously, "Where is Kit?" and Constance pointed. Maggie had Kit in her arms. Connor strode to the maid and she gave him the sleeping baby.

Maggie whispered, "Miss Constance asked me to bring him to you, Sir. She was most insistent."

The figure on the bed stirred, her eyelids, purple as gentian, moved. Ellen went to the bed. She raised Oriana's hand to kiss it, cradling the cold, dry fingers in her own. "Cousin. Dearest Oriana."

Look after the children. The voice was a thread. *Love them. Love him. For me.* Those tired eyes stared at Ellen before the heavy lids closed once more.

"Oriana?" Poor man. Poor, stricken husband. With Kit in his arms, Connor lay down beside the girl on the bed. He clasped her hands to warm them. "We are all here, my darling. And I *shall* love them. I shall do as you ask. Do not strain to talk."

Slowly, as if she was managing a great weight, Oriana moved her head. Her eyes opened again. Staring at Connor, she said, "Dearest man. Ellen? Connor. Constance. Kit. Mama." She spoke each name with punishing effort. And Ellen knew. Oriana had spoken to her alone. This was what she meant. *Love them. Love him.*

Kit woke. Seeing all those he knew so unhappy, he started wailing. Oriana faintly smiled and her arms, so limp on the counterpane, stirred. "Give him to me. And Constance. Come." The whisper was very faint.

Connor placed the crying baby beside his mother as Connie scrambled closer to Oriana, reaching out to kiss her. For a moment, father and mother and the two children were united, and the little boy ceased to cry. With his small, damp hand he touched his mother's face.

And then, as Constance held her hand, as her baby snuggled against her breast, as Connor kissed her brow, and Ellen embraced Daisy to keep her from falling, Oriana Moncrieff left this world.

CHAPTER 44

A WEEK, THAT was all. Only seven days since the moment her cousin took a last, deep breath, as if to store air enough for the long journey to come. But Oriana had never taken another, and they, her family, were left bereft.

Ellen and Connie were sitting quietly in Oriana's dayroom. All the mourners had departed and, at Connie's request, Ellen had a book of fairy tales on her lap.

"Which one would you like first?"

The little girl shrugged. "You choose, Mama."

Ellen opened the book and scanned the index. "This is one of your favorites. The girl who was given three wishes."

Connie muttered, "I want only one."

Ellen softly closed the book. "If we could bring her back to you, Connie, we would."

Connie stared past her mother toward the garden. "Sometimes, I look up and expect she will be there. But she never is."

Ellen spoke carefully. "I, too, have wished, so often, to hear her voice, to see her. Even one more time." She stopped again. Taking Connie by the shoulders, Ellen turned the child gently to face her. "She wants us to take comfort in each other, Connie."

Connie stared at Ellen. "But you will go back to London."

The words were a blade. Something wicked and thin that brought only pain. "You are my daughter, Connie. *Nothing* is more important to me than your happiness."

"Then stay here. Do not leave. Marry Uncle Connor. Kit will be my brother and he will be my father. Properly. Forever. I miss having a daddy so." Connie, sobbing, buried her face in Ellen's lap.

Ellen stroked Connie's curls. She spoke with effort. "Uncle Connor loved Aunt Oriana very much. Just as he loves you. That will never change. And he and I are beloved friends. That is as it should be."

"Then he will marry someone else one day and I will have to leave Clairmallon and I will never see Kit or Aunt Daisy again. Why does everyone have to go away?" Connie could not speak for sobbing.

"These are groundless fears." *Were they?* "This is your home. It always will be. And mine also."

When she returned to the family salon Connor was there, staring into the fire.

"Aunt Daisy?"

"Has gone to her bed."

Ellen nodded. Pretending for the sake of the children had been hard for them all. She shivered. "It is cold tonight, cousin."

"Draw nearer to the fire. Warm yourself."

They spoke over each other. And hesitated. And laughed. The first light moment in many days.

Ellen held her hands to the flames as Connor said, "Perhaps it is easier for you. I hope with all my heart that it is."

She frowned. "Easier?"

"The female sex is expected to express emotion. We men, however . . ." The lightness of the moment was lost.

Ellen could bear no more. There was only a step between them. Seizing his hand with both of hers, she pressed it to the side of her face with painful strength. "I loved her also, Connor. She became my sister, my real sister."

This was too much. Connor Moncrieff swept Ellen against his chest and they wept.

Swollen-eyed, at last he released her and said, "Forgive me. My loss of control is—"

"A comfort. To me at least." Ellen's voice shook. Propriety. How it crippled true feeling. She would not be embarrassed that they had held each other so close. That would be to shame the moment.

Connor gestured to a chair. "Sit, cousin. I beg you sit. Or I shall fall down." An aching, terrible laugh.

Ellen's head was lighter than feathers. A great tide had washed through her being, carrying a part of the anguish far away. But only a part. She did not want to sit. She wanted his arms around her still. Connor's strength supporting her, nothing more. Was that so wrong? *Oriana, forgive me. I know you understand.* But she did as he asked.

They were silent, then Connor said, "We must talk of the future. That is what she wanted us to do."

Where was that familiar voice, the inner being who conveyed advice good and bad? Ellen heard nothing. But a response was expected from her. She said, "Yes. There is much to speak of, many matters of business and other things as well, but I shall make no sense tonight." *Business?* She did not care about business at all.

Connor murmured, "Will you permit Connie to stay on at Clairmallon?"

Permit? Ellen swallowed. "I know that is her dearest wish."

Connor's face brightened. "I am so grateful." His laugh was shaky. "Sometimes, as Oriana did, I find myself believing Connie is my own child. And she so loves Kit." He spoke low, staring into the fire. "I have thought often it would be cruel to part them."

Ellen expelled a slow breath. "You are very good to her. To us. If Constance misses the father she has never known, your love lessens that sadness." She stared blindly at the dark beyond the windows. How she longed, tonight, to tell Connor the truth. To ask his advice about her daughter.

But Connor broke the silence. "Perhaps you have not heard that Shene has finally been sold? Daisy will continue to live here with us. That was Oriana's dearest wish. Your aunt will not leave either of the children. Or me, it seems. I welcome her presence." A sweet smile. "But you are a gracious woman, Ellen Gowan."

"Gracious?" Ellen shrugged helplessly. "You have given us a home and opened your heart to Connie. And to me. You have helped me create our business so that, one day, I may be independent and give my daughter a future. You say *I* am gracious?" Tears ran from her eyes. She did not try to stop them. "Oriana spoke of herself as a lucky woman. She was to have so many years of happiness here."

"But not enough. Never enough."

"For either of us." Ellen pressed the heels of her palms to her eyes.

Reverie filled up the growing silence. Perhaps, when Oriana had spoken of luck, she had discounted the full meaning of the word. To be loved as she had been loved by this man would be a rare experience.

"We should speak of business tomorrow, then?"

Ellen nodded.

Connor plunged an iron into the heart of the blaze. "Then, may your sleep be dreamless, Ellen."

When Ellen closed the door he stared for a long time at the space she had occupied.

A casement was open and the curtains rippled in the night breeze. In the window seat, Ellen laid her face against the glass. It was cold as a pool. The sky was cloudless and a three-quarters moon edged the trees with silver. Ellen leaned out to close the casement. And saw.

Someone was standing at the edge of the lake. The figure moved, and when it turned, a silver face gazed toward the house. Toward her. *Oriana?*

How long before Ellen stood by the lake's verge? She did not know. She was panting and there was a pain in her side. She must have run. This was the place she had seen the figure, beside the bench where she and Oriana had sat and talked so many times. But she was alone.

One light burned still among the many windows of Clairmallon. Hers. Would she wake, soon, in her bed? Was she dreaming?

"Oriana?" No answer but the reeds. That dry, soft clatter as they shifted. Despairing, Ellen turned back toward the house.

Something warm bounced at her throat as she walked. It was the locket.

Ellen stopped. She opened the case. There was enough light to see, if she held it very close. Was this her mother's face or little Connie's? Or was it she, or Oriana? Hair. Eyes. Mouth. In the moonlight there seemed no difference.

Ellen clutched the locket in both hands. "What does it mean? Tell me!"

Do not go back to London. Connie's voice was in her head.

Ellen's heart was a fragile thing. And she had thought herself so strong. "But I must. You know I must. Oh, what should I do?"

The sky and the garden were silent. They had no answer.

CHAPTER 45

WINTER MISTS, so pretty in Clairmallon's valley, lay over the city as if, by smothering, they might choke life from the streets.

Ellen had been at Berkeley Square for some weeks. In full mourning for Oriana, most days she wore iron black velvet. Sorrow had hollowed the space beneath her eyes and cheeks, but this had the effect of sculptural magnificence. As if her destiny had been fulfilled, she was as imposing, as severe as a nun. But only discipline, and the routine of work, provided sanctuary from thought. As she had done every morning since her return, she sat at her desk, selected a fresh sheet of paper from an ample supply, arranged her pencils, her brushes, her paints, and an India rubber. And began to draw. Sketches of clothing certainly, but faces also. Oriana, Connie, Daisy, Kit. And Connor. He was staring up at her today, half-smiling. Ellen covered him up, and continued to sketch a riding costume as if she were an automaton.

"Coddled eggs." Polly was at the door. She did not knock because she did not want to be sent away. In her hands was a covered tray.

Ellen did not look up from her work. "Do not be angry with me, Polly. I have no time to eat. These are needed. I did not finish them last night."

Conveniently deaf, Polly marched through the door and put the tray down on the table. With a snap, the cloth settled in a drift of white linen. Polished glassware and silver followed, precisely arranged on that pure surface. They had the money, now, for pretty things.

Polly said, pleasantly, "Come. Sit. You will work better with food beneath that belt." The new Mrs. Redcliffe was a determined woman. She had won the battle with her mother-in-law. Will had backed her. She would continue to work with Ellen until she found herself with child. For now, Madame Ellen was still her charge.

Ellen looked down at her hands and frowned. They were shaking. Had she eaten last night? She could not remember. "Very well. But I am not hungry."

Polly swallowed a pleased smile. *We shall see about that.*

The coddled eggs and warm rolls were set down before Ellen. Curls of pale butter, Stilton cheese, and crab paste in white pots were placed beside a dish of gammon and mustard pickles. There were white peaches and grapes, too, imported out-of-season exotics from the market.

"All this for breakfast? The fruit must have been so expensive!"

Polly was unrepentant. "So, relish it. And if you do not finish each and all, I shall want to know why."

"*Such* a bully. I cannot be force-fed like a goose."

Polly grinned. "Goose or not, food is what you need." She pretended to flounce from the room as if mortally offended.

Dearest Polly. Ellen smiled fondly. The scent of hot bread was beguiling. Her stomach growled. She was hungry, she really was. Ellen drew the basket of rolls closer. Eat first, think later.

Real hunger sharpened the savor, and if her corsets pinched tighter, a punishment for indulgence, Ellen decided she did not care. It was rare to feel so satisfied. But as she finished the last of the peaches, her desk, finally, would not be ignored.

Other work lay waiting there. A thick packet of documents wrapped in brown paper was addressed to her. Ellen had seen it last evening but forgotten to open it when more urgent tasks absorbed her.

Ellen cut the string with the bread knife. Inside, there was a single sheet of letter paper and two thick documents. She unfolded the first and almost dropped it. This was the deed for Berkeley Square but the owner's name had been changed. *Her* name was there in place of Connor and Oriana Moncrieff's. Ellen's pulse quickened as she leafed through the pages to find Connor's signature. She touched it disbelievingly. He had signed there. It was real. Urgently, she riffled through the other deed. It was the loan agreement for the business. It had been canceled.

She picked up the letter. It was from Connor. Her hands shook so much she laid it on the desk. And read.

8th December, AD 1854
Clairmallon
Near Norwich

My dear Ellen,

I hope the documents that accompany this letter are welcome.

Before Oriana left us, she asked me to do two things. The first was to place the title of Berkeley Square in your name, which I have done. The second was to cancel the loan for the business. This, too, has been arranged. You are now the sole owner of both.

We salute you. Through your own efforts and the talent with which you were born, you had already begun to secure the future for Constance, and for yourself, which we both knew to be your dearest wish. With these gifts we hope to complete that process and help consolidate all that you have achieved.

Oriana asked me to say that she wished you joy in the continuing success of what is, now, your own enterprise. To which I desire to add my own congratulations and admiration.

But do not forget us at Clairmallon. Constance, Kit, Daisy, and I eagerly await your return.

With good wishes for the continuing prosperity of Chez Miss Constance.

Your true and respectful friend,
Connor Moncrieff

"Dearest God!"

Ellen's scream brought Polly to the door. "What is wrong?"

As if the victim of a fit, Ellen opened and closed her mouth though no sound emerged.

"Do not try to speak." Polly tried to raise Ellen from her chair. "I shall get you to bed and call the doctor."

"No, Polly." At last Ellen began to resist. "I can stand. Really."

But Polly would not listen. "I knew. I knew something bad would come from this. No sleep for days, nothing to eat of any consequence."

Ellen, exasperated, said, "Look! Look at what is written here!" Clutched in her fist was the letter.

A cautious pause as Polly began to read. She looked narrowly at Ellen. And then at the text of the letter, mouthing the words one by one. Her eyes grew very wide. "But this says?"

Ellen nodded. "It does. I own the business." She began to sob, wailing louder by the second.

Polly gaped. "Why are you crying?"

"Because I do not deserve . . . This is not right, and . . ." She gasped and cried harder.

Polly subsided to a chair, and began to laugh. "Of all the sillies." She, too, was gasping.

Ellen's sobs dwindled as Polly, doubled over, rolled from side to side. And that set Ellen off, gulping between laughter and tears as Polly's guffaws grew louder still.

Polly calmed first. She pressed a hand to her side. "My ribs hurt." She sighed. "She knew, your cousin. How hard you have worked. How much you have given up. I should think about *deserve,* if I was you. It is time, my girl, for you to reap joy, not tears."

Ellen wiped her eyes. Her breath came in hiccups. "And so, too, for you, Mrs. Redcliffe. If it is really mine to give, then a share of this business is in order."

"For me?" Color drained from Polly's face.

Ellen held out her arms. "For you, old friend. If sadness plows the field, joy is a crop we can both gather in."

It was near sunset before Ellen found time alone. Work had engulfed her during the day and there had been little time to think. Now the dull yellow afternoon had turned cold. Soon the air would thicken. Fog would occupy the windless sky, blurring the sharp edges of the buildings to something soft and strange as night fell.

"I shall go for a walk."

"It will be dark soon, Madame." Frances, the assistant that Polly had found for Ellen, did not wish to offend her new employer but London was London. Even in the best parts of town a woman walking alone was vulnerable.

Pulling on her gloves, Ellen said, pleasantly, "I have been working since before daylight. The cool air will clear my head." She smiled at the anxious girl. Frances was not to know how much Ellen had to think about. All of it glorious.

"Will you take this, at least?" A large black umbrella was proffered. "It has been raining."

"Now, Frances, do not fuss."

The young woman gulped. But she said, bravely, "We can walk together, if you would like company?"

Taking the umbrella, Ellen hesitated on the step. "Thank you for your concern. I shall return in an hour." But she did not look back as she tripped quickly down the steps to the wet street. She was smiling.

Pulling down her veil, Ellen walked in the direction of Westminster. This was a path she had taken many times, and the quick tapping of her feet ticked off the seconds with the regularity of a clock. She needed London tonight, needed the sense of all the other lives lived in this place and the pleasure of anonymity.

Berkeley Square was quiet, the noise of the city muted by the buildings on either side. It was that uneasy time between dusk and the lighting of street lamps. Ellen quickened her pace. A sharp wind skirled past, and the last autumn leaves lifted from the pavement, as if to escape.

She heard the other footfall five houses from the end of the square. It kept pace with her own so perfectly that, at first, she did not notice, until the scuffle of a double-step directly behind her.

Ellen stopped: And doubted her senses. Less than thirty yards away was the corner that led out of the square. It was lit there. Here, where she was, shadows lay.

Ellen grasped the handle of the umbrella firmly. She set out for the corner, her feet a quick scatter of taps on the paving stones. Unblinking, she fixed on the goal ahead and the promise of the brighter street beyond.

And heard it again.

A hard leather heel on stone, the interval between each step longer than her own. A man's stride. Moving quickly. She whirled about.

"Mrs. de Valentin. Good evening." Raoul lifted his hat.

Ellen gasped as he sauntered forward.

"Surprised to see me?"

She did not step back. It pleased her that her voice was steady. "What do you want, Raoul?"

He smiled, that confident smile women found so charming. "I am delighted to see you again, Ellen, after all this time. And looking so well."

Astonishment sharpened Ellen's tone. "You followed me. Why did you not come to the house?" Contempt lent an edge. "Let me guess. Chicken hearted." She turned back. She could see her house ahead. *Her* house. She stepped out steadily.

Raoul matched her stride. He was still smiling. Light spilled from a window and Ellen could see every detail of his face. Her nostrils flared at the tang of him. That faint odor of musk and tobacco she had once adored was nauseating now.

"Why so unfriendly, *ma chère*? All I desire is a little conversation. A gentleman and a lady exchanging memories. Talking of the future."

If he could smile, so could she. "Memories?" Ellen stopped. And turned to face him. "You were never a gentleman, Raoul. You just looked like one. I have acquaintance with the real thing, now."

He gripped her arm but said, pleasantly, "However, we shall speak together, *ma chère*. I insist." The hold tightened.

Ellen stared at his fingers. "We have nothing to discuss, Raoul." They were close enough that a passerby might have thought them lovers.

Raoul collected himself. He dropped his hand and shrugged. "On the contrary, there is a great deal of which we must speak. But you are right. It will be more agreeable if I call on you. Tomorrow evening. Important matters must be addressed."

"Ellen!" Polly had seen Raoul and was running toward them from the house.

"Until then." Raoul raised his hat and walked toward the corner of the square. Sauntering at first, he picked up pace quite quickly.

"That man! What did he want?" Polly, panting, arrived at Ellen's side.

"I do not know."

Polly snorted, and answered her own question, "Nothing good, I'll be bound. The nerve of him!"

"He says he will call, tomorrow night."

"Ah well, that's easily fixed. I shall get my Will to greet him at the door. They'll remember each other. You shall not be bothered again."

"Raoul said it was important." Ellen was troubled.

"Important? For you or for him? Do not trust him, Ellen."

Ellen turned and stared toward the end of the square. Raoul had gone. "I would not use that word in conjunction with his name."

"Come back to the house before this fog gets in your lungs."

Ellen nodded, but she asked, "Is that a whip?"

Polly colored and hid the offending item behind her skirts. "What of it?"

"Did you really think to use it?"

Polly tossed her head as she chivvied Ellen up the steps. "Does not matter now. He walked away pretty quick when he saw me."

"But a whip, Polly?"

The door closed behind them, shutting out the night. "Too good for the likes of him."

It was late the following evening when the carriage drew up outside. In the hall, Ellen composed herself. She stood on the second-lowest step of the staircase as the knocker sounded.

"Are you sure about this?" Polly had refused to go home. "I can send him away, I promise you."

"Open the door, please."

"Very well." Polly stamped away with bad grace. Ellen smiled mirthlessly. *The contest begins.*

The tall door opened to a dank mist and Raoul de Valentin appeared, a black-suited conjurer. Polly followed, scowling.

"Ah, Madame Ellen. It delights me to see you again. Your servant." Raoul bowed with particular grace. He ignored Polly.

Polly said impassively, "Will that be all, Madame?" She glared at Raoul's back.

"If I need you, I shall call."

Pausing at almost every step, Polly trailed toward the baize-covered door beneath the stairs and finally went through.

Ellen stared at her husband. Raoul de Valentin's brow creased.

He coughed. A signal, a pause offered, in which Ellen should properly indicate a salon, or some other room in which they might speak. When she did not, he said, "This is a most handsome house, Madame. Delightful. A worthy setting for the jewel it contains." He bowed again. Ellen did not respond. Smoothly, he continued, "And I trust your lengthy sojourn in the country was agreeable?"

Now that they were alone, the French vowels slid imperceptibly away.

How did he know? Ellen said, short, "No, Sir, it was not. A friend, a dear friend, passed away."

"I grieve for your sorrow." His expression was grave.

Ellen said, politely, "You have never felt either emotion, Raoul, except when it touches yourself."

Raoul flushed. Controlling his voice with an effort, he said, "Emotion at such a time is to be expected." He advanced a step or two. She stood above him, a black pillar, and did not move. The higher ground was hers tonight.

"I had forgotten. You think us the weaker sex, do you not? Irrational and flighty, incapable of constancy or purpose?" Her glance was cool.

A full moon was rising behind the houses, and a pale corona formed around Ellen from an easterly window. The effect was eerie. A silver woman in a black dress lit by candlelight from below. "Interesting as it is to see you here tonight, Raoul, I must ask what it is you want?"

Raoul blinked. "Whatever the general opinion of men might be, I know you to be different from most of your sex. Not just exquisite appearance sets you apart." A graceful compliment, gracefully delivered.

But she would not play this game. "I repeat, what do you want?"

He shrugged. "I am hurt, *chérie*. Why would this visit not be to speak of old times, renew old bonds?"

Ellen laughed incredulously. "I am a busy woman, Raoul. If this is all you have to say to me, I shall say good night."

She went to pull the bell cord but he gripped her wrist. She did not struggle but stared at him with raised brows. He said quickly, "Your business, Madame. That is what interests me." He released his grasp. Glancing around the hall he observed, pleasantly, "You have done well."

Too hastily, Ellen said, "None of this is mine. I have an investor. His loan is still to be repaid." It had all been true. Yesterday.

He laughed tolerantly. "Dearest Ellen, I know you so well. You lie poorly. Such an honest face."

As if dealing with a fractious child, he said, "Recall, my dear, that we are married. As your husband, I have interests identical to yours. By law, I own what you own."

"Blackmail, Raoul? How odd. I find myself unconvinced by threats." But Ellen's heart hammered.

He sighed. "Very well. Let us not speak of money. There are things of greater importance. The loss of a child, for instance. A sorrow from which a grieving parent never recovers. To think I have never known my daughter, that she was taken from me at birth."

That was too much. Ellen was enraged. "You wanted to *sell* her."

Raoul gazed at her sorrowfully. "After all these years, after so many sleepless nights, I find to my astonishment that she lives. And so pretty. The image of her beautiful mother."

Ellen swallowed. *He has seen Connie.* "Your interest in Connie is remarkable after so many years of absence." *Do not debate with him!*

Raoul knew that he had the advantage now. He said, musingly, "By Connie you must mean Constance? A name I should not have chosen. But then, I was not consulted. Not even in the naming of my daughter. That was not wise." He stared at Ellen. His eyes were as dark and shiny as flint.

"Alas, we did not know where to find you." The polite understatement was considerable. "And now this conversation is at an end. I bid you good evening." Ellen's hand went to the bellpull again.

Raoul waved airily. "Do not trouble. I shall see myself out." He bowed, and strolled to the door. Pulling it open, he turned. "I wish to assure myself of the safety of my daughter, that is all. I am sure you find, as I do, that a child on the streets of London is always to be considered vulnerable. Especially the daughter of a wealthy woman. So many who would take advantage of innocence for gain."

Do not react! Ellen tried to school her features, but his satisfied smile said she had not succeeded.

"Any unpleasantness, of course, can depart from your life immediately, as I shall, on payment of one thousand pounds. Gold is to be preferred, and by the end of the week. If this sum is not deposited with my bankers by that time, I shall bring proceedings of divorce. I shall also apply to wind up the business so I may obtain my fair share of its value."

Raoul placed his card delicately in a silver dish on the hall table.

"And please to remember that no court in the land will permit that you have custody of our daughter. You unlawfully deprived me of her presence by the use of violence. And now you dwell apart from Constance, and allow our child to be brought up by others. An unnatural and neglectful mother. Ah yes, I know all that you do, Madame Ellen. I have made it my business to understand your life."

The barb struck home. It was tipped with the poison of Ellen's own self-reproach, but she would not let him see that.

"I shall countersue, of course. By your previous behavior to me, I shall have ample grounds for a divorce since there are numerous witnesses to your behavior. And very few fathers attempt to sell their newborn child to avoid debtors' prison."

Raoul stiffened.

"And I, at least, have money for lawyers, where as I doubt that you do." Ellen had no concept of her rights at law, but she was certain he knew less than she did. Raoul was a lazy man. Ellen Gowan might be many things, but she was not lazy.

Raoul mustered an insouciant shrug.

"It saddens me, Madame, that we have so little to say to each other. I had thought the tenderness we felt once should allow this matter to conclude with dignity. You have much to be grateful for, and my mother's teaching, and my own, has played no small part in your success."

That was the wrong tone. Raoul saw it immediately as the pupils of Ellen's eyes contracted. If she had been angry before, now she was coldly furious. "Leave, Raoul." Her glance was bleak as bitter winter.

Raoul said, hastily, "By Friday, then, Coutts and Company shall be alerted to expect your draft." He replaced his hat and, walking through the open door, addressed Ellen from the step. "Madame, it remains only to wish you the very best of good nights. After this most delightful of evenings, be sure I shall count the moments until I may return. All felicitations of the season. *Au revoir.*"

"Good morning, Polly." Ellen was at her desk, neatly dressed. She was writing.

Polly blinked. She struggled from the embrace of the chair. Ellen had woken from a nightmare in the early hours of the morning, after Raoul had left, and Polly had gone to comfort her friend, and fallen asleep before the fire.

"I know how my granny felt, now. On winter mornings she'd say, 'Seized up like an old clock, that's me.'"

Ellen did not respond as she scratched words rapidly across a sheet of paper.

Polly frowned. She angled her head, trying to see what was being written, but Ellen leaned over her work, one arm curled around the paper.

"Tea, that is what we need."

Ellen slewed around in her chair. Her eyes were chips of stone. "No." She turned back. "I am busy."

It took a great deal to reduce Polly to tears, but the stress of the last days was too much. She blinked rapidly. "I am only trying to help."

"Leave me *alone!*" Ellen crashed her fist on the desk, and a black flood streamed across the page. She jumped up, trying to stem the flow with her hands. "My letter!" The stain spread over her skirt. Ellen's movements grew increasingly wild.

Polly ran forward. She clasped Ellen tightly in her arms, though the girl tried to push her away. Abruptly, Ellen ceased to struggle, and slumped against her friend.

"Sit here, sweetheart. In my chair." Ellen did as she was told—her docility as unnerving as the rage. Polly mopped up the ink on the desk as calmly as she could. "Not much damage. Nearly done. Just give me your hands."

Obediently, Ellen lifted first one black hand and then the other for Polly to wipe.

Ellen sighed. "I have to stop him. Connie must be protected. I was trying to write to Connor."

"Of course." Polly tried to assess the damage to Ellen's dress. The stain had spread to a great degree, though fortunately the skirt was black.

Utterly defeated, Ellen said, "I did not tell you last night. Raoul has threatened to take the business, and this house."

Polly blanched. "But, he cannot."

"He can. He is my husband. And worse, he will kidnap Connie if I do not pay him a great deal of money."

Polly's mouth dropped open. *God damn that man to Hell!*

"He would not dare. How could he? At Clairmallon?"

"But she is coming here next week. I cannot take that chance! He called me neglectful of Connie. And I have been. What mother deserts her child?" She began to cry. Heaving, piteous sobs. Polly was crying, too. Ellen's pain was too much to bear.

"You made the decision to come to London *because* of her."

"How can I face Constance when she knows the truth? Or Connor?"

"Connor Moncrieff is a good man. He will understand. So will Connie. One day." So Polly devoutly hoped. "Be brave. You have always been brave."

12th December, AD 1854
Berkeley Square
Westminster
London

Dear cousin,

I wonder if I might ask a favor? With Christmas close, we have been very busy here. Constance is expecting to visit Berkeley Square next week. However, I am concerned she will not have my entire attention. I feel her visit must be canceled.

I have never done such a thing before, and Connie will be confused, and possibly upset. But it is better, believe me, that she does not come. Would you be so kind as to break this unwelcome news?

I shall write again very soon.

Forgive the brevity of this letter.

Your grateful cousin,
Ellen

"Uncle Connor, you are frowning." Connie was feeding Kit porridge. They were enjoying the game greatly as, for each spoonful he swallowed, another decorated his face, his hands, and his hair. And Connie's apron, too.

"Am I?" Connor was distracted. He folded the letter and slipped it beneath his breakfast plate.

Connie navigated a last spoonful to the baby's mouth. "There, Kit. All gone." Kit began to wail. "But you can have some toast if you like?" The yelling stopped. A fat hand reached out and Connie, fatally, inserted a wedge of toast slathered with blackberry jam.

Connie pointed proudly at her cousin. "He likes that, Uncle Connor. Look." Jam had joined the porridge in decorating Kit's cherubic face.

"Time for Maggie, or we shall have to dunk him in the horse trough." Oriana's maid had become Kit's nanny. They loved each other dearly. Connor picked up the breakfast bell and rang it.

"Was the letter from Mama?"

"What very sharp eyes you have, child."

Connie grinned. "As the wolf said to Little Red Riding Hood! I recognized her writing."

"Maggie, Master Kit is in need of your services. And a nap, I should think."

The girl curtsied as she entered. Kit waved at her cheerfully. "He certainly is, Mr. Moncrieff. Come along, young man."

The baby squealed at being removed from all the entertainment, but as his wails receded along the corridor, Connie asked casually, "And so, what does Mama say?"

"Not a great deal. Christmas is causing a rush of business. She has suggested we postpone your visit next week until—"

"Not go to London?" Connie's eyes welled up. "But, Mama was going to take me to the jewel room in the Tower."

"Well now, that is certainly a wonderful treat, *but* . . ." Connor paused with great theatricality.

Connie sniffed. "But what?"

"I had not intended to tell you until you returned." Another artful pause.

Connie sat up. "Tell me? What did you want to tell me?" Her eyes grew round. "Not the hunter?"

With pretended reluctance, he said, "Since you ask." He nodded.

"She is coming before Christmas?"

"She is indeed. In two days' time. Your bonnie Irish mare. There, you see, everything works out. In the end."

"Oh!" Connie rushed from her seat to embrace Connor. "You are so kind. I must tell Granny Daisy!" She hurtled from the breakfast room as fast as she could.

Connor's fond smile faded. He picked up the letter and scanned it again, carefully. He knew Ellen well. Too brief and too agitated. Something was wrong.

Perhaps it was time for him to pay his own visit to London.

CHAPTER 46

"M R. PRIKE, Sir?"

The solicitor frowned. The practice clerk was agitated. This was unusual. "Yes, Alderney. What is it?"

"An urgent consultation, Sir. A young lady. Referred to us by Lady Hawksmoor."

Mr. Prike was instantly alert. The countess was a most valued client. He asked, "Does this young lady have a name?"

The clerk shook his head. "No name."

Mr. Prike sighed. Anonymous ladies guaranteed difficulty. He consulted the clock. "Very well. I shall see her. But we must finish precisely at ten. I rely on you, Alderney, to remind me." He could not imagine the countess having many nameless ladies among her acquaintance. Still, human nature was often surprising. And the ways of the aristocracy most surprising of all.

"Mr. Prike will see you now, Madame."

During the minutes in which Ellen had waited on Mr. Prike's pleasure in the dusty outer office, her resolve—so strong after receiving the recommendation from Lady Hawksmoor on "a personal matter, Countess, but legal advice is required"—had steadily withered. If the solicitor was to help her, she must tell the truth. Ellen swallowed.

"If you will sit, Madame?"

Just in time, Mr. Prike observed the wedding ring as the lady removed her gloves. He indicated a chair on the far side of his desk. His voice was as dry as the countless books on his shelves.

But the solicitor was impressed. His visitor was expensively dressed, and by the color of her gown, a widow. And though her face was deeply veiled, the voice that addressed him was cultivated. A peeress in trouble, perhaps?

"Sir, I have come to consult you about divorce. Mine. Or that is what I think I shall most likely need." Anxiety made Ellen blunt.

The lawyer cleared his throat. He said, carefully, "I must tell you, Madame, that divorce is difficult to obtain. It is only granted by an act of parliament and is an expensive process. It is not common, therefore, to be uncertain before one attempts a road so arduous."

Ellen responded politely, "Mr. Prike, I married my husband very young. Ours was an unhappy story. We became destitute and he deserted me before our baby was born."

Destitute. Not a peeress, then. Mr. Prike watched as his potential client made courageous efforts not to cry. He felt the stirrings of compassion. This was unusual. The anonymous lady seemed to be telling the truth, though many of his clients could quite sensibly manage that impression. Useful with juries, in his experience.

His visitor went on. "My husband, you see, drank. Our business failed, and he had debts. The loans were called in and he sought . . ." Ellen swallowed. In a stronger voice she continued, "He promised to sell our daughter to expunge his obligations." The lady paused.

Mr. Prike's eyebrows rose. As a solicitor he was unsurprised by the vagaries of his clients, and yet his visitor's case was certainly unusual. Unusual was often lucrative. "Continue, please."

The lady cleared her throat. "I was very ill, you see. Without my friends, he would have succeeded in his aim. He deserted me for the second time. But then, a night or two ago, after an absence of many years, he followed me from my home. And, attempted blackmail. My daughter thinks her father dead. As does my family. And I had hoped, also . . ."

The black dress was witness enough to the lady's hopes. Mr. Prike leaned forward. "And also?"

Turning slightly, Ellen raised her veil to blot the tears on her face. Mr. Prike sat up. The lady's expression was tragic, but the degree of her beauty was unusual. But then, very pretty women often led extraordinary lives. That, too, was lucrative. Sometimes. He said, politely, "We should begin at the beginning. You say the marriage was contracted in extreme youth?"

Ellen dropped her veil. Steadying her voice by an act of will, she replied, "I was fifteen on that same day. We married at St. Olave's, near the Tower, by special license."

Mr. Prike carefully pared a goose quill. He continued to use one deliberately. Thinking time was useful. He began to take laborious notes. *Underage: Bride.* "And this was with the consent of your parents or your legal guardian?"

Ellen shook her head. She said, softly, "By that time I was an orphan. I had no guardian."

The pen poised over the paper. "The groom then? What age was he?"

"Nineteen, I think. But I am not certain." The pen scratched on. *Under-age: Groom?* "Therefore, his parents had consented—or *his* guardian? The legal age of marriage, Madame, is twenty-one years in this country."

"No. I do not believe so, though my mother-in-law provided my wedding dress." Ellen frowned. "Or, that is what Raoul told me."

The solicitor crossed out the question mark and wrote, *No consents, either party.* "Had banns been called in your parish three weeks before?"

"No." Ellen's face felt hot. It was as if she was guilty of a crime she could not name.

No banns was scratched down. The list was longer by the moment. "Was there a special license obtained?"

Ellen nodded with some relief. "Yes. I was shown that document." Mr. Prike wrote *Special license.* "Which bishop, archbishop, or vicar general granted the license, and in what diocese?" The lady shrugged helplessly. He crossed out *Special* and wrote *Suspect*.

"Do you have a copy of the marriage certificate? And, was your marriage entered in St. Olave's registry?"

Ellen said, slowly, "There is no certificate, though I signed a Deed of Marriage in front of the sexton. He was our witness."

"The sexton?" the solicitor repeated. He was beginning to feel sorry for his little client. Almost purely because the story was unlikely, he had decided to take the case.

Ellen said, slowly, "None of our family was present, you see, and they said the registry had been damaged by a fire the preceding week." Her voice faded. "Mr. Prike, does this seem odd to you? My marriage, I mean? It does to me, as I speak of it."

Mr. Prike's eyebrows twitched, but he diligently wrote, *Marriage deed—not certificate—signed before witness,* before he said, "I am not able to fully assess this matter until I have all the facts before me. And yet there are certainly irregularities, as you describe them."

"What might that mean, Mr. Prike?"

He studied his list. And paused. He was about to say a very serious thing. "Madame, it *may* mean that you were not legally married."

Ellen whispered, "Not married?"

The solicitor had been afraid of this. Even behind the veil he could see the lady had blanched. "I repeat. Without documents to assess, it is not possible to be certain. However—"

"But this is wonderful! If we are not married, he has no right to take Constance? Or my business?"

The solicitor, a man little given to enthusiasm, responded carefully, "Your business? No indeed, if you are not married the man who claims to be your husband may appropriate none of your property. Under law, you are still a feme sole, not a feme covert. That is, a married lady. A man may have possession of his wife's goods or earnings only when they are one person in the eyes of the law. She having become his responsibility on their marriage day, since he is the legally answerable entity."

Ellen asked urgently, "But my daughter, Mr. Prike? Could he still take her from me?"

"Your daughter, Madame, is not real property. In the case of bastardry . . ." Ellen flinched, and Mr. Prike, too, winced. It was an ugly word, even he would acknowledge that. "There are no obligations under law on the part of either parent. Custody is not an issue in such a case."

Ellen stared at the solicitor with great intensity. "I cannot believe it. Not married?"

Mr. Prike nodded cautiously as the clock began to strike. A knock sounded at his door. Alderney had done his duty. Rarely had an appointment passed so quickly.

"Madame, I urge you to seek evidence of your marriage from St. Olave's. This is most important if I am to help you in this matter."

"Mr. Prike, I am grateful indeed that you will take my case, and shall do as you suggest. Good day, Sir."

The solicitor rose and bowed as the lady left, but with unlikely sprightliness, he hurried to the window of his room. A moment passed before his new client emerged to the street below. He watched as she hailed a hansom cab, and drove away.

He must remember to thank Lady Hawksmoor for the kind referral. What a very interesting beginning to the day this had been.

Things had reached an uncomfortable pass for Raoul de Valentin. Some days had elapsed since his call upon Ellen, and today when he had presented himself at the offices of Coutts and Company in the Strand, nothing, neither gold nor a banker's draft, had been deposited into his account. That was disheartening enough without the discreet reminder that unless the already existing arrears of more than thirty pounds was discharged, no more funds could be provided. His checks, in short, would be dishonored.

Almost worse than this, the previous evening had been an occasion of some unpleasantness with Letitia Ondle. If he were not able to buy an engagement ring very soon, he might be forced to acknowledge, if only to himself, that his long and careful campaign to marry the widow would not bear fruit.

And yet, yesterday evening all had seemed so promising. With the hope of money to come, Raoul had called around to Letitia's town house in the very best of spirits, expecting an intimate dinner.

He had knocked with confidence, even admiring the set of his hat in the polished knocker before the door was opened. "Is your mistress at home, Clarke?" But the man, though impassive, as all good servants are, seemed uncomfortable. Thinking back, that should have been enough to alert him.

"Alas, Monsieur le Marquis, Mrs. Ondle has departed for the evening. I am not expecting my mistress to return until after ten at the earliest."

"Indeed?" Raoul flattered himself that well-practiced aplomb held good when he said, "Perhaps I was mistaken. I had thought my dear friend asked me to call. No matter. I shall go to my club. Let her know of my visit, if you would?"

Raoul had slipped a shilling into the man's white-gloved hand. It was almost the last in his pocket, but he regarded such things as an investment. Servants are useful to those who tip them well. Clarke's wide smile had been his reward, or so he had thought. "I shall indeed, Sir. Madame will be sorry, I am sure, to have missed you."

Raoul twirled his cane and paused, gazing up and down the charming street. Where would he go? He was hungry, and the remaining change would buy dinner only at an Ordinary. So be it.

Giving Clarke a last smile as the door closed, he took the first step down to the street.

Was that laughter he heard? Female laughter?

Raoul stared at the blank-faced house. Surely not? But he knocked again. When Clarke opened the door, he narrowly observed that this time, the man could not disguise embarrassment.

"Yes, Sir?"

There was no need for Raoul to say anything. In that very moment, Letitia's laughter, no silver tinkle but an explosive snort, was heard. She was in the drawing room. Raoul drew himself up and fixed Clarke with a glance that he knew would be described later, in the servants' hall, as cold.

"My hat." He stalked past the servant and did not wait to see if the man received his precious topper in, no doubt, his nerveless fingers.

"Sir, Madame is not at home!"

Ignoring the manservant's desperate bluster, several long strides took Raoul to the closed drawing room doors.

"Letitia?"

Surprise has some advantages but is not always wise. The door opened on a scene he could not have imagined, and certainly did not wish to see. Letitia Ondle, *his* Letitia, was perched on a satin sofa far, far too close to a pretty boy who was only then removing his hand from a décolletage best described as ample.

Raoul, sweating at the remembrance, was at least comforted that impeccable manners, perhaps the most useful part of his inheritance as a de Valentin, had been employed to withering effect.

"You have me at a disadvantage, Sir. I do not believe we are acquainted?"

The boy, for boy he seemed since he was three or four years younger than Raoul, laughed easily. Standing, he advanced with his hand held out. "Liam O'Connell, Marquis. I know who *you* are, of course." He cast a laughing glance at his hostess who tried, in vain, to hide her giggles behind a fan.

A charming Irish accent and a bright, hard pair of eyes. And excessively too well-dressed. *Fortune hunter.* What else could the youth be? Raoul had a rival.

Ignoring the hand, ignoring the boy, Raoul instead addressed the widow with the smallest of bows. "Do not allow me to disturb your evening, Mrs. Ondle. I had thought to engage in a discussion of some seriousness tonight. One that spoke of the future. But now is not the time. I shall bid you good evening."

Head held high, he had sauntered from the room. The craven Clarke silently proffered Raoul's hat as he passed by. Raoul removed it from the man's fingers, set it gently in place, and waited for the door to be opened. Behind, in the drawing room, there was silence. Until she giggled.

In pain, Raoul briefly closed his eyes, but he departed with all the dignity of his ancestors displayed in the graceful set of his shoulders, his measured stride. A de Valentin does not make a fuss when others prove unworthy.

The question now was, What should he do? Ellen was his only hope. He did not want the business, he certainly could not be burdened with a child, but he did need that thousand pounds. It was the key to everything. If he must abandon the widow, a little fresh capital would set him up for the next pursuit.

Seething Lane, close by St. Olave's Church, was a busy place. It took Ellen some minutes before she could safely navigate a passage across the street to reach the church. She had not seen this place since her wedding, and now so much was bound up in what she might, or might not, find.

It was a cold day with a low sky. The settled chill, growing by the hour, suggested there would be snow before dusk. Ellen shivered. London seemed very dark on this comfortless morning. Standing before the outer door of St. Olave's, she hesitated. *Oriana, lend me your courage.* Then, clasping the handle of her umbrella tighter, she turned the ring to lift the latch. Nothing would change without action.

Ellen had thought she might not remember much of the interior of the church. The day of her marriage was a blur, still, of piecemeal recollections. But there was the altar at which they had stood together, and even on this gloomy day, the reds and blues and greens of the medieval window cast color out beyond the altar rail. She remembered Raoul's face in the pretty light when he had made his vows to her.

The church seemed cared for now. The brass polished, the pulpit dusted, fresh flowers on the stands. Even the grave slabs in the floor seemed cleaner, as if the lettering had recently been retouched.

"May I help you, Madame?"

Ellen jumped. A kind-faced, respectable-looking man stood beside her. Her first instinct was to decline the offer. "Thank you, Sir." But she hesitated. Should she ask him?

"Private worship is, of course, always encouraged in our church." The sexton nodded pleasantly. The lady seemed troubled. Perhaps silent prayer would assist in the carrying of her private burdens. He bowed and stepped away. His next task was to count the prayer books at the entrance and remove all those that must be replaced. The new vicar was particular about the condition of the prayer books.

"Sir?" The stranger seemed breathless. Her face was obscured by a veil, but he sensed a growing agitation. He responded, patiently, "Yes, Madame?"

"Sir, I was married in this church quite some years ago."

"I am happy to hear it, though it will have been before my time." The sexton thought he understood. The lady was dressed in black. Perhaps the widow had returned for comfort after the death of her husband. She, no doubt, wished to relive that joyful day in this place.

"Could I see the parish register, if you please?"

The sexton said, smilingly, "Of course. This way. We keep it in the vestry." If the lady wished to see her name and that of her husband written in the record, he was happy indeed to oblige. Anything to help the bereaved.

Ellen followed the man. Proud of the church, he chatted happily of the history of the building to set the visitor at ease.

"Perhaps you do not know, but we have some notable graves here. Mrs. Elizabeth Pepys, for instance." The sexton pointed, and stopped to explain a few choice facts, but they were wasted on Ellen. The words washed past unheeded, as with each step she drew closer to the vestry. "And here we are, Madame."

A very large book lay on the oak table in the vestry. The very one at which she sat to sign her marriage declaration. Ellen swallowed. "How very interesting St. Olave's is. Such a wonderful history. But was there ever a fire here?"

The man stroked his chin. "Well, yes. The Great Fire of London certainly, in 1666. We nearly lost the building along with so many of the other medieval churches. However—"

Ellen broke in, "Forgive me. I should have asked if there was a *recent* fire. One which damaged the parish register. In July 1845, perhaps?"

The sexton frowned. "I do not believe so. Or, at least I have never heard of such a thing." He opened the leather-bound book. It was extremely thick. "This volume takes us back to, let me see. Here it is, January first, Anno Domini 1835. Let me look at July in the year you mention."

The man leafed on, year after year, page after page, July first, second, third, fourth, 1845. "Nothing so far." Seventeenth, eighteenth, nineteenth, twentieth . . . Ellen's breath was ragged. "No damage that I can see . . ." Twenty-ninth, thirtieth, thirty-first . . . "Nothing. No sign of fire. No scorching." He peered closely at the last page in July.

"And what marriages do you have recorded on the first of August, 1845?"

Time slowed as the page was turned over and the first day of August was revealed. The man's finger moved carefully down from line to line. "Two baptisms in the morning. And then a third. In the afternoon. No marriages. Nothing else of any kind." The sexton

risked a glance at his visitor. He cleared his throat. Her very still-
ness made him nervous.

"You are completely sure? No note of a marriage between Miss
Ellen Gowan of Wintermast, and Monsieur Raoul de Valentin of
Richmond? They were married by the Reverend Lydgate. They,
that is I, signed a declaration of marriage at this table. The parson
said the register had been damaged by fire, and when it was returned to the church, our details would be recorded and a copy of
the marriage lines sent on to my husband."

The sexton was sweating. What a shame, what a very great
shame. Here was another one deceived. He looked with compassion at the lady. "I am sorry to tell you no such record of that marriage is recorded in the register."

"Look again. Please be absolutely sure."

"Of course. But it will do no good. Please see for yourself." He
stepped aside to provide room for the visitor. She raised the veil
from a face that was white and strained. The sexton was put in
mind of a good piece of marble, lovingly carved.

A deep sigh. "You are quite correct. Nothing is written here." A
gloved hand dropped the veil back to its place.

"I am sorry indeed, my dear. From Reverend Lydgate's time at
St. Olave's certain, well, irregularities have come to light. Some other
ladies have found themselves in a similar situation to your own."

"Do you mean," asked the stranger, her voice low and deliberately steady, "that others found they had not actually been married,
though a service was performed?"

The sexton sorrowfully nodded. "It is very wrong, and though
I hesitate to speak ill of the dead, the Reverend Lydgate was the
victim, we now believe, of an uncontrollable habit. An addiction. It
seems he took money to perform, well, sham marriages for reasons
that were, perhaps, less than honorable." He gulped. This poor
girl must have been so young, and doubtless far too trusting. The
wickedness of some men was beyond understanding.

"Shall I call the Reverend Moxton? He is the parson here now, though only recently appointed. He may be able to help you further. Some weeks ago we had another lady in the same situation as yourself. She was very upset. Doctor Moxton took her case to the bishop."

"And what did the bishop do?"

The sexton shook his head. "Alas, nothing. Well, that is to say, the lady asked for an annulment but because there had been no marriage, that was not possible. At least, though sorrowful, she had the satisfaction of her situation being confirmed."

He cleared his throat. It escaped him how any satisfaction could have come from knowing that her children were bastards and that she had lived in sin for close to ten years.

Ellen nodded. "I should like to see the Reverend Moxton very much. I need a letter attesting what you have said. A letter for my solicitor."

"I shall fetch him from the rectory directly." As the sexton hurried from the vestry, he experienced confusion. He could not be entirely sure, but perhaps the lady seemed happy, and might even be smiling behind the veil. That was a first.

The horse's hooves scattered on the cobbles as the coach rounded the corner into Berkeley Square. Alarmed, the driver shortened the reins in his fist. He had not seen the ice in this freezing mist. The gelding might slip. "There now. Gently does it."

His passenger called out, "There is the house, cabbie. Here. For your trouble." The man took the steps in a flurry of black. The driver stared at the gold coin in his hand. *Someone's in a hurry.* He moved his cab into the road as smartly as he dared, in case the passenger changed his mind. It should have been a shilling fare from the station.

The knocker crashed against the plate resoundingly. Downstairs, in the workshop, Polly heard the bell, too. *Another one!* So many people did not read what was written beside the bellpull.

Chez Miss Constance is closed for the present. Every effort will be made to accommodate all changes of appointment. Please kindly place your card in the letter-slot and we shall contact you directly.

"Shall I go, Mrs. Redcliffe?"

"No, Frances. You get on with what Madame has asked you to do. Some of the clients have been a little difficult." Polly cast a critical glance at Frances's work as she passed her drawing table. Not bad. Not perfect, but not bad. The girl was coming on.

Under the portico, Connor Moncrieff read the note with interest. His instinct had been correct. Something *was* wrong. He lifted his hand to knock again as the door opened.

"Mrs. Redcliffe. Is Madame Ellen at home?"

"Sir . . ."

Connor did not wait for an answer. He strode past into the hall, removing his hat, his scarf, and his coat. Holding them out to Polly, he said, "She wrote to me. Is all well?"

Connor may have been a young man but he had a very direct glance. Polly schooled her face to bland politeness. "If you will wait in Madame's salon, I shall let her know you are here." She caught Connor's eye again and thought of saying more. But did not. These were Ellen's secrets, not hers.

"Very well. Thank you." Connor paused before he crossed the black and white tiles of the hall. The house was well ordered and showed no signs of crisis. Elegant furniture was grouped against the walls in the usual way. Gilded sofas in the French style upholstered in gray or rose silk, single armchairs of the same, and alabaster-topped tables placed between them. The latest illustrated papers of fashion from Paris were neatly arranged on every surface, and flowers, forcing house roses and camellias, spilled in profusion from crystal bowls. Huge mirrors covered almost every wall.

Connor could not avoid his reflection. His hair stood up in tufts from removing his hat. He raked his fingers through the disordered mass. Perhaps it was better, perhaps not. He was impatient of appearances at the best of times. And this was not that.

There were two pairs of identical doors at the end of the hall; lacquered ivory with gilded moldings. Which one should he choose?

"The larger salon is to the left, Connor."

He slewed around. "Ellen!" He said, simply, "I was worried."

Ellen stood on the lowest stair in a gown of soft white. "Polly told me. But you did not need to come all this way." After a brief shock at first, Ellen was actually glad Connor had come to London. She wanted to be brave. She wanted to tell him the truth. She had lived too long with lies. But could she really say what must be said?

A fire was burning in the grate to warm the salon, and ratafia biscuits and a flask of sherry were arrayed on a side table. "You must be cold after your journey?" Ellen picked up the sherry.

"Let me." Connor took the flask from her hand—he had seen it tremble slightly. He removed the stopper, and handed her a brimming glass.

"Sit down, Ellen. And tell me what is wrong."

"Wrong?" She tried not to sound nervous, but drank too much of the sherry, which he saw. He sat back in his chair and waited, saying nothing.

Ellen began again. "I am, of course, grateful that you have taken the trouble to . . ." She stopped. He waved his hand as if to say, *Go on.* She bit her lip, and would not look at him.

"Whatever you have to say to me, it cannot be as bad as the expression on your face." A trace of humor.

Ellen shot back, "You do not know. There is so much, so many secrets." She stared at him. Agitated, she drank the rest of the sherry in a gulp.

He picked up the flask. "Dutch courage. Named for good reasons. Now, what secrets? What is so difficult to say?"

Words stumbled out of Ellen's mouth. As each one was said, it became less possible to lie. "I am not who I thought I was."

He looked at her quizzically. The pause before he spoke was torture. "And who did you think you were?"

"Ellen de Valentin. If we were married, that is. But perhaps we did not. And then, after the business failed and Connie was born, he tried to sell her. He thought I would not know because I was so ill. But Polly found a man, her husband now, who broke his nose. And *she* wrote to Oriana. And I ended up at Clairmallon. But I had not seen him in all this time until . . ." She jerked to a stop. "It is all such a terrible mess."

Connor rose and drew Ellen to the sofa beside the fire.

"Sit. Speak. Tell me from the beginning."

"The beginning?"

He nodded. "We have all evening . . ."

Ellen's hands were twisted in her lap. The fire had burned low while she told her story. ". . . and then he threatened me. He wants money. A thousand pounds in gold."

She picked up the glass and drank the sherry down like medicine. Her fourth. Or perhaps fifth. Connor had filled that deceptive little glass too many times. But if Ellen was dizzy, she did not care. "Because we were married, *he* said, he could take the business, and the house. And this was only the day after I received your letter."

Connor nodded. "The title deeds."

"Yes! And the discharge of the loan. But it was worse. He threatened to take Connie as well. '*A child on the streets of London is always to be considered vulnerable,*' he said." Ellen made a disgusted noise. "His own daughter."

Connor's expression was unreadable. He nodded. "And that was why you wrote to me?"

Ellen nodded. "It was. I could not take that chance. And I knew she would be safe with you."

"Did you not think you could tell me the truth?"

"How could I? To tell you about Raoul was to confess that my husband was still alive. And then Connie would know. And she would hate me. As you would also." This last was said in a small, forlorn voice. She raised her head. "I lied, Connor. To everyone. To you. And Oriana. To Aunt Daisy. But, worse, I have lied to Connie her whole life. And I do not know what to do." The events that Ellen spoke about were sordid, but the relief of telling the truth at last to someone she cared for was very great.

Connor prized fairness and he prized decency. "Your actions in these past years have been to protect Constance and secure her future. It seems to me you have tried, within dreadful constraints, to behave in an honorable manner."

Connor believed her. He was on her side. Ellen's heart felt suddenly light. It was rising like a feather in her chest.

She said wonderingly, "But I cannot credit, I truly cannot, that I have told you. I have been so frightened." She shook her head. "And the telling does not resolve what I should do."

Connor put his head to one side. "I think we must see Mr. Prike so that he may read the parson's letter from St. Olave's. And then, when the solicitor confirms the unlikeliness of this marriage—as I suspect he will—we shall beard Monsieur de Valentin together, in his den."

"But I have not paid over the money to Raoul. Because I did not have it. He may be desperate. I would not forgive myself if, through some action of mine, you were harmed."

Connor's tone was judicious. "You need have no concern for me. You have told me all your secrets. And his." Connor's tone turned at *his*. It became remarkably hard. "Raoul de Valentin will not take money from you, not one penny. It shall not be permitted."

Leaning forward in his chair, Connor stared at Ellen with great intensity. "You were fifteen, and alone. He preyed on your youth and situation to secure what he wanted. You were both underage and there seem to be so many irregularities, I cannot believe this marriage was more than a sham. That shall be confirmed with the help of your Mr. Prike, I am certain of it. But if divorce should be necessary, it shall be accomplished. *That* I promise also. For your sake and in memory of Oriana. She would not want you to carry this burden. You must be free of the past that has so nearly destroyed you."

"But Constance? What shall I say to her?"

He picked up one of Ellen's hands. "Trust Connie, Ellen. She is her mother's daughter, not her father's. We will help her to embrace the truth, together." He smiled at her with great sweetness.

CHAPTER 47

THE RAP on the door of the house at Cheyne Walk was decisive. Raoul de Valentin cursed beneath his breath. Cautiously, he drew back the tasseled edge of a curtain and peered out. Strange. From this angle, his front door seemed deserted. Someone had mistaken the number.

He dropped the brocade with relief. Several duns had called in recent days. One demanded payment so vigorously, Raoul had escaped through the back door and run down to the mews without his hat, to the loudly expressed delight of the urchins who congregated there. They liked to see toffs discomforted.

Money. It was such a curse when one had too little. Raoul sighed gloomily. Ellen was wrong. He had considerable distaste for blackmail. It was wearing.

He listened carefully. All was quiet from the street.

"Good day, Raoul."

Raoul jumped. The voice was *behind* him. He turned. "Ellen!"

But Ellen was not alone. A well-dressed man accompanied her. The pair had entered from the domestic offices at the back of the house. Ellen said pleasantly, "We knocked, but there was no answer."

Raoul was resentful. Haughtily, he asked, "And who, Madame, is your companion? I do not recollect issuing an invitation for strangers to enter my house."

Ellen smiled, but not warmly. "This gentleman is eager to be introduced to you. Mr. Moncrieff, may I present the Marquis de Valentin?"

"Monsieur." The man bowed to a small extent and said politely, "But I am not at your service."

Normally quick witted, Raoul gaped. Recovering, he attempted hauteur. "English manners. An oxymoron, evidently."

He edged closer to the door, but Ellen got there first. Coolly, she turned the key in the lock.

"That is mine." Raoul's voice was not entirely steady, which annoyed him.

Ellen inspected the key. "Is it? Your neighbor told me that you lease this house."

Raoul said, with dignity, "I regret, Madame, that you have been misinformed. And now, I must ask you and your *friend* to leave." The sneer was foolish.

Connor advanced a step, his walking stick pointed at the middle button of Raoul's waistcoat.

"And yet, we have so much to talk about."

Raoul drew himself up. He was a tall man, but not, he saw, taller than his visitor.

"I cannot imagine why you should think that."

He edged away. Too late he saw that he was being herded to the drawing room, since Ellen, behind him, blocked the way to the back of the house.

"Just one step farther, Marquis. If you please." Connor's glance was discomfortingly steady.

Raoul tried not to swallow. He attempted the same sangfroid. He turned his back and sauntered toward the sofa. Fortuitously, it was close to the window. If he pulled down the curtain over Moncrieff, he could throw it open and leap into the street. Undignified, yes, but prudent, certainly.

"Not the sofa."

The stick pointed to the elegant dining table. It had only two chairs. Perfect for impromptu suppers beside the fire.

"There, if you please, the chair against the wall."

Connor clicked the handle of his walking stick. "Madame has

some questions that must be answered." A long, very thin blade slid out. "Old-fashioned in these civilized times. But effective when you know how to use it." Connor smiled politely. "It was my father's. He taught me. A celebrated duelist, in his time. Illegal of course."

The point of the sword stick touched the cushion in the chair's back. "Sit."

Aristocratic good manners, that ancient family armor, buttressed Raoul's spine. He bowed gracefully. But sat just the same.

Without hurry, Connor pushed the table closer. Raoul was forced to shift backward until his chair was jammed into a corner. Connor sat on the other chair. He nodded to Ellen.

"Very well. Madame. Please continue."

Ellen had observed the little ballet from beside the door. She walked over to the window. The light was behind her and Raoul could not easily see her expression.

"Thank you, Mr. Moncrieff. Raoul, I shall ask you a number of questions and you will reply with the truth."

Icily, Raoul replied, "I do not lie, Madame. A de Valentin has no need of lies."

Connor leaned forward. "Have you not?" He pressed the point of the rapier into the cloth of Raoul's waistcoat. Raoul's head began to ache. This was not going well.

Ellen coughed, and the pressure of the blade was withdrawn. A little.

"I went to St. Olave's, Raoul."

"Indeed, Madame?" The Marquis de Valentin only evinced polite interest.

Ellen nodded. "I had expected it to be a place of pleasant memories."

Raoul did not like Ellen's tone. It was ironic.

"Perhaps you will be surprised to know that I could find no record of our marriage?"

"If you recall, the register was damaged."

"I do remember the Reverend Lydgate told me it had been. By fire?"

Raoul nodded. "Just so." He shifted in his chair. He did not look at Connor but, from the corner of his eye, saw the blade now rested across the man's knees.

Ellen said, without emphasis, "There was no fire, Raoul. And no marriage."

"You are mistaken, Ellen. I obtained a special license, which you saw. And we both spoke the responses before the priest. The marriage took place."

The point of the blade whipped to Raoul's throat just below the Adam's apple. The touch was light but depressingly accurate.

Connor said, "A form of words was spoken. However, the marriage was not legally binding. You will confirm that fact." The point was insistent. In a moment, the skin of the neck would be punctured.

Raoul sat very still. "The information you seek has value."

Ellen laughed incredulously.

Connor blinked. The man's nerve was certainly remarkable. "You wish to *bargain*, de Valentin?"

Raoul shrugged. He had nothing to lose except his life, and he doubted it would come to that. Cheyne Walk was not Minories Court.

"I had requested a thousand pounds."

"So that you would not snatch your daughter from the street, and use her to bargain for more? The baby you wanted to *sell* for your debts?"

Ellen leaned toward Raoul. He squinted uncomfortably. He heard, rather than saw, her contempt.

Connor said, without heat, "I think your life, de Valentin, is sufficient payment for the facts we require."

The ache in Raoul's head got worse. He disliked bargaining very much. "If I answer your question, you will both leave my house? On your word as a gentleman, Moncrieff?"

Ellen stared. Her eyes were pitiless. "Why should Connor not break his word as you have done, so many times?"

Raoul shrugged. He was sweating—an uncomfortable trickle down his sides.

Connor measured Raoul de Valentin with a glance. He withdrew a folded document from an inside pocket. "You will sign this. It has been drawn up by a solicitor."

Raoul tried not to show relief. He said, sullenly, "I said I would answer your questions. I did not agree to sign anything."

Connor stood. "I am sorry, Ellen, but we tried. You will be well rid of this fool." The blade glinted as he drew it back.

"Very well!" Raoul did not quite squeak, but the tone of his voice was certainly elevated. "Give me the paper."

Ellen looked around the pretty room. An inkstand and a pen lay on a boulle desk. She dipped the nib in the ink and offered it to the man she had always thought of as her husband.

Raoul took the pen with ill grace. "What does it say?"

Ellen hesitated. "It is a deed drawn up by a solicitor which attests that no marriage took place between us because of manifold irregularities. That the 'special license,' so called, was a forgery. That the Reverend Lydgate feloniously, and for gain, pretended to marry us in full knowledge of the illegal act he was performing. And that you have no claim now or in the future on my business, my property. Or my daughter."

Raoul stared at Ellen for a long moment.

Connor cleared his throat. He pointed at the document. "Sign here, if you please. Just above your name. Where it has been printed. And the date."

Raoul defiantly scrawled his signature and wrote, sixteenth December. "And the year." Raoul doggedly added the year. Connor smiled as if to encourage a recalcitrant child. "And now, the seal, if you please."

Ellen held a lit candle. Connor used the flame to melt wax onto the page from a stick he produced from his pocket.

"Impress the ring, Raoul. It is all that remains." Ellen spoke quite softly.

"A little subdued, Madame la Marquise?" Raoul smiled crookedly. "I did love you. And I saved you. I was a fool to do it, and you cost me a good deal of money, but whatever this paper says, I regarded our marriage as real. Remember that."

He impressed his signet ring in the cooling puddle of wax.

She nodded. "For a little while you loved me. Until it became too hard. But we were not married."

Connor rose. "I suggest you leave England, de Valentin. Today." He waved the document gently to dry the ink. "If you return, please be assured you will be prosecuted to the full extent the law allows. There are a number of crimes to your account already, it seems. False pretenses, money extracted on promise of marriage. That sort of thing."

Raoul stood, and nonchalantly stretched. "But, I know something else. Something that will interest you, Mr. Connor Moncrieff, very much." A last roll of the dice.

Connor put the point of the sword stick into a fine Persian carpet, and leaned on it. "Well?"

Raoul winced. *Barbarian.*

"What would this information cost me?"

With creditable composure, Raoul said, "A thousand pounds."

Something warned Ellen. Perhaps it was the glittering smile Raoul directed at her. "Connor, we have what we need. Let us go."

But Connor had seen the smile also. "Go on, de Valentin. But what is money among gentlemen? You are a man of honor, you say."

Raoul laughed. "Touché. Very well. I shall tell you. For nothing." He swept out his arm, a flamboyant gesture of generosity. "She was in love with you. Green love, but important, I think." He pointed at Ellen. "She confessed it to me on our wedding night. But of course, married or not, I had her first, not you."

Connor traversed the space between them in a blur and hurled the table away with such force, it broke against the marble fireplace. Kicking Raoul's feet from beneath him, he straddled the man's chest, the blade pressed hard against his throat. Raoul's head hit the wall as he went down, and a gash above his eyes opened. Blood blinded him.

"Was Ellen married to you? Tell me." Under the circumstances, Connor spoke with restraint.

Raoul tried to blink the blood away, and gave up. "No."

"Swear it. To her."

The blade was drawn slowly across his throat. Raoul, with utter horror, felt the blood trickle down. "I swear. I swear!" He closed his eyes. This was the end. Perhaps it was not so bad. He was weary of the life he led.

But Connor got up. He wiped the blade on Raoul's sleeve and said, dispassionately, "You are not to attempt to contact Miss Constance Gowan in any way. Not now, and not in the future. And, if you remain in London for a period greater than today, I shall go to the police."

He paused, fingering the blade. "Prison, at the very least, I believe, is what can be expected for blackmail of this kind. Transportation to the colonies, too, if not hanging. And, if I ever see you again, I shall kill you. I hope you understand." He adjusted his hat, which had become a little dislodged in the fracas.

Perhaps Ellen was shaken, but she hid it well.

"Do not get up, Raoul. We shall see ourselves out." She paused for a moment as Connor unlocked the door. And for that instant, Raoul thought she might say farewell.

But Ellen Gowan did not look back. She was free.

It was late when Ellen and Connor returned to Berkeley Square. Past hunger, past thirst perhaps, she was empty of all feeling, too.

A light was burning in the hall, and lamps stood in the windows of Ellen's apartment on the third floor. Frances had waited up to see them home. But Ellen opened the great front door quietly. She would not engage in trivial pleasantries tonight.

"Shall we go to the salon?" She led the way.

Firelight picked out gilding and deepened the silk from rose to scarlet, gray to soft black. The crystals of the chandelier moved in the warm air beneath the ceiling. More gold than silver, they took the light and held it, shimmering. The effect was very beautiful. Connor sauntered to the fire and held up his hands. The silence between them was comfortable. After a moment, he asked, "Are you hungry?"

Connor's expression was kind, but the experience of the afternoon, and the unhappiness of her marriage, made it hard for Ellen to believe that men could be so very different from one another. She hesitated. Then nodded.

"Well then, I shall find my way to the kitchens. And raid the pantry." He smiled. "Presumptuous, I know."

"Not presumptuous. Natural. This was your house. I still think of it as yours."

He said, lightly, "Well, it is not."

Ellen did not reply. But she was grateful for the soft cushions, grateful for the warm room. She closed her eyes. She could see the glow of the flames through her lids.

"Do you trust me, Ellen?" Had he read her mind? "I understand if you do not."

Ellen was tired. Not knowing how to answer Connor, she made an effort to sit up.

"Rest." He smiled. "I shall hunt a little and return with what I capture."

Ellen did not want to fall asleep but time passed. Five minutes, ten, perhaps half an hour. Half an hour in which Raoul's face and Connie's somehow became her mother's. And there was her father in his academic gown. He was warning her, but of what? Ellen jumped as a gentle hand was placed on her shoulder. She woke to find Connor close.

"I startled you. I did not mean to." He drew back.

Ellen blinked. As if in her own bed, she yawned and stretched. He chuckled.

She became self-conscious. "Forgive me, I was still half-asleep."

Setting dishes down on a side table, he said, cheerfully, "I know. Shall I serve?"

"Yes. Please." How long had she known this man? And yet, alone with him now, she felt suddenly shy. And did not know what to say. She cleared her throat. "You hunted well, it seems."

"There was no need. Frances had left these excellent comestibles laid out for us. She found me in the kitchen. Good girl, that one." He flourished a carving fork. "Ham? There are very good deviled eggs also. And a pork pie."

Ellen nodded. She did not really care.

Connor brought over loaded plates and sat down in a chair beside hers. "De Valentin lives well, for a man with no money."

Ellen grimaced. "Perhaps he has other wives as well. And wealthy patrons."

"Patrons can be useful, it is true." It was said lightly.

Ellen colored. "You have been so good to me, Connor. Much more than good."

"Stop." He leaned forward. The gap between the chairs was small. "I learned something today."

She was locked by his eyes. She had to ask the question. "What did you learn?"

"That I worry about you more than is sensible." He smiled faintly. She liked the way his mobile face changed when he smiled. "And that . . ." He paused.

She started to speak. But said nothing.

Connor put down his plate. He was very close to her now. And changed tack. "What will you do with your freedom, Ellen? Now that you know it to be real?"

She hesitated. "I am not certain."

Connor took her plate of uneaten food and set it aside, and pinioned one of her hands between both of his.

"There is something I would like you to consider."

Her throat was so dry, it was painful to swallow. "What is it?"

"I love Constance as my own child. I always will. And it is clear that she must have a father. A proper father. Not a borrowed one." That faint smile again. *These are the words Connie used,* Ellen thought. "And though she is resilient, and knows that we all love her, she will need her family, each one of us, when she learns the truth about Raoul as, one day, she must."

"Whatever I do, whatever I say, I am so afraid that she will despise me. That I will lose my daughter."

He laid a finger on her lips.

"Dearest Ellen, you have borne burdens alone that would have destroyed most people. You are strong. And clever. But heartsore with all you have endured. Let me help you. I loved Oriana, very much, and cannot hope to replace what we shared in our marriage, but we are dear friends, you and I. We find peace with each other. And you need never doubt my loyalty or my regard."

He was so sincere and so tender, but Ellen's spirits sank with each word he spoke. Companionship. Peace. Kindness. Loyalty. These were all precious things. But Connor did not mention love.

Ellen closed her eyes, upbraiding herself. *Of course he would not speak of love!*

Connor continued. "If you would consent to marry me, Ellen, our children would rejoice, Daisy would be delighted, and I should be honored indeed." He faltered. She had not spoken.

"Tell me what is in your mind. And in your heart."

My heart is weeping.

Ellen tried to smile. It was hard to frame the words, exactly as she meant them. "I thank you for this kindness. But these last months . . ." She shook her head. How hard it was to speak of her feelings and not cry. She would not cry. "Have been more than sad. For us both."

In the firelight, Ellen's eyes were huge and deep. And hurt, somehow. Had he miscalled the timing of his proposal? And yet it had seemed so sensible, the solution to so many things.

"Do not answer me tonight, Ellen. Rest. Body and spirit. I know you carry affliction with grace, but a lesser soul would have been overwhelmed today."

Ellen's eyes welled. She could not prevent them. But she was able to say, with great sincerity, "I am so truly grateful for your friendship, Connor. And for the love you bear my daughter. You have been so kind to us. But you are correct. My mind, tonight, is clouded by the past. I must find my way to a different, more hopeful country. The country of the future—Daisy said that to me, once. And then you shall have your answer."

It was Connor's turn to feel discomfort. *Kind?* The understanding was not welcome, as he saw, now, that *kind* was not enough. For either of them. But he said, "All the time you need, dear Ellen, is yours. We have the rest of our lives."

He rose, and Ellen began to stand, too, but he pressed her gently on the shoulder. "Rest. Sleep."

Ellen heard his footsteps cross the hall. Heard the door creak open, and then close. Her hand strayed to her shoulder, to where he had touched her. If she looked beneath the silk, would his fingers have left marks on her skin?

And when she slept in her bed, at last, Ellen dreamed of the children's ball.

CHAPTER 48

ELLEN WOKE with a start. London was quiet. No carriages rattled on the roadway below. No boots on the pavement, or the voices of maids, chatting as they swept the steps or shook the doormats outside the houses. The light in her room was different, too.

"Snow!"

Throwing the coverlets off, she hurried to the window. Her breath melted the frost skin on the glass, and she gazed through the clear circle thus created. Below, Berkeley Square wore white like a counterpane of feathers, as if all the houses, and the gardens, had been tucked up and encouraged to sleep and now were reluctant to wake. Only the birds were about. Sparrows and some seagulls, a long way from the sea, were lined up and fluffed out on the backs of benches, as if conferring on important matters.

Flakes began to fall past Ellen's window. Slow at first, they wandered in spirals and then fell faster. And faster still and thicker. Soon the world was obscured, the very air as opaque and pale as milk.

Ellen turned back and luxuriously stretched. Snow turned to ice in the streets beneath carriage wheels. If the drift continued all morning, she would have few clients. She went to ring the bell for water. And paused. Last night. Had Connor really proposed marriage? No. Not so much marriage as an alliance. An aligning of interests. And it all made such good sense.

"But I am young!" Ellen was standing in front of her dressing mirror. She stared at her face. And her body. *Too young for a passionless marriage.*

Her feet were cold. Shivering, she hurried to the dressing chair. There was a robe and a shawl and silk-lined slippers. Cold sharpened the mind and the senses, but that was no help. This was not about the mind.

Ellen stared around her room. She had made this place. Bought the bed, sewn the coverlet of sprigged silk. The workshop had cut the curtains of indigo blue velvet, and she had had such delight in finding, piece by piece, the wardrobe, her dressing chair, her two glassed bookcases, one on each side of the fireplace. And she had read every book on those shelves. She had even found the fire tongs and the little sofa at the market.

Polished the first until it shone, covered the last in straw-colored silk. She liked to sit there on cold nights, sewing, as the wind tapped at the window glass.

And, on each wall there were the sketches and paintings of Connie she had made, or things her daughter had given her. The perfect skeleton of a sycamore leaf from Clairmallon. A birthday card, painted for Ellen when Connie was five. A scribble that suggested a frog. She liked frogs. And here was a drawing that her daughter had done of the ravens in the Tower only this year. Ellen smiled. Another of Connie's odd enthusiasms, the ravens. She said she liked their bright eyes.

Ellen walked around the walls, touching each precious object, the things that tracked the trajectory of her life. Here was Connie at only a few weeks old. The sleeping baby was exquisite, vulnerable. Ellen traced the line of those closed lids, the eyelashes, the perfect mouth. She had drawn the image while recovering from the birth, after Raoul had gone but before she went to Clairmallon to live. And Connie at six, just before Ellen had decided to come to London. She took down the framed little drawing and gazed at it.

Connie stared back at her, her expression so grave and so alive. *I observe*, the drawing seemed to say. *I watch and I see more than you think I do.*

"You do indeed, Constance." Ellen touched the sweet mouth as if her fingertips could kiss the living child. She hung the drawing again, and lit the coals laid in the fireplace. As she waited for the flames to catch and grow, she thought about Connor. Could she untangle the things that she felt?

There was her desk. Of course. Ellen pulled a piece of paper from the top of a new ream. White and pure as the snow outside, perhaps she did not need to write on it. Perhaps, if she just stared at that perfectly blank, perfectly featureless object, an answer would come as if she were looking into a crystal ball.

But it was not Ellen's way to be passive. Dipping her pen, she drew a steady black line from the top of the page to the bottom, dividing the space. *I will marry Connor* was written on the left-hand side. *I will not marry Connor* on the right. Then she proceeded to make the list.

He is kind.	To everyone.
He loves Connie.	She is not his child.
We get on well.	I get on well with Polly!
Kit will have a sister.	I am not marrying Kit.
Security.	I have that now.
Clairmallon.	I like my work in London.
He is fond of me.	Fond? Is that enough?
Love will grow.	He does not mention love.
He wants to marry me.	I am second best.
I felt passion for him, once.	Do I love him, now?

Ellen frowned. Love. What did she know of that? What did she know of anything?

There are some things you do know.

"What? What do I know?"

Ellen roamed to the mirror. She began to unplait the braid in which she had slept. Her hair sprang loose. She shook her head deliberately. Let the curls be as wild as they chose.

The voice in her head spoke patiently. *You know, most of all, that you do not want to lose Constance. You want her to be happy. And independent.*

It was true. Ellen sighed and sat before the mirror. She brushed her hair slowly. She had created this business for her daughter. She and her mother had been victims of circumstance, but little Connie need never be humiliated by dependence, regardless of what she chose in life.

But happiness? That was different from security.

What had her daughter said? *Marry Uncle Connor. Live here with us.* Connor was offering them both a real home, a home in which they belonged. The certainty of a family living together. No longer a guest, no longer a poor relation, but Mrs. Connor Moncrieff, of Clairmallon.

"But what about love?"

Ellen touched the naked skin of her shoulder. She had thought herself frozen. But she was not. The specter of Raoul had been defeated. And it was as if, after a long and desolate winter, the earth was breaking up with new life, green shoots thrusting up through the frozen ground.

Yes, Connor had been her first love. But she had set aside those feelings long ago, and thought of him all these years—most deliberately—as her friend. Yet something had stirred last night, when he had touched her. What if she found herself in love with Connor and he could not love *her* in return?

She would not be that loveless girl again, not after all she had been through.

And what if Oriana, that beloved shade, came between them for as long as they lived?

Ellen avoided her anguished reflection. She paced up and down, up and down as the snow fell ever faster beyond the window glass.

Connor had treated her with respect in their business partnership. He had been more than fair. If they married, he would not try to control her, as Isidore had crushed Daisy and Oriana, before she escaped.

He would not lie to her or abandon her as Raoul had done. And there would be more children.

What did she think of that? What would Connie think of more brothers and sisters?

"I cannot decide! I really cannot."

Soft flakes clung to the freezing glass. The wind rose and they were whirled away, flung out, absorbed into the white beyond, all sense of the single lost in the whole.

Ellen stood in the muffled silence. Her room had become a box with white walls. Oriana had been buried beneath white flowers, the petals thick as snow in the soil as she was laid to rest.

Oriana. Help me.

Oriana's voice had been so faint as she lay dying. *Love them. Love him. For me.*

Oriana had stared at her with such intensity before the heavy lids closed. Forever.

The trees in Clairmallon's park were naked and stark and black, but Ellen had deliberately waited for the first sight of the house as she always did when she returned.

She pulled down the carriage window, and the air turned her nose and cheeks an instant apple pink. Even gloves had not kept out the cold on this long day's journey, and her boots felt as if they had an inner skin of ice. Yet as the carriage turned into the forecourt of the house, Connie ran, screaming for joy, beside the wheels, and at her heels, two leggy puppies, one large, one small, barked and yipped, distracting the horses and displeasing Giles.

All young dogs, like half-grown boys, were fools, in his opinion.

"Connie, be careful!" It did no good. Ellen had an adventurous daughter and she hurtled, panting, into Ellen's arms as soon as her mother stepped down.

"Constance! Let your poor mama breathe."

Connor had followed more slowly from the house, with Daisy.

He had Kit in his arms. The pandemonium of welcome pleased him.

"Dearest Daisy. And Kit!"

Ellen tried to embrace her aunt and kiss the little boy, who wriggled and giggled, but Connie had hold of her arms and was pulling her toward the house.

"Come to my room, *please.*"

Ellen said, helplessly, "If nothing else is planned?" Connor waved genially as Ellen was swept away.

He and Daisy contemplated each other over Kit's head. It was as if a gale had raged through the forecourt. Daisy put her hand on her son-in-law's arm. "I am so glad Ellen has returned for Christmas, Connor."

Though she mourned her daughter, and would each day of her life, she knew more, perhaps, than he thought she did.

Connor patted Daisy's hand. He called out to a manservant, "Allen, take Madame Ellen's trunk and bag to her old room, please?" Did he say it more loudly than required?

He and Daisy strolled back to the house. Daisy said, "She seems well, Connor. I am very glad of it. I had expected . . . well, I had not known what to expect."

"No more did I."

Was it only so few days since he had asked her to marry him? Time had stretched and then collapsed. And now Ellen had returned to Clairmallon. He had been patient. Would she answer him? He could not tell. Ellen had not seemed distant. She had smiled at him. She was different, though. More vivid. More alive.

"It is not good, you know, to compress the emotions. They do not become more manageable. One fine day they will not be contained, and then . . ."

He stopped as Kit struggled to get down from his arms. "Now why, dearest Daisy, did you think to say that?"

She gently straightened a lapel on his jacket. "Because I have eyes. And ears."

He ruminated. "And I have need of advice. If you will give it to me?"

"With all my heart." They had arrived in the winter drawing room, a place of thick curtains and soft cushions, the walls lined with books.

"Very well, young man." Connor put the baby down on the carpet. He watched fondly as Kit determinedly set off, crawling rapidly, toward the sofa. It was a good height on which to haul himself upright. As Connor warmed his hands and his back at the fire, he said, "There are things Ellen will wish to tell you when she is ready. But there are others that I prefer you hear from me."

Connor sat beside his wife's mother. "Daisy, I must tell you a story."

"I have missed the stories. Uncle Connor is not as good as you." Connie was perched in the nursery room window seat.

"Then you shall have one tonight." Ellen stroked Connie's curls lovingly. Perhaps, in some ways, they were a little alike.

"A made-up one. About London?"

Ellen laughed. "If you wish."

Connie laced her fingers through Ellen's. "We have all been very excited you were coming. Uncle Connor most of all."

"Really?" Of course, this was only a child's opinion. Constance yawned as she nodded, and leaned against her mother. "You are tired."

Connie said indignantly, "I am not tired. I am never tired."

"Are you not? Not ever?"

"No. Too much to do, now that you have come home." That smile caught Ellen's heart and turned it over.

"Is something wrong, Mama? Did you not want to come back?"

Ellen hugged Connie fiercely. "I wanted to come back very much. For you. And for everyone. I wanted my family. All of you.

But especially Miss Constance Gowan." Should she tell Connie about Connor's proposal? But Connie's expression had changed.

"In London, did you think about Aunt Oriana?"

Ellen said, "I think of her every day. And not just in London. I miss her."

Connie's eyes filled. Ellen held her daughter close. She berated herself for a clumsy fool. "We miss her, too. So much. But it is better when you are here. Uncle Connor was very worried about you. I could tell. That is why he went to London. He thought I did not know, but I did." Connie played with the buttons on Ellen's jacket.

Ellen hugged her daughter. Yes, it was right to be at Clairmallon this Christmas. She was needed here.

But Connor? What did she feel for him?

You will know. Do not be frightened. Ellen blinked.

Constance sniffed. "Did you say something, Mama?"

Ellen found a handkerchief tucked in the cuff of her gown. She handed it to her daughter. "No. But we must go down, or we shall miss the fun. The guests will be here very soon."

A pine tree had been set up in the center of Clairmallon's hall, and from it the green smell of the winter forest, that wild, still place, scented the air with resin. Daisy and Ellen stared up. It was their task to dress the tree. Daisy said anxiously, "It is really very big, Connor. How shall we reach the top? Someone has to place the star."

Constance said, promptly, "Can I climb it?"

Ellen looked at Connor imploringly, as she tried to dissuade her daughter. "Now, Connie, this is not an apple tree and—"

"But I climb the trees in the park. Big ones. You have seen me, Mama. Uncle Connor, *please*? You know I can."

Connor's face crinkled. "It is true. You are a tremendous climber. But for the sake of your dear mama's nerves, I think it better to place the tree closer to the minstrels' gallery. You can dress the very top from there. What do you say to that, Miss Constance?"

Connie's face fell, but Daisy said, firmly, "Though I am sorry to inconvenience the gardeners by moving it again, I do agree." She eyed her disappointed great-niece, and then her son-in-law. "But come with me, Constance. Let us see if we can help cook. She might have a treat for us. I saw shortbread this morning."

"Shortbread?" Connie ran ahead of Daisy, shouting happily, "I love Christmas!"

"Shall I come? Perhaps I can help, too?" Ellen called to their retreating backs.

Over her shoulder Daisy said, "Settle the tree, first."

Anxiety fluttered in Ellen's belly like a living thing. It was best that there was too much to do to get ready for the party. Less time to think.

Last night in London, as hour after hour fled past, she had lain in her bed without sleep. How many times had she rehearsed the moment when she would say to Connor . . . what? She still did not know.

"Ellen, where should we place the tree to best advantage?"

She started. What had he said?

Connor was as nervous as she. "Come up to the gallery. We can see better up there."

"Of course. You are right." *If I reached out my hand, now.* But Ellen did not.

Ellen climbed the steps behind Connor. She shivered. A conscious act of will, her will, kept them apart, but her will was not always strong.

"If the tree is placed directly below"—he was pointing—"both halves can be easily dressed. The top from here." They were only a small distance apart. He was staring at her. "Come closer, you will see better."

It was only a step or so. "Yes. That will be perfect." But she did not move.

"Ellen." His hand reached out. She would not look at him. She could not.

"The decorations! And the holly, too, I should . . ." *Coward!* She turned and would have fled.

But he said, "Do not go."

She stopped.

"You are shaking." He had closed the distance between them.

Ellen shook her head. She would deny the obvious if she could.

"I spoke of friendship, in London. Companionship. Of our children." Connor could not control his voice. "Ellen. Look at me. I cannot talk to your back." A ragged half laugh. "I know that you want . . ." But he did not finish the sentence.

Would breath give her strength? Ellen turned, and saw such emotion in his eyes, she was shocked.

He said, softly, "I know that you want more. More than an agreement."

"Don't you?" This was it. This was the question that must be answered.

Connor Moncrieff had beautiful hands. Long-fingered, strong. He cupped Ellen's face and tilted it. She could not look away. "I do." And smiled. A tender, curving smile. And then his eyes darkened. "Could you love me?"

"Love you?" The anguish peeled all pretense away. "You do not understand. Raoul spoke the truth. I saw you at the children's ball and loved you in that first moment. But you only saw Oriana. And married her. And I married *him,* or rather, I did not—thinking that love must be different from what I first thought.

"Connor, you restored my belief in so many things and gave me hope again, though I do not understand men and perhaps never will."

William Greatorex flashed into her mind, and Raoul, looking at her so adoringly in the church.

"I do not know what to do. I would break, really break, if through foolishness I made such a mistake again. And I love my business, too. And my daughter. Though differently." The words died away.

The look between them seemed eternally long. Imperceptibly, he was drawing her closer.

She said, "Could you love *me,* one day?" Her voice broke.

He kissed her. Softly. "One day?" His hands dropped to her waist. "This day. And for as many days as you choose."

As inexorable as the pull of the moon upon the earth, he brought her closer.

"I had faith, you see. And time to consider our conversation. I remembered the little girl at the ball, too. And then I thought about the woman."

Ellen was dazed. "I have had to be practical, all my life. I could think of nothing but survival. After Raoul."

He touched her face gently, tracing the shape of her upper lip. "I am not Raoul. And you do not have to be practical tonight." That drew a giggle.

He tightened his hands around her waist. "Trust. Believe."

Ellen went to protest. And then *she* kissed him.

Dusk had claimed the distant hills, but in Clairmallon's valley the alchemy of last light transformed the winter garden.

Standing trees became pillars of gold, and the black shapes of the topiary might have been carved from ebony. Nothing was different from other winters past. . . .

But I have changed, thought Ellen Gowan as she sat by the lake's edge, watching as the light dwindled. *I do not have to be who I was.*

"Oriana? Can you see me?" Ellen closed her eyes. "Do you know, now, wherever you are? Are you glad? Please bless us, dearest friend." Ellen felt a hand on her shoulder. And screamed.

"I did not mean to startle you!" Daisy quickly sat beside her niece. "I am so sorry. Constance told me you had gone for a walk before the party. I know you love this place."

In some confusion, Ellen went to stand. "Of course. The guests will soon be here."

Daisy put a hand on Ellen's arm. "Stay. Talk to me."

There was a quiet pause, then Ellen asked, "Did I upset you just now, Aunt Daisy? I was talking to Oriana. You must have heard me." She laughed nervously.

"No. I do it all the time. So does Connie. It helps us both."

Daisy touched Ellen's cheek. "From when we first met, you have been my other daughter."

"You are kind to say such things."

"It is hard sometimes, to be a mother. So much is sacrifice."

The rushes moved and whispered. Daisy said meditatively, "I would give much to see you happy, child. We all would. Constance and Connor and me. Oriana most of all."

She knows. Timidly, Ellen said, "If I were to tell you . . ." She cleared her throat, and began again. "Aunt Daisy, in London, Connor asked me a question. One that I could not immediately answer."

"Go on." Smiling gently, Daisy gazed out over the serene water.

"Would you mind very much if he and I were to marry?" Once she began, the words hurried out. "Not yet, of course, and if the thought upsets you or Connie, of course, well then, we would not for the world pursue the idea."

"It will not upset Connie. It does not upset me."

Daisy took her agitated niece in her arms. "Child, I have prayed for this. For you both. For us all."

Ellen sagged. How hard this had been to say. Daisy continued, "If there was a path to Hades, I would take it to bring Oriana back. But there is not. She is gone, and you are here. Be happy. For her. And for me. Connor is a very good man."

Daisy stood, and pulled Ellen after her. Catching her wrist, she said, "Come with me to the house."

☙

Daisy stopped before a door, and took a key from her reticule.

Ellen said, slowly, "But this . . ."

Daisy nodded. "Yes. Oriana's dressing room." Unlocking the door, she pushed it open. "I have not been in here since that day." She hurried to the windows and, one by one, drew back the curtains. The sky lay beyond. A perfect night, still and glittering.

"Do not wear black tonight. Choose something pretty and bright. She would want you to." So many cupboards, all full of Oriana's clothes. Daisy quickly opened each of the doors. A garden of color.

"She was always so generous." Ellen stopped. Here was the dress she had made for Oriana—the one her cousin had worn at Connie's birthday party. Blue and white. That had been the day she had decided to leave Clairmallon. And now she had returned.

"This one." She held it against herself.

Daisy said, dubiously, "Will you not be cold?"

Ellen stared in the triple mirror. She was transformed. The fresh blue and white complimented her bright skin, her shining hair. Even her eyes looked different. They seemed a color between jade and topaz tonight. "It is silk, and the hall will be warm."

Daisy nodded. "Very well. But we must find a wrap. Something lined. The season is so treacherous."

"You worry too much." Ellen caught her aunt's hand. Cradled it against her cheek.

"One cannot be too careful." Daisy bustled away to search the cupboards. Ellen watched her aunt affectionately. All three of her reflections smiled as, looking down, she began to undo the laces on Oriana's gown.

She felt the soft kiss on her cheek. "Thank you, Aunt Daisy. You have been so good to me." But it was not her aunt.

Behind Ellen's shoulder stood Oriana Moncrieff. She met her cousin's smiling eyes.

"What did you say, dear?"

Ellen blinked. Oriana was gone. Ellen said, slowly, "Just that you have been so good to me, dearest Aunt."

Daisy beamed. She hurried forward. She had a short cape in her hands, white velvet banded with miniver. "Will this do? The fur will keep you warm." She stood behind Ellen, just as Oriana had.

Ellen opened her mouth. And said, "The very thing."

She saw herself in the mirror. Like a swimmer close to the surface, her perception cleared. She *could* be happy.

EPILOGUE

THE AUTUMN of 1856 was long and glorious, summer heat lingering into October.

Lush and abundant, the valley of Clairmallon had never been so fruitful, so blessed with flowers and vegetables and grain. And each day that the weather held, the threshers went out into the fields and the air was filled with the scent of mown hay. There would be no rest for any at Clairmallon until all the harvest was gathered in. And though rain threatened, it did not fall, and at last the estate was put in order for the winter to come.

The family chapel, however, was still decked out for the Harvest Home. It had been held especially late this year, and as the successive hymns drifted out over the garden and the fields, and prayers—question and answer—were heard, a new sound joined the voices of adults and children. The cry of an indignant baby.

Connor, in the chapel, watched more than anxiously as the water from the font was dripped on his daughter's forehead. She screamed lustily, though he knew the water was warm. He had seen to that himself.

"And I baptize thee, Oriana Moncrieff, in the name of the Father, the Son, and the Holy Ghost. Amen."

The parson handed the outraged infant to her mother, the very pretty Mrs. Ellen Moncrieff, who quickly swaddled little Oriana in the Christening shawl, watched by her proud great-aunt, her older daughter, her stepson, and Mr. Connor Moncrieff, her husband.

There was a collected exhalation in the church. It was accomplished. Ellen turned to display the baby in her arms and, against all the rules of correct behavior, the entire congregation applauded.

At last, Connor found he could breathe again. As Ellen and he walked from the chapel, smiling to friends and neighbors, he murmured, "I do not know why I have been so nervous. About the Christening, I mean. I was more worried when little Oriana was born, of course, but I so wanted this to go well. For you."

Ellen looked lovingly at her husband. "For all of us, Connor."

Connie, so decorous to this point, stared pleadingly at her mother. "Mama, you said."

"So I did. Connor, Connie asked if she might play after the service? There are so many children here."

Connor ruffled his stepdaughter's curls. "Very well, Miss Minx. But where is Kit?" He looked back toward the chapel.

"Here we are, Connor. All is well." Daisy had hold of his son's small hand, and Polly, down from London with her husband, was holding the other. The business had been closed in honor of the day. Polly was managing Berkeley Square now, with capable help from Frances. Ellen sent designs by mail and personally consulted a few clients by special arrangement, including Lady Hawksmoor.

Connor grumbled happily, as they came out of the shadows of the church, "Two children, and now three. Where will it end?"

Ellen laughed. "You are far too young to talk like an old man, dear husband."

Daisy strolled happily beside her son-in-law, holding Kit's hand as, slowly, the procession from the chapel wound toward Clairmallon, laughing and talking. All the windows were thrown wide, and garlands twined around each open door. New life was always welcome beneath this generous roof.

Ellen paused, allowing the crowd to stream past.

"Do you see, my darling?" she said softly to little Oriana. "This is your home. You live here with your family."

Introducing her daughter to the house, Ellen held the baby proudly in her arms as she turned a slow circle. "This is your garden." She showed Oriana the trees, the lawn, the yew walk. "And there is your lake."

A light wind raced through the trees, and a scatter of leaves fell around the mother and child. The child laughed and held up her naked arms.

Ellen hugged the baby closer. How much she had been given. The love of her father, and her mother. Oriana, Daisy, and little Connie. And now Connor. And Clairmallon. She had a family, and the dark days, the days haunted by Isidore and Raoul and Carolina Wilkes, had been banished. Yet in the end even *they* had all given her the gift of strength. She knew that now.

"Mrs. Moncrieff?" Connor hurried across the lawn. He was carrying Kit and had Connie by the hand.

Ellen laughed. "Yes, Mr. Moncrieff?"

"The guests are waiting. They all want to meet our newest daughter." He kissed Ellen and Oriana. "Connie, shall we remove your mother to the house?"

"Yes, Papa." Connie beamed at Ellen. "You look very happy, Mama."

But Ellen hung back one moment more, her youngest child in her arms. *Thank you, Oriana.* She sent the thought from her heart.

And slowly, whispering to her daughter of the joys that would fill her life, Ellen Moncrieff walked away from the past.

And into the country of the future.

ACKNOWLEDGMENTS

The Dressmaker has taken me a long time to write. At the beginning, I set out to create another novel entirely but Ellen Gowan, who had been a minor character in the first draft, would not be denied. Draft by draft she became stronger and, in the end, this book is her story.

Writing is an odd process. Who knows where characters come from, or why they do what they do. And, because this book took its own sweet time to write, I do owe more than usual thanks to a number of people who, for instance, helped me find my way back to the story when it went missing (as it did, not once but several times, during particularly fraught periods).

First, to Judith Curr, Publisher of Atria Books, Simon & Schuster, New York City. Thank you indeed for the opportunity to write my books with Atria Books at Simon & Schuster. This is the fourth, there'll be a fifth, and each time I finish a book I find it easier to say, "Yes, I'm a writer." That's down to you. You took the punt in the first place.

I have two editors—one in Sydney, and one in New York. Both are invaluable. I mean that. Price above rubies!

Nicola O'Shea has worked with me (patiently) over some years and three books, *The Dressmaker* being the most recent. She knows how to talk to writers in despair, but also to tell it like it is. And, too, what must be faced if the story is to be dug out of the mire of a shaggy, baggy first, second, or even third draft. Nicola, over these last years, has also spent time house-sitting in Sydney—she likes our cats—when I have run away to Tasmania to write in solitude, removed from the white noise of the city. I look forward to the day that you come and stay with us in this small southern island, Nicola. Tasmania is a tonic to the senses and the spirit.

And, Sarah Branham lives in New York and works with Atria Books, Simon & Schuster there, the publishers of this book. This is the first manuscript she and I have spent time on together and most of our working relationship has been conducted via cyber-space. (I like email. What writer doesn't?) I also have a penchant for leaving loooong and sometimes anguished telephone messages in the middle of the New York night. I must be the voice-mail caller from Hell. How Sarah stays sane when dealing, day after day, with battalions of neurotic novelists is a mystery to me. But I'm very grateful you respond to my calls, Sarah. I truly value your support and belief in this book.

Between these two compassionate and clever people I've been held up, helped, encouraged and, always, offered good advice—not to mention route maps when I got lost among the words.

I want to thank, also, my friends at Simon & Schuster in Australia. Lou Johnson and Tina Gitsas most particularly. It's been a great experience getting to know each of you. And thank you so much for trusting me to shoot the cover images for the Australian edition—and make the trailer for the novel—with my small band of great, great practitioners. A unique experience and one I think we've all enjoyed.

I'd also like to pay tribute to Franscois McHardy. Thank you, Franscois, for your belief in *The Dressmaker*. You've had to wait a long time to see it in print. It takes another writer to know, some-times, how daunting carving a delinquent mass of words into a pleasing shape can be.

Carolyn Caughey at Hodder Headline. You've always been a bracing presence throughout the writing process. I've greatly valued what you've had to say—and loved our most recent meal together on that particularly chilly night in London.

Rick Raftos and Rachel Skinner. My two agents (though Rachel has now run away to New York as well). That's another unfathomable occupation to me—being an agent—but how grateful I am to know I can ring you up and just talk. Longtime collaborators and friends, your support is and always has been precious.

And, of course, my family. Having a writer around with that abstracted look in the eye must be odd sometimes. Thank you for your tolerance, your kindness, and your interest.

Andrew, it was such a relief when you read the manuscript and liked it!

With my love and thanks to you all.

Posie

POSIE GRAEME-EVANS
TASMANIA, 2010

The
Dressmaker

POSIE GRAEME-EVANS

A Readers Club Guide

INTRODUCTION

Ellen Gowan's childhood in the wilds of Norfolk is a happy one. Ellen's parents are deeply in love, and their quiet family life is rich with affection and respect yet poor in worldly goods. But a tragic accident on Ellen's thirteenth birthday changes the course of her childhood forever, and Ellen must find courage and strength of will beyond her years to face the hardships that follow. But undeniable artistic talent, wit, and an indomitable spirit carry her from Norfolk to London, and in time she is transformed into Madame Ellen: dressmaker to the nobility of England, the Great Six Hundred.

Beautiful Madame Ellen is burdened by the secrets she has been forced to keep along her journey, ones that could destroy the success and happiness she has fought so hard to create. She will need all that she has—will, strength, talent, and passion—to find and hold a place for herself in an unforgiving era in which women's involvement in the world of business is a rarity.

QUESTIONS AND TOPICS FOR DISCUSSION

1. The title of the novel is *The Dressmaker*. Discuss how Ellen's inborn talent impacts her life at its various stages. What do you think might have happened to her had she not possessed such a skill? Do you think she's defined by her role as a dressmaker? Do you think this title—her title—speaks to Ellen's role in the lives of those around her in a symbolic as well as a practical way?

2. Choose one adjective you think best sums up the character of Ellen Gowan and share it with the group. Were you surprised by how others in your group perceived Ellen? What are her strengths and her weaknesses? How are your perceptions of these altered throughout the story?

3. How do you view the various examples of marriage and romantic relationships in this novel (some to consider: Edward and Constance, Daisy and Isidore, Oriana and Connor, Ellen and Raoul, and Ellen and Connor). Based on your reading, what do you make of attitudes about marriage during this time? What about attitudes regarding fidelity, sex, or love?

4. The novel ends with Connor and Ellen together, though it seems, earlier on, that he never considered her in a romantic way. Did you see it as a marriage of convenience (normal at the time), or do you believe they had something more? Do you think they will eventually come to be truly *in* love, in a way comparable to what Connor and Oriana had?

5. When Daisy comes to Clairmallon upon Isidore's death, Ellen observes: "Cruelty. Weakness. Perhaps they were the same. In effect" (p. 293). Discuss power and weakness as related to gender and class in this novel. Do you agree with Ellen's insight? Why or why not?

6. Raoul de Valentin, though the antagonist, is a complex character. Do you believe that he truly loved Ellen, at least in the beginning? If so, discuss his motivations in faking the marriage. If not, why do you believe he went through the charade in the first place, when he could so easily have taken advantage of Ellen after Constance's death with the aid of Carolina? If their business attempt had succeeded, do you think Raoul would have stayed? Do you feel there was any point in the book where Raoul had a true opportunity for redemption and failed to grasp it?

7. Ellen and Oriana have very different childhoods and each endure unique hardships as they grow into womanhood, but in many ways they are also quite similar. Compare and contrast their characters as a result of the experiences that shaped them. Did you find yourself identifying more with one than the other through-

out the book? What did you think of Oriana's request for Ellen to leave Connie at Clairmallon? Do you think Ellen would have asked the same of Oriana, had their positions been reversed?

8. The novel is full of examples of blighted ambition and characters trapped by circumstance. Do you feel that deep unhappiness excuses the scheming behavior or betrayals of some of the more antagonistic characters (consider Miss Wellings, Carolina Wilkes, Isidore Cleat, and Raoul de Valentin)? Or did you find them entirely unsympathetic?

9. The theme of appearance (versus reality) recurs constantly throughout the book, from the moment in Norfolk when Constance laments that Ellen is "too pretty" (p. 25) and will thus be feared. What are some obvious (and not so obvious) examples of this idea? Why do you think people put such stock in appearances at the time, when it was common knowledge that darkness and debauchery lurked behind many closed doors? Do you see appearance as a shield of sorts (in Ellen's case), or is it more of a mask (as with Raoul)?

10. Madame Angelique says " 'it is sad to find ability in the hands of one who will never use it to real effect . . . [you], with all that this world provides, do not have the need, or the hunger, to pursue such talent. God grant that remains the case' " (p. 114). What do you make of this assessment? Do you think, even if Isidore had not thrown them out, Ellen would have pursued her talent? Do you believe her life would have been better if she hadn't, as Madame Angelique seems to think?

11. *The Dressmaker* has a cast of strong, supporting female characters. Think about all the different women who impact Ellen's life: Polly, Oriana, Madame Angelique, Mrs. Ikin, Constance, Daisy, and even little Connie. What does Ellen learn from each of these women at various points of the novel? What do they learn from

her? Think about the women who play a significant role in your life. What can you learn from them?

12. Consider this quote: *" 'Mama? All will be well, will it not?' Ellen asked only what all children ask for: certainty in an uncertain world"* (p. 88). Do you agree with the idea that everyone—not only children—seek out certainty in an uncertain world? Do you think that this desire greatly influences and motivates Ellen, who is forced to act more grown up than her age on multiple occasions? Is the quest for certainty an important one, for all the characters, in one way or another? What about for you?

ENHANCE YOUR BOOK CLUB

1. Read and discuss Posie Graeme-Evans's previous works, the Anne de Bohun trilogy (*The Innocent, The Exiled,* and *The Uncrowned Queen*). Compare Anne to Ellen. Do you see any similarities between the two heroines? Is there a time period you prefer to read about?

2. Do some research on the fashions of Victorian England in the 1850s. Have everyone bring in an image of their favorite. If you're feeling truly adventurous, have everyone re-create the styles and turn your club into a costume party for the evening!

3. Learn more about the author at www.posiegraemeevans.com.

A CONVERSATION WITH POSIE GRAEME-EVANS

When Ellen is attempting to discover her misstep in translating Lady Hawksmoor's dress from paper to reality, she tells herself:

"Method. Examine each aspect, each element of the gown. Then look at the whole" (p. 318). **Do you feel a kind of kinship to Ellen in this approach, in regards to your writing process?**

Yes I do. My whole working life, TV as well as writing novels, has been about trying to understand the structure of something. If you can make the structure work, you have a fighting chance of creating a satisfying whole, be it a script, a film, or a book. And taking things apart, piece by piece, helps you avoid panic when things aren't working (and you just can't avoid that truth!).

From Norfolk to London to Clairmallon, the novel is rich in sense of place and atmosphere. Is a lot of this "setting of the stage" created out of heavy research? Do you tend to gather all the research and map out your story before you begin, or do you prefer to make discoveries as you write?

I have always loved England—its landscape, its architecture, its history. I travel as much as I can to the places I'm going to write about, too. Not to take notes so much, more just to stand somewhere and look and feel, taste the air (somehow), sense what might have happened there. But then, yes, once I begin to write, I think the story discovers me. I do read around the subject and look at books and search on the net for details of the era I'm trying to conjure from thin air, but I don't plot the story out. Television writing is always so disciplined, so plotted and pored over in group meetings, that it's a relief for me, just a single person facing a blank page, to wait until words begin to form and characters step forward from the mist. Then I wait to see what they're going to do and try to write fast enough to get it all down!

There are obviously gaps and missing pieces in historical evidence; how do you make the determination whether or not an imagined event, dialogue, or action is authentic or possible? What questions do you ask yourself? Do you consult others for verification?

Each book is different, but I find I'm very influenced, always, by the writings from a particular era. I try to read as much as I can about the time I'm targeting, and also, perhaps, search for the authentic voices of the people who lived then—diaries, letters, etc. Then one of the most important things for me to do is to write myself into the "voice" of the book. With *The Dressmaker,* I knew I wanted, very much, to capture the different ways people used language in the mid-nineteenth century, however, I also did not want a contemporary reader to find the words I used, or the ways the characters spoke, too hard to read. A tough balance, because I adore language, adore obscure but rich words. All I can say is that this book had draft after draft after draft and it took me a loooong time to feel satisfied that I had given the world I'd invented, and the people in it, reality in their, and my, terms. They won't be told, sometimes. They'll say what they say!

What responsibilities do you, as a writer of historical fiction, feel toward your audience? Do you think those responsibilities would be different if you were a nonfiction writer?

I want the worlds within my books to be as real as they can possibly be. But, also, I want the story to be engrossing and satisfying and for the characters to be as rich and multilayered as I can make them. These, above all, are my responsibilities to my readers, I think. However, I could not live with myself if I thought that the details of the world within the book were not correct. I really do try to make sure that I can answer every question that might be asked of me. And then, of course, like almost every novelist, I do give myself license, from time to time, to make facts bend a bit for the purposes of drama. Not too much . . . but some.

You say in the acknowledgments that Ellen began as a minor character in an entirely different story. What made you decide to abandon that original story and tell hers instead? Was she always a dressmaker? If not, why did you choose to make her one?

I didn't really decide to abandon the other story—it just became clear that I had to. It wasn't working, simple as that. And my Australian editor, Nicola O'Shea—who is good at tough love—pointed out that inescapable fact. Boy, did I find that truth hard to hear! But she was right. She very often is. And, in a way, when I surrendered and stopped trying so hard, Ellen's story flowed on to the page, and I just scrambled to keep up with what she was doing. And, yes, she always *was* a dressmaker. I became interested in the fact that for the longest time, the whole world thought fashion began and ended in Paris (has anything changed? Maybe.). The English of the nineteenth century just didn't value their own creators and designers. I decided Ellen would break that mold, but I wanted it to be a real journey. The things that matter are not easy, they do have to be practiced and learned, I believe.

Do you have a particular interest in the fashions of the age in which Ellen lives? Or just a general fascination with Victorian London? Was it fun delving into the details of the styles and fabrics of the time (particularly the decadent description of Lady Hawksmoor's ball gown)?

I adored it all! It *was* the best fun looking at the clothes of the time (the crinoline, uncomfortable as it must have been to wear, what with corsets and all, has to rank as one of the most flattering and romantic garments of all time). And then, placing those clothes in their time, almost as a symbol *of* that time, was like composing a painting. All color and movement and texture—fleeting glimpses of this and that to think about and draw upon. When I write, it's as if a movie plays in my head—and I loved looking through the highways and byways of Victorian England with Ellen beside me.

Many authors find that their characters are extensions of themselves, in one way or another. Do you find that to be true? Which character do you identify with most? Are any of the characters in *The Dressmaker* based on people you know?

An interesting observation. But I've been a storyteller in another form for a very long time and I find it hard to untangle the various influences that inhabit and form my characters. I know that I'm watching and listening all the time. People I meet, places, events, bits of conversations in public places (are all writers born voyeurs? I think so!). So, is any of it me? Hmm. Attitudes here and there perhaps, in various characters. I don't look like any of them, I know that. But, rather than taking elements of myself, I think the characters are amalgams of many, many people—and then they become themselves as they are written. I certainly identify with Ellen's struggle, however, and I like Polly very much, too. And I think Mrs. Ikin, a minor character though she is, would be someone I'd like to know. Raoul interests me, too, and Carolina Wilkes. Love the baddies as much as the goodies. I could go on and on! But all the characters develop so much as they are written, draft to draft, and I think that's what we all do in the course of a life.

Was it always your intention to end the novel with Connor and Ellen together? Do you believe it's truly possible for them to fall in love with each other without the shadow of Oriana—someone they both loved—coming between them (especially for Ellen)?

What an interesting question. Did I always intend for them to be together? Hmmm. Perhaps I did, but then I never know until I come down right toward the end. By that, I mean the ending declares itself. I think Ellen does truly love Connor, right from the start. It happens. Though rarely. And he is loyal to Oriana, so she chokes off any feeling she might have had for him. I think the human heart is a very enigmatic but flexible organ. Would Oriana come between them? Actually, I don't think so. Ellen seeks permission to love Connor, somehow, and gets it from her cousin. But she dithers right until the last moment. In the end, I'm glad she takes the plunge. People do that: throw the dice. And she's brave enough and strong enough to do it. I like, though, that she tells him the truth and says she could not bear it if he did not love her. He doesn't have to marry Ellen, but he does. I like to think he's sincere. I like to think that they will be happy. But maybe that's because I believe happiness and love are both possible between people.

All of your novels feature a female protagonist. Do you find it easier to write from a woman's perspective? Do you imagine that women at the time had more interesting stories to tell?

I like writing about women because . . . I do. The obvious answer, I suppose, is because I'm a woman. But then, I like writing about men

as well. If I write about the past, at the moment, it's because I enjoy the look of the canvas, i.e., the appearance of things—clothes, buildings, food, everyday life. But most of my TV drama is contemporary. I think people *always* have interesting stories. My next book is set in the present (in North East Scotland) and a thousand years ago. Perhaps that counts as moving closer to now. Strangely (!) there's still a bunch of strong women in this next story. I suppose that's not a coincidence.

A significant idea in the book is learning to live in the present, for the future, instead of dwelling on the past. Is that a mantra you live by?

Yes, it is. It's what producers do all the time—and I've been a producer for thirty years. However, I'm also trying to teach myself to just live in the present and *not* to think so much about everything that might go wrong in the future.

This is your fourth novel. Your previous three novels all center on Anne de Bohun, who was a real historical figure. Was the experience of writing Ellen, a completely fictionalized heroine, very different?

You bet it was! In the previous book I had a real framework to hang things on—and the architecture of actual events and people. Here everything blurred and spread out without defined boundaries—until I learned to corral the story a bit better. It wasn't harder as such, but it sure was different.

The story of Anne was a trilogy; do you plan to do the same with Ellen and/or the Moncrieff family? If not, what are you working on next?

I think *The Dressmaker* is a one-off—at the moment (never say never!). I'm currently working on a third draft of *The Island House*. It's set on a small imaginary island off the northeast coast of Scotland in the present and, in parallel, around 850 AD, the time of the Viking raids. It's about the discovery, in the present, of a buried Viking ship. Two skeletons lie in that boat, surrounded by treasure, and the girl in the present who finds the grave has a link to those men. It's a love story and a ghost story, and I hope to have the novel finished early next year.